PENGUIN BOOKS

FAIRACRE ROUNDABOUT

Miss Read, or in real life Mrs Dora Saint, is a teacher by profession who started writing after the Second World War, beginning with light essays written for *Punch* and other journals. She has written on educational and country matters, and worked as a script-writer for the BBC.

Miss Read is married to a retired schoolmaster and they have one daughter. They live in a tiny Berkshire hamlet. She is a local magistrate and her hobbies are theatregoing, listening to music and reading.

Miss Read has published numerous books, including *Village School* (1955), *Village Diary* (1957), *Storm in the Village* (1958), *Thrush Green* (1959), *Fresh from the Country* (1960), *Winter in Thrush Green* (1961), an anthology, *Country Bunch* (1963), *Over the Gate* (1964), *The Market Square* (1966), *Village Christmas* (1966), *The Howards of Caxley* (1967), *The Fairacre Festival* (1968), *News from Thrush Green* (1970), *Tyler's Row* (1972), *The Christmas Mouse* (1973), *Farther Afield* (1974), *Battles at Thrush Green* (1975), *No Holly for Miss Quinn* (1976), *Village Affairs* (1977), *Return to Thrush Green* (1978), *The White Robin* (1979), *Village Centenary* (1980), *Gossip from Thrush Green* (1981), *Affairs at Thrush Green* (1983), *Summer at Fairacre* (1984), *At Home in Thrush Green* (1985), *The School at Thrush Green* (1987), *The World of Thrush Green* (1988), *Mrs Pringle* (1989), *Friends at Thrush Green* (1990) and *Changes at Fairacre* (1991). Many of Miss Read's books are published by Penguin, together with six omnibus editions: *Chronicles of Fairacre*, *Life at Thrush Green*, *More Stories from Thrush Green*, *Further Chronicles of Fairacre*, *Fairacre Roundabout* and *Christmas at Fairacre*. She has also written two books for children, *Hobby Horse Cottage* and *Hob and the Horse-Bat*, The Red Bus series for the very young (published in one volume by Viking as *The Little Red Bus*), a cookery book, *Miss Read's Country Cooking*, and two volumes of autobiography, *A Fortunate Grandchild* (1985) and *Time Remembered* (1986).

MISS READ

———

FAIRACRE ROUNDABOUT

TYLER'S ROW
FARTHER AFIELD
VILLAGE AFFAIRS

ILLUSTRATED BY JOHN S. GOODALL

PENGUIN BOOKS

PENGUIN BOOKS

Published by the Penguin Group
Penguin Books Ltd, 27 Wrights Lane, London W8 5TZ, England
Penguin Books USA Inc., 375 Hudson Street, New York, New York 10014, USA
Penguin Books Australia Ltd, Ringwood, Victoria, Australia
Penguin Books Canada Ltd, 10 Alcorn Avenue, Toronto, Ontario, Canada M4V 3B2
Penguin Books (NZ) Ltd, 182–190 Wairau Road, Auckland 10, New Zealand

Penguin Books Ltd, Registered Offices: Harmondsworth, Middlesex, England

Tyler's Row first published by Michael Joseph 1972
Published in Penguin Books 1975
Copyright © Miss Read, 1972
Illustrations copyright © John S. Goodall, 1972

Farther Afield first published by Michael Joseph 1974
Published in Penguin Books 1978
Copyright © Miss Read, 1974
Illustrations copyright © John S. Goodall, 1974

Village Affairs first published by Michael Joseph 1977
Published in Penguin Books 1979
Copyright © Miss Read, 1977
Illustrations copyright © John S. Goodall, 1977

Published in one volume as *Fairacre Roundabout* in
Penguin Books 1990
Reprinted, also including the original illustrations to *Farther Afield* 1992
1 3 5 7 9 10 8 6 4 2

All rights reserved

Printed in England by Clays Ltd, St Ives plc
Filmset in Bembo

CONTENTS

Tyler's Row

For Helen
with love

CONTENTS

PART ONE

Outlook Unsettled

1. *Up for Sale*

Nobody knows who Tyler was.

In fact, the general feeling in Fairacre is that there never was a Tyler, male or female.

'I can assure you, Miss Read,' the vicar, Gerald Partridge, told me one day when I inquired about the subject, 'that there is *not one* Tyler in the parish register! It's my belief that someone called *Taylor* built the four cottages. Taylor, as you know from your own school register, is a very common name in these parts.'

He rubbed his chin reflectively, a little concerned, I could see, about further explanation. The vicar, a living saint, dislikes hurting people's feelings, but is transparently truthful.

'"Taylor" can be so easily debased to "Tyler" if the diction is at all impure. It must have occurred many years ago, before schooling was so er – um . . .'

'Widespread?'

'Exactly. I doubt if it could happen now.'

I was not in agreement with the vicar on this last point, but forbore to say so. I am constantly correcting 'pile' for 'pail', 'tile' for 'tale'; arguing about 'pines of glass', 'rine-drops', and people arriving 'lite' for school. The vicar, though, would be most distressed at the thought of casting aspersions on my teaching, or the purity of the vowels of my pupils.

'I'm sure you're right about it once being "Taylor's Row",' I agreed. 'But it's too late to change it now.' We parted amicably.

Although mystery surrounds Tyler of Tyler's Row, yet the date of the building is in no doubt, for on the end cottage of the four is a carved stone bearing the inscription:

1763 A.D.

in beautiful curlicues, now much weathered by the sunshine and storms of two centuries, but still decipherable.

13

The row of four cottages stands at right-angles to the village street and faces south. Under its dilapidated thatch, it drowses in the sun behind a thorn hedge, causing cries of admiration from visitors who are charmed by the tiny diamond-paned windows and the ancient beams which criss-cross the brick-work.

'Pretty enough to look at from outside,' I tell them, 'but you wouldn't want to live there. All four riddled with damp, and there's no proper drainage.'

'I expect plenty of people lived happily enough in them, over the years,' they retort defensively, still dazzled by Tyler's Row's outer beauty. One tenant, years ago, trained the thorn hedge into an arch over the gateway, and this enhances the charm of the view beyond.

A brick path, rosy with age and streaked with moss, runs along the front of the row, and there are narrow flower borders beneath the windows. There's no doubt about it. On a fine summer's day, with the pansies turning up their kitten-faces to the sun, Tyler's Row makes a perfect subject for a 'Beautiful Britain' calendar. After a spell of drenching rain and wind, when the sagging thatch is dark with moisture, and the brick path is running with the rain from the roof, Tyler's Row looks what it is – a building fast reaching the end of its days unless something drastic is done to restore it.

Of course, as the besotted visitors point out, it has housed generations of Fairacre folk. Carters and ploughmen have brought up their families here – mother, father and the latest baby in one bedroom, girls in the other, and boys downstairs. Shepherds and shoe-menders, dress-makers and washer-women, all have called Tyler's Row home over the years. At one time, at the end of Victoria's reign, there was even a poet beneath the thatch. He lived there alone, when his mother died, for many years, and the older people in Fairacre remember him.

Mr Willet, who is my school caretaker, sexton to St Patrick's, our parish church, and holder of a dozen or so important positions in our village, told me a little about him. The poor fellow had been christened Aloysius (locally pronounced as Loyshus), and was much given to reciting his works at local functions, if given half a chance.

'Lived to a great age, Loyshus did,' commented Mr Willet. 'Well, to tell you the truth, Miss Read, he didn't do much to wear himself out. That garden of his was like a jungle. The neighbours in Tyler's Row went on somethin' shockin' about it. No, he never put hisself out much. Never even bothered to wash hisself the last year or so. Smelt like a proper civet's paradise that house of his, when they finally came to clear up after him.'

Aloysius's poems are sometimes quoted in the *Caxley Chronicle*. In our part of the country, at least, a prophet is not without honour. Occasionally someone writes a short article about our local poet. The poems are pretty dreadful. He had a great fondness for apostrophes, and one of his better known works begins with the formidable lines:

> Ere e'en falls dewy o'er the dale,
> Mine eyes discern 'twixt glim and gloam

It goes on, if I remember rightly, for a hundred and sixty lines, with apostrophes scattered among them like a hatful of tadpoles.

'He were a holy terror at church socials,' recalls Mr Willet. 'Get old Loyshus on the platform, mumbling into his beard, and you could count on a good half-hour gettin' on with your game of noughts and crosses in the back row. 'Twere easy enough to get him up there, but getting him down was murder. They took to putting him on just before the Glee Singers. They used to get so wild waitin' about sucking cough-drops ready for "When you Come Down The Vale, Love", that they fairly man-handled Loyshus back to his chair, as soon as he stopped to take a breath.'

'He sounds as though he was a problem,' I said.

'A problem, yes,' agreed Mr Willet, 'but then, you must remember, he was a *poet*. Bound to turn him funny, all that rhyming. We was half-sorry for Loyshus, really,' said Mr Willet tolerantly. 'I've met a sight of folk far worse than Loyshus. But not,' he added, with the air of one obliged to tell the truth, 'as smelly.'

When I first became head teacher at Fairacre School, Tyler's Row belonged to an old soldier called Jim Bennett. The rent for each cottage was three shillings a week, and had remained at this ridiculous sum for many years. With his twelve shillings a week income, poor Jim Bennett could do nothing in the way of repairs to his property, and he hated coming to collect his dues and to face the complaints of the tenants, most of whom were a great deal better off than he was himself.

The Coggs family lived in one cottage. Arthur Coggs was, and still is, the biggest ne'er-do-well in Fairacre, a drunkard and a bully. His wife and children had a particularly hard time of it when they lived at Tyler's Row. Joseph Coggs and his twin sisters frequently arrived at school hungry and in tears. Things seem a little better now that they have been moved to a council house.

The Waites lived next door, a bright, respectable family who also moved later into a council house.

An old couple, called John and Mary White, both as deaf as posts, sweet, vague and much liked in the village, occupied another cottage, and a waspish woman, named Mrs Fowler, lived at the last house. She was a trouble-maker, if ever there was one, and Jim Bennett quailed before the lash of her complaining tongue when he called for his modest dues.

The Coggs were moved out first, and an old comrade-in-arms, who had served in the Royal Horse Artillery with Jim Bennett in the First World War begged to be allowed to rent the house. Jim Bennett agreed readily. Sergeant Burnaby was old, and in poor health. His liver had suffered from the curries of India, when he had been stationed there, and bouts of malaria had added to the yellowness of his complexion. But he was upright and active, and managed his lone affairs very well.

The Waites moved and their cottage remained empty for some time, and then, soon afterwards the old couple grew too frail to manage for themselves, and went to live with a married daughter.

Now the two middle cottages of the row were empty, and Jim Bennett decided that it was as good a time as any to sell the property as a whole. Mrs Fowler at one end, and Sergeant Burnaby at the other, were not ideal tenants, and the fact that they were there at all must detract from the value of Tyler's

Row, he knew well. But frankly, he had had enough of it, and he told his sister so.

They lived together at Beech Green in a cottage quite as inconvenient and dilapidated as any at Tyler's Row.

They sat on a wooden bench at the back of the house, in the hot July sunshine. The privet hedge was in flower, scenting the air with its cloying sweetness. Blackbirds fluted from the old plum tree, and gazed with bright, dark eyes at the blackcurrant bushes. Old white lace curtains had been prudently draped over them by Alice Bennett to protect the fruit from these marauders. From the plum tree they watched for an opportunity to overcome this challenge.

'We'll have to face it, Alice,' said Jim. 'The time's coming when we'll have to find a little place in Caxley – one of these old people's homes, something like that. If we sell up Tyler's Row we should have enough to see us pretty comfortable, with our pensions, until we snuff it.'

'You'll miss the rent,' said Alice. Her brother laughed scornfully.

'A good miss, too! Traipsing out to Fairacre every week, to be growled at by Mrs Fowler, isn't my idea of pleasure. I'll be glad to see the back of Tyler's Row, and let someone else take it on.'

'Who'd want it?' asked Alice reasonably. 'With those two still there?'

'We'll see. I'm going into Caxley tomorrow to get Masters and Jones to put it on their books. Some young couple might be glad to knock a door between those middle cottages to make a real nice little house.'

'They won't fancy old Burnaby rapping on the wall one side, and Mrs Vinegar Fowler on the other, if I know anything about it.'

'That's as may be. I'm getting too old to trouble about Tyler's Row. I'm content to take what the agents can get for it, and be shot of the responsibility.'

He knocked out his cherrywood pipe with finality. Alice, knowing when she was beaten, rose without a word, and went indoors to cut bread and butter for tea. Jim might be getting on for eighty, but there was no doubt he could still make up his mind.

And what was more, thought Alice, his decisions were usually right.

In no time at all it was common knowledge in Fairacre, Beech Green, and as far afield as the market town of Caxley, that Tyler's Row was up for sale. No advertisement had appeared, no sales board had been erected, but nevertheless everyone knew it for a fact.

The reasons given varied considerably. Some said that Mrs Fowler was buying it, having won several thousands from

a. the football pools
b. a tea competition
c. an appearance on a TV commercial advertisement.

('What for?' asked one wit. '"Use our face cream, or else?"')

Others held the view that the Sanitary People had condemned the property and it was going to be pulled down anyway.

Nearer the mark were those who guessed that Jim Bennett had had enough, and he was selling whilst there was a chance of making a few hundred.

The wildest theory of all was put forward by no less a person than the vicar, who was positive that he had heard that a society for the revival of Victorian poetry was buying the property, and proposed to open it to the public as a shrine to Aloysius's memory.

Certainly, within a week of the conversation between Jim and his sister in the privacy of their garden, everyone knew of the intended sale. He had told his tenants, of course, as soon as he had made up his mind, but they had said little. It was yet another case of air-borne gossip, so usual in a village as to be completely unremarkable.

Mrs Pringle, a glumly formidable dragon who keeps Fairacre School clean, and who polishes the tortoise stoves with a ferocity which has to be seen to be believed, told me the news with her usual pessimism.

'So poor old Jim Bennett's having to sell Tyler's Row.'

'Is he?' I said, rising to the bait.

'Some say he's hard put to it to manage on his bit of pension, but I reckons there's more to it than that.'

There was a smugness about the way Mrs Pringle pulled in her three chins, and the purse of her downward-curving mouth which told me that I should hear more.

She put a pudgy hand on my desk and leant forward to address me conspiratorially.

'It's my belief he's Got Something. Something the doctors can't do anything about.'

'Oh, *really* . . .' I began impatiently, but was swept aside.

'Mark my words, Jim Bennett knows his Time Has Come, and he's putting his affairs in order. By the time that sales board goes up, we'll know the worst, no doubt.'

An expression of the utmost satisfaction spread over her face, and she made for the lobby with never a trace of a limp – a sure sign that, for once in her martyred existence, Mrs Pringle was enjoying life.

2. Prospective Buyers

But, amazingly, the board did not go up. While Fairacre speculated upon this, the firm of estate agents in Caxley had informed several clients already seeking country houses that Tyler's Row was now for sale, and they enclosed glowing reports on the desirability of the property.

Among those who received a letter from Masters and Jones was Peter Hale, a schoolmaster in his fifties. He sat at his breakfast table, toast in one hand, the letter in the other and read hastily through the half-glasses on the end of his nose.

Every now and again he glanced at the clock on the mantel-piece. At half-past eight every morning of term time, for just over thirty years, Peter Hale had set off down the hill to Caxley Grammar School where he taught mathematics and history to the lower forms.

He walked the half-mile or so regularly, for the good of his health. As a young man he had been a sprinter and a hurdler, and the thought of losing his athletic figure, as so many of his fellow colleagues had done, was anathema to him. To tell the truth, exercise was something of a fetish with Peter Hale, and his family and friends were sometimes amused, sometimes irritated, by his earnest recommendations of a 'good five-mile walk', or 'a run before breakfast' for any minor illnesses, ranging from a cold in the head to a wasp sting. His wife declared that he had once advised one of these sovereign remedies for her sprained ankle. It might just have been possible.

She was a small, plump, pretty woman with a complexion like a peach. Once fair, her hair was now silvery-grey and softly curled. She was very little changed from the girl Peter had met and married within a year. There was a gentle vagueness about her which won most people's affection. The less charitable dismissed Diana Hale as 'rather bird-brained', which she most certainly was not. Beneath the feminine softness and the endearing good manners was a quick intelligence. Her anxiety not to hurt people kept her sharpness sheathed like a sword in its scabbard: but it was there, nevertheless, and this awareness of the ridiculous and the incongruous gave her much secret amusement.

The clock said twenty-five past eight and Diana waited for the last quick gulp of coffee and the rolling of her husband's table napkin.

He tossed the letter across to her, and lifted his cup.

'What do you think of it? Shall we go and have a look?'

'Fairacre,' said Diana slowly. 'Wouldn't it be rather far?'

'Six miles or so. Not much more. And lovely country – good downland walks. High too. Wonderful air.'

Peter Hale tucked his spectacles into their case, checked that he had his red marking pen safely in his inner pocket, his handkerchief in another and his wallet in the back pocket of his trousers. 'So much more convenient for the pickpockets,' as Diana had told him once.

'Must be off. I'll be late back. Staff meeting after school.'

He gave her forehead a quick peck, and was gone.

Diana poured a second cup of coffee and thought about this proposed move.

She wasn't at all sure that she wanted to move anyway. They had lived in the present house for almost twenty years and she had grown very attached to it.

It had been built early in the century, in common with many others, on the hill south of Caxley. Mostly they had been taken by professional and business people in the town, who wanted to move away from their working premises, yet did not want to be too far off.

They were well-built, with ample gardens whose trees were now mature and formed a screen against the increased traffic in the road. Diana had worked hard in the garden, scrapping the enormous herbaceous border which had been the pride of a full-time gardener in earlier and more affluent times, and the dozen or so geometrically shaped garden beds which had been so beautifully set out with wall-flowers, and then geraniums, in days gone by.

The two long rose-beds were her own creation, and a new shrubbery, well planted with bulbs, gave her much satisfaction and less backbreaking work. She would hate to leave her handiwork to others.

The house too, though originally built with accommodation for at least one resident maid, was easily managed. Here she and Peter had brought up their two sons, both now in the Navy, and the place was full of memories.

And Caxley itself was dear to her. She enjoyed shopping in the town, meeting her friends for coffee, hearing the news of their sons and daughters, taking part in such innocent and agreeable activities as the Operatic Society and the Floral Club. Her nature made her averse to committee work. She lacked the drive and concentration needed, and had never been able to whip up the moral indignation she witnessed in some of her friends who were engaged in public works. She admired their zeal sincerely, but she knew she was incapable of emulating them.

She knew so many people in the town. After all, Peter was now teaching the sons of his former pupils, and every family, it seemed, had some tie with the Grammar School. The young men in the banks, the shops and the offices of Caxley were almost all Old Boys, and knew her well. Wouldn't she feel lost at Fairacre?

She told herself reasonably that she would still run into Caxley to shop and meet friends, but it would mean a second car. She knew that any buses from Fairacre would be few and far between. Had Peter considered this, she wondered, in his desire to get into the country?

He had wanted to do this for years now. Circumstances had kept them in the town, the boys' schooling, the convenience of being within walking distance of his work, and Diana's obvious contentment with her way of life. But the boys were now out in the world. The house was really too large for them, and the garden, with no help available, was soon going to prove too much for them.

'Now's the time to pull up our roots,' Peter had said, at least a year earlier. 'We're still young and active enough to settle into another place and to make friends. I'd like to get well dug in before I retire.'

He looked at his wife's doubtful face.

'If we don't go soon, we never will,' he said flatly. 'It's time we had a change of scene. Let's go and look at a few places anyway.'

During the past few months they had visited a dozen or so properties, and each time they had returned thankfully to their own home.

At this time, estate agents could laud their wares to the skies and many a 'desirable residence in charming surroundings' could have been more truthfully described as 'Four walls and a roof in a wilderness'. Sometimes, it was enough to read the agent's description, and the Hales did not bother to visit the establishment. Other factors weeded out the possibles from the impossibles. For instance, Peter Hale refused to have anything to do with a property advertised ''twixt' this and that, or as 'prestige'.

'Listen to this,' he would snap crossly. '"'Twixt downs and salubrious golf course." And here's another, even worse. "A gem set 'twixt wood and weir." Well, they're out for a start! I'm not living 'twixt anything.'

There would be further snorts of disgust.

'It says here that "Four prestige houses are planned in Elderberry Lane". Such idiotic phrases! And pandering to the vanity of silly people! Who's going to be gulled into thinking Elderberry Lane's any catch, anyway, stuck down by the gas-works?'

They knew the district well, after so many years, and Fairacre was one of the villages which attracted them. In open country leading to the downs, it remained relatively unspoilt, yet there were one or two useful shops, a Post Office, a fine church, and enough inhabitants to make life interesting.

'This might be a possibility,' said Diana to herself, studying the glowing account of Tyler's Row's attractions.

'Suitable for conversion into one dignified residence', probably meant it was falling down and needed prompt support internally and externally.

'Half an acre of mature garden' could be construed as two ancient plum trees, past bearing, standing among docks and stinging nettles, and 'leaded windows' would be the deuce to clean, thought Diana.

But the price was unusually low. Why, she wondered? Was it even more dilapidated than she imagined?

And then she saw the snag.

'Two of the cottages at present occupied.'

Hardly worth bothering to go and look then. They certainly wouldn't want neighbours at such close quarters.

'Still,' thought Diana reasonably, 'it does mean that the cottages are capable of being lived in.'

Perhaps they would run out to Fairacre after all.

As it happened, the Hales did not visit Fairacre until the following week, for end of term was upon them, involving Sports Day, a tennis tournament arranged by the hard-working Parents' Association to raise funds for the school's swimming pool, a dinner for three of the staff who were retiring, as well as the usual end-of-term chores such as reports, last-minute advice to panicking school-leavers looking for jobs, and so on.

'Well,' said Peter Hale, arriving home on the last day of term, with a broad smile, 'now we've broken up, and my peptic ulcers can recover gently.'

He flopped into the settee, put up his feet and surveyed the ceiling blissfully.

'Think of it – seven weeks of freedom. Time to do just as we like.'

'If you still want to look at that place at Fairacre, perhaps we could drive out tomorrow,' suggested Diana.

'Tomorrow, the day after, the day after that, any day you like, my dear. I'm a free man,' declared Peter rapturously.

'If we leave it too long,' pointed out his wife, 'it will have been snapped up.'

'So it might,' agreed her husband, coming abruptly to earth. 'Let's go tomorrow morning.'

It was a perfect day to drive the six miles northward to Fairacre. They picked up the key as they drove through Caxley, and were soon out of the town, driving through leafy lanes, and rising steadily as they approached the downs.

The sky was cloudless, and a blue haze shimmered over the wide fields. Honeysuckle and a few late wild roses embroidered the hedges, and when Peter stopped the car to fill his pipe, Diana heard a lark scattering its song from the sky. A blue butterfly, native of the chalk country, hovered over the purple knapweed on the bank. Nearby was a patch of yellow and cream toadflax, vivid in the sunshine, and everywhere was the scent of warm grass and leaves – the very essence of summertime.

'Wonderful country,' said Peter dreamily, gazing into the blue distance, above the leaping match flame.

'In this weather,' replied Diana. 'Could be pretty bleak in the winter. And lonely.'

'You don't sound very enthusiastic,' said Peter, turning to look at her. 'Shall we go back?'

'Not till we've seen Tyler's Row,' said Diana firmly. 'We'll know what to think then.'

Peter started the engine and they made their way slowly through Beech Green and on to Fairacre, without speaking further, until they reached the Post Office in the centre of the village street.

As it happened, Mr Lamb, the postmaster, was in his front garden cutting back rose suckers with a fierce-looking clasp knife.

'Tyler's Row?' called Peter, winding down the car window.

'Eh?' said Mr Lamb, startled.

'Tyler's Row – Mr Bennett's property,' enlarged Peter, knowing that it is far better to name the owner than the house in rural parts.

John Lamb, who had not heard Peter properly at first, was a trifle nettled at having Bennett's name brought in. He was postmaster, wasn't he? He knew Tyler's Row well enough, after all these years, without some foreigner trying to tell him his business!

He answered rather shortly.

'On your left. Matter of a hundred yards or so. You'll see the thatch over the hedge-top.'

'Thanks very much,' said Peter, equally shortly. Diana turned her gentle smile upon John Lamb, to soften her husband's brusqueness.

'Surly sort of devil,' commented Peter, eyes alert to the left.

'I thought he looked rather a dear,' said Diana. 'Look, that's it!'

They pulled up by the tall hawthorn hedge.

'That archway's rather attractive,' said Diana. 'Shall we go in?'

The gate was rickety and dragged on the ground. A semicircle had been worn into the earth, and the pressure had caused some of the palings to hang loose.

'Tut, tut!' clicked Peter, who was a tidy man. 'Only the hinge gone. Wouldn't have taken five minutes to replace.'

They stood just inside the gate and surveyed Tyler's Row. The cottage nearest them had a fine yellow rose climbing over it. The dark foliage glittered in the sunshine as brightly as holly leaves. The windows were closely shut, despite the heat of the day, and Diana was positive that she saw a curtain twitch as though someone were watching them.

They moved a few steps along the brick path. A bumble bee wandered lazily from rose to rose, his humming adding to the general air of languor.

The two empty cottages, their windows blank and curtainless, looked forlorn and unloved. The paint peeled from the doors and window frames, and a long, skinny branch of japonica blew gently back and forth in the light breeze, scraping across the glass of an upstairs window with an irritating squeaking noise.

'Turns your teeth to chalk, doesn't it?' remarked Peter. 'Like catching your finger-nail on the blackboard.'

'Or wearing those crunchy nylon gloves,' added Diana.

'I've been spared that,' said Peter, stepping forward and pressing his face to the glass.

At that moment, a woman came out of the last cottage, flung a bucket of water across the garden bed, in a flashing arc, and stood, hand on hip, surveying the couple. Her face was grim, her eyes unwelcoming.

'Can I help?' she asked tartly. It looked as though it were the last thing she wanted to do, but Diana answered her softly.

'No, thank you. We'll try not to bother you. We have the key to look at these cottages.'

At the same moment, the door of the other occupied cottage opened, and out stepped Sergeant Burnaby. His face was as yellow as his roses, but his bearing was still soldierly.

'Yes, sir,' he said briskly. 'Anything I can do to help, sir?'

'Nothing, thanks,' said Peter, with a smile. 'Just taking a look at the property.'

'In a very poor way, sir. Very poor way indeed. My old friend Jim Bennett hadn't the wherewithal to keep it together. No discredit to him. Just circumstances, you understand. A fine man he was, sir. We served together for –'

A violent snort from the woman at the end interrupted the old soldier's monologue, and Peter Hale took the opportunity of turning the key in the lock and opening the door of one of the cottages.

'We mustn't keep you,' he said firmly, and ushering Diana inside, he closed the door upon the two remaining tenants of Tyler's Row.

Despite the summer heat which throbbed over the garden, the cottage interior was cold and damp. This was the Waites' old home, and had been empty now for a long time.

27

Cobwebs draped the windows and a finger of ivy had crept inside and was feeling its way up the crack of the door. Diana could smell the bruised aromatic scent where the opening door had grazed it.

The floor was of uneven bricks, and snails had left their silver trails across it. The old-fashioned kitchen range was mottled with rust, and some soot had spattered from the chimney to the hearth.

But the room was unusually large, with a window back and front, and there were several fine oak beams across the low ceiling. There were two more doors. One opened upon a narrow staircase, and the other led to a smaller room.

Above stairs were two fair-sized bedrooms, and the view at the back of the cottage was breath-taking. Mile upon mile, it seemed, of cornfields, just beginning to be tinged with gold, stretched away to the summit of the downs. A hawk hovered nearby, a motionless speck in the clear blue, and from every-where, it seemed to Diana, came the sound of larks singing.

She forced open one of the creaking windows, and the sweet air lifted her hair. Peter came behind her, and they gazed together in silence.

Immediately below them lay the four long, narrow gardens. Sergeant Burnaby's had a row of runner beans growing in it, and a strip of bright annuals, poppies, cornflowers, marigolds and nasturtiums, growing higgledy-piggledy together near the back door.

A ramshackle run containing half-a-dozen hens and a splendid cockerel completed Sergeant Burnaby's garden, with the exception of a stout wooden armchair, much weather beaten, that stood on the flag-stones in the shelter of the house.

Mrs Fowler's garden had a concrete windmill, two stone ducks, a frog twice as large as the ducks, and a neat rose bed planted with a dozen standard roses. Beyond this stretched the kitchen garden, ruled neatly into rows of onions, beetroot, parsnips, carrots, and a positive sea of flourishing potato plants. A clothes-line, near the house, bore a row of fiercely white tea-towels and pillow-cases which Diana guessed, correctly, had been bleached within an inch of their lives.

Between the two gardens lay the wide, neglected area of

grass, docks and nettles which Diana had envisaged. There seemed to be a square of fruit bushes, almost shrouded in weeds, towards the end of one garden, and a rustic arch leant, like the Tower of Pisa, halfway down the other. It was a sad scene of desolation, but for some reason it did not depress Diana. Her gardener's heart was touched at the sight of so much neglect, but unaccountably she wanted to shout from the window to the beleaguered plants, telling them to hang on, to cling to life, that help was coming, that she would save them. She was surprised, and slightly amused, at the vehemence of the feeling which shook her. She was becoming bewitched!

Peter was now stamping on the ancient floorboards, which stood up to this onslaught sturdily. His eyes scrutinized the beams for woodworm, his finger-nails peeled a little of the damp wallpaper, and he sniffed the air, like a pointer, for any trace of dry rot.

They went down the squeaking stairs and into the next cottage. It was a replica of the first, with another large room adjoining a small one, and two bedrooms above, but the staircase here was broken and dangerously splintered, and the dampness, if anything, more noticeable.

'What do you think?' asked Diana.

'Humph!' grunted her husband enigmatically.

'Do you want to look at the other two? I suppose we can?'

'Not now, anyway. I've seen enough, I think. Let's go back and think about it.'

There was no sign of Mrs Fowler or Sergeant Burnaby as they closed and locked the doors, but martial music was issuing loudly from the latter's radio set and competed with the humming of insects enjoying the downland sunshine.

They closed the broken gate carefully, and looked through the archway at the scene which had fascinated so many sightseers before them.

'It would never do, of course,' said Diana, at last. 'Although it's a heavenly spot – ' Her voice trailed away.

Despite her words, she had the odd feeling that the forlorn cottages and the smothered garden were beseeching her for help. Could she withstand that piteous cry?

29

'I need my tea,' she said forcefully, turning her back upon Tyler's Row.

She made her way, almost in panic, it seemed to her surprised husband, back to the haven of the car.

3. Local Competitors

The Hales, of course, were not the only people to visit Tyler's Row, and as the village watched the callers, speculation grew animated.

'One chap came from Lincolnshire,' said Mr Willet. 'Said he knew these parts from the fishing, and might retire here. I met him outside "The Beetle". Very civil-spoken, he was too, coming from so far away.'

Mr Willet spoke as though this were extremely odd, as if Lincolnshire people might be expected to have their heads growing from their breasts, like the natives described by medieval travellers in distant lands.

But most of the visitors came from Caxley or neighbouring villages. One indeed came from Fairacre itself, and he was Henry Mawne.

Henry Mawne and his wife have lived in Fairacre for some time. He is a renowned ornithologist, but better known in our village as a zealous churchwarden and parish councillor. He and his wife occupy part of a fine Queen Anne house at the end of the village. Why should he want to move?

'Finding them stairs too much, I don't doubt,' said one.

'Needs more room for all them books and papers of his,' said another.

'Wants his own home, I expect,' said a third. 'Who wants to die in a rented place?'

As it happened, all three reasons had something to do with Mr Mawne's interest in Tyler's Row. Both he and his wife had twinges of arthritis, and the idea of making a home on the ground floor appealed to them.

Then, their present abode was some distance from the hub of the village. The post office, the shops, the church, and the bus stop were close to Tyler's Row. And his books grew more numerous as the years passed and, despite his wife's threats to throw them out, Henry Mawne refused to part with a single

31

volume. At least one room downstairs could be set aside as a library-cum-office, and the lesser-used books could be housed upstairs.

And then, Tyler's Row had always attracted him. The long thatched roof, silvery with age, its southern-facing aspect, making it bask like a cat in the sunshine, its thick hawthorn hedge screening it from the road, had all combined to delight Henry Mawne whenever he passed the property.

His wife was less kindly disposed. A forthright woman, who has upset many a Fairacre worthy with her bluntness, she told her husband just what she thought of the project.

'Nothing but a hovel, and those two old people a positive menace. There's nothing wrong with this present place, except the stairs and your books. We can still manage the first, and if you would only weed out the second we should be perfectly happy.'

Henry Mawne doubted this privately, but had the sense to hold his tongue. He dropped the argument for the time being, but returned to it several times in the next few days, for it was a matter which obsessed him.

His wife remained adamant, but was beginning to realize that she was up against unusually stubborn opposition. Henry Mawne had been back and forth to the estate agent's and to Tyler's Row, and had even gone so far as to get the place surveyed.

'You see, my dear,' he told his wife, 'this might be an investment. It is ridiculously cheap because of the tenants and the dilapidation. I know we should have to spend a lot on it, but we've enough behind us to cope with it. We could make a start on the empty pair, making them one, and let it when it was done, until we felt we wanted to move in ourselves.'

'You mean, stay here indefinitely?' asked his wife suspiciously.

'I don't see why not. We should be on the spot for watching the building's progress, and as you say we can manage here for some time yet.'

'I'll think about it,' said Mrs Mawne cautiously.

'Well, think quickly,' adjured her husband. 'There are other people interested in Tyler's Row.'

But his heart leapt, nevertheless, at this tiny chink in his wife's armour. Dare he hope?

Much the same debate was going on at the Hales' house. The comparative cheapness of the property appealed particularly to Peter, for schoolmasters are usually hard up and this seemed to be a sound investment.

'The site alone is worth best part of the money,' he told his wife. 'Plots of land fetch astronomical prices now round here. We should get a good price for this place, and it would be comforting to have something in the bank. We'll be down to half our income when I retire. We must look ahead.'

'I know that,' answered Diana unhappily, 'but I really think that we shall find those two old things a terrible headache. If we could be sure they would be leaving soon – '

'If Nature takes its course properly they'll be leaving in the next year or two. That old soldier is truly in the sere and yellow. I doubt if he'll last the winter.'

'Don't be so horribly calculating.'

'Who started it?'

'I didn't so much mean *dying* – ' began Diana, prevaricating.

'Well, they're not likely to move out just to oblige us,' said Peter flatly. 'They're fixtures all right, and we shall have to face the fact.'

'I hate being hustled,' said Diana, changing her tactics.

'Me too. I don't propose to leave this place until the next is habitable. That's understood. But if we made up our minds now, I could spend quite a bit of time during the summer holidays going over the plans with the architect, and doing a certain amount myself.'

'I do see that, but oh dear!' sighed Diana.

'Look at it this way,' said Peter, pressing home the attack. 'It's nearer the mark than anything else we've seen so far. We've always liked Fairacre. It's only twenty minutes from Caxley, and the site of the house is perfect. Faces south, just enough garden, endless possibilities with the whole row to consider – '

'You sound like Masters and Jones rolled into one. Are you sure you're not being too optimistic?'

'Are you sure you're not being downright awkward?' retaliated Peter. 'What, in heaven's name, beside the two tenants, have you got against the place?'

'It's dark. It's damp. It's falling down.'

'So was that mill house the Kings bought ten years ago. When I went to see it with him, a mother rat the size of a rhino met us at the front door, with about twenty-five babies tagging along behind. Now it's superb, and would sell for a bomb. Tyler's Row could be even better than that.'

'If I could be *sure*,' said Diana slowly, 'that the middle part would be absolutely ready to move into, and that there was some possibility of those two going in a reasonable time, so that we could incorporate their cottages eventually, then I think I'd agree.'

Her face lit up, as an idea struck her.

'Couldn't we offer them alternative accommodation? I'm sure I've heard something about it.'

'They'd have to be willing to go, and you know what it's like finding something suitable. Still, I could find out about it.'

'Give me until tomorrow to get used to the idea,' said Diana. 'I think making decisions is the most exhausting thing in the world.'

'You want practice,' commented her husband drily.

She woke at two o'clock in the morning, the problem still unresolved. She had gone over the pros and cons so many times that her head buzzed.

In the other bed Peter snored rhythmically. Moonlight flooded the room, and an owl's cry wavered from the trees which edged the common some quarter of a mile away.

Diana lay there, savouring the quietness. It would be quieter still at Fairacre, she supposed, remembering the vast sweep of downs behind the village.

The remembrance of the neglected garden in the foreground flooded back to her, and she was shaken, yet again, by the longing to rescue it from decay. It could be so lovely in that setting, and the soil was rich, as the fine plants in the neighbours' gardens proved. Pinks should do well on that chalky soil, and lavender. A lavender hedge would grow easily . . .

Her mind drifted vaguely, and then came back to Peter. It was only fair that he should have his way in this matter. For years he had put up with Caxley for the sake of the family, always longing to settle eventually in the countryside nearby. This was their chance.

Diana sighed, and decided to creep downstairs to warm some milk. It might make her sleep. Experience told her that nothing short of clashing cymbals would stir Peter from his rest, but nevertheless, she went on tiptoe from the room and down the stairs. The moonlight was so bright that there was no need to switch on lights until she entered the kitchen.

The cat gave a welcoming chirrup, stretched luxuriously, and descended from its bed on the kitchen chair near the stove. It watched Diana expectantly as she poured milk into a saucepan. A little snack in the middle of the night never came amiss.

Diana shared the milk between her mug and the cat's saucer, and stood warming her hands as she sipped.

'How'd you like to live in the country, puss?' asked Diana, watching the pink tongue at work. But the cat, strangely enough, never answered questions, and Diana carried her mug and her problems back to bed.

'Go ahead,' she said next morning, when Peter awoke.

'Go ahead where?'

'With the house.'

'The Fairacre one?'

'What else?' said Diana, slightly nettled. Peter never came to full consciousness until after breakfast. This morning he seemed more comatose than usual.

'You're sure?'

'No, I'm not, but I think we could make something of it, and if we're going to move, then now's the right time.'

There was silence for a time, and then Diana heard humming from the other bed, proving that her husband was feeling contented. It was difficult to recognize the tune. It might have been 'Onward Christian Soldiers', 'Take a Pair of Sparkling Eyes' roughly transposed for a tuneless baritone, or possibly the marching music from 'Dr Zhivago'. Peter's repertoire was limited, but gave him a great deal of private pleasure, and Diana a keen appreciation of variations on several themes.

'Better get up, then,' said Peter, throwing aside the bed-clothes. 'I'll get down to Masters and Jones as soon as they open.'

Still humming – the *Dr Zhivago* motif coming through strongly now – he made his way to the bathroom.

Masters and Jones estate agents' office presented a fine Georgian front, all red brick and white-painted sash windows, to Caxley High Street. It looked what it was, a long-established prosperous family business which had served Caxley and its neighbourhood well for four generations. William Masters had founded the firm in the year of the Great Exhibition of 1851, and three of his descendants were still active in the firm. Clough Jones, a foreigner from Pontypool, joined the firm in 1920, and so was a comparative newcomer to Caxley. His beautiful tenor voice was soon taking the lead in Caxley's Operatic Society and he was reckoned to be 'a very steady sort of chap'. Some added: 'For a Welshman', in the year or two after Clough's arrival, but this proviso was soon dropped – proof that he had shown his worth.

Peter had taught two of the Masters' boys and Clough's only son Ellis. It was the younger of the Masters' boys, now a man of twenty-eight, who welcomed Peter to the office and set a chair for him on the other side of the desk.

The interior of the house was disappointing. The large square rooms on each side of the hall had been divided into four, with partitions of flimsy wood topped with reeded glass. Occasionally one would catch sight of a head, curiously distorted, in the next compartment, elongated like a giraffe-woman from Africa, or bulging sideways like a squashed Christmas pudding, according to the angle of the glass through which it was visible.

The floors were covered with linoleum of a pattern purporting to be wood blocks. As these were of such unlikely colours as pale blue, orange and pink, the effect was unconvincing, and to Peter, eyeing it distastefully, thoroughly shocking.

'Very nice to see you, sir,' said young Masters deferentially.

It seemed only yesterday that he was waiting outside the detention room door under Mr Hales' stern direction. Something to do with the unification of Germany and Italy, if he remembered correctly, had brought him to that pretty pass, and now he came to think of it, he was still not much wiser on the subject, detention or no detention. But he had always felt a healthy respect for old Hale, and even now a slight tremor affected his knees at the thought of past bondage.

'I've come about this property at Fairacre,' said Peter. He looked over his spectacles at the young man. David, Paul, John? What the deuce was the boy called?

'Can't remember your name, I'm afraid,' he added.

'Philip, sir.'

'Ah, yes, Philip. Second fifteen full back.'

'Well, no, sir. That was my brother Jack. I wasn't much good.'

'Forget my own name next,' replied Peter cheerfully. 'Well, I'm thinking of going ahead with Tyler's Row. Better have a survey. Sooner the better.'

'Yes, indeed,' said Philip, with more confidence. 'You will

certainly need to get moving, sir. Another gentleman is being rather pressing.'

Peter Hale looked sternly across his spectacles.

'Is this the truth?'

Philip was instantly transformed into a wrong-doing first-former, despite his six feet in height.

'Yes, sir. Honestly, sir,' he heard himself saying nervously. Heavens above, his voice seemed to have become treble again! He took a grip upon himself, and cleared his throat. Dammit, this was his office, wasn't it?

'A gentleman already resident in Fairacre –'

'"Living in" or "residing", if you must,' corrected Peter automatically. Philip, clinging to his precarious confidence, ignored the interruption.

'He is very interested in the property and has already had it surveyed. I think it's quite likely he will make us an offer. Probably in advance of the selling price.'

'More fool him,' said Peter flatly. 'I'm not bribing anybody.'

'Of course not, sir. But I should advise you to get a survey done immediately. I could go out myself.'

'Do that then, Philip, will you?'

'I'll just jot down one or two reminders.'

He pulled a sheet of paper towards him and began to scribble diligently with his left hand.

Terrible writing that boy always did, remembered Peter, watching his old pupil at work. Felt sure he'd be a doctor with that scrawl, but not enough brains really, nice fellow though he was. He looked at the bent head, the beautifully clean white parting, the well-shaven cheeks, and felt a warm glow. Should be able to trust him – solid chap, nice family, respectable firm. Why, young Philip might bring Tyler's Row to him eventually! He was smiling when the young man looked up.

'You'd be happy there, sir,' he said, stating a fact, not asking a question.

'I think we should,' agreed Peter.

He rose and went to the door, his gaze on the linoleum.

'Who chose this?' he asked, pointing a toe.

'I did, sir,' said Philip proudly.

'Pity,' said Peter, in farewell.

4. Mrs Pringle Smells Trouble

Who was to be the new owner of Tyler's Row? This was the question which exercised the minds of his future neighbours in Fairacre.

Henry Mawne had been the favourite for so long that it was something of a shock to learn that he had retired from the race, and that an outsider was the winner.

The news came to me from Mrs Pringle during the summer holidays. She spends one morning each week 'putting me to rights', as she says, and although her presence is more of a penance than a pleasure, the results of her hard work are excellent. I try to do any of my simple entertaining on Wednesday evenings. It is the one day in the week when the place really shines.

'That sitting-room of yours wants bottoming,' said Mrs Pringle dourly. This, construed, meant that a thorough spring-cleaning was considered necessary.

'Looks all right to me,' I replied, quailing inwardly. Mrs Pringle, bottoming anything, is one of the major forces of nature, something between a volcano and a hurricane, and certainly frightening and uncomfortable.

'Seems to me you just lays a duster round when you feel like it. That side table's a fair disgrace, all over hot rings where you've put down your cup, and ink spots no honest woman could get off.'

'Well, I sometimes – ' I began, but was swept aside. The hurricane was gaining force nicely.

'Mrs Hope, poor soul that she was, was a stickler for doing the furniture right. Every piece was gone over once a week with a nice piece of soft cloth wrung out in warm water and vinegar.'

When Mrs Hope's example is invoked I know that I may as well give in. She lived in the school house many years ago. Her husband is remembered as an unsuccessful poet who drowned his sorrows in drink, and was finally asked to leave. But Mrs

39

Hope has left behind her a reputation for cleanliness as fierce and unremitting as Mrs Pringle's own.

'Mrs Hope didn't have to teach all day,' I said, putting up a poor defence.

'*Mrs Hope*,' boomed Mrs Pringle, 'would have kept her place clean AND taut! Nothing slipshod about Mrs Hope.'

'You win,' I said resignedly. 'Shall I make coffee now?'

Mrs Pringle inclined her head graciously.

'And put it on a tray. I've enough marks to rub orf the table as it is.'

Over coffee, she told me the news.

'Mrs Mawne put her foot down, so I hear. Never liked the idea of moving so Mrs Willet said. Her sister was doing a bit of ewfolstery for her –'

'A bit of *what*?'

'Ewfolstery. Covering chairs, and couches and such-like. Well, as I was saying, Mrs Mawne told her plain that they had looked at Tyler's Row and decided against it. *She'd* decided, she meant! Anyone could see the poor old gent would have loved it.'

'So it's on the market still?'

Mrs Pringle swelled with the gratified pride of one about to impart secret knowledge.

'I've been told – by One Who Should Know – that Mr Hale from the Grammar School's having it.'

'Probably just rumour,' I said off-handedly. A cunning move this, to learn more, but I still smarted under the threat of being bottomed.

Mrs Pringle rose to the bait beautifully. Her wattles turned red, and wobbled with all the fury of an enraged turkey-cock.

'My John's sister-in-law cleans at Masters and Jones and she's seen Mr Hale in and out of that place like a whirligig! And what's more, he's been to Tyler's Row hisself nigh on half-a-dozen times in the last fortnight, fair bristling with foot-rules and pencils and papers. He's having it all right, mark my words!'

'Well, well! We'll have to wait and see, won't we?' I said, with just a nice touch of disbelief. 'Anyway, he'd be a pleasant neighbour.'

'*Respectable*,' agreed Mrs Pringle, accepting a second Garibaldi biscuit graciously. 'Friendly, too, they say. Though he fair lays about those boys, from what my nephew says, if they don't work.'

'I'm glad to hear it,' I said. 'He sounds a man after my own heart. When's he coming?'

'You tell me!' replied Mrs Pringle emphatically. 'He's got an architect *and* a builder, so between 'em both that'll hold things up. The architect was out doin' what Mr Willet tells me is a survey, though he saw young Masters doing one too, a week or so back. Shows he's serious, doesn't it? Having two people to look at it, I mean?'

She dusted a crumb or two from her massive bosom, and rose to continue her labours.

'If he's in by next spring, he'll be lucky,' she foretold gloomily. 'And then I wish him joy of his neighbours, poor soul.'

I must confess that the future of Tyler's Row did not concern me greatly, although I have as keen an interest in village affairs, I think, as most people in Fairacre.

But I had troubles of my own at this time. As well as the

intimidating prospect of Mrs Pringle's bottoming in the near future, I was also threatened with the formation of a Parent–Teacher Association at Fairacre School.

For generations any association between parents and teachers has been a natural one – sometimes enthusiastically co-operative, sometimes acrimonious, according to circumstances. But always it has been of an informal type – and it has worked very well.

I don't mind admitting that I am a non-committee woman. The very sight of an agenda fills me with dreadful boredom, and all that jargon about 'delegating authority to a sub-committee', and 'forwarding resolutions' to this and that, renders me numb and vague. The thought of an association which met once a month and involved speakers and demonstrations, and general sociability, filled me with depression. It would mean yet another evening away from my snug fireside, sitting in the draughty schoolroom and acting as reluctant hostess to a bevy of parents whom I saw quite enough of, in any case.

The moving force behind this sudden activity was a newcomer to the village, Mrs Johnson. The family had moved into a cottage in the village street once occupied by a lovable slattern called Mrs Emery and her family. Mr Emery had worked at an establishment, some miles away, known to us as 'the Atomic'. Mr Johnson also worked there, and was a somewhat pompous young man of left-ish tendencies, who had some difficulty in finding cruel masters grinding the faces of the poor, but lived in hope.

His wife, rather more militant, held strong views on education. She brought three young sons to the school soon after the summer term started. They were pale, bespectacled children, fiercely articulate, in contrast to my normal placid pupils, but quite amenable and keen to work. We got on very well.

But their mother was a sore trial. She met them at the school gate every afternoon, and button-holed me. I was subjected to tirades of information – usually faulty – on such topics as the dangers of formal teaching, the necessity for monthly intelligence tests, absolute freedom of thought, word and deed for each child and, of course, the complete rebuilding of Fairacre school.

There are very few teachers who welcome this sort of thing

at four o'clock in the afternoon after a hard day's teaching. My civility soon grew thin, and I was obliged to tell her that any complaints must be dealt with at an appointed time. After this, I had fewer face-to-face encounters at the gate, but a number of letters, badly typed on flimsy paper and running to three or four pages, setting forth half-baked theories on education bearing no relevance, that I could see, upon present circumstances.

Unfortunately, Mrs Johnson and Mrs Mawne became close friends, and Mrs Mawne is one of the school's managers.

Whether she was still smarting from the wounds inflicted in the battle of Tyler's Row, from which she had emerged the victor, I shall never know. But certainly, soon after Mrs Pringle's conversation, the pressure for the formation of a Parent–Teacher Association was intensified. The vicar, who is chairman of the managers, mentioned the matter on several occasions.

'I really think it is unnecessary,' I told him, yet again. 'Fairacre's managed very well without one, and it's going to be a real headache finding something to do regularly every month, or whenever it is proposed to meet. If I felt that the majority of parents wanted it, then I'd submit with good grace, but I feel sure Mrs Johnson's at the bottom of this, and I don't suppose that family will stay in the village any longer than the Emerys did. I give them two years at the most.'

The poor vicar looked unhappy.

'We have a managers' meeting tomorrow, and this is one of the matters to be discussed, as you know.'

I did not, as a matter of fact, as the notice had been thrust, unread, behind the clock on the mantelpiece from whence I should snatch it one minute before the meeting.

'Do consider it, my dear Miss Read,' said the vicar, his kind old face puckered with anxiety. 'And what does Mrs Bonny think about it?'

I realized, with a shock, that I had never even thought of consulting Mrs Bonny, the infants' teacher, about this possibility. This was remiss of me, and I must put the matter right without delay.

When the vicar had gone, his cloak swirling in the fresh

summer breeze from the downs, I made my way to the infants' room where Mrs Bonny was walking among her charges' desks, admiring plasticine baskets of fruit, crayoned portraits of each other, notable for rows of teeth like piano keys, and inordinately long necklaces of wooden beads which trailed over the desks like exotic knobbly snakes. It was a peaceful scene, and Mrs Bonny, a plump pink widow in her fifties, added to the air of cosiness.

'Very nice,' I said, to an upheld blue banana.

'Beautiful,' I said, to a picture executed by one of the Coggs' twins, showing her sister with one mauve eye, one yellow, and a mop of what appeared to be scarlet steel wool at the top of the portrait.

By this time, every piece of work in the room was raised for my inspection and approval.

'Wonderful! Very good effort! Lovely beads! Neat work! You have tried hard!'

The comments rattled out as evenly as peas from a shooter. Then I clapped my hands, and told them to continue.

'Sweets for quiet workers,' I added, resorting to a little bribery.

'The vicar's been talking about this idea of a Parent–Teacher Association,' I began to Mrs Bonny.

A bright smile lit her face.

'It's a marvellous idea, isn't it?' she said enthusiastically, and I felt my spirits sink. 'All the Caxley Schools seem to have them, and the parents are wonderful – always raising money for things, and in and out of the school, helping, you know.'

My face must have registered my misgivings, for she gazed at me anxiously.

'You don't think it would work here?' she queried. There was a pause whilst she darted to the front row and ran an expert finger round the inside of a child's mouth and removed a wet red bead.

'That would *hurt* if you swallowed it,' she said sternly. 'And what's more,' she added practically, 'we're very short of beads.'

She turned to me.

'Sorry, Miss Read. What's your objection to a P.T.A.?'

I told her, somewhat lamely, I felt. It was quite apparent that she was strongly in favour of setting up one, and I could see I was going to be heavily outnumbered.

'I think you would find it a great help,' she assured me. 'I'd welcome it myself.'

She stopped suddenly, and her pink face grew pinker.

'But there – I might not be here to enjoy it,' she said, looking confused.

Novelists talk about a cold hand gripping their heroine's heart. Two cold ones gripped mine, and fairly twisted it into oblivion. The thought of losing Mrs Bonny and all that that entailed – the succession of 'supply' teachers, if any, or, much more likely, the squashing of the whole school into my class-room for me to instruct for some dreadful interminable period, froze my blood. It has happened so often before, and every time, it seems, is more appalling than the last.

'Mrs Bonny,' I said, in a voice cracked with apprehension, 'what do you mean?'

She rearranged her pearls self-consciously, slewing them round with energetic jerks to get the clasp tidily at the nape of her neck.

'I was going to tell you on Friday,' said Mrs Bonny. To give me time, I thought despairingly, to recover from the news during the weekend.

'I am getting married again. In the Christmas holidays, in fact.'

I professed myself delighted, and waited for a bolt from heaven to strike me dead.

'A friend of my husband's,' she said, warming to her theme. 'He's always been so close to our family. In fact, he's godfather to my boy.'

'Well, he's jolly lucky,' I said, and meant it, stopping a string of beads which a boy was whirling round and round in a dangerous circle, and getting a bruised hand in the process. The occupational hazards of an infants' teacher are something which would surprise the general public, if explained.

'I don't want to give up teaching, at least for some time. We want to save as much money as we can for when we retire. Anyway, I should miss the children terribly.'

'That's a relief,' I told her.

'We thought we'd see how things go. Theo says that if I find it too much, then I must stop, of course. But I shall stay as long as I can.'

'Let's hope it's for years,' I said.

'So you see,' concluded Mrs Bonny happily, 'although I think the P.T.A. is a marvellous idea – and I think you will too, if it happens, Miss Read – I won't press you one way or the other, because it won't really affect me, will it?'

'No,' I said morosely. 'I quite see that.'

I renewed my congratulations, smiled brightly upon the infants, and returned to my own classroom.

There I found that the children had put away their work, books had been stacked neatly on the cupboard, the large hymn-book had been propped upon the ancient piano in readiness for the next morning's prayers, and all that the class awaited was the word to go home.

Certainly, the clock's hands were at five to four, but I felt slightly nettled at such officious time-keeping. The children, however, arms folded, stout country boots neatly side by side, were so pleased with their efforts that I had not the heart – broken-spirited woman that I was – to chide them.

They sang grace lustily, and then tumbled out into the lobby, while I locked my desk. An ear-splitting shriek, followed by a babble of voices, took me to the lobby in record time.

Mrs Pringle, broom upheld like Britannia's trident, gazed wrathfully upon the horde milling round her.

'If I'm laid up tomorrow,' she boomed, 'lay it at the door of that boy.'

She pointed to Joseph Coggs, whose dark eyes looked piteously towards me.

'Stepped full on me bunion with his great hobnail boots! Enough to cripple me for life!'

I looked at the terrified Joseph.

'Have you said you were sorry?'

'Yes, miss,' he whispered abjectly.

Mrs Pringle snorted. For some unworthy reason my spirits rose unaccountably.

'Ah well, Mrs Pringle,' I said, with as much gravity as I could muster, 'we all have our troubles.'

5. Making a Start

Trouble was certainly looming for Peter Hale. The two surveys confirmed that there was dry rot in the ground floor of the cottages, and in one king beam, and that rising damp at the back of the property was causing considerable damage to the fabric of the outer walls.

'Nevertheless,' said Mr Croft, the architect, 'there is nothing to worry about. All these little matters can be put right.'

He leant back in his swivel armchair and surveyed Peter Hale benevolently. He was the senior partner in the firm of Croft and Cumberland, and something of a personage in Caxley. He was a man of unusual appearance, affecting from his youth rather long hair and a style of dress which blended the artist with the country gentleman.

His tweed suits were pale, and with them he wore a bow tie which carefully matched them in colour. His shirts were always made of white silk, and he wore a wide-brimmed hat at a jaunty angle. Someone once said that Bellamy Croft was the cleanest man in Caxley, and certainly his face shone with soap and his hair, now white, formed a fluffy halo round his gleaming pink scalp. A whiff of eau-de-Cologne accompanied him, and was particularly evident when he shook out the large vivid silk handkerchiefs he affected.

Caxley's more sober citizens thought Bellamy Croft rather a popinjay, but as time passed he was looked upon as a distinguished member of the community, and the results of his work were much admired.

As a young man, he had spent some years in India when the British Raj held sway. Indian princes had employed him, and he had worked on some projects instigated by Sir Edwin Lutyens himself. Caxley was impressed by this exotic background, but even more impressed with the solid work he did in their own neighbourhood when he settled there.

Now, nearing seventy, he took on only those projects which

47

he liked, and certainly only those within easy range of the Caxley office. The conversion of old property was a speciality of his, and Tyler's Row attracted him.

Peter Hale knew he was lucky to have his services, but was a little apprehensive about the cost of the job.

'I don't want Bellamy Croft to run away with the idea that I'm one of his Indian-prince clients with strong-rooms stuffed with emeralds and rubies of pigeon-egg size, and diamonds too heavy to lift,' he said to Diana. 'Do you think he has any idea of teachers' salaries?'

'Of course he has,' replied Diana robustly. 'Anyway, ask him. If he's outrageously expensive, we'll manage without him.'

'Impossible,' said Peter. 'He knows his stuff, and will see that old Fairbrother gets on with the building properly. I don't grudge Croft's fee – it'll be an investment – but I must see that he doesn't get carried away with all kinds of schemes for improving the place.'

'What do you expect? A miniature Taj Mahal rising between Mrs Fowler's and Sergeant Burnaby's?'

'Not quite, but I intend to keep a tight rein on him. He's already contemplating shutters, and a sort of Chinese porch which would set us back a hundred or two. I can see he'll want watching.'

Now, on this bright August morning, Peter did his best to impress upon Bellamy Croft the absolute necessity of keeping costs as low as possible.

'This dry rot. What will it cost to put right?'

Bellamy told him, and Peter flinched.

'And a damp course?'

'I should prefer to tell you that after I have had a longer look at the place. But we ought to make a good job of it while we're about it. No point in cheese-paring.'

'Naturally. The essentials must be done, and done well. But I simply haven't the money to indulge in extras such as this porch you show in the plan. Heaven knows what I'll get for my present home – a lot, I sincerely hope, but the bridging loan from the bank must be met eventually, and I'm determined to cut my coat according to the cloth. Maybe we can do all the fancy bits when the other two cottages become vacant.'

'Ah yes, indeed! Stage two,' said Bellamy, shuffling enormous sheets of crackling paper upon the desk. 'I quite appreciate your position – and frankly, I'm glad to work for a man who knows his mind. Stage one, the conversion of the middle two cottages, we can keep very simple, and by the time we've reached stage two we shall know how much more you feel able to embark upon.'

His bland pink face was creased in smiles. He looks happy enough, thought Peter, but then he doesn't have to foot the bill. Was it a hare-brained project he had started? What other snags, besides dry rot, rising damp, two awkward tenants, a jungle of a garden and an architect with alarmingly lavish plans did the future hold?

Was he going to bless or curse the day he decided to buy Tyler's Row?

Time alone would tell.

What with one thing or the other it was well on into August by the time the contract was signed and the die cast.

One sultry afternoon, Diana and Peter drove over to their new property with a formidable collection of gardening tools in the back of the car.

'Do you really think you'll need that enormous great pick-axe?'

'It's a mattock,' corrected Peter. 'And the answer's "Yes". It will probably be the most useful tool of the lot. You won't need that trowel and hand fork, you've so hopefully put in, until next season.'

The gate still scraped a deepening semi-circle in the path as they pushed it open.

'I must see to that,' said Peter, shaking his head.

They carried the tools into the back garden and surveyed the jungle with mingled awe and dismay.

'Look at the height of those nettles!' said Diana.

'Take a look at the brambles! Tentacles like octopuses – or do I mean octopi? And those prickles! We really need a flame-thrower before we can begin with orthodox tools.'

He picked up a bill hook and stepped bravely into the weeds, followed by Diana carrying a pair of shears.

'We'll start at the bottom of the garden and work our way towards the house,' Peter said. 'Knock off the top stuff first, and burn it as we go.'

It was hot work. Far away could be heard the rumblings of a storm, and dark clouds massed ominously on the horizon. Thousands of tiny black thunder-flies settled everywhere, maddening them with their tickling, and swarming into their hair, ears and eyes. Their labours were punctuated by slapping noises as they smote the unprotected parts of their bodies which were under constant attack from the tormentors.

They had been working for about an hour, and cleared a strip about two yards wide across the width of the garden, when they became conscious of Mrs Fowler watching them sharply over the hedge.

'Oh, good afternoon,' called Diana, wiping her sticky face on the back of her glove. 'As you see, we're just making a start on this terrible mess.'

'There's some good rhubarb just where you're standing,' replied Mrs Fowler austerely. 'And there used to be a row

of raspberry canes. Looks as though you've cut them down now.'

Diana refused to be daunted.

'Well, there it is,' she said lightly. 'We shall have to start from scratch, it's obvious. It's impossible to tell weeds from plants now that it's got to this state.'

'Should have been seen to weeks ago,' continued Mrs Fowler. 'All them weeds have seeded and blown over into my garden. Never had so much groundsel and couch grass in my life.'

Peter straightened his back and came to his wife's support.

'And ground elder,' went on Mrs Fowler, before he could say anything, 'and them dratted buttercups. Bindweed, chickweed, docks, the lot! All come over from this patch.'

'Any poison ivy?' asked Peter mildly. 'Or scold's-tongue?'

Mrs Fowler looked suspicious.

'Don't know those, but if there's any over there it'll be in here by now.'

'I'm glad to see you, anyway,' said Peter. 'I was going to knock to tell you we're going to make a bonfire of this lot, in case you had washing hanging out, or wanted to close the windows.'

Mrs Fowler drew in her breath in a menacing manner, but said nothing. She nodded, and retired to her house. A few sharp bangs told the toilers that the windows were being slammed shut.

'What an old bitch she is!' remarked Peter conversationally, slashing at a clump of nettles.

'Peter, don't!' begged Diana. 'She'll hear you.'

'Do her good,' he said, unrepentant. 'Pass the rake, and we'll get the bonfire going before it rains.'

At that moment they heard a loud cough. Sergeant Burnaby's sallow face loomed above the other hedge like a harvest moon.

'Good afternoon, sir. Just made a pot of tea, and hope you and the lady will do me the honour of takin' a cup.'

'How kind,' said Diana. 'I'd love one.'

Peter looked less pleased. He was a man who liked to finish the job in hand.

'I want to get the bonfire started before the storm breaks.'

'Let me take the green stuff over the hedge for my fowls,' urged Sergeant Burnaby eagerly. 'They dearly love a bit to pick at, and it'll help you get rid of it.'

'Fine,' said Peter, brightening. He gathered an armful of grass, docks, hogweed and sow thistle and staggered with it to the hedge.

There was a flustered squawking as Sergeant Burnaby flung it over the wire, and then a contented clucking as the hens scattered the largesse with busy legs.

'May as well let them have the lot,' observed their master, after the fourth load had been deposited.

Peter obediently scraped together the last few wisps, and as he did so, a crack of thunder, immediately above, made them jump. A spatter of raindrops fell upon them.

'Come straight in, ma'am,' called Sergeant Burnaby, retreating up the path.

'Run for it!' shouted Peter, snatching the tools together, and within two minutes they were in the old soldier's kitchen, shaking the rain from their clothes.

Everything looked remarkably clean and tidy, thought Diana, when one considered that the lone occupant was approaching eighty.

There was a kitchen range identical with their own in the next cottage, against one wall, but this one was glossy with blacklead, and on the mantelshelf above were several brass ornaments, including a large round clock, all shining.

Among them Diana saw a little embossed box, and following her gaze, the old man took it down for her to handle. It was quite heavy, and bore a medallion showing the heads of George V and Queen Mary.

'Sent to us in the Great War,' said the sergeant, with pride. 'We was in the trenches at the time. Christmas present, it was, filled with tobacco. We all thought a lot of that, I can tell you. My old pal, Jim Bennett, he treasured his too. It gets a rub-up every Saturday.'

'I should think that all your lovely things get a rub-up weekly,' said Diana, handing back the box. 'Does anyone come to help you?'

'Not a soul,' said Sergeant Burnaby proudly. 'I don't want no help. That Mrs Fowler come once, early on, but it was only to snoop round. I sent her packing.'

He stirred his cup with a large teaspoon, and looked fierce.

'I'm not one to speak ill,' he continued. Diana waited for him to do just that, and was not disappointed.

'But that old besom needs watching, sir. Tongue like a whip-lash, and not above nicking anything that's going. Why, the moment the Coggses and Waitses left, she was in them gardens diggin' up what she fancied! They come back, a week after they'd moved, to dig up a row of potatoes, but they was gone. "Next door," I told 'em! "You have to look in the shed next door. You'll find 'em all right. Sacked up for the winter!"'

He sniffed at the remembrance.

'Them Waitses never done nothing about it. Too easy-going by half. Always was. But good neighbours to me. I miss 'em.'

Diana exchanged a glance with her husband. Peter's face bore the impatient look of a schoolmaster suffering tale-telling, and about to take retaliatory action.

'Your flowers are so pretty,' said Diana hastily, rising to look out of the window.

The rain drummed down relentlessly, spinning silver coins on the flagstones and the seat of the wooden armchair outside the back door. The bright patch of marigolds, cornflowers and shirley poppies, was a blur through the streaming window, but Diana's comment had succeeded in stemming the old man's venom and in soothing her husband's irritation.

'I like a bit of colour,' said Sergeant Burnaby. 'I dig over a bit near the house and fling in packets of seeds – annuals, you know, all higgledy-piggledy. Don't take a minute, and there's a fine bright sight for the summer.'

He turned to Peter.

'You plannin' to do anything about the thatch?' he asked.

Peter looked cautious.

'Not at the moment,' he replied. 'The architect is still studying things.'

He did not care to tell the sergeant that the thatch would probably be renewed, or at least repaired in stage two, after the demise of his host.

'The window frames are rotten,' continued the sergeant. 'And my chimney don't look too healthy.'

'They'll be seen to,' said Peter, more frankly. These things were included in stage one, he seemed to remember. 'Can't do it all at once, you know, but we'll put things ship-shape as soon as we can.'

'You see,' said Sergeant Burnaby, filling Peter's cup again before he could refuse, 'my end of this row gets all the weather. You'll find that's true, sir. Now, old Mrs Vinegar-Bottle up the other end, she'll worry the guts out of you – pardon me, ma'am – about what she wants doin', but her place is a king to this. Sheltered, see, from the westerlies. And her old man kept things up together, so I'm told, when he was alive.'

He spooned sugar briskly from a glass bowl into his cup.

'One, two, three, four,' he counted under his breath. Diana suppressed a shudder. It must taste like thin golden syrup.

'Poor devil!' commented the sergeant. 'He's better off, wherever he is. That old cat must have helped him to the grave, I don't doubt.'

Peter drained his cup, and stood up.

'Time we were off. Very kind of you to give us tea.'

'Very kind,' echoed Diana.

The old man looked suddenly old and pathetic.

'Must you go? Don't see much company, you know. No need to hurry away on my account. I've got some old photos of this place you might like to see.'

He began to open the table drawer, in a flustered way. Diana's heart smote her.

'We'd love to, some other time. We really must go now, and pack up our tools.'

'But it's still raining,' protested the old man, trying in vain to keep his guests.

'Can't be helped,' said Peter firmly. 'We'll have another go at the garden as soon as we can. And there's plenty of marking waiting for me at home too which I must go and tackle.'

He held out his hand, and smiled at Sergeant Burnaby.

'I know you'll forgive us for hurrying away,' he said with sudden gentleness. 'But you'll be seeing quite a lot of us in the next few weeks. Too much probably.'

They escaped into the pouring rain, collected their things, and drove home through the storm to Caxley.

*

54

The Hales spent the grey, wet evening in their armchairs. Diana's hands were busy with knitting a pale-blue coat for a god-daughter's baby. Her head was busy with thoughts of their two tenants.

What on earth had they taken on?

Peter's thoughts were engaged with his history marking. His red pencil ticked and slashed its way across the pages. Every now and again he gave a snort of impatience.

'Sometimes I wonder if Lower Fourths can take in American history,' he said, slapping shut one grubby exercise book. 'Young Fellowes here informs me that the Northern Abortionists – a phrase used five times – were extremely active in the nineteenth century.'

'Northern Abortionists?' echoed Diana, bewildered.

'"Abolitionists", to everyone else in the form,' explained Peter, reaching for his pipe. 'But not to young Fellowes, evidently. He's the sort of boy who writes the first word that enters his head. It might just as well have been the Northern Aborigines, or Abyssinians, or anything else beginning with Ab.'

He patted the books into a neat pile.

'That'll do for tonight,' he said firmly. 'They don't have to be returned until term starts.'

'Only another fortnight,' said Diana, 'and so little done at Tyler's Row.'

'What's the hurry? Look upon it as a hobby. It's no good fretting about delay, and we're in the hands of Bellamy and the builder anyway.'

'But nothing seems to be happening.'

'It will soon enough,' Peter assured her.

He spoke more truly than he knew.

6. The Problem of Tyler's Row

Work began at Tyler's Row towards the end of September, and Diana and Peter grew quite excited when they saw how much had been accomplished after ten days.

Everything movable, the old kitchen range, the light fittings, the worm-eaten dresser – even some of the wallpaper – had gone, and the two cottages appeared to be stripped for action.

What they failed to realize, in their innocence, was the fact that the first stages of any building work are rapid and quickly apparent. It is the last stages which are so maddeningly prolonged, when plasterers wait for plumbers, and plumbers wait for electricians, and decorators wait for the right paint and wallpaper, and the owners wait to get into the place, with the growing conviction that the mad-house will claim them first.

Those despairing days were still in the future, but already things were becoming complicated for the Hales in the early part of the term. The headmaster, knowing that Peter was intending to move, asked if he might buy his present house.

'My son John comes back from Singapore before Christmas. They've three children now, and another on the way, and your house would be ideal.'

'We shan't be out of it until well after Christmas,' said Peter.

'Surely a couple of cottages won't take all that time to put to rights?'

'They're doing pretty well at the moment,' replied Peter, 'but Bellamy Croft won't be hurried, and I think John will have to look elsewhere if he wants to bring the family straight into a house.'

'He might get temporary accommodation,' mused the headmaster aloud. 'Until you're ready, I mean.'

And a very pleasant situation that would be, thought Peter, with a harassed family man breathing down his neck, urging him into a half-finished Tyler's Row. He was not going to be hustled into anything, he told himself sturdily.

But this was only the beginning. It was amazing how many people decided that Peter Hale's house was exactly what they, or their relations, had been waiting for, and he found himself accosted in Caxley High Street on several occasions by would-be buyers. He had two stock answers. The house was not on the market yet, and wouldn't be until Tyler's Row was ready. Masters and Jones would be the people to approach. He was not handling it himself.

It was all a trifle wearing, although it was some comfort to know that it looked as though the house would sell easily.

And then there was the architect. Peter had said that Bellamy Croft would not be hurried. He was beginning to wonder if he went to Tyler's Row at all. There were several things he wanted to talk to him about, but he never seemed to be in the office, and his secretary was a past-master in covering up for him. Always, it appeared, Bellamy was at work in some remote village, or had gone to consult someone at Oxford or London or Cheltenham.

'I'll ask him to ring you,' was the nearest Peter ever got to seeing the elusive fellow, but he waited in vain for the telephone to ring. And when, after several frustrating weeks it did, Bellamy's apologies were so profuse and disarming that Peter's ire evaporated.

However, it was soon revived by discovering that Bellamy had returned to his fight for a mock-Gothic porch in the centre of Tyler's Row.

'I'm not having it!' he told Diana firmly. 'I'm not being saddled with a Chinese–Chippendale porch, with a pointed lead roof, costing about two hundred smackers, when I want a simple affair with a thatch on top!'

'You did ask him to do the job!' pointed out Diana.

'If I asked the butcher for two pork chops,' replied Peter heatedly, 'I'm damned if I'd accept a saddle of mutton just because he wanted me to have it. My God, what a battle it all is!'

As term progressed, the outlook grew steadily gloomier. Peter began to get headaches – a most unusual thing for so healthy a man.

'Nothing that exercise won't cure,' he insisted, setting out on a four-mile walk whenever he was so afflicted.

'Perhaps you need new reading glasses,' suggested Diana solicitously.

'No, no. These are perfectly adequate. A spell of fresh air and plenty of muscle-work's the answer.'

And he would vanish for an hour or so, and return rather more exhausted than when he set out; certainly in no mood to tackle the piles of marking which always stand about a schoolmaster's sitting-room.

It was at this stage that Diana found their rôles reversed. She who had been so full of doubts about the move, now did the comforting.

'It will sort itself out. There are bound to be set-backs. All progress goes in fits and starts – two steps forward, and one back – and if you think of Tyler's Row a couple of months ago, and then today, it's really quite heartening.'

Peter refused to be consoled.

'The time they take!' he stormed, raising fists to heaven. 'You'd think three men plus an architect would get the place done in a month! When I think that this is only *stage one* of Bellamy's plan, I wonder if I'll ever live to see stage two. Or even if I *want* stage two, or will be able to raise the money for it. As far as I can see, we'll be looking for a nice little Eventide Home for the Aged by the time stage one's done.'

Autumn gales, of unprecedented ferocity, ripped away tarpaulins fixed over empty window frames and created more work at Tyler's Row. Copper piping and bathroom fittings, left overnight in the empty cottage, disappeared in the small hours and had to be replaced, with infuriating difficulty. Mr Roberts' cows, in a field adjoining the property, pushed their way into the garden and helped themselves to the freshly-planted perennials which Diana had spent three afternoons arranging carefully in a newly-dug border. The garden was pock-marked with large holes where they had browsed undisturbed for hours.

At one point, Bellamy Croft, in an expansive mood, had said that there was a possibility of moving in by Christmas. In January he said, somewhat more cautiously, that it might be possible at the end of the month.

In February he said what a trying winter it had been for

builders ('And for schoolmasters!' Peter had snarled), and he was truly surprised to find how much there still needed to be done. Perhaps, in early March . . .?

In the middle of that month, with the end of term in sight, Peter issued an ultimatum.

'We're moving during the Easter holidays, come hell or high water,' he told Bellamy. 'My own house is sold, and the chap wants to move in. Put some dynamite behind old Fairbrother and his minions, or they'll find themselves having to work round us. They've got three weeks to finish.'

Bellamy Croft professed himself pained and astonished at such impatience, though, in truth, he met with it often enough with his clients. However, Peter's forbidding detention-for-you-boy look had some effect, and a slightly brisker pace of progress began at Tyler's Row.

Although there were cupboards still to be fitted, some topcoat painting to be done and the lavatory window was still missing, Peter and Diana pressed on with their preparations for the move, and named the day as the twentieth of April.

'The relief,' sighed Diana, 'at having something settled at last! Who was it kept saying his patience was exhausted, Peter?'

'Hitler.'

'Are you sure?' Diana sounded startled.

'Positive. His patience was exhausted just before he snapped up yet another country.'

'Well, I never expected to ally myself with that man, but at the moment I can sympathize with his feelings.'

Fairacre, of course, had watched the progress of conversion with unabated interest. The theft of the copper piping was attributed at once to Arthur Coggs, although no one had a shred of evidence to prove the charge. It was noted, however, that Mrs Coggs was unusually free with her money at the Christmas jumble sale, even going so far as to expend a shilling on a fur tippet, once the property of Mrs Partridge's mother. This, said some, proved that there was more money than usual in the Coggs' household and where had it come from? Funny, wasn't it, they said, that the copper piping had vanished only a few days earlier?

Others pointed out that any proceeds from the sale of the stolen goods would have been poured promptly down Arthur Coggs' throat in 'The Beetle and Wedge'. Mrs Coggs would have been the last person to receive any bounty from her husband.

Sergeant Burnaby enjoyed every minute of the builders' company, sitting in his old armchair in the garden and carrying on a non-stop conversation with anyone available. He had never had so much excitement and company before. Every day brought another enthralling episode in this living serial story, and he delighted in regaling Peter and Diana with a blow-by-blow account of all that went on between their visits.

Mrs Fowler, on the other hand, behaved with mouth-pursed decorum.

She knew, however, quite as much about the doings next door as did Sergeant Burnaby, and kept a watch upon the workmen as vigilant as his, but more discreet.

The schoolchildren were equally interested, shouting to the builders as they passed on the way to school, begging for pieces of putty, nails, strips of wood, pieces of wallpaper, broken tiles and anything else to be treasured.

Mrs Pringle and I were in rare unity in trying to discourage them from pillaging in this way, and from bringing their loot into the school. Well-worked putty leaves finger-prints on exercise and reading books, and the children's fingers were grubbier than ever with handling their newly-found possessions.

I tried to convey to them the fact that they were stealing, with small success.

'But they was going to be thrown out,' they told me. 'Them workmen said as these bits was rubbish.'

'And the putty?' I would persist remorselessly.

'Jest an odd bit, miss,' they would plead.

'Who do you think pays for the putty?'

'Don't know, miss.'

'Mr and Mrs Hale are paying for it. You are just as bad as the thief who took their copper piping.'

'But the workmen – '

'The workmen have no business to give the things away.'

I made little headway with my arguments. The magpie instinct in children is strong, and they could see endless possibilities in the odds and ends so easily obtained. I have always kept a large box in the classroom filled with such oddments as cotton-reels, matchboxes, odd buttons, scraps of material, lino, off-cuts of wood, corks and so on, in which the children love to rummage. From this flotsam and jetsam of everyday life they produce dozens of playthings for themselves, and prize them more than any 'boughten' toy, as they say.

One bleak January morning, after prayers had been said and the register marked, there came a crash from the lobby and a loud wail.

On investigation, I found Joseph Coggs surveying the fragments of a tile scattered over the brick floor of the cloakroom. His dark eyes were shining with tears.

'And what,' I said sternly, 'makes you so late?'

'I bin to get this for my mum.' He pointed a filthy finger towards the pieces.

'From Tyler's Row?'

'Yes, miss. It's going to be – ' He sniffed, and corrected

himself. 'It *were* going to be a teapot stand. For her birthday, miss. Saturday, miss.'

'I shouldn't think your mother would want a stolen teapot stand,' I said, improving the shining hour.

'She wouldn't know,' explained Joseph patiently. Despair began to grip me. Should I ever succeed in my battle?

'You are late. You have been pilfering, despite all I've said, and you've made a mess on Mrs Pringle's clean floor. Sweep it up, and come inside the minute you've finished.'

'Yes, miss,' said Joseph meekly, setting off for the dustpan and brush.

He was disconsolate for the rest of the morning. I could see that he was grieving for his lost treasure, and when he refused second helpings of school dinner – minced beef with mashed potato and gravy followed by treacle pudding – my hard heart was softened a little.

When they went out to play, in a biting east wind, I returned to the school house across the playground, and sorted through a number of objects to join the other contents in the rubbish box.

'You are free to choose,' I told the children when Handwork lesson began that afternoon. 'You can paint a picture, or get on with your knitting, or you can make something fron the rubbish box.'

Half-a-dozen little girls drew out their garter-stitch scarves and composed themselves happily with their knitting needles. About the same number of both sexes made for the paints and brushes, but the larger proportion of non-knitters rushed excitedly to the box. Some had seen me adding material and were agog to have first pick.

As I hoped, Joseph was among them. I watched him remove a piece of lino with one hand, and a large wooden lid, once the stopper of a sugar jar – with the other. His expression was one of mingled hope and anxiety. Which, he seemed to be asking himself, would make a replacement for the broken tile?

He took both objects back to his desk, and studied them closely, stroking them in turn. Around him work began on the construction of dolls' beds, dolls' chests-of-drawers, paper windmills and cardboard spinning tops. There was a hubbub of conversation among the manufacturers, but Joseph remained silent, engrossed in his problem.

At length, he set aside the lino and put the flat circle of wood in front of him. Then he went to the side table which holds such necessary equipment as nails, paste, gummed paper, string and so on. He selected some squares of gummed paper, yellow, green, and red, returned to his desk and cut out a number of bright stars.

For the rest of the lesson he stuck them on the lid in ever-diminishing circles. Despite the finger-prints, the result had a primitive gaiety, and it was good to see the child growing happier as the wood was covered. When the last star was in place, he sat and gazed at it enraptured. Then a thought struck him. He came to my desk.

'Will them stars come off under a teapot?'

'Not if you varnish them,' I told him. He made his way to the side table again without a word, and tipped a little varnish into the old saucer kept for the purpose. When the lesson ended the teapot stand was put on the piano to dry, with all the other objects.

'You've made some nice things,' I told the children. 'Are you pleased with your teapot stand, Joseph?'

'Yes, miss. It's for my mum's birthday, miss. Come Saturday, miss.'

'And it's honestly come by,' I said meaningly.

'And all out of bits thrown away,' commented Ernest glee-fully.

'Like my tile,' added Joseph.

I opened my mouth but thought better of it and closed it again.

'There's a fine old mess in my dustpan,' grumbled Mrs Pringle when she arrived after school that afternoon. 'Full of bits of broken tile or something.'

'Joseph should have tipped that in the dustbin,' I said.

Mrs Pringle snorted.

'Been pinching again? Them Coggses is all tarred with the same brush, if you ask me. Tyler's Row, I suppose? Wonder that place isn't gutted by now. Don't know what children are coming to these days. We'd 'ave got a good leathering when I was young, but today – why, the kids don't seem to know right from wrong.'

'It's not for want of telling,' I told her, with feeling.

PART TWO

Some Squally Showers

7. Moving Day

Providence, kindly for once, sent sunshine on April 20th. Diana had dreaded the day of departure from her old home, but when it arrived, the house looked so strange and bare that she felt as though the parting with it were already over.

Then, too, there was so much to do that there was little time to wax sentimental. Much of the stuff was already at Tyler's Row, for they had been taking over boxes of books, china and cutlery during the last week or so.

They ate their breakfast in the depleted kitchen, with boxes of kitchen utensils stacked around them. The final stages of packing Diana found completely numbing.

'What on earth shall I do with this milk?' she asked, looking hunted, as she held up a jug.

'Chuck it down the sink,' said Peter robustly. 'And throw the rest of the cornflakes and bread to the birds.'

She obeyed, and then stood, looking bewildered.

'Suppose we want a drink later on? I ought to have kept out the flasks, you know, and filled them with coffee.'

'There's a pub at Fairacre, and old Burnaby will be making pots of tea like mad. Don't fret so,' said Peter impatiently.

Diana moved dumbly about her tasks. Most women, she told herself, would have thought about flasks and sandwiches and all the preparations for a move. She felt decidedly inefficient and slightly despairing. What, for instance, did she do with the last wet teacloth?

The removal men were due at nine-thirty. Peter was going ahead to let them into Tyler's Row, and Diana was left behind to see things out. Later, Peter would return to fetch her, and Tom the cat, whose basket stood on the kitchen dresser in readiness.

'You must leave Tom's saucer,' said Diana, watching Peter cram the last-minute objects into the laundry basket. 'He likes a drink about eleven.'

'Oh my lord!' moaned Peter, clutching his head. 'Tom'll have to go without today. Anyway we've thrown away the milk.'

'Oh dear! He'll go next door for Charlie's. You know what he is!'

'He won't if you shut him in the bedroom,' replied Peter firmly. 'Now, I'm off. Don't panic. Leave it all to the men, and I'll pick you up as soon as I've seen the furniture settled. Probably soon after one.'

Within minutes of his departure the furniture vans arrived, and from then on four hefty men took over. Diana wandered vaguely from room to room, trying to keep out of their way. They seemed remarkably calm and efficient, with their tea chests and mounds of newspapers, and pieces of sacking and polythene sheeting.

She watched the largest of the four deftly wrapping her best tea-set in pieces of newspaper, his great red hands handling each piece much more delicately than she could herself.

There was something very sad about uprooting all these things – worse, in a way, than uprooting oneself. A box of oddments, left for the daily woman, seemed particularly pathetic to Diana. There was the blue and white mixing bowl which Mrs Jones had always admired, and over there, waiting to be packed, was the blue and white flour dredger which had always stood beside it. It seemed wrong that they should be parted after so many years. Somehow, Diana was reminded of a family dispersed, a bond broken, each wrenched from a common home, and scattered afar.

By mid-morning the upstairs floor was stripped, and Diana's roving feet echoed dismally on the bare boards. In the spare bedroom, a disgusted cat lashed his tail and did his best to escape as the door opened. He was as upset as Diana by this outrageous shattering of routine. No after-breakfast stroll in the garden, no visiting of Charlie, the next-door Siamese, to polish off his breakfast, no mid-morning snack – it was enough to put a cat in a rage, and Tom indulged his fury to the utmost. He repelled Diana's sympathetic advances, wriggling from her arms, and gazing at her malevolently from the window sill. He had noticed the hated cat basket earlier in the day, and knew that something unpleasant was afoot. Another trip to see the vet? Another stay at the kennels? Whatever was planned was not going to be approved by Tom, and he showed his displeasure plainly.

Diana left him to his sulking, and went from bedroom to bedroom to make sure that nothing had been overlooked. The rooms, without the curtains, were amazingly light, and the walls seemed remarkably dirty. There were grubby lines where the chests of drawers and chair had stood. There was even a patch on the wall above Peter's bed, where his head must have rested when he read at night. Diana had never noticed it before, and thought the rooms looked startlingly seedy without their furnishings.

The oddest things seemed to have come to light. Whose was this grey hairpin by the skirting board? She had never used a hair-pin in her life, and certainly not a grey one. In the boys' old room, a china bead and the bayonet broken from a lead soldier glinted in the crack of the floorboards. A papery butterfly clung to their window, and in a dark corner were a few minute shreds of paper which looked suspiciously like the work of a mouse.

It was a good thing that Mrs Jones was going to scrub the place from top to bottom, thought Diana, or the new owners would think that they had lived in absolute squalor. No one, looking at the bare rooms now, would believe that they were thoroughly spring-cleaned each March, and zealously turned out once a week.

By mid-day the vans were packed, and they rumbled away down the drive. Automatically, Diana looked at the empty mantel shelf to see the time, and even wandered into the kitchen to consult the non-existent wall clock there. Her neighbour had invited her to lunch, and she made her way next door, glad to leave the uncanny silence of her own home.

'How's it going?' asked her hostess.

'Very well, I think. But I feel as though I've been put through a wringer.'

'What you need is a meal,' said her neighbour practically, leading the way.

Over at Tyler's Row the day grew more hectic as it advanced. Peter knew exactly how he wanted the unloading done, and had given explicit directions about labelling the tea-chests so that they could be taken to the right room without any delay.

'Carpets down first,' he had told Diana. 'Then cover them where the men will be treading, and simply put each piece of furniture in place as it's unpacked. It shouldn't take much more than an hour.'

Of course, it did not work out like that. The men had packed the vans with pieces which fitted well together, irrespective of the rooms for which they were intended. A little desultory labelling had been done in the early stages, but most of the tea-chests bore no labels at all. Poor methodical Peter felt his blood-pressure rising as the boxes came into the tiny hall, one after the other, with the cheerful cry: 'Where do you want this, sir?'

Diana's camphor-wood blanket chest, brought back from China by a long-dead seafarer in the family, proved to be too large to go upstairs to the landing which was to have been its resting place.

'But it *must* go up,' said Peter distractedly, watching the men twist it and turn it. The stair wall and the banisters were escaping damage by a hair's breadth. 'I *measured* the thing.'

'But did you measure these 'ere stairs?' puffed one man.

'Of course I did,' snapped Peter.

'Measurements don't help,' said the second man lugubriously. 'When you comes to it, there's always summat as sticks out. Legs, maybe, or an 'andle – or the staircase bulges. I've seen it 'appen time and time again.'

'We could take it through the bedroom window,' suggested the other, 'if we could get it out of the frame.'

'And what about the bedroom door?' cried Peter. 'That's about half the width of the window. No, no. It will have to stay downstairs for the time being.'

'In the 'all?'

'A fat lot of good that would be,' said Peter, sorely tried. 'We can't move as it is for all these unlabelled boxes. Take the thing into the garden shed for now. At least it's out of the way.'

Despite his meticulous work with pencil and paper in the preceding weeks, there were other things besides the blanket chest which Peter found to be too large or too wide for the places appointed. The kitchen door opened on to the cooker. The saucepan shelf proved to be just the right height for the handles to jut out into passers' eyes. The hall floor was so

uneven that the grandfather clock leant drunkenly this way and that and they were obliged to put it into the drawing room, displacing a bookcase which eventually joined the blanket chest in the limbo of the garden shed.

But the final straw came when an underfelt was discovered in the van and proved to be the one which should have been put down under the main bedroom carpet, upon which all the heavy furniture was now in position.

The day had been punctuated by visits from Sergeant Burnaby, loving every minute, who offered cups of tea, coffee and general advice non-stop. At four o'clock, exhausted by his tribulations, Peter reeled next door and partook of a cup of well-stewed tea sweetened with condensed milk, which he drank standing, saying, truly, that if he sat down he felt he would never rise again.

At five o'clock the men departed, cheerful to the last, and Peter set off to fetch Diana and Tom.

'I feel about a hundred,' he thought as he drove through Beech Green, dodging a pheasant bent on suicide. 'Talk about preparing for retirement! I doubt if I'll live to see it at this rate.'

And then his spirits rose. They were actually at Tyler's Row! After all the vicissitudes, it was theirs at last! In a few minutes, he and Diana would be driving away from their old home for the last time.

He stepped on the accelerator and sped towards Caxley.

But he had reckoned without Tom. Diana greeted him in some agitation.

'I went to get Tom a few minutes ago, and I swear the door wasn't open wider than three inches! He shot out through the back door, and he must be about six gardens away. I've called till I'm hoarse. What shall we do?'

'Tell Kitty next door. He's bound to turn up tonight for his food, or for Charlie's. We'll come over last thing to collect him, or tomorrow morning.'

Diana departed, and Peter took a look at the empty house. He could understand Diana being upset about the move, he realized suddenly. Such a lot had happened here. Almost all their married life had been spent under this roof. The house had served them well. He hoped the newcomers would be as happy in it.

Diana returned much relieved.

'Kitty will look out for him. It's a pity we're not on the phone yet at Tyler's Row, but she says we're not to dream of turning out again tonight after such a day. She'll keep him in her house overnight.'

They drove slowly down the familiar gravel path.

'Trust Tom,' said Peter, smiling. 'I thought this would be our final exit, but what's the betting we are back and forth like yoyos fetching that dam' cat?'

'How's the house?' said Diana.

'A shambles,' replied her husband happily, 'but I've found the drink and the glasses to celebrate getting in at last. We've made it, my dear!'

Later, when the celebratory drinks were over, Diana became unusually business-like.

'Now, the first thing to do is to hang the curtains. Then we must make up the beds and put in hot bottles.'

'What, in this weather?'

'The sheets have been packed in a suitcase for the last two days. They may be damp.'

'Which suitcase?'

'The red one,' said Diana briskly. 'I put everything we should need for the beds in it. Including the bottles.'

'Well, where is it?'

Diana's confidence wavered.

'Here, somewhere. Upstairs, I should think.'

There was no sign of it upstairs. Downstairs, a pile of boxes, holdalls, cases and bundles yielded no red suitcase. Diana, by now, was reduced to her more normal state of vagueness.

'Did you see it go into the van?'

'No. We brought it over ourselves one day this week.'

'Are you sure?'

'I'm not sure of anything now,' cried Diana hopelessly. 'I swear I'll never move again. It's all too exhausting.'

'Have another drink,' said Peter, watching his wife sink on to the settee between a pile of curtains and a mound of *The National Geographical Magazine*.

'No, I'm tiddly enough as it is.'

She pushed her fingers through her hair distractedly.

'I *know* it's here,' she said firmly. 'Think, Peter. You must have seen it during the day.'

She fixed him with a glittering stare.

'You frighten the life out of me,' said her husband, 'looking like the Ancient Mariner.'

He stared back, then put down his glass and left the room. In a moment, he returned carrying the case.

'Under the stairs,' he said triumphantly. 'Come to think of it, I put it there myself. I thought it had dusters and brushes and things in it.'

He looked at it more closely.

'But you said "a red case". This is brown.'

'It's maroon or burgundy,' said Diana, snapping it open with relief. 'That means red.'

'The only red I recognize is the colour of a pillar box,' said Peter, following his wife with an armful of bed-linen.

By the time the beds were made and the curtains hung in their bedroom and the sitting room they were too tired to do much more.

'I should like a mixed grill,' said Peter. 'A large one – with plenty of kidney.'

'Well, you won't get it, my love,' replied Diana cheerfully. 'I propose to give you a tin of soup prepared by Messrs Crosse and Blackwell's fair hands. That is, if we can find the tin opener. And we might rise to bread and cheese after that. And if you really want high life, you can top up with a banana, rather squashed.'

'It sounds delightful,' said Peter resignedly. 'Do we get breakfast?'

'With luck,' said Diana. 'We'll have to be up early, by the way, to let in the workmen.'

'Well, let's have this rave-up of a meal now,' suggested Peter. 'I'll go out and lock up the shed, and see everything's to rights.'

Outside, a full moon was rising, glowing orange through the light mist that veiled the downs. The air was as fresh as spring water, and the scent of narcissi came from Mrs Fowler's trim garden next door.

Peter breathed in deeply, savouring the beauty of the night, and relishing the thought of happy years to be spent in Fairacre. He turned to look at Tyler's Row.

Through the curtainless kitchen window he could see Diana at the stove. He hoped she would be as happy as he was about the house. She had been so content in Caxley. It would be terrible if she found Fairacre lonely or uncongenial. He must make sure that she settled here easily. It was a good thing, he told himself, that term did not begin for another week or so. They could get the place straight together, and ease the change-over.

Dimmer lights than their own kitchen one shone from the two cottages at each end. A greenish one at Mrs Fowler's suggested that she was watching television. Sergeant Burnaby's glowed as orange as the moon, behind his buff curtains.

'If only all four were empty!' thought Peter. 'If only we could start stage two!'

If, if . . .

His grandmother used to have some tart remark about 'ifs and buts getting you nowhere', he remembered. Maybe she was right. It was enough, for the moment, to be in Tyler's Row, to sleep under its thatch and to have his first meal – austere though that promised to be – in its kitchen.

With a last look at the exterior of his domain, Peter turned to go indoors.

8. An Exhausting Evening

'They're in then,' said Mr Willet as I crossed the playground to go into school. He was perched on a stepladder tying back the American pillar rose which scrambles over the side of the school, clashing hideously with the brickwork, but delighting us all with its bountiful growth.

'Who are?'

'Them new people. Hales. Schoolmaster up Caxley. Took Tyler's Row.'

Mr Willet's staccato delivery was caused more by rhythmic lunges at a high shoot than by impatience with my stupidity.

'Oh yes! I forgot they were moving in. Yesterday, wasn't it?'

'And a nice day they had for it too,' said Mr Willet, coming down the ladder. 'Very lucky, they was. Not all plain sailing though, from what I hear. Them removable men was a bit slap-handed, and they found the underfelt after they'd put everything in the bedroom.'

'Good lord!'

'You might well say so. Then their blessed cat run off in Caxley and they're having to fetch it today.'

I began to wonder how Mr Willet knew all this. As if he guessed my thoughts, he spoke deprecatingly.

'Not that I know much about it, of course. I'm not one to meddle in other folk's affairs, but you can't help over-hearing things in a village.'

'So I've noticed,' I said, one hand on the school's door-handle.

Mr Willet pointed roofwards.

'Couple of sparrows making a nest up the end there. I suppose I dursen't pull it out?'

'No indeed,' I said firmly. 'I like sparrows.'

'Not many does,' commented Mr Willet.

'I know. I can't think why. I once knew a kind, good-hearted man, very much respected everywhere, who used to catch sparrows and pull off their heads. Quite unlike him really.'

'Very sensible he sounds,' said Mr Willet approvingly. 'They're pestses, is sparrows. Worse'n rats, I reckon.'

'That's as maybe,' I replied, using one of Mrs Pringle's favourite phrases, 'but you can leave that nest alone.'

My caretaker beamed indulgently, and I left the bright sunshine to enter Fairacre School, knowing that the sparrows would be spared.

Later that morning, I decided it was too splendidly sunny to stay indoors, and bade the children dress and accompany me on a saunter round the village. This invitation was received with rapture.

These occasional sorties are officially known as 'nature walks', and to make these outings seem more legitimate we collect such things as twigs, flowers, mosses, feathers, snail-shells and other natural objects to take back to the classroom for study. Naturally, other objects, far more attractive to the children, have to be discarded.

Cigarette cartons, bottle tops, nuts and bolts, crisp bags, lengths of wire, tubing, binder twine, broken plastic cups, pieces of glass from smashed windscreens and rear-lights and a hundred other manifestations of civilization are collected, only to be thrown into the school dustbin, amidst general regret.

This morning the April sunshine was really warm, a preview, as it were, of summer days to come. Enormous clouds towered into the blue sky above the downs, moving slowly and majestically in the light breeze. A bevy of larks mounted invisible stairs to heaven, letting fall a cascade of song as they climbed. Cats and dogs sunned themselves on cottage doorsteps, and here and there a budgerigar had been hung outside in its cage to enjoy the early warmth and fresh air.

A red tractor, bright as a ladybird, crawled slowly up and down Mr Roberts' large field behind the school, and the children waved energetically to the driver.

'My dad,' said Patrick proudly.

'My uncle,' said Ernest, at the same moment. They were both right. And that, I thought, sniffing at an early white violet, is the best of a village school. It remains, even now, a family affair.

We took the rough lane that leads uphill to the bare downs. For the first hundred yards or so, a few trees and bushes line the path. The thorny sloes were already pricked with white blossom, and the black ash buds were beginning to break into leaf along the pewter-grey stems.

Joseph Coggs knelt suddenly down in a patch of dry grass by the side of the lane.

'Got a nail in me shoe,' he explained.

'Us all 'ave,' retorted Patrick, convulsed by his own wit.

Eileen gave a sudden shriek.

'There's a snake, miss! Look, by Jo!'

Sure enough, the last few inches of a small grass snake could be seen slithering for cover among the bushes. Obviously, it had been sunning itself in the grass and was disturbed by Joseph.

'Kill 'un!' shouted some of the boys, advancing with sticks upraised.

'No, it's cruel!' shrieked the girls.

'Leave it alone,' I said firmly. 'It doesn't do any harm. In fact, it does quite a lot of good.'

'That's right,' agreed Ernest, siding with me. 'Grass snakes eat beetles, and frogs, and tadpoles, and earwigs, and worms, and spiders, and slugs, and maggots, and snails and . . .'

He paused for breath.

'Brembutter?' asked someone sarcastically. 'Old knowall!'

This shaft of wit caused more general hilarity. The boys smote each other with juvenile joy. The girls tittered behind their hands, and the snake made good his escape in the general furore.

'See who can get to the top first,' I said suddenly, and watched them stampede uphill, screaming with excitement. I followed at a more sedate pace, relishing my temporary solitude and mentally congratulating the sparrows and the grass snake on their escape from their male predators.

The children's spirits were still high when we returned to the school room, but mine had suddenly plummeted. This very evening the first meeting of the Parent–Teacher Association of Fairacre School was to be held.

My struggles against the formation of this association had

been prolonged but necessarily half-hearted. If popular demand clamoured for such a thing, then a headmistress must bend, particularly if she wished to live in amity with her neighbours.

It had been decided by half the committee to make the first meeting a purely social occasion, but the other half had felt that something more earnest and meaty should mark the event. Mrs Johnson and Mrs Mawne were both of this faction.

'I happen to know the president of the Caxley P.T.A. group,' Mrs Johnson said, with some pride. 'I'm sure I could persuade her to come and give a talk about the aims of the movement.'

After some discussion, a compromise was arranged. Mrs Jollifant would be invited to give a *short* talk, 'a *really brief* talk,' emphasized the vicar, our chairman, 'say, of about fifteen to twenty minutes in length.' This, we all felt, need not take too much time from the main activities of the evening, which would be eating, drinking, listening to a duet played on the school piano by Ernest's mother and aunt, 'Three Little Maids from School' sung by three of the younger mothers, and looking at slides of Mrs Mawne's holiday in Venice, that is if we could find the right plug for the projector. Mrs Johnson had offered to prepare a quiz ('Make it *simple*,' begged the vicar), and would supply pencils and paper for this excitement.

'Now leave your desks tidy,' I exhorted my flock at the end of their school day. 'Your parents may want to look at your books, and they don't want to see half-sucked sweets and lumps of putty, any more than I do.'

There was a feverish scrabbling among their possessions, and the waste-paper basket overflowed in record time. I saw them out thankfully, did my own tidying, and went across to the school house to have an hour or two's breather before facing the rigours of a social evening.

At seven-fifteen, clad in my best black frock which Fairacre knows only too well, I went back to the school room bearing a handsome bowl of King Alfred daffodils which I was lending for the occasion.

It looked rather splendid, I thought, on top of the ancient piano. Mrs Johnson, rushing in two minutes later, stopped short in her tracks and threw up her hands.

'Well, that thing can't stay there,' she said, advancing upon my beauties. 'The window sill, I think.'

'It's not wide enough,' I said mildly. 'Anyway, what's wrong with the top of the piano? They show up rather well there.'

'The piano,' explained Mrs Johnson, with ill-concealed impatience, 'is to be *in use*. It will have to be *open* for the duets and the accompaniments.'

'You'll be lucky,' I told her. 'It's never been opened since the skylight dripped on it and the wood swelled.'

Mrs Johnson breathed heavily and turned a little pink, but banged the bowl back on the piano top, and turned away.

Parents began to arrive thick and fast, and I kept a sharp look-out for my old friend Amy, whilst welcoming them at the door. Amy is not a parent at all, but she was at college with me and sometimes does a little 'supply' teaching to keep her hand in. At this time she was helping at the same Caxley school at which our speaker, Mrs Jollifant, was a member of staff. Consequently, Amy had double entry, as it were, into tonight's festivities.

I saw her soon enough, in an exquisitely cut burgundy-red wool frock. One large cabuchon garnet swung on a long gold chain about her neck, and her dark red shoes I mentally priced at twelve pounds. We kissed each other with real affection. Amy, though she tries to boss me, is very dear to me, and the memory of horrors shared at college binds us very close.

'Put me somewhere at the back,' she said, with unusual modesty.

'Not in that frock,' I said. 'You'll sit in the front and delight all eyes.'

The vicar settled matters by taking her arm and leading her to a seat next to his own, and very soon afterwards he opened the proceedings with an admirably clear explanation of the reasons for our being gathered together.

'We are particularly fortunate in having Mrs Jollifant for our speaker,' he said. 'She will be with us in a few minutes, but has to attend another meeting in Caxley first. Meanwhile, we will have a short session of community singing, if someone will give out the booklets.'

I rose to oblige. These dog-eared pamphlets date back to the days of war – the last war, I hasten to add – though you might not think so on reading the contents.

'Pack Up Your Troubles In Your Old Kit-bag' and 'Tipperary' are there, relics of World War One, and 'Goodbye, Dolly, I Must Leave You' carries us right back to the Boer War seventy-odd years ago. However, 'Roll Out The Barrel' redresses the balance a little, and 'She'll Be Coming Round the Mountain' seems positively up-to-date.

At any rate, all Fairacre knows them well, and we sang lustily, to Mrs Moffat's somewhat erratic accompaniment on the piano. The daffodils nodded vigorously on the tightly-closed lid, much to my satisfaction.

When we were exhausted, the vicar introduced Mr Johnson as our next contributor to the general gaiety.

'He is going to sing to us,' said the vicar, with a hint of resignation in his tone which I thought misplaced.

Mr Johnson, clutching a sheet of music, made signals to Mrs Moffat. What would it be? I half-hoped for a spirited rendering of 'The Red Flag'. His three ebullient children had taught the rest of the school a lively ditty in the playground which had become very popular.

It went:

> Let him go or let him tarry,
> Let him sink or let him swim,
> He doesn't care for me
> And I don't care for him:
> For I'm the worker, he's the boss
> And the boss's day is done,
> But the worker's day is coming
> Like the rising of the sun.

But Mr Johnson did no more than sing 'Bless This House' in a pleasant baritone, and with the mildest of expression. I felt cheated, but the general applause was warm.

Mrs Jollifant arrived at this juncture, a dazzling figure in a trouser-suit of shimmering metallic thread. There were some looks of disapproval from the older ladies in the audience, but the young mothers gazed in open admiration.

Her hair was piled high in a tea-cosy style, and was of that

intense uniform blackness which only a hairdresser can achieve. She carried a beaded and fringed handbag and an ominously large bundle of notes.

After polite clapping, Mrs Jollifant began her little talk. The time was eight o'clock.

At twenty past, she had covered what she described as 'The preliminary steps to forming a Parent–Teacher Association'. By eight-thirty we had heard of the Necessity For Co-operation, Keeping Abreast of Modern Methods, and the Need for Constant Discussion Between Parent and Teacher.

The two tea-ladies here tip-toed out across the creaking floorboards to turn down the boiler which was bubbling in readiness for the tea and coffee. I noticed that they did not return.

By ten to nine, a certain amount of fidgeting began, and one or two young mothers whispered agitatedly to each other. Mrs Jollifant's address flowed on remorselessly. Amy, sitting betweeen the vicar and me, sighed noisily, and crossed one elegant leg over the other. I admired the beautiful shoes without envy, and hoped that the rumbling of my stomach was not heard by anyone but myself. A cup of coffee would have been welcome half-an-hour ago. Now it was needed as a desperate restorative.

St Patrick's church clock struck nine, but this did not perturb our speaker. We had now reached the Benefits To Our Children stage, with a lot of stuff about Flowering Minds, Spiritual Needs and the Sharing of Love and Experience. Every profession, I thought wearily, has its own appalling jargon, but surely Education takes the biscuit.

At nine-fifteen Mrs Mawne rose, with considerable clattering, and said she really must go, as it was getting *so late*. Mrs Mawne does not lack moral courage, and though the general feeling was, no doubt, of disapproval at such behaviour, there was a certain amount of envy as we watched her depart into the night.

The two tea-ladies, emboldened by Mrs Mawne's gesture, now put their heads round the door and asked if they should make the tea.

Mrs Jollifant, not a whit abashed, said she would be exactly five minutes, was exactly fifteen, and at length sat down to thunderous applause activated by relief rather than rapture.

Stiffly, with creaking joints, rumbling stomachs and slight headaches, we made an ugly rush upon the tea, coffee and sandwiches, before embarking on a shortened second half of our social evening.

Later by my fireside, Amy and I caught up with our own affairs. James, her husband, now had to go to London regularly twice a week, and stay overnight, she told me.

'An awful bore for him,' said Amy, fingering her gold chain. 'He brought me back this garnet last week.'

Amy has a collection of beautiful jewellery which James brings home after his business trips. Sometimes I wonder if Amy has suspicions, but she is a loyal wife, and says nothing.

'It's simply lovely,' I said honestly.

'You should wear red,' said Amy, studying me, and looking as though she found the result slightly repellent. 'I've told you before not to wear black. It positively *kills* you.'

'But I've got it! I must wear it. It's hardly been worn at all.'

'Now, that's a flat lie. To my knowledge you've had it four years. You wore it first to my cocktail party.'

'I may have had it four years – that's nothing in Fairacre. I don't get much opportunity to wear this sort of frock. It'll do for another four easily.'

'Put it in the next jumble sale, and buy yourself a red one. Give Fairacre a treat. Or what about a sparkling trouser-suit like Mrs J's?'

'No thanks.'

Amy lit a cigarette.

'Detestable woman! I try and avoid her at school. She wears emeralds with sapphires.'

'Bully for her,' I said. 'I'd like the chance to wear either of 'em. My Aunt Clara's seed pearls are about the nearest I get to the real thing.'

Amy blew three perfect smoke rings in a row, one of the ex-curricular accomplishments I watched her learn at college.

'She's such a phoney,' said Amy. 'All that terrible stuff we heard tonight! If you could only see her three children!'

'No Flowering Minds? No Sharing of Love and Experience?'

'Plenty of that all right,' said Amy darkly. 'The two youngest are at school. The eldest, an unattractive amalgam of hair and spots, is at one of the danker universities in the north. He brought his girl-friend home for the entire vacation. Heavily pregnant too.'

'Is he going to marry her?'

'Well, it's not his baby, so he says, so probably not. Could you squeeze another cup of coffee out of that pot?'

I poured thoughtfully.

'What about the other two?'

'Both on probation. One steals, the other fights, and they both lie. I'd give them two years before the mast rather than probation, but of course it does mean Mrs Jollifant gets seen too by the probation officer when he visits.'

'You'd think she'd keep quiet about children,' I said, 'having such horrible children of her own.'

'The Mrs Jollifants of this world,' Amy told me pontifically, 'do not recognize horrible children – least of all their own. By

the time your Parent–Teacher Association has brain-washed
you, with half-a-dozen speakers like Mrs J, you'll think they're
all perfect angels too.'

'That'll be the day!' I told her, reaching for the coffee-pot.

9. Callers

May, that loveliest of months, surpassed itself as the Hales settled into their new home. Shrubs, which had stood half-hidden by dead grass and weeds when Peter and Diana had first visited Tyler's Row, now flowered abundantly. Lilac bushes, pink, white and deep purple, tossed their scent into the air, and a fine cherry tree dangled its white blossom nearby. Unsuspected bulbs had pushed up bravely, and delighted them with late flowering narcissi and tulips. Those perennials which had escaped the notice of Mr Roberts' cows, flourished in the fine dark soil, and Diana already made plans for new beds in the autumn.

She was so busy that she had no time to miss the whirl of Caxley's social life. It was a relief, she found, to be free of coffee mornings, bazaars, cheese and wine parties, and all the other fund-raising affairs which she had felt obliged to attend. The invitations still came, but she was able to answer truthfully that she had too much to see to at the moment.

The workmen were still with them, and at times Peter wondered if they would ever go.

'I confidently expect to wrap up Christmas parcels for them,' he commented gloomily, watching their van depart one tea-time. 'I shall give Bert a bottle of shampoo, and Frank a belt to keep up those filthy jeans. Binder twine doesn't appear to do the job.'

Bert and Frank were two cheerful youths, self-styled 'subcontractors', who were engaged in the last stages of the outdoor painting. They were accompanied everywhere by a transistor radio which blared out a stream of pop music to the unspoken despair of Diana, and the very outspoken fury – when he was there to hear it – of Peter. As they plied their brushes, squatting on their haunches or balanced on ladders, they shouted above the din to each other. Diana heard their exchanges and found them incomprehensible.

''E fouled 'im right 'nuff. Ref be blind 'arf the time.'

'Ar! Wants to drop ol' Betts. Never make the fourth round with 'im in goal. See 'im Sat'day?'

Football appeared to be the only topic of conversation, and this was punctuated with occasional bursts of discordant song with transistor accompaniment.

At eleven each morning, Diana made coffee for them. She carried it into the sunshine, and they knocked off with alacrity and sat on the garden seat. Sometimes she sat with them and they told her about their families. To her eyes they appeared only children themselves, but Bert had two boys of his own, and Frank three girls.

After ten minutes, Diana would hurry back to her work, but the two young men remained sitting and smoking until half-past eleven or twenty to twelve.

'Ah well,' one would say, rising reluctantly, 'best get back, I s'pose.'

'Ar! Get the ol' job done,' the other would agree, and they would amble back to their paint brushes, much refreshed.

And their wives, thought Diana, are scrubbing, and washing, and ironing, and cooking, and shopping, and dressing and undressing young children, and generally running round in circles. And when their husbands get home, no doubt the wives will think indulgently: 'Poor things, they've been working hard all day! Must give them a good meal, and let them have a nice rest while I wash up and put the children to bed!'

Diana's immediate neighbours were not greatly in evidence, she was relieved to find. Certainly, Sergeant Burnaby tended to hover near the dividing hedge whenever she had occasion to go into the garden, and was pathetically eager to prolong any little conversations they had. But her fears that he might make frequent calls proved groundless, and only the rattle of his poker in the grate next door, or the sharp tap-tap caused by knocking out his pipe on the fire-bars, called his presence to mind.

From Mrs Fowler's side, nothing was heard. 'Keeping herself to herself' was one of her prides, and Diana only had a rare glimpse of her when she hung out some of her dazzling washing, or took a bowl down the garden path to pick some greens.

But if Diana saw little of her neighbour, the same could not be said of Mrs Fowler, who knew nine-tenths of the newcomers' movements. Before a week was out she knew that the Hales preferred brown bread to white, took one pint of Jersey milk a day, sent sheets, pillowslips, towels – even tea-towels and dusters, which Mrs Fowler thought scandalous – to the laundry, and that Peter Hale used an electric razor, and that the bed-side alarm went off at seven o'clock sharp.

Diana was unaware of the intense interest that the village as a whole took in their affairs. She would have been surprised and amused to know that Mr Lamb at the Post Office knew where her two sons were stationed, that the Hales banked with the National Westminster and had monthly accounts with a Caxley garage, butcher, and hardware store. He had still to find out who the titled lady was to whom Mrs Hale wrote regularly. (It was, in fact, an elderly aunt.) He was intrigued too by the number of letters addressed to a certain Oxford College in Mr Hale's neat hand, but Mr Lamb was used to biding his time, and was confident that all these things would be made clear to him, if he waited long enough.

There had been several callers at Tyler's Row. The vicar, the Reverend Gerald Partridge, and his wife were the first to come, and later Mrs Mawne descended upon Diana when she was engaged in the almost impossible task of pinning up the hem of a frock whilst wearing it. She opened the door to her visitor, very conscious of her uneven hem-line and the half-dozen pins threatening her stockings.

'I know that calling is out-of-date these days,' said Mrs Mawne when they were seated in the drawing room, 'and a great pity it is, I think. One can feel so lonely in a new place. I know I was quite daunted when I first came to Fairacre. Luckily, my husband had been here for some little time before me, and of course he'd made a number of friends.'

'I thought I would join the Women's Institute,' said Diana. 'It's a very good way of meeting people.'

'*Excellent!*' agreed Mrs Mawne, with energy. 'We can always do with new members, especially on the committee.'

'Well, I don't know – ' began Diana, somewhat taken aback.

'Your leg,' said Mrs Mawne, peering through her glasses, 'appears to be bleeding.'

'Confound these pins!' exclaimed Diana, leaping to her feet, and explained her predicament.

'Well, we'll soon put that right,' said Mrs Mawne, and fell upon her knees on the new carpet. 'Hand me the pins and a ruler.'

'They're upstairs,' said Diana. 'One moment, and I'll fetch them.'

For the next five minutes the ladies were engrossed in their task, and Diana thought that Mrs Mawne, formidable though her manner was, certainly had her practical side.

'Now stand still while I crawl round,' said her visitor. She thumped down the school ruler on its end, by one side seam.

'Seventeen,' puffed Mrs Mawne, circumnavigating her hostess, and pausing at intervals with the ruler.

'Seventeen, seventeen, seventeen-and-a-quarter — blast-it! Hold hard a minute!'

After a short battle with the pins, Mrs Mawne professed herself satisfied, and scrambled with difficulty to her feet.

'It's terribly kind of you,' said Diana. 'You couldn't have

called at a better time for me. Now let me brush your skirt. This new carpet is shedding whiskers madly.'

Mrs Mawne gave the skirt a perfunctory bang with a massive hand.

'Don't vacuum clean it too much just yet,' she advised. 'Hand brush for a few weeks, I always say, until it's settled in.'

'Let me give you some tea.'

'No, no. I've the dogs to exercise, and Henry wants me to type a talk he's giving in Caxley.'

'It was good of you to come, and kinder still to help with my pinning up. You must bring your husband to meet mine before long.'

She accompanied Mrs Mawne to the front door.

'How do you get on with the next door folk?' asked Mrs Mawne in a voice which was much too loud for Diana's peace of mind. Through one hedge she could see Mrs Fowler, bent to weed her path, but strategically placed to see and hear all that transpired. Intermittent coughing came from beyond the other hedge where Sergeant Burnaby sat enjoying the sunshine. His hearing, for so venerable a man, was amazingly acute at times, as Diana well knew.

'Very well. Very well indeed,' said Diana firmly. 'We're extremely lucky.'

'Glad to hear it. Neighbours can be a curse or a comfort,' boomed Mrs Mawne. She dropped her voice a trifle and spoke now in a tone which was possibly more penetrating than before.

'You'll have to watch Mrs Fowler. A very awkward woman, I hear, and apt to be vindictive. Not to be trusted. Not to be trusted at all. Remind me to tell you a tale next time we meet. More in the nature of a *warning*, you understand.'

'Thank you again for calling,' said Diana. 'I shall look forward to seeing you at the W.I. meeting.'

Mrs Mawne stumped off to the gate, and Diana watched her departure with relief. The bent figure next door straightened itself with a loud sniff, and the banging of Mrs Fowler's front door seemed to prove the point of the old adage that eavesdroppers hear no good of themselves.

*

The W.I. meeting did not take place for a week or more, but before that event occurred Diana met a great many more of Fairacre's inhabitants.

The village shop, which was also the bakery, proved to be as much a club as a business, and here she was introduced to other customers.

The owner was an old boy of Caxley Grammar School and knew Peter well. Old boys were ubiquitous within a radius of ten miles around Caxley and turned up as electricians, plumbers, nurserymen, as well as bank managers, solicitors, accountants and other men of business. The family feeling engendered by this tie was very reassuring, Diana found.

Mr Willet was one of the first friends she met at the shop.

'I'm going your way,' he said on the first occasion. 'Give us your basket, while you carry the cornflakes. That's one's work alone, them great packets.'

They walked amicably along the village street.

'That's my place,' said Mr Willet. 'You must meet my wife some time. She tells me you're going to join the W.I.'

'Yes, I am.'

'Jumble-jam-and-Jerusalem!' commented Mr Willet, with a rumbling laugh. 'That's what they calls it, eh? Well, keeps you ladies out of mischief, I suppose. You want to watch they don't get you on the Committee though. Fair sharpens their knives there, I understand.'

'Oh, I haven't been here long enough for that honour,' said Diana.

'It's the new ones that get copped,' replied Mr Willet shrewdly. 'You take a look round. You won't find many of the old sort running things in Fairacre – they're too fly. They likes to sit back and watch the newcomers make a mess o' things, and then they can criticize.'

They approached Tyler's Row and slowed to a halt.

'You all right for help in the house?' asked Mr Willet solicitously.

'At the moment, yes, thank you. Mrs Jones who worked for me in Caxley comes out once a week.'

'Good. 'Tisn't easy to get a decent body as you can trust.'

He handed over the basket.

'Well, I must be off to the school. Caretaker, see. Odd job man, like. Be plenty of coke spread about the playground for me to sweep up, I've no doubt. Still, did the same meself when I was there fifty years back.'

He gave a smile which creased his weathered face, reminding Diana of a wrinkled apple.

'If you wants anything, let me know. Or your husband now, if he needs a load of logs or someone to fix that gate of yourn, tell him to come and see me. I've heard plenty about him from my two nephews as goes to his school. They've got more up top than I had at their age.'

'I very much doubt it,' said Diana with conviction.

On the following afternoon Diana went to Caxley, and returned to Tyler's Row to find that the first salvo had been fired in a battle which was to last for months.

A light breeze was blowing, and Diana had noticed faint wisps of smoke drifting from the Sergeant's garden across their own, towards Mrs Fowler's property. The bonfire was at the end of the garden, and could have given no offence to anyone, at the stage when Diana first saw it.

She was just peeling off her gloves, when the knock came at the front door. On opening it, she was confronted by Mrs Fowler, dressed very neatly in an afternoon frock, and surmounted by a hat. It was of a masculine nature, something of a trilby modified for feminine wear, but still uncompromisingly severe. Beneath it, Mrs Fowler's grim countenance appeared more formidable than ever.

'Will you come in?' said Diana, regretting the invitation the moment she had made it.

She showed her visitor into the sitting room, and both perched on the edge of their chairs. Mrs Fowler wasted no time.

'I'm here to make a complaint,' she said formally. Her quick eyes were flickering about the room, noting everything. She would be the winner at any Kim's game, thought Diana, with wry amusement.

'I'm sorry to hear that,' she replied. 'Have we done something to offend you, Mrs Fowler?'

'It's not you, ma'am. It's 'im!'

She jerked a thumb at the dividing wall, in the direction of Sergeant Burnaby's abode.

''E does it for sheer devilment,' she went on, her face becoming flushed. 'Waits till 'e sees it 'anging out, then gets to work.'

'Sees what?' asked Diana, understandably bewildered.

'The washing. The clothes. Waits till I've pegged out the lot, and then lights 'is bonfire. Time and time again it's 'appened. All over smuts, they get, clear-starched, fresh-boiled, hand-washed woollies – 'e don't care.'

Diana had often heard of people bridling, and had never quite known what this meant. Now she saw it in action. Mrs Fowler fairly bubbled over with her grievances, but with an air of militancy which boded no good to any who crossed her path just then.

'Surely,' she began gently, 'he doesn't do it intentionally?'

'Oh, don't 'e!' exclaimed Mrs Fowler vindictively. ''E watches the weather-cock on the church to see when 'is ol' bonfire can do most damage! I've seen 'im at it.'

'Then why not go to him and put your complaint directly? What can I do?'

'Well, he's your tenant, same as I am. 'E takes no notice of what I say. Laughs in me face, 'e does. But if you – or, say, Mr Hale – should have a word with the old devil – pardon my language, ma'am – there's a chance 'e might see reason.'

Diana sighed.

'I don't like it at all, Mrs Fowler. We all live at close quarters, and we simply must be understanding and tolerant.'

'I've been that long enough,' retorted Mrs Fowler, buttoning up her mouth.

'Well, I'll tell my husband that you called,' said Diana, rising to her feet, 'but I don't promise that he will intervene. I still advise you to mention the matter politely to Sergeant Burnaby. It's probably just male thoughtlessness. After all, he's getting very old, you know.'

'It's the old 'uns,' said Mrs Fowler darkly, as she crossed the threshold, 'as is the worst!'

*

93

'Bad-tempered old harridan,' was Peter Hale's comment that evening when he arrived home from school and was told the tale.

'Let them get on with it. We're not taking sides. Anyway, it's only a storm in a tea-cup. That woman's liverish. You can see that plain enough from her complexion. What she needs is more exercise. A sharp three-mile walk daily would soon put her right.'

'I'll leave you to tell her that,' commented Diana dryly.

10. *Awkward Neighbours*

No more was heard of this incident, and as Sergeant Burnaby refrained from lighting a bonfire during the next few days, Diana hoped that all would be well. Fairacre was so lovely in the May sunshine that nothing could daunt her spirits for long. They soared even higher when Bert told her that they reckoned to be finished in a week.

'Marvellous!' cried Diana, with heartfelt relief.

'Been a nice job, this has,' said Bert, turning up the transistor's volume a trifle.

'That's right,' shouted Frank, above the racket. 'Peaceful out here. I like a bit of country myself.'

'What say?' bellowed Bert, climbing the stepladder.

Frank executed a few intricate dance steps round a paint pot and ended up nearer his friend.

'Eh?'

'I said "What say?"' repeated Bert, fortissimo.

'Dunno what you're on about,' yelled Frank cheerfully, moving on a yard or two, and beginning to ply his brush languidly.

Diana retreated from the din, savouring this most welcome news. At last, to have the house to themselves!

She told Peter as soon as he came in.

'Now that', he said approvingly, 'calls for a glass of sherry. And it will give me strength to tackle Form One's History essays.'

His glass was empty, and the pile of exercise books reduced by half, when he sat back, sighing.

'Do they teach spelling these days?'

'I think so. Why?'

'Well, it appears from this young man's account of the finding of the treasure ship at Sutton Hoo, that "they discovered golden bowels, spoons and things". What d'you think of that?'

'Odd.'

'Very. Mind you, I must admit to getting a bit tangled with "necessary" and "occurred" myself.'

'And "antirrhinum",' agreed Diana thoughtfully.

'Luckily,' said Peter, 'that doesn't seem to crop up very frequently in History.'

He resumed his marking doggedly.

Now that the house was almost straight, the Hales began to entertain their friends. In a cottage as small as theirs, the perfect way to see one's friends was to invite two, or at most four, to dinner.

Diana enjoyed cooking, and the frequent dinner parties which they gave in the early summer evenings gave everyone much pleasure.

The weather was so warm that it was possible to have drinks, and sometimes after-dinner coffee, in the garden. Mrs Fowler and Sergeant Burnaby were interested and not-too-well-hidden spectators on these occasions.

One evening, the Hales had an old college friend of Peter's for the evening. He had been invited to talk to the boys, have tea with the Headmaster, and then drive out to Fairacre.

'Poached salmon?' said Diana. 'Everyone likes it, and if it's cold we needn't hurry with drinks.'

'Fine, fine,' replied Peter, hastily finishing his breakfast.

Diana spent most of the day on her preparations, poaching and skinning the fish, making a green salad, scraping new potatoes, whisking a strawberry mousse, and beating up fresh mayonnaise.

By six-thirty the table was set in the diminutive dining room and Diana awaited their guest. How many years since she had seen Robert, she wondered? The boys had been at school, she remembered. It must be more than ten, though he and Peter had met occasionally during that time.

She dwelt, with some satisfaction, on the meal she had prepared. Everything had gone well. It was bound to be appreciated.

The car arrived and after affectionate greetings, they took their drinks into the garden. The windows of all three cottages stood open. There was no breeze, the air was warm and still, disturbed only by a flight of swifts that were screaming round the village and passed over Tyler's Row, now and again, in their career.

'It's good to be back,' said Robert, his face tilted to watch the birds. 'Do you know it's three years since I've been in England?'

'Is Hong Kong so attractive?'

Robert was in banking and had been abroad for over seven years.

'It is, of course. But it's not that. Somehow I seem to have spent all my leaves elsewhere. My mother and sister are in France now, and I usually go there.'

'How did the boys enjoy your talk?' asked Diana.

'Never seen them so attentive,' said Peter. 'Not since we had that aged general who kept walking about so near the edge of the platform that they held their breath waiting for him to fall off.'

Robert laughed.

'The slides accounted for the attention. Hong Kong is very photogenic. But tell me all the news. How are the boys? And what about the Caxley friends? And how is it working out here? I must say, it all looks marvellous. You've done some good work in this garden.'

'Come and see the vegetable patch,' said Peter, when Robert had finished admiring the flowers. 'Not that we grow much, but Diana thinks a few early potatoes are worthwhile, and lettuces and runner-beans.'

'I grow peas too. Not potatoes though. Never touch 'em. My waist-line won't stand it.'

Diana congratulated herself silently on the large green salad which awaited them. The new potatoes, simmering gently on the stove, would obviously only be eaten by the Hales.

'Sometimes I wonder,' went on Robert, gazing at the young lettuces, 'if exercise helps at all.'

'Of course it does,' said Peter, mounting his hobby-horse. 'Half today's ills are caused through lack of exercise and fresh air.'

'Well, I play golf regularly, and spend a month salmon-fishing with old Craig. Remember him?'

Peter nodded.

'Salmon's rather fattening, I believe,' said Peter.

'I never eat the stuff, anyway,' said Robert. 'Friends get any I catch.'

Peter opened his mouth, caught Diana's eye, and said nothing.

'I must go and dish up,' said Diana, hoping that the tin-opener was in working order. At that moment, the sound of a brass-band, energetically playing 'The Turkish March', came from Sergeant Burnaby's windows. The old soldier must have had the volume well turned up, for the rhythm throbbed through the still air, shattering the evening's peace.

'Well, let's hope that soon stops,' commented Peter, watching his wife disappear.

They ate their melon to a musical accompaniment, although the sound was slightly less formidable indoors.

'Ham and tongue,' announced Diana, bearing in the dish.

'Delicious!' said Robert, rubbing his hands together.

Peter said nothing, as he took up the carving knife and fork, but his look of conspiratorial admiration pleased his wife.

Just then, Sergeant Burnaby's radio let forth a prolonged scream, then some whoops, and finally settled down to emit a strident tune with plenty of tympani in evidence. The cottage shook, and a copper bowl on the Hales' mantelpiece began to throb in sympathy.

'I do apologize for this,' said Peter. 'It's worse than it's ever been.'

'Tell me about your neighbours,' said Robert. 'I'm really interested. I never see mine in Hong Kong. I take it one of yours is deaf?'

Diana laughed, grateful to him for the easy way in which he was dealing with the situation. He seemed genuinely amused by the racket next door. Peter, on the other hand, was becoming more furious each minute.

During the strawberry mousse the music changed to a comedy programme of some sort which was interspersed with frequent screams, claps and laughs from what appeared to be a near-demented audience. Sergeant Burnaby's own laughter, punctuated by fits of raucous coughing, could be clearly heard, and added to the general rumpus.

Peter threw his napkin down and pushed back his chair.

'Excuse me. I'd better go and see the old boy. This is unbearable.'

At that moment, they heard Sergeant Burnaby's door being thrown open, the radio blared forth, louder than ever, but above the noise was the shrill screaming of Mrs Fowler's voice. The language was strong, but Sergeant Burnaby, whose voice had been trained in the barrack squares of India, not only shouted her down, but used earthy expressions of Anglo-Saxon origin which were quite new to Diana, but sounded terrifyingly abusive.

'Don't interfere,' said Diana nervously. Peter's face bore that grim look which generations of youthful sinners had come to fear.

'That's exactly what I'm going to do,' he said ferociously, making for the door.

Within two minutes the voices were silent, the set switched off, and the distant sound of the swifts could be heard again. A bee bumbled against the window pane. Peace had returned.

'Our tenants', said Peter, passing the cheese-board to his guest, 'are something of a problem. Let's hope we'll hear no more of them.'

The evening passed pleasantly, and without further alarms and excursions, but Diana thought it prudent to have coffee indoors after all.

When they had said goodbye to Robert, they returned to the cottage. An owl was hooting far away, and the scent of early roses hung about the garden like a blessing.

Tyler's Row, quiet now as the grave, looked the epitome of tranquillity.

Peter sighed happily.

'Despite those two, it's a good spot to be,' he commented.

Diana agreed, bending to stroke Tom who was just setting out on his nightly activities. There were far more mice to attend to here than in Caxley. It kept a cat pretty busy, he found.

'By the way,' said Peter, as they mounted the stairs. 'I can get home to lunch tomorrow. Is that all right?'

'Splendid,' said Diana warmly. 'You can guess what it will be!'

*

Peter's hope that they would hear no more of their tenants was a vain one.

Certainly, Sergeant Burnaby's radio set seemed to be put on less frequently, but when it was then the volume was inordinately loud. Diana was positive that the old man's hearing was deteriorating. She had overheard visitors and tradespeople shouting messages at him, in a way which she had not noticed before.

'Well, he'd better get head-phones,' said Peter, when she put forward her suspicions. 'This is no joke.'

Both neighbours were now less friendly to their landlord. Mrs Fowler went indoors, and slammed the door pointedly, if Diana appeared in the garden. Sergeant Burnaby ceased to put his head over the hedge to pass the time of day. Diana found this withdrawal sad, but something of a relief. In any case, there was little she could do.

A week or two after the visit of Robert, a new tactic was tried in the hostilities. Mrs Fowler, more vinegary of countenance than ever, came to the door one evening to complain that the kitchen tap was leaking.

'Needs a new washer, I expect,' said Peter, and in a burst of generosity offered to replace it. Half an hour had gone by before he returned, looking exasperated.

'I fell into that trap very successfully,' he told Diana. 'Our friend took me all over the house to point out jobs that need doing. The bedroom ceiling needs replastering, two doors have dropped, the rain comes in the spare room window, and something's amiss with the guttering.'

'But you had it looked at when we took over,' protested Diana.

'Maybe she's got grounds for a certain amount of dissatisfaction. I've promised to have a look at these things. Old property wants looking at every week, it seems to me.'

'Was she friendly?'

'Far from it. Frosty, I'd say, with just a hint of a knife up the sleeve somewhere.'

'Oh dear, it is a wretched business! They've been awkward ever since you ticked them off.'

'Well, what do you expect me to do? We do our best not to disturb them. They must do the same.'

Two days later Sergeant Burnaby presented himself at the door and was invited in.

'I hear you're having the workmen along to see to Mrs Fowler's guttering and the window,' said the old soldier. 'Thought it might save them another trip if I showed you the mess the overflow pipe's making down the wall. Wants seeing to badly.'

Peter followed him resignedly.

'What else is wrong?' asked Diana when he came back.

'Damp kitchen floor, stove wants replacing, and the sink's cracked.'

'True?'

'We-e-ll – ' drawled Peter, spreading out his hands like a Frenchman, 'nothing's altered since it was inspected three months ago. I can't help feeling that our two tenants are doing their best to get their own back.'

'And what have you told him?'

'That the men will come and have another look round. Incidentally, I think you're right about his hearing. He couldn't hear me at all when I was speaking normally. I wonder if the doctor should see him.'

'We shall need to be on better terms before we can broach that subject,' said Diana firmly.

Meanwhile, as the days passed, Diana became convinced that, as with so many deaf people, Sergeant Burnaby heard a great deal more than others imagined.

Mrs Fowler's niece, who lived in Caxley, occasionally came to see her aunt, bringing her two young children with her.

On this particular afternoon, while the women talked over a cup of tea in the kitchen, the children were sent to play in the garden. To Diana, writing the weekly letters to her sons abroad, the sound of their chattering and laughter was very pleasant. Sergeant Burnaby evidently found it otherwise, for, to Diana's astonishment, she heard his voice bellowing across the garden.

'Keep them bloody kids quiet, will you? Get 'em indoors!'

Immediately, he was answered by Mrs Fowler.

'You mind your own business. They make less noise than you do. And get indoors yourself.'

'Fat lot of good trying to get a nap with that row goin' on.'

Another female voice now joined the battle.

'I can look after my own kids, thank you, without any help from you. Just a trouble-maker. I knows you!'

'*Trouble-maker!*' shouted the old soldier, and broke into a terrible fit of coughing. Diana felt that it was time she asserted herself. This was the first occasion on which the battle had been carried on across her premises, and it was going too far.

She emerged from the cottage and approached the two furious women. They looked startled to see her, and Diana suspected that they thought she was out.

'If you've anything to say to Sergeant Burnaby, please go to see him. *Don't* shout across my garden. It's extremely disturbing.'

'Sorry, I'm sure,' said Mrs Fowler insolently, but she turned to go indoors and the children and their mother followed her.

Sergeant Burnaby, still coughing, and scarlet in the face, peered over the hedge.

'I advise you to go indoors and calm down,' said Diana. 'You are only making yourself worse by flying into such a temper. If you want to speak to Mrs Fowler don't do it across our premises.'

'That old besom,' gasped the sergeant, 'eggs them kids on to make a row. Does it for spite. She knows I has a nap afternoons. If it's not children, it's that dam' dog of hers.'

Still spluttering, he stumped indoors, and Diana watched him go with a sinking heart. The dog, an attractive mongrel bitch, was a new acquisition next door, and Diana had wondered how soon this would be yet another bone of contention. Obviously, Sergeant Burnaby was going to be alert to any little misdemeanours on the dog's part which might be an excuse for further battles.

She went indoors, finished the second letter and read it through, but her mind was elsewhere. It harked back to the quiet privacy of the garden at the old house.

There had been neighbours there, but at four times the distance, and they had been people who behaved in an adult and civilized way. To be in the cross-fire of two such opponents as Mrs Fowler and Sergeant Burnaby, barely twenty or thirty yards apart, was as frightening as it was exhausting. Life at Tyler's Row was going to be impossibly difficult if this sort of conduct continued. Diana had never quarrelled with anyone in her life. This ever-increasing hostility made her acutely unhappy.

She stamped her letters abstractedly. In them she had dwelt on the pleasant side of life at Tyler's Row, the flowers now blooming, the friends who had called, village activities and news of the family. There was no point in burdening the boys with her growing doubts about the wisdom of the move. It would be disloyal to Peter, and in any case, the neighbours were really the only fly in the ointment.

There was one other matter which Diana kept to herself, but one which she knew she must tell Peter before long. For the past few days this fear had haunted her so terribly that she had tried to evade making a decision.

A mole on her neck which had been there for several years was beginning to grow at an alarming rate. She noticed it first as she was drying herself after a bath. It seemed slightly painful and definitely larger than usual.

She watched it anxiously for the next three or four days, and was now positive that it was growing steadily. Could it be malignant? Could it be cancerous? She knew so little about these things, but remembered reading somewhere that moles sometimes became a menace.

She knew quite well that she must go and see the doctor. He would probably allay her fears, and if he could not, then the sooner the wretched thing was removed the better.

It was telling Peter which worried her so much. As a family they had all been so wonderfully healthy that any kind of illness seemed doubly horrifying to them. No doubt, thought Diana, with a wry smile, Peter would prescribe a good walk to scotch her trouble.

He had enough to think about, in all conscience. Tyler's Row had cost more than at first estimated, as is usual. The problem of their irascible tenants was going to grow, and he was anxious, Diana knew, that she should settle happily.

Well, one could not arrange these things, thought Diana, taking up her letters. Illness struck without warning. She had lived with this fear now for a week. She must not delay further. This evening she would share the problem with Peter and make an appointment with their doctor first thing in the morning.

She stood up and looked into the sunlit garden. The single roses were wide open in the heat, showing their golden stamens. A yellow and orange butterfly fluttered over a lavender bush, and a blackbird scratched busily under the lilacs.

It was so beautiful. How could she bear to be taken from it? And how would Peter manage if she died?

Her vision was suddenly blurred by tears, and she pulled herself together. No more morbid thoughts, she told herself. Indulging in self-pity helped no one. She would take her letters and walk in the sunshine to Mr Lamb's Post Office to calm herself.

But a line of poetry throbbed in her head as she walked beneath the trees up to the village:

> Look thy last on all things lovely
> Every hour . . .

and, despite the sunshine, Diana was shaken with the chill of fear.

11. A Village Quiz

'I warn you,' said Mr Willet, one June morning, 'Mrs Pringle's comin' up the village street draggin' her leg.'

'Oh, no!' I cried, my heart sinking. 'What's wrong then?'

'Didn't you ask her to pull out that cupboard to see if there was a mouse there?'

'I asked her to have a look when she swept – yes!'

'Well, she did, and there was, and she says she's strained herself.'

This was dispiriting news. If Mrs Pringle feels that too much has been asked of her, which is a frequent occurrence, then it has dire consequences upon her bad leg. This limb reflects the state of Mrs Pringle's temper and martyrdom as surely as a weather-cock shows the prevailing wind. It 'flares up', as Mrs Pringle puts it, at the slightest provocation. Any little extra effort, such as moving a cupboard, aggravates this combustible quality of her leg, and we all behave with circumspection when Mrs Pringle appears with a limp.

'Let her get on with it,' advised Mr Willet sturdily. 'Pretend you don't notice it, silly old faggot.'

At that moment the door-scraper clanged, and Mrs Pringle appeared over the threshold.

'Lovely morning,' I ventured, with forced cheerfulness.

Mrs Pringle advanced, limping heavily, her head out-thrust like a bull whose patience is fast running out.

'Not if you're In Pain,' boomed Mrs Pringle.

'I'm sorry to hear that,' I replied mendaciously. Mr Willet looked out of the window, smirking quite unnecessarily.

'I've tore my back muscles and my bad leg, pushing that great cupboard to one side last night. Not that it wasn't needed. That mouse must've been there for weeks. He'd got a fair collection of nuts and berries and rubbish off of the nature table. You know what I'm always saying. That nature table's an open invitation to pests. Stands to reason mice is going to come in for that stuff, spread out for them to help themselves.'

I know quite well, and Mrs Pringle knows that I know, that it is not the mice she dislikes, but the extra debris which the nature table sheds occasionally on to the floor, and which makes more work for her. Mrs Pringle's leg was badly affected on the day some branches of blackthorn capsized, sprinkling the floor heavily with petal confetti.

'What's more,' went on Mrs Pringle remorselessly, 'he's had the corner off of one of them map things. That one with the gentleman made of india-rubber.'

This I rightly construed as the wall chart showing 'The Muscles of The Human Body', an alarming diagram which has not been in use very much since my arrival at Fairacre school. As far as I was concerned, the mouse was welcome to it, but I forebore to say so.

'He's been and chewed it up to shreds so it's no good hopin' to fix it back on, or cryin' over spilt milk.'

'I'm not,' I assured her.

'I shall have to take things easy today,' announced Mrs Pringle, putting a large mauve hand on the small of her back – if so extensive an area of anatomy can be thus called – and limping towards the door.

Mr Willet watched her go solemnly, turned to give me a sympathetic wink, and followed her into the lobby.

A minute later, presumably in the lady's absence, I heard one boy call out: 'You wants to watch it! Ma Pringle's leg's 'urting 'er. You'll get the back of 'er 'and if she sees you doing that!'

The retort was in terms more suited to the public bar of 'The Beetle and Wedge' than the playground of a Church of England primary school.

I decided that I had not heard it.

The days that followed were still darkened by Mrs Pringle's gloomy mood, but the limping seemed to ease a little as the days went by, and we became cautiously hopeful.

The high spot of the week was a visit from Amy. She brought with her a niece of James's, called Vanessa, an eighteen-year-old dressed fashionably in a motley collection of shapeless woollen garments in shades of mauve, grey and black. Three sleeves overlapped, the first layer appearing to be some sort of garment which my mother would have called a spencer, then another three-quarter length one, topped by a cardigan which reached the knees but, surprisingly, had short sleeves.

A dull brown stone on an inordinately long silver chain swung over her attire and hit her teacup, every now and again, when she tossed back a mane of long black hair. The stone reminded me of one shown me once by Mrs Pringle. She had told me, with much relish, that it came from her mother's gall bladder and was much treasured in the family. I am a squeamish woman, and have never quite got over this shattering experience. To have Vanessa's stone swinging about the tea-table was very unnerving.

She was a silent girl, ate very little, and appeared thoroughly bored with our company. As soon as tea was over, Amy dispatched her to the village stores to buy some cigarettes.

'Sorry about this,' said Amy, 'but she's in love. Eileen, James's sister, is at the end of her tether, and I said I'd have her for a few days.'

'What's he like?'

'Unsuitable.'

'How unsuitable?'

'Well, do you remember dear Joyce Grenfell's sketch where the bewildered mother says: "Daddy and I are delighted that you are going to marry a middle-aged Portuguese conjurer, darling. But are you sure he will make you happy?" It's rather like that.'

'Married?'

'Four times already. Has six children, one eye and a cork leg.'

'You're making it up!'

'Cubs' honour!' said Amy, drawing a finger across her throat for added measure. 'May I slit my throat, if I tell a lie, and all that. He was wounded in a war in Bolivia.'

'This gets more unbelievable every minute.'

'It's gospel truth, darling. He recently came as a rep, to the firm where she fiddles with the typewriter all day – one can't call it proper typing. She offered to do some letters for me yesterday, and every one began: "Dear Mr Who-ever-it-was Halfpenny".'

'She has my sympathy,' I said.

'Maybe. You taught yourself, but Vanessa had over a year at some ruinously expensive place in town where she met dozens of perfectly normal cheerful young men of her own generation. But no – she must fall for Roderick.'

'I suppose Eileen's talked to her?'

'Till she's blue in the face. So have I. It makes no difference. She eats next to nothing, dissolves into tears, has constant headaches, and threatens to do away with herself.'

'Can't she change her job?'

'She doesn't want to. She can see the wretched fellow this way. I've offered to take her abroad for a few weeks – James is willing – but Eileen's doubtful, and to tell the truth, I don't know if I could stand it, after having her at close quarters these last few days.'

'What is she interested in?'

'Roderick.'

'I know, silly. But besides Roderick?'

'More Roderick,' said Amy emphatically. 'I tell you, my dear, that child has absolutely no other thought in her head at the moment. Her parents, at their wits' end, have offered her a car, hoping she would find some other interest, but she's even refused that! Have you ever heard of an eighteen-year-old turning down a car?'

'Never!'

'That shows you. Incidentally, James pranged ours last week. He rang up to tell me, and of course I said, "Are you all right?" and I couldn't think why he laughed so much. Evidently, a man in his office always maintains that wives always say this on these occasions. If the *wife* rings up, of course, after an accident, the husband always says: "Is the *car* all right?" So we ran true to form.'

Vanessa appeared in the doorway, holding the cigarettes. She handed them to Amy without a word, and sank, exhausted, into an armchair.

Amy and I stacked the tray and I carried it into the kitchen.

'Come and see the pinks,' I said. 'Would Vanessa like to come in the garden?'

'I should leave her,' said Amy, and so we wandered together down the path, enjoying the June sunlight and the heady scent from the cottage pinks.

'I really can't see why love is cracked up so much,' I said thoughtfully. 'As the Provincial Lady once said, good teeth and a satisfactory bank balance are really much more rewarding.'

'You always were cold-blooded,' said Amy. 'I can remember how you treated that poor young fellow at Corpus Christi when we were at college.'

'If you mean that sanctimonious individual with a name like Snodgrass or Culpepper who was going to be a missionary, he deserved all he got. He was simply looking for someone to accompany him to the poor unsuspecting head-hunters in Africa. Anyone strong and female would have done. Of course I turned him down! So did about a dozen more.'

'Not as flatly as you did. I think you are the most unromantic woman I've ever met.'

'Maybe,' I said, threading a pink in her button-hole, 'but when I meet the Vanessas of this world – and many of them years older, and with less excuse for such follies – then I am sincerely thankful that I am a maiden lady, and likely to remain so.'

Amy laughed indulgently, and we went back to the house to collect her comatose niece. She drifted to the car behind her aunt, but, once inside, remembered her manners sufficiently to thank me in a listless voice.

As Amy searched for her car key, Vanessa made her first voluntary contribution to the conversation. There was even a faint hint of animation in her tone.

'What a pretty village this is!'

Amy's mouth dropped open in astonishment. It was good to see her smitten dumb for once. It so rarely happens.

A few days after the visit of Amy and the lovelorn Vanessa, the next meeting of Fairacre Parent–Teacher Association took place.

As I had feared, these monthly meetings seemed to occur much too frequently, and I had reason to dread the present one, rather more than usual, for I had agreed, in an off-guard moment, to be on the panel of a quiz game.

'The vicar will take the chair,' Mrs Johnson told me, 'and you and I will be the female pair of the quartet. Basil Bradley and Henry Mawne are willing to come too, so I think we shall be a well-balanced team.'

Basil Bradley is our local celebrity, a writer who produces an historical novel yearly. The plot is much the same each season: a Regency heroine, all ringlets and dampened muslin, having an uphill time of it with various love affairs and disapproving parents and guardians, and a few dashing bucks in well-fitting breeches and high stocks, rushing about the countryside at breakneck speed on barely-schooled horses, trying to win her hand, or to stop someone else from winning it.

He sells thousands of copies, is much beloved by many women – and his publisher – and we are very proud of him indeed. He is a gentle, unassuming soul, given to pink shirts and ties with roses on them. The men tend to be rather scornful about Basil, but he is a great deal more astute than his somewhat effeminate appearance leads one to believe.

'We're very lucky to get him,' I said to Mrs Johnson.

'I caught him at the end of a chapter,' she said. 'He was feeling rather relaxed.' She sounded smug, as well she might. Basil Bradley is adept at eluding such invitations.

On the great night, I put on my usual black, with Aunt Clara's seed pearls, and was glad that Amy was not there to protest at my dowdy appearance. With her words in mind, I took a second look at myself in the bedroom mirror. She was right. I did look dreary.

I routed out a shocking pink silk scarf, brought back from Italy by a friend, and tied it gipsy-fashion round my neck, putting Aunt Clara's seed pearls back in their shabby leather case. Greatly daring, I put on some pink shoes bought in a Caxley sale, and took another look at myself. A pity Amy wasn't coming, I thought.

Feeling like the Scarlet Woman of Fairacre, and rather enjoying it, I picked my way carefully across the playground to the school where the quiz was to be held. All the village had been invited, and the place was full.

Mrs Pringle was just inside the door. Her disapproving gasp, on viewing my unaccustomed finery, raised my spirits still higher. Mr Willet, arranging chairs on the temporary platform, gazed at me with open admiration.

'Well, Miss Read,' he said, puffing out his moustache, 'you certainly are a livin' doll tonight.'

I began to have slight qualms. As someone once said: 'No one minds being thought wicked, but no one likes to appear ridiculous.' But I had no time for doubts. The other members of the team arrived, and we took our places meekly.

Basil Bradley, who sat beside me, easily outshone me sartorially. His suit was dove-grey, his shirt pale-blue, and his colossal satin tie matched it perfectly. His opposite number, Henry Mawne, was in his church suit of dark worsted, and Mrs Johnson had on a green clinging jersey frock which could have done with a firm corset under it. The vicar, in the chair, looked as benevolent as ever in one of his shapeless tweed suits well known to all in the parish.

Having introduced us, 'just in case there is anyone here who has not had the pleasure of meeting our distinguished panel', the vicar called for the first question. Mrs Johnson had sternly told us that she was not letting us know the questions beforehand, which I thought rather mean of her, so we were all extremely apprehensive about the questions which, no doubt, would be hurled at us like so many brick-bats.

We need not have worried. As with most village affairs, any invitation to speak in public, 'making an exhibition of meself', as Fairacre folk say, was greeted with utter silence and a certain amount of embarrassed coughing and foot-shuffling.

At last, when the vicar could bear it no longer, he pointed to one of the young mothers in the front row, who was clutching a shred of paper which looked suspiciously like a page torn from the laundry book.

'Mrs Baker, I believe you have a question?'

The young woman turned scarlet, stood up, and read haltingly from the laundry book's page.

'How much pocket money do the team think children should get?'

We were all rather relieved at such a nice straightforward question to open the proceedings. Knowing Mrs Johnson, I strongly suspected her of planting a few questions about the hall on such knotty subjects as Britain's rôle in the Common Market, the rights of parents concerning their children's education, or the part played by the established church in village life.

Henry Mawne was invited to speak first by the vicar. He was admirably succinct.

'Not too much. Give 'em some idea of the value of money. I had a penny a week till I was ten. Then tuppence. Bought a fair amount of hardbake toffee or tiger nuts, tuppence did.'

The mention of tiger nuts brought some nostalgic comments from the older members of the audience, and the vicar was obliged to rap the table for order.

I was next and said that I felt sure it was right to grade pocket money according to age, and that as children grew older it might be a good idea to give them a quite generous fixed amount, and let them buy some of their clothes.

Mrs Johnson felt that there should be a common purse for all the children in the family, each taking from it what was needed, thus training them in Unselfishness and General Co-operation.

This was greeted in stunned silence, broken at last by the vicar who observed mildly that surely a greedy child might take it all in one fell swoop, which would be a bad thing?

'In that case,' answered Mrs Johnson, 'the other siblings' disgust and displeasure would bring home to the offender the seriousness of his mistake.'

'Wouldn't 'ave worked in our house,' said a robust voice from the hall, and the vicar turned hastily to Basil Bradley, who contributed the liveliest theory that children appreciate material things so keenly that it was vitally necessary for them to have enough to enjoy life. His passionate descriptions of the joys of eating dairy-flake chocolate stuffed into a newly-baked bun and eaten hot brought the house down.

We were then asked if we approved of corporal punishment in schools. The men said 'Yes' and gave gruesome accounts, much embellished, I suspect, about beatings given them at school, both ending on the note: 'And I'm sure I was all the better for it!'

Mrs Johnson abhorred the whole idea, and thought infliction of bodily pain barbaric. It simply encouraged sadism in those in authority and, she implied darkly, there was quite enough of that already.

I said that I thought most people found that there were a few hardened sinners for whom the cane was the only thing they feared. Thus I should like to see the cane kept in the cupboard. The mere fact that it was there was a great deterrent to mischief-makers. I added that in all my years at Fairacre I had never had to use it, but that I thought the total abolition of corporal punishment was a mistake.

There was so much interest in this question that it was thrown open to discussion, much to the pleasure of the four of us on the platform, who were then relaxed enough to blow our noses, look at our wrist watches and, in my case, loosen the shocking pink scarf which, though dashing, was deucedly hot.

Mr Willet held the floor for a good five minutes describing his old headmaster's methods at Fairacre school.

'Mr Hope give us a good lamming with the cane whenever

113

he thought it was needed,' he ended, 'and it never done us a 'aporth of 'arm. Boys needs the strap to teach 'em right from wrong. Look at Nature,' he exhorted us.

'Look at a bitch with pups, or an old stag with a young 'un playing up. They gives a cuff or a prod where it hurts, and the young 'uns soon learns.'

There was considerable support for Mr Willet, and it would appear that, in our neck of the woods at least, most of us favour a little corporal punishment in moderation.

We then romped through such questions as: 'Does the team approve of mini-skirts?' Answer: 'Yes, if the legs are all right.'

'Are we doing enough about pollution?' Answer: 'No' – this very emphatically from Henry Mawne, who expatiated on the state of the duck-pond near his house, and the objects he had picked up in the copse at the foot of the downs, for so long that the vicar had to pass to the next question rather quickly.

Reading methods, the debatable worth of psychiatric reports on difficult children, nursery schooling, pesticides, subsidies to farmers, the team's pet hates and where they would spend a holiday if money were no object, were all dealt with, before a halt was called, and we were allowed to totter down from the platform to be refreshed with coffee and a very fine collation of tit-bits prepared by the ladies of the committee.

Mr Johnson offered me a plate, and a paper napkin with Santa Claus and some reindeer on it. Obviously, someone had over-estimated the number needed last Christmas. I was glad to see that they were not being wasted.

'I was very glad to hear your remarks about corporal punish-ment,' he said, in a low voice.

I stared at him, too astonished to reply. My impression had been that he was, if anything, more bigoted than his wife about such things.

'My wife feels very strongly about correction, or rather, non-correction, but there are times when I wonder if a quick slap on the arm or leg isn't a better way of dealing with disobedience or insolence than a rather lengthy discussion. Children aren't always reasonable, I find. Now and again, I must admit, I have doubts.'

'They do you credit, Mr Johnson,' I assured him. 'They do indeed.'

I raised my coffee-cup and looked across at him with new respect.

Perhaps, after all, a Parent–Teacher Association had its good points.

12. A Fateful Day

On the last day of June, Diana drove to Oxford by herself. There she had an appointment with a specialist at two-thirty, for although her own doctor had been most reassuring, he was taking no risks.

Peter, much alarmed by Diana's disclosure, had wanted to come with her to the appointment, but she had dissuaded him. She always preferred to face such crises alone. It was less exhausting than trying to put on a brave front in the presence of someone else. Frightened though she was, she wanted to tackle this in her own way, without the effort of calming another's fears as well as her own.

She decided to go in the morning, do a little shopping, have a quiet solitary lunch and have plenty of time to drive to north Oxford where the specialist had his surgery.

Two days of heavy rain had left the countryside fresh and shining. The sun was out as Diana drove away from Fairacre, turning the wet road to black satin, and sparking a thousand miniature rainbows from the raindrops on the hedges. Steam rose from the backs of the sheep as they grazed on the downs, and little birds splashed in the roadside puddles. There was a clean sweetness in the morning air, as the sun gained in strength, and Diana turned down the window of the car, revelling in the freshness. How could one be despondent on such an exhilarating day? How could anything go wrong?

Her mind, suddenly anxious, turned back to the household details. Had she locked both doors? Had she switched off the cooker, the kettle and the electric fire? Had she left water as well as milk and fish for Tom? Had she remembered to put out the bread bin with a note to the baker? Was the shed unlocked so that the laundryman and the butcher could leave their deliveries? Had she put her cheque-book in her handbag, and the shopping list and the card giving particulars of her appointment? Really, going out for the day demanded a great deal of physical and mental activity before it even began, thought Diana! Perhaps she was getting old. As a young thing, she could not remember making such heavy weather over such simple preparations.

This brought her mind back to the nagging worry which had been her constant companion for the last week or two. Could life really be so cruel? Would there be months of pain to face? Death, even? Just as retirement was in sight, and all the simple pleasures that that promised? How truly dreadful suspense was! If only she knew – even the worst could not be more torturing than this gnawing anxiety and apprehension. Well, today might supply the answer. She put her foot on the accelerator and sped forward to her fate.

Oxford's parking problem was as formidable as ever. Diana did the usual round stoically. The car park opposite Nuffield College showed its FULL sign smugly. So did Gloucester Green's. A slow perambulation of Beaumont Street and St Giles showed a solid phalanx of cars, with not one space to be seen. Broad Street appeared equally packed, but to Diana's relief a large bearded man entered an estate car, grinned cheerfully at her to show he was about to go, and drove away, leaving her to take his place gratefully.

The sun had dried the pavements, but the battered heads of the Roman emperors outside the Sheldonian still had one wet cheek where the sun had not yet reached it, and roofs in the shade still glistened with moisture. The city had a freshly-washed air, and a glimpse through the gates of Trinity at the cool beauty of the grass made Diana decide to collect a picnic lunch later on and take it into the hospitable grounds of St John's.

She bought some knitting wool in Elliston and Cavell's, a pair of white sandals in Cornmarket and wandered round the market, enchanted as ever with the bustle and variety. While she was busy in these small affairs her fears were forgotten, but when she stopped for a cup of coffee at Fullers, they came crowding back again, as sinister as a cloud of black bats. If only she knew, if only she knew!

She made herself walk briskly back to the car to deposit her shopping, doing her best to conquer her fears. She would make her way to the Ashmolean. There, among the treasures of centuries, she knew she would find peace. To be in their presence, in the tranquillity of the lovely building, put things in perspective.

On her way she bought a ham sandwich and a banana for lunch. Not exactly a well-balanced meal, she thought with amusement, but easy to handle on a garden seat.

Inside the museum she turned left and made her way to the room she loved most, crammed with a wonderful collection of Worcester china. As usual, it was empty, and Diana sat down on the bench and gazed about her enraptured. There was the set of yellow china she loved particularly, as sunny as primroses, as pretty as Spring itself. There were the handsome tureens and plates, the jugs and sauce-boats, which always gave her pleasure. And there was her particular pet – the little white china partridge that she greeted every time she visited the room.

There was something very soothing about these beautiful objects. Perhaps their domestic usefulness, their perfect combination of service and splendour was of particular appeal to a woman. Whatever their magic, Diana found it of enormous solace and comfort during that dark hour of anxiety, and she went on her way to St John's in a calmer state of mind.

She walked through the quadrangle to the gardens at the rear. Here it was very quiet. Only the pyracantha petals, falling like confetti over paths and seats, and the fluttering of a few small birds, disturbed the stillness.

The lawns had just been mown. Stripes and swirls across the grass, where the mower had been used, were like gigantic green silk ribbons. In the borders delphiniums and peonies towered, a glory of blue, pink and cream, and in front of them clove pinks sent out their spicy fragrance.

Diana settled herself on a seat in the sun, and took out her ham sandwich. Instantly, a robin appeared, then another and another, until four robins eyed her brightly from very near at hand. She threw them crumbs, relishing their boldness, their soft feathered rotundity, and the swiftness of their movements.

Before long, a few more people wandered into the garden with their packets of lunch. Diana was struck by their general air of happiness. Most of them were women, faces upturned to the sunshine, half-smiling – children again in a world where flowers and birds, quietness and fragrance, took precedence, and one had time to observe, to reflect, to wonder and to be glad.

One middle-aged woman in particular, dressed in a floral summer frock covered by a shapeless cardigan, settled not far from Diana. Her face was so serene, her happiness so apparent, that Diana began to wonder, not for the first time, if women imbibed the atmosphere of a place more quickly than men. Had they a more ready response to surroundings?

A young girl, plain to the point of ugliness, peering through thick glasses between two swinging bunches of matted hair, suddenly knelt down on the damp path by the pinks, her arms crossed over her breast, and bent down to bury her face in them. She looked as though she were making obeisance to beauty, and when she sat back on her heels, Diana saw that her face was transformed. Sheer bliss had made her, suddenly and miraculously, into a beauty.

Diana finished her simple meal, tidied away her rubbish and gave the last few crumbs to the attentive robins who, by now, had been joined by a hopeful band of sparrows. For a few minutes she leant back in the seat, just another middle-aged woman, enjoying the benison of June sunshine on her face, and gave herself over to the peace of the place.

She must have dozed, for when she looked at her wrist watch she saw that it would soon be two o'clock. Reluctantly, she returned to this world, making her way towards the gate, stopping only to smell a single pink rose by the path. It seemed perfect, its petals translucent in the sunshine, cupping a glory of golden stamens; but, as she bent to smell it, Diana saw a small green maggot in its depths, and she drew back with a shudder.

She regained the car, turned its nose northward, with a sinking heart, and began to thread her way through the traffic.

The quiet world was behind her. Now she must face the darker side of reality with what courage she could muster.

The specialist was a tall, lantern-jawed Scotsman, infinitely gentle and reassuring. He examined Diana with concentrated deliberation, and finally told her that the chances of the growth being malignant were slight, but that he would like to have some tests made to make quite sure.

He gave her a card to take to an Oxford hospital in the following week for this to be done, bade Diana a courteous farewell, and accompanied her to her car solicitously.

Another delay, thought Diana, near to tears as she drove home to Fairacre. Another whole week to live through, frightened and apprehensive.

She tried to concentrate on the words of comfort the Scotsman had given her, but doubts kept breaking in. It was very hot now, and the car seemed stifling despite having all the windows open. The distant downs shimmered in the heat.

A dog lay panting on a cottage doorstep. His master, sitting on a wooden kitchen chair beside him, dozed with a panama hat tipped forward on his nose. Some children were coming out of school in one of the villages. Even they appeared languid in the brilliant sunshine, drifting along, their hands brushing the long grasses by the hedge, instead of jumping and shouting as children normally do when released from their desks.

For the last few miles of her homeward journey, Diana deliberately wrenched her mind from her troubles and tried to relive the pleasure of the morning. She thought of the loveliness of rain-washed ancient streets and monuments, the garnered treasures in the Ashmolean, the exquisite beauty, ravishing all the senses, in the garden of St John's.

But always, at the back of her consciousness, was the niggling fear of what might be. It reminded her of that rose – so perfect, it seemed, but with 'a worm in the bud'. A world, full of delights, was about her, but fear ate her heart, and spoilt perfection.

Peter was home early, waiting to greet her and to hear how she had fared. He shared her dismay at yet more suspense, but did his best to cheer her.

They sat in the garden, under the shade of the old plum tree, and sipped tea. The neighbours were very quiet, and Diana commented on it with relief.

'They weren't half-an-hour ago,' said Peter. 'The old man met me on the doorstep when I got back. He was absolutely furious.

'It seems that Mrs Fowler's dog got into the garden and buried a bone in his border. Heaven knows it's not all that spick and span! I should have thought he would have welcomed a bit of digging. However, he took umbrage, they evidently had a slanging match during the afternoon, and he was waiting to "complain about my tenant"!'

'What did you do?'

'Told him to forget it. I also told him that we were getting absolutely sick of these upsets, and that he might have to think of finding another place to live if he couldn't come to terms with things here.'

'We certainly can't go on like this,' said Diana.

Tom approached languorously, his tail flicking from side to side. He disliked the heat, but had stirred himself from under the shade of the lilac bushes to investigate the clinking of china and teaspoons. A saucerful of milk was always welcome.

Diana watched him lapping, taking the milk fastidiously round the edge of the saucer. Her mind dwelt on the scene Peter had described.

She knew why he had been so ruthless this time. He was anxious about her, and determined that nothing which he could prevent should worry her further. She herself could never have brought such pressure to bear on poor old Sergeant Burnaby, but she was glad that the words had been said. Their neighbours were fast becoming the serpent in their little Eden.

'Worms in the bud,' quoted Diana aloud, with a sigh.

'Where?' said Peter. 'I'll get the spray.'

Diana laughed. 'Just a figure of speech. Our neighbours – a canker at the heart of things – spoiling it all.'

Peter looked grim. 'They won't be at the heart of things much longer, if they don't mend their ways. I know we can't give them notice, but I can tell them to mend their ways. They're living on the edge of a volcano, if they did but know it, and it's liable to erupt at any moment!'

'Perhaps they'll heed your words of warning.'

'They'd better,' said Peter shortly.

13. Dog Trouble

'What d'yer think of it?' inquired Mr Willet, proudly holding a small wooden structure before me. It looked like a miniature dog kennel without sides, but I guessed, accurately for once, that it was a rather superior bird-table.

'Lovely!' I replied. 'Did you make it?'

'Yes. It's for Mr Hale. They've got one already, and I copied it for him. Wondered if you could do with one, miss? I've got plenty of wood, and that old one I did you hasn't got a nice little roof like this. Keeps the birds' food nice and dry when it rains, this does.'

'Yes, please. I'd love one.'

'You can 'ave it on a stout pole, or 'ang it up by a bit of chain off of a bracket,' said Mr Willet, warming to his work. 'What say?'

'Give me till tomorrow to decide,' I said, after some thought. 'I'll try and fix on a good spot where I can see it from the house.'

'Fair enough,' agreed my caretaker, lodging the edifice carefully on the side desk which supports everything from models, paintings waiting to dry and large garnered objects such as a sheep's skull from the downs, bleached white and papery, down to packets of biscuits and half-sucked lollipops carefully shrouded in a scrap of grease-proof paper, awaiting their owners' attention at playtime.

'Nice people them Hales,' went on Mr Willet conversationally. 'Friendly, but don't push in, like. For a schoolmaster he's really a very nice chap indeed. I mean, teachers can be funny old things. The women all teeth-and-britches, and the men a bit toffee-nosed, by and large.'

He stopped suddenly, his rosy face turning an even deeper rose with embarrassment. It is not often one sees Mr Willet discomfited. I quite enjoyed the occasion.

'There now!' he exclaimed, slapping his thigh with exasperation, 'I ought to be shot, that I ought. Talk about the tongue being an unruly member! I'm truly sorry I spoke as I done, Miss

Read. I meant no offence. You're the last one to call a teeth-and-britches-madam. Why, you looked a fair picture the other night in that pink tippet you had round your throat.'

'You're very kind,' I said, 'and don't bother your head about your very fair assessment of some of my profession. I'm glad Mr Hale passes muster.'

'It'll teach me to guard my tongue. What a thing to say! I'll be hot and cold for weeks every time I remember it!'

'Don't remember it then. It's not worth worrying over. If I took to heart all the bloomers I've made in my life, I should have slit my throat by now,' I assured him.

'That Mrs Hale now, she's a real lady. Don't look very well to me though. Always busy in that house, getting it straight, you know, and only that Mrs Jones to help her once a week. They do say she's giving up. Have you heard?'

I said that the grape-vine had not extended as far as the school house yet, but no doubt word would reach me before long.

Mr Willet coughed delicately, and looked about him for any eavesdroppers.

'It's like this. *If* Mrs Jones is leaving, my wife would dearly love a little job at Tyler's Row. She's been in good service, as you know, and we're only a few steps away. It would fit in lovely with her own bits of house-keeping. Should I mention it, do you think?'

I felt a rare pang of envy. Mrs Willet is a sweet little mouse of a woman, wonderfully capable at running a home, discreet, kindly – in fact, the proverbial treasure. I should dearly love to have invited her to work for me, but my house is so small, needing only one morning's work a week, and Mrs Pringle, alas, already has the job. It would be open warfare to change the arrangements, even supposing Mrs Willet wished to come. I dismissed the happy dream with a sigh.

'If Mrs Willet's agreeable,' I said, 'I don't see why not. Then it's up to Mrs Hale, if she needs her at any time. I may say, I think she's jolly lucky. There's no one in the village I should like more than your wife to work for me.'

'Well, that's very handsome of you, miss, particularly after all I blurted out just now. Yes, my Alice is pretty good, I must say. Pretty good! I expect she'd like the chance to work for you, but then you're suited, aren't you?'

'"Suited" isn't the word I'd choose,' I told him. 'Let's say I am unable to alter present arrangements.'

'Here comes the old bird now,' said Mr Willet, hurriedly picking up the bird-table. 'You let me know where you wants yours, when you've decided, and I'll be up one evening to fix it up for you.'

'I shall look forward to that,' I told him.

'With a smart contraption like this,' he said, smiling, 'you'll be gettin' all the fowl of the air. Tits, robins, nut-hatches, chaffinches – maybe hoopoes and peacocks!'

'You'd better make it twice the size then,' I shouted after his retreating back.

The week in which Diana Hale waited to go for her hospital tests seemed to be the longest of her life.

Not that it was without incident. Mrs Jones, who had agreed to come once a week 'just to see how it goes', found that the journey made the day a long one, and having expressed her doubts about being able to continue, particularly during the winter, finally gave her notice during the week of waiting.

Both women were genuinely sorry to part. Mrs Jones had been a faithful servant for many years, a staunch friend to the Hales and their two boys. But she was getting on in years, and Diana could see that she was wise to give up.

'I shan't leave until you've found someone else,' declared Mrs Jones. 'But I thought you should know the minute I'd made up my mind. There'll be plenty in the village, I don't doubt, as would jump at the job.'

'Well, I hope so,' admitted Diana, 'but it will be hard to find someone as reliable as you are.'

She pondered the matter in bed that night, as Peter slept dreamlessly.

Should she advertise in the *Caxley Chronicle*? Or would a postcard put up in Mr Lamb's Post Office be better? Or simply let him know that she was looking for domestic help?

The night was warm, and the smell of jasmine crept sweetly through the open window. Somewhere, across the village, an owl hooted in the darkness. There seemed to be rustling sounds, too, in the garden. Tom, perhaps, stalking a poor mouse, or even hedgehogs on the prowl. They could make quite a lot of noise for such small animals.

Suddenly, the unearthly howling of a dog split the silence, followed by a sharp yapping, and then the unmistakable shindy of a dog-fight just below the window. More barking added to the din.

Peter sat up, jerked from slumber.

'What the devil's going on?'

'I don't know. It's only just started.'

Before he had time to get out of bed to investigate, there was the sound of a window opening next door. Mrs Fowler was obviously making her own investigations.

'Push off!' screamed the lady, beside herself. 'Get off home! Be off with you!'

There was the sound of another window opening. Sergeant Burnaby, it seemed, had also been disturbed, despite his deafness.

'Stop that hollering!' commanded the sergeant, in a voice that had made itself heard under heavy shell-fire in its time. 'How d'you expect law-abiding Christians to sleep with that racket going on?'

'If I had a gun,' said Peter grimly to Diana, 'I'd train it on our neighbours in turn, so help me. As it is, I suppose I'd better lean out and read the riot act.'

'Not for a minute,' begged Diana. Who knows what he might say in the heat of the moment!

'You mind your own business,' yelled Mrs Fowler, evidently retreating for a moment, but returning to her post bearing something that chinked against the window fastening.

The dog-fight seemed to be continuing a little further down the garden, but there were whimpering sounds and more barking near at hand, as if a dozen or more dogs were still close to the house.

A sloshing noise, followed by wild yelping and what sounded like a stampede of elephants, indicated that Mrs Fowler had tipped the water from the bedroom ewer over her unwelcome guests.

'Let that be a lesson to you!' she shouted, slamming shut the window with such force that all four cottages in Tyler's Row shuddered.

There was an answering slam from Sergeant Burnaby's window, and then silence from each side of the Hales' abode. Outside, the noise of snuffling, whining and yelping went on, but with slightly less energy. Mrs Fowler's activity with the water jug seemed to have some effect. Certainly the two main contestants seemed to have retired, probably to carry on their dog-fight in some other quarter of the village.

'I suppose that dam' dog of hers is on heat,' said Peter gloomily. 'How long does that last?'

'About three weeks, I believe.'

'That's jolly. I suppose we'll have all the dogs of the neighbourhood growling and prowling round, like the hosts of Midian. Do the garden a power of good, that will!'

He sighed gustily.

'I wonder if we've been fools to come here? I must say I never envisaged this sort of persecution when we took on the tenants. What d'you think, Di?'

He sounded unusually downcast, and Diana rallied herself to speak cheerfully, although she too was full of doubts lately.

'It will turn out all right. They are bound to settle down before long. You've told them. It's up to them to have a little sense. I can stand it, if you can. We've put all we can spare into this place, and we'll jolly well see it gives us pleasure – neighbours or not.'

'That's how I feel. I just can't bear to think I've landed you with this lot. After all, I'm out all day. You're the one who has to put up with it, and you've got enough to worry you just now without these two pests.'

'Forget it,' said Diana comfortingly. 'Let's go to sleep.'

To the faint sound of mingled whimpers and snuffles, the Hales sought slumber.

The next morning a collection of dogs of all shapes and breeds were visible through Mrs Fowler's hedge, clustered hopefully at her back door. There were plenty of paw marks on the Hales' garden beds, and two of Diana's cherished penstemons were broken down.

She was understandably nettled, but tried not to show it before Peter, who was worried enough anyway. He drove off to school, and Diana set about her domestic chores.

The morning was punctuated by commotions from Mrs Fowler's side of the hedge. Every time she opened the back door, she emerged either with a stick or a jug of water to send off the amorous invaders.

At the same time she let fly a stream of invective which quite unnerved Diana. She wondered how soon it would be before Sergeant Burnaby retaliated.

She did not have long to wait.

A peremptory rapping at the back door came about ten o'clock. On opening it, Diana faced Sergeant Burnaby, very spruce, his waxed moustache tilted heavenward and his yellow face unusually stern.

'Come in,' said Diana, with a sinking heart.

'Thank you, ma'am. I shan't keep you long. My business won't take more than a minute or two.'

'Do sit down,' invited Diana.

'No, thank you, ma'am. I'll say what I have to say standing. I only come because I respect your wanting to 'ave a bit of dignity over Mrs Fowler's and my upsets. This 'ere bawling that she does is no way to go on.'

Diana, remembering the Sergeant's stentorian bellows in the night, found herself speechless.

'I'm here to lodge a complaint,' went on the old man, 'a *formal complaint*. If your blasted tenant can't keep her blasted bitch under control I give fair warning I'll take the matter to the police.'

This was said in Sergeant Burnaby's most polite tones, and Diana was hard put to it not to show her amusement.

'Sergeant Burnaby,' she said, in the cooing voice which had melted many men's hearts, 'you are making yourself so unhappy – and us too, you know – by taking offence at every little thing which goes wrong. Of course it's annoying to have all these dogs about, and I intend to visit Mrs Fowler to see what can be done about it. We can't have our sleep broken as we did last night, but *please*, Sergeant, try to be a little more forbearing. We've simply *got* to shake down together peaceably. You must see that.'

Diana thought she detected a little shame in the old soldier's countenance, but his answer was as belligerent as ever.

'I've done my best, ma'am, as you know. That woman's more than flesh and blood can stand, and that dam' dog of 'ers has caused my garden to be turned into a fair wilderness with all them others rooting about. I means it when I says I'll see the police!'

Diana put a hand upon his arm pleadingly.

'Now don't do anything hasty. I shall see Mrs Fowler myself. We all want an end to this unpleasantness.'

The old man stumped towards the door, his back as straight as a ramrod, his moustache bristling.

'Well, I've made my complaint. I can't do more. But she'd better watch out!'

Diana abandoned her soft womanliness and assumed a sterner tone.

'Sergeant Burnaby, you must do your part in a little give-and-take. As my husband has told you, if you can't settle happily at Tyler's Row it may be best for you to find somewhere else to live.'

If Diana expected a change of attitude, she was to be disappointed. The old man said nothing, but gave her a glance so full of venom that she felt shocked.

The door slammed behind him. It was plain that Sergeant Burnaby was unrepentant.

Later that day she called upon Mrs Fowler with much the same result. It had needed considerable courage to visit her neighbour, but Diana felt that it must be done.

Eight dogs waited hopefully in the garden, and watched Diana as she approached.

'Better come in, I suppose,' said Mrs Fowler sourly, eyeing the expectant crowd. 'It's about *them*, no doubt.'

She shut the door behind her visitor and motioned Diana to a battered sofa.

'Yes, it is, I'm afraid,' said Diana. 'Not only on our behalf, but on Sergeant Burnaby's as well.'

Mrs Fowler gave a contemptuous laugh.

'Should've thought he could have done his own dirty work.'

Diana decided to ignore this, and pressed on.

'It's very difficult when you have a bitch, I know – ' she began.

'I won't have that word mentioned in my house,' said Mrs Fowler loftily. She folded her arms across her pink cardigan and glared at poor Diana. 'I always say *lady-dog*. It's politer.'

'Just as you wish,' agreed Diana hastily. She was devoutly thankful that Peter was not present, or she might have broken down. 'I just wondered if you knew that there is something available for bitch – I mean, for lady-dogs – which can be put on them when they're on heat. It keeps the dogs away, and is so simple.'

Diana's innocent suggestion brought a blush to Mrs Fowler's withered cheek, but whether it was caused by outraged modesty or plain temper it was difficult to guess.

'I know the stuff. My niece brought me a tin last night.' She turned round to root among a number of medicine bottles and aerosol tins on the dresser, and held up a large yellow canister proudly. Bright red letters across it said: KUM-NOT-NY.

'Haven't had time to use it yet,' went on Mrs Fowler, 'and I don't know as I intend to. Nature knows best, my mother always said.'

Diana, who had now recovered from the shock of the name, decided that a firmer line was needed.

'I should certainly use it *immediately*, or I fear Sergeant Burnaby will be sending for the police. My husband and I are sympathetic to your difficulties, but they can be overcome, and you really can't want to upset your neighbours like this. If you don't want to use this stuff, then why not put the dog into kennels? It's often done.'

Mrs Fowler bridled.

'And who's going to pay for that, may I ask?'

'The dog is your responsibility,' replied Diana steadily. She got up from the little-ease of a sofa, and made her way to the door. Mrs Fowler looked thoughtful.

'I might have a word with my niece when she brings the children to tea,' she said, in a less belligerent tone of voice.

'Do,' replied Diana. 'And please remember that we all want to sleep at nights – *all of us* – in Tyler's Row.'

Luckily, Diana's words bore fruit. She saw the niece depart, after tea next door, complete with children and the dog. Kumnot-ny must have been applied with a heavy hand, for no dogs followed the little group towards the bus stop, and Tyler's Row was destined to have peaceful nights for over a fortnight.

Diana saw the family waiting for the bus when she went to the post office with her carefully written postcard asking for domestic help, on one or two mornings a week, times and wages to be arranged.

'I'll put this up first thing tomorrow,' promised John Lamb. 'I'm sure you'll be suited without much bother.'

He watched Diana depart, and put the card carefully on one side. He must look out for Bob Willet. This was just the job his missus was looking for, he knew.

There was not much that John Lamb did not know in Fairacre.

By eight-thirty the next morning Mr Willet knew about the post, as he returned from his early duties at the village school. After a brief word with Mrs Willet, he collected the bird-table and made his way to Tyler's Row. Diana was dusting, but went out into the morning sunshine to admire the bird-table.

'It's really splendid,' she cried. 'Do you want to put it up now?'

'Better wait till Mr Hale's here,' advised Mr Willet. 'I'll call back this evening, if it's convenient. I'll be going up to choir-practice and I should be back here by eight or so. Mr Annett's written a descant to "Pleasant are Thy courts above". We're doin' it Sunday.'

'How clever of him,' commented Diana.

'Well, that's as maybe. It's my belief he's tone-deaf when it comes to makin' up tunes. This 'ere fairly pierces yer eardrums. Atonal, he called it. That's one way of describing it, I suppose.'

'Modern music does take some getting used to,' agreed Diana diplomatically.

'I was having a word with John Lamb,' said Mr Willet. 'He tells me as you need a bit of help here. I was wondering if Mrs Willet might come and see you? She's looking for a light job, and you wouldn't get nobody better, and that's the truth.'

Diana gasped with pleasure. She had met Mrs Willet at the Women's Institute, and frequently in the lanes of Fairacre. This seemed heaven-sent.

'This is good news. Would Mrs Willet like to call here soon and have a look at the work? At the moment I am paying Mrs Jones twenty-five an hour. She might like to know.'

'Twenty-five?' said Mr Willet, puzzled.

'New pence.'

'Ah!' Mr Willet's brow cleared. 'Five bob! This decimation gets you down, don't it? By the time I've decimated shillings and pence, I don't know if I'm on my head or my heels. D'you have trouble decimating, Mrs Hale?'

'It's getting easier. It's pints into litres and ounces into grammes I'm dreading.'

'Well, now. What about Mrs Willet comin' next Tuesday, to see the job?'

'Fine,' said Diana, then checked suddenly. 'No, sorry, I have to go to hospital that day.'

She regretted the disclosure the minute she had made it. Mr Willet's face crumpled with concern. She hoped he would not mention the matter to others. However, nothing could be done.

'Nothing serious,' she said lightly. 'Just a routine check.'

'Good. Good,' said Mr Willet, looking relieved. 'Then perhaps Monday would be better?'

'Ideal. Would two o'clock be a good time?'

'Do fine. We've washed up and had a bit of a ziz by then. Forty winks, after a bit of dinner, is a very good thing, Mrs Hale.'

He put the bird-table in the porch, and surveyed it with his head on one side.

'Looks a treat, don't it?' he said disarmingly. 'I enjoyed makin' that.'

'We'll enjoy using it,' Diana told him, with conviction.

PART THREE

Settled, With Some Sunshine

14. Amy's Invitation

The fact that Diana Hale had to go to hospital was soon general knowledge in Fairacre. To give Mr Willet his due, he mentioned this interesting item of news to his wife alone. Whether she inadvertently let the cat out of the bag, or whether Sergeant Burnaby or Mrs Fowler overheard the conversation in the garden, or whether, as is quite likely, that mysterious communication system, the village grapevine, which works with a life of its own, was to blame, no one can tell, but the village knew quite well that on Tuesday next Mrs Hale was going to hospital.

Why, and which one, were matters of debate. Some said the appointment was at Caxley-Cottage, others Up-the-County, and those who guessed aright plumped for Oxford. These last admitted that there were so many hospitals in Oxford that it was anyone's guess which it would be. By the law of elimination they cancelled out That Bone Place (Orthopaedic) and That Loony Place (Nervous Diseases), on the grounds of Diana's physical activity and her obvious mental composure. Further than that they were unable to go, to their infinite regret.

The reason for the visit engaged the villagers' interest pleasurably. Heart trouble and hernias, goitre and gall-stones, diabetes and deafness were all discussed with lively conjecture, and gruesome accounts of relatives' sufferings when similarly afflicted.

Even the school children discussed the subject, seriously and with sympathy. I overheard two of them, as they squatted on their haunches by a sunny wall, waiting to come into school.

'What's up, d'you reckon, with that new lady up Tyler's?'

'Nothin' much. Havin' a baby, I expect.'

'Get away! She's too old. She must be sixty or seventy. My mum says you can't have a baby after forty.'

'That's where she's wrong then. Our mum had our Linda when she was forty-three. So there!'

135

There was silence for a moment before Mrs Hale's case was resumed.

'Don't expect it's an operation. More like getting old. Bits of you wears out, like an old bike does.'

'She ain't all that old. Not much more'n Miss Read.'

'Well, *she's* no chicken! I bet she's got bits of *her* wearin' out pretty fast.'

Too true, I thought, tottering into the playground to call them in. I felt decrepit for the rest of the day.

On Wednesday morning Mrs Pringle told me, with evident disappointment, that Mrs Hale had been seen busy weeding the borders on Tuesday evening.

'Can't be much amiss there,' grumbled the lady. Then her eye brightened.

'Unless the doctors have missed something,' she continued. 'Some of these young fellers – no more than bits of boys – simply give you a quick prod, here and there, and look at your tongue, and that's it. Easy enough to miss the Vital Symptom.'

'I feel very sorry indeed for Mrs Hale,' I began severely, about to embark on a short pithy lecture on the theme of prying into the affairs of others, but Mrs Pringle forestalled me as successfully as ever.

'Oh, so do I. So do I. There's not one in the village as doesn't feel the same. Mrs Fowler reckons it's liver. Sergeant Burnaby reckons it's a judgement, whatever that may mean, and John Lamb says he's never been one to talk about women's ills and then shut up like a clam!'

'Sensible man,' I said.

'I wonder what that poor soul's doing at this very minute,' pondered Mrs Pringle lugubriously.

'Minding her own business perhaps,' I retorted tartly.

And, for once, I had the last word.

More news came from Tyler's Row within the week. Mrs Willet was going to work for Mrs Hale!

'She's very lucky,' I said feelingly to Mrs Pringle when she told me.

'She is indeed. Five shillings an hour!'

I had meant that Mrs Hale was lucky, and said so.

'Well, yes,' Mrs Pringle conceded doubtfully. 'Alice Willet's a good worker and a very nice little carpet beater, considering her arms.'

Mrs Willet's arms, compared with Mrs Pringle's brawny ones, are certainly rather wispy, but I was not surprised to hear her praised as a carpet beater. As far as I could see, Mrs Willet would be competent at anything she undertook, and I said so.

Mrs Pringle seemed to resent my enthusiasm, and began to look mutinous. Before long, I knew from experience, spontaneous combustion would occur in her bad leg, and we should all suffer.

'Alice Willet,' said Mrs Pringle heavily, 'doesn't have what others have to put up with.'

This barbed remark might have referred to me, or to the children, or to us both, but prudence kept me silent. With only the slightest limp Mrs Pringle made her way to the lobby.

'Don't come walking all over my clean floor with your feet!' I heard her shout to the oncoming children.

'Just walk on your hands,' I said.

But I said it to myself.

During that week I had a surprise visit from Amy. Her car was waiting in the lane as the children left school, and I greeted her warmly.

'Come and have some tea.'

'Lovely. But nothing to eat. I'm getting off a stone and a half.'

'How do you know?'

'Because that is what I *intend* to do,' said Amy sternly, locking the car door – a wise precaution, even in comparatively honest Fairacre.

'Good luck to you,' I said, leading the way to the school house. 'I lose four pounds after three weeks of starvation, and then I stop.'

'Wrongly balanced diet,' began Amy, then stopped dead, listening.

A distant mooing noise came from the direction of the school.

'What on earth's that? One of the children crying?'

'Mrs Pringle singing. She usually practises the Sunday hymns as she sweeps up. That sounds like "Eternal Father strong to save", unless it's Mr Annett's new descant.'

'It sounds to me like murder being done,' said Amy, picking her way carefully across the stony playground to my gate. Her cream suede shoes were extremely elegant, but really too beautiful for walking in.

'I'm starving,' I told her, as I put on the kettle, 'and intend to have a large slice of Dundee cake. Shall I eat it out here in the kitchen to save you misery?'

'No,' said Amy, weakening, 'cut me a slice too!'

Later, demolishing the cake as hungrily as we used to at college, so many years ago, Amy came to the reason for her visit.

'I wanted to tell you the latest news of Vanessa and also to invite you to a little party. I've got such a nice man coming.'

I began to feel some alarm. Every now and again, Amy tries to marry me off to someone she considers suitable for a middle-aged schoolteacher. It is rather wearing for all concerned.

'Who is he?' I asked suspiciously.

'A perfect dear, called Gerard Baker. He writes.'

'Oh lor!'

'Now, there's no need to take that attitude,' said Amy firmly, picking a fat crumb from her lap and eating it with relish. 'Just because you took a dislike to that poor journalist fellow at my cocktail party – '

'A dislike! I was terrified of him. He was a raving lunatic, trying to interview me on Modern Methods of Free Art over the canapés. What's more, his beard was filthy.'

'Well, Gerard is clean-shaven, and cheerful, and very good company. He's writing vignettes of minor Victorian poets.'

'How I hate that word "vignettes"!'

'And he's here for a few weeks,' went on Amy, carefully ignoring my pettish interjection, 'because he is finding out about Aloysius Someone who lived at Fairacre years ago and wrote poetry.'

'What! Our dear old Loyshus? Mr Baker must meet Mr Willet.'

'And what can he tell Gerard?'

'Everything. How his cottage smelt like a "civet's paradise", and how long his poetry readings were – oh, hundreds of things.'

'They don't sound quite the things for vignettes,' said Amy pensively.

'He'll have to call them something different then. I've no doubt he'll work out some horribly whimsical title like "Baker's Dozen".'

'Now, now! Don't be so tart, dear. I know you'll get on very well, and for pity's sake don't wear that black rag. If you can't afford to buy a new frock, I'll be pleased to buy you one.'

'Thank you,' I said frostily. 'But I haven't sunk to that.'

'Hoity-toity!' shrugged Amy, quite unconcerned. 'Friday week then? About six-thirty?'

'Lovely,' I said gloomily. 'Now tell me about Vanessa.'

Amy lit a cigarette luxuriously, put her beautiful shoes up on the sofa, and settled down for a good gossip.

'That wretched man was *married*.'

'I know. Four times. You told me.'

'Yes, but he'd tried to make Vanessa believe that he'd tidied all four away by death or divorce. Actually, he is still married to Number Four. Just think of it! If Vanessa had married him, he would have been a bigamist!'

'How did Vanessa find out?'

'Oh, Somebody knew Somebody, who knew Somebody whose children went to the same school as his and Number Four's. You know what London is – just a bigger Fairacre when it comes to it.'

'Is she very upset?'

'Dreadfully. She can't decide whether to go into a convent or to take up the guitar.'

'I should try the guitar first,' I said earnestly. 'It's not quite so final.'

'I really believe she's beginning to grow out of this awful infatuation at last. At least her mind is turned towards these other two subjects. When she was with me she thought solely of Roderick. There seems to be a ray of hope.'

'Is she coming to the party?'

'Now that's an idea. I think it might be a very good thing.

She would meet a few new people, and she liked you, strangely enough.'

'There was no need for the last two words.'

'I suppose there was a fellow feeling,' mused Amy, tapping ash into the fireplace absently. 'Two spinsters, you know.'

'I'm not crossed in love,' I pointed out.

'You might well be, after meeting Gerard,' said Amy smugly. 'We shall have to wait and see.'

Term was due to end within three weeks, and already I was beginning to quail at the thought of all the things that had to be done before the glad day arrived.

I had to find out about new entrants to the school in September, when the school year began. There were reports to write, cupboards to tidy, present stock to check, new stock to order, the school outing – a time-honoured trip to the sea with the choir and other church workers – and our own Sports Day, which involved giving refreshments to parents and friends of the school.

It was whilst I was contemplating this daunting prospect that Mrs Bonny dropped her bombshell. She has been a tower of strength ever since her arrival at the school, and in one as small as Fairacre's, with only two on the staff, it is vitally important that the teachers get on together. Mrs Bonny and I had never had a cross word, and I had hoped that she would continue to teach for many years, although I knew there was some doubt when she remarried at Christmas.

She came into the playground as I sheltered in a sunny recess made by one of the buttresses. My mug of tea was steaming nicely, and playground duty was quite pleasant on such a blue-and-white day, with rooks cawing overhead, and the ubiquitous sparrows hopping about round the children's feet, alert for biscuit crumbs.

'Gorgeous day,' I remarked.

'Well – er – yes,' said Mrs Bonny vaguely. She twisted the wedding ring on her plump finger, and I wondered why she appeared so nervous.

'I've something to tell you.'

'Fire away,' I said, heading off one of the Coggs twins who was about to collide with me and capsize the tea.

'I've only just made up my mind,' said Mrs Bonny, looking singularly unhappy.

'What about?' I asked. Ernest and Patrick were fighting on the ground, rolling over and over in the dust, legs and arms flailing. I don't mind a certain amount of good-natured scrapping, but on this occasion their clothes were suffering, and Ernest's head was dangerously near to a sharp post. I left Mrs Bonny to part them.

When I returned, she was twirling the wedding ring even more violently.

'I must go,' she blurted out.

'Where?' I said, bewildered.

'To Bournemouth.'

I stared at her. For one moment I thought she had gone off her head.

'To Bournemouth? Now?'

Mrs Bonny took a grip on herself.

'No, no. I'm explaining things badly. I mean, I shall have to leave the school. I must give in my notice. Theo thinks it's best. We've talked it over.'

This was dreadful news. I looked at my watch. It was rather early, but this must be discussed in the comparative peace of the classroom.

I blew the whistle, and we took the reluctant children into school.

'Now, tell me,' I begged, when we had settled the children to work, and she had come into my room, leaving the adjoining door open so that the infants could be under observation while we talked.

'It's my daughter, really,' explained Mrs Bonny. 'She's been pressing us for some time to go and live near them. She's got two young children, as you know, and another due at Christmas. I could help her a great deal, and I said that if she could find a suitable flat for us, we'd think about going.'

'Oh, Mrs Bonny,' I wailed. '*Must* you go?'

The thought of finding another teacher filled me with despair. I have endured, in my time, a succession of temporary teachers, known as 'supply teachers', and though some have been delightful, more have been deplorable. Moreover, it is very unsettling for the children to have so many changes.

'I'm sorry it's such short notice,' said Mrs Bonny. 'I thought of leaving at the end of October – at half term. That would have given you plenty of time to find someone else. But this flat has turned up.'

I laughed hollowly. Finding a good infants' teacher is like searching for gold dust.

'And we should have had time to get the flat ready at weekends and during the summer holidays. But we've had a good offer for our house, and we feel we must sell it and go now.'

She seemed to have given the matter much thought, and obviously her mind was made up. I did my best to look at it from her point of view, but I felt sad and apprehensive.

A pellet of paper, obviously catapulted from a bent-back ruler, landed on my desk, and for a minute my staffing problems were forgotten.

Ernest, still holding the ruler, was scarlet in the face.

'I never meant – ' he began fearfully, noting my expression.

'No play for you this afternoon,' I told him. 'You can write out your multiplication tables instead.'

Meekly, he picked up the pellet and put it in the waste-paper basket.

At the same moment, a bevy of infants converged upon the communicating door, babbling incoherently.

Mrs Bonny and I went to see what was the matter.

Beneath one of the diminutive armchairs a pool of water darkened the floorboards. The children pointed at one wispy five-year-old accusingly.

'Rosie Carter went to the lavatory,' said one self-righteous little girl.

'*That*,' said Mrs Bonny, with awful emphasis, 'is exactly what she did *not* do.'

We postponed our plans for the future to deal with more urgent problems.

15. *Sergeant Burnaby Falls Ill*

For some days after the departure of Mrs Fowler's dog, peace reigned at Tyler's Row.

Sergeant Burnaby maintained an offended silence when his path crossed the Hales'. Even his radio seemed quieter, although his cough, Diana noticed, became more hacking daily. She wished he would smoke less, but it was really none of her business, she told herself, and there were very few pleasures left for the old man to enjoy.

Mrs Fowler, too, seemed unusually quiet, and was inclined to toss her head and look the other way when Diana met her. It was a pity that she felt like this, thought Diana, but nothing could be done about it, and at least things were more tranquil.

She was glad of the respite, for she awaited the results of the tests with acute anxiety. She did her best to put aside her fears, busying herself with the house and garden, and with entertaining all those Caxley friends who wanted to see their new home, but now and again the grim doubts would break through her defences, and she would be beset by dark thoughts.

She felt sure that the wretched mole, which had started all the trouble, was growing. It was certainly giving her twinges. If only she could know! Even the worst news would be better than this torturing suspense.

It was during this waiting period that the Hales invited the Mawnes to dinner. Peter's headmaster, another keen ornithologist, and his wife, were also invited.

'Henry Mawne,' said Diana, as she set the table, 'reminds me of one of my old flames.'

'Which one?' asks Peter. 'That terrible tennis-player I met?'

'No, no. He didn't last long. D'you know, I can't for the life of me remember this man's name.'

Diana paused, forks in hand, and gazed into the middle distance.

'He had just been jilted by another girl called Diana, and he seemed to think it was the hand of God – meeting me, I mean. He was really rather persistent.'

'I expect you encouraged him,' said Peter primly.

'That I didn't! He was frightfully old, forty at least –'

'Poor devil!' commented Peter.

'And I was only twenty. He had a silver plate in his head, or a silver tube in his inside – something metallic one wouldn't expect – and such a nice voice.'

'What an incoherent description!' remarked Peter. 'I wouldn't trust your choice in an identity parade.'

'It's all I can remember,' protested Diana, resuming her work with the forks. 'Anyway, Henry Mawne is rather like him. How I wish I could remember his name!'

The headmaster and his wife arrived first. They were sticklers for punctuality, and if the invitation was for seven-thirty, they were there on the dot, if not a trifle earlier.

Diana, in common with most people, disliked visitors who kept one waiting whilst the meal grew browner and drier in the oven, but she sometimes wondered, when the Thornes appeared so promptly, if it were not harder to appear sincerely welcoming when one's back zip was still undone.

The Mawnes appeared at twenty to eight. Mrs Mawne, whom Diana had only seen in tweed suits or sensible cotton shirt-waisters, was resplendent in red velvet, cut very low, her substantial bosom supporting the sort of ornate necklace of gold, pearls and garnets, which Diana had only seen in the advertisements of Messrs Sotheby. She would really look more at home, thought Diana, at a gala performance at Covent Garden, rather than a modest dinner party in a cottage.

However, it was good of her to do the occasion so much honour, and she certainly looked magnificent. Henry, in his dark church suit, made a suitably restrained background to so much splendour.

The two men took to each other at once, and such terms as 'lesser spotted woodpeckers', 'only a *cedar* nesting box attracts them', 'migrator habits' and 'never more than one clutch a season', were batted between them like so many bright shuttle-cocks.

The two women found that they had attended the same

boarding school, and though they were both careful to make no mention of dates, thus giving away their ages, they remembered a great many girls and members of staff.

'And do you remember Friday lunch?' asked Mrs Thorne.

'Friday lunch,' said Mrs Mawne, with feeling, 'is permanently engraved – scarred, perhaps I should say – upon my memory. Those awful boiled cods at the end of each table, swimming in grey slime, with their poor eyes half out.'

'They might have looked better on a pretty dish,' said Mrs Thorne, trying to be fair. 'But those thick white dishes added to the general ghastliness.'

'At least you knew what you were eating,' said Diana. 'At my school we had fish-cakes every Friday, concocted from sawdust and watered anchovy essence, as far as I could see. The irony of it was, they used to be dished up with a sprig of fresh parsley – the only thing with any food value in it at all – and, of course, that remained on the dish.'

'Have you noticed,' said Mrs Mawne, stroking her red velvet skirt, 'that everyone talks about food these days? I think we got into the way of it during the war, and now whenever women meet they swap recipes or reminiscences.'

'I know,' said Mrs Thorne. 'I remember my mother drumming into me as a child that a well-brought-up person never talked of politics, religion, money or food. We should all be struck dumb these days.'

Diana retreated to the kitchen to dish up. Mrs Willet was coming later to make the coffee, and to wash up when the meal was over. It was a long time since she had taken on such an engagement, and she had welcomed Diana's tentative invitation with as much relish as if she were having an evening at the theatre. Diana hoped she would get a glimpse of Mrs Mawne's magnificence. It would please her so much.

The meal was a great success, the duck succulent, the fresh young vegetables, some from Mr Willet's garden, at their best, and Diana's strawberry shortcake sweet much admired.

Nothing, mercifully, could be heard of their neighbours. Ever since the earlier catastrophic dinner party when Robert was present, Diana had been painfully aware of how easily their peace could be shattered. The weather, perhaps, had something to do with it. The fine spell had broken, and heavy summer rain lashed the windows and dripped steadily from the thatch.

'Good for the grass,' commented the headmaster, who was a great gardener. The talk turned to flowers and trees, and then, suddenly, to neighbours.

'And how are you getting on with yours?' asked Mrs Mawne.

'Not very well,' confessed Peter, and told them a little of their troubles.

'You really must get rid of them,' Mrs Mawne maintained robustly. Diana hoped that Mrs Fowler's ear was not glued to the adjoining wall. Mrs Mawne's voice was notoriously carrying.

'That's easier said than done,' said Peter. 'They're sitting tenants.'

'I haven't seen the old soldier,' said Mr Mawne. 'At least, not since the week-end. Is he all right?'

'As far as I know,' said Diana. 'I think I saw him yesterday. Or was it the day before?'

'We often meet at the shop,' said Henry. 'I usually go to the post office at four, and he's going to buy his baccy. Interesting old fellow, but you don't want to be in a hurry. He'd talk till Kingdom Come if you'd let him.'

'He's lonely, I expect,' said Mrs Thorne. 'Particularly now, if he's taken umbrage about something, and isn't speaking to you.'

Diana began to feel worried. The conversation went on to other matters, but she had an uncomfortable feeling that it was quite two days since she had seen Sergeant Burnaby about. She must investigate as unobtrusively as possible. It was dreadful to think that the old soldier might be incapacitated so near at hand.

'I don't think we recognize,' she heard the headmaster saying, 'how much the country lost when that generation was wiped out in the First World War. All the best, you know – the finest minds. Must make a difference to have all those potential fathers gone. I used to have *My Magazine* as a child. There were pages of photographs of some of the chaps who died. The Grenfell brothers, Raymond Asquith, Rupert Brooke, Charles Sorley and someone in a bush hat called Selous, as far as I remember. Just a handful of well-known men, of course. When you multiply that by hundreds, it makes you think of what we are still missing.'

'I had *My Magazine* too,' cried Diana. 'My parents thought I should learn such a lot from it. The first thing I did was to turn to "The Hippo Boys"! They once made a sledge out of an upturned table, and flew Union Jacks from all the legs.'

'A fat lot of education you seem to have gleaned from *My Magazine*,' commented her husband. 'I don't think you picked up many of the pearls cast by the editors before all the young piglets. I had *Rainbow*, and was brought up on Mrs Bruin. I wonder why she had her frock decorated with a poached-egg pattern? It used to intrigue me.'

'Easy to draw, I expect,' said Henry Mawne. 'I wasn't allowed such luxuries, but I used to buy Sexton Blake in secret when I was at school, and read him under the bed clothes with a flickering torch.'

The party broke up about eleven. The rain still tumbled down. The Thornes had come from Caxley by car, but the Mawnes had come on foot, sheltering under golf umbrellas. By this time, there were formidable puddles everywhere, and despite protestations by Henry Mawne of enjoying a good splash through the rain – Mrs Mawne, for once, remaining silent – the Thornes insisted upon taking them home, and the Hales waved them all goodbye.

Diana looked anxiously towards Sergeant Burnaby's cottage. It was in complete darkness, as was Mrs Fowler's, but this was only to be expected at that time of night.

She found herself listening for sounds of life, as she lay in bed an hour later. It was very quiet, and she made up her mind that she would call next door first thing in the morning, and risk the old man's wrath.

Then, faintly, she heard coughing. It was the old familiar rasping cough of the heavy smoker.

Much relieved, Diana turned over and fell asleep.

It was still raining the next morning when Peter went off to school. A long puddle, dimpled with raindrops, lay along the edge of the brick path, and the trunks of the trees were striped with little rivulets.

Still anxious, Diana peered through the hedge at Sergeant Burnaby's doorstep. She was shocked to see two full bottles of milk standing there in the rain. This must be the third day that the old man had been unable to go outside.

At that moment, the postman arrived. He called at the soldier's house first and then came to Diana's door. She enquired if he had seen Sergeant Burnaby.

'Come to think of it,' said the young man, dripping droplets from his peaked cap over the letters in his hand, 'I haven't. He's usually up and about. And now you mention it, yesterday's letter was still stuffed in his letter slit. You reckon he's okay?'

'I'm not sure,' replied Diana, 'but I'm going round immediately.'

'Shall I come too?'

'No, you've got your duties to do, many thanks. I'll manage. If need be, I can telephone for some help.'

The postman looked a trifle disappointed, Diana thought, at being denied a little drama, but she was sure that the fewer people who visited Sergeant Burnaby the better. No doubt she would get a hostile reception anyway, but she was willing to take the risk.

She shrugged on a mackintosh and splashed her way to the adjoining cottage.

The door was shut. She knocked and waited, watching the raindrops slide down the wood, and noting that all the windows were securely shut. After a minute or two, she tried the door handle.

The door was not locked or bolted, she was thankful to find. She opened it a little way and called. There was no answer.

Now she began to feel afraid, and wished she had accepted the offer of the postman's company. Suppose the old man lay dead? The house was unnaturally quiet, and had the frowsty smell of an old house shut up for days without air.

She picked up the milk bottles. They rattled together in her shaking hand, and seemed to make a terrible din.

Taking a deep breath, she entered the living room. The fireplace had a few cold ashes in it. The windows were slightly misted with condensation. A crumpled newspaper lay on the floor by the old man's armchair. It was dated, Diana could see, three days earlier.

Behind the door were more newspapers and two or three letters. She picked them up and put them on the table, still listening intently for any sound.

'Sergeant Burnaby!' she called at the foot of the stairs. There was no reply.

She called again, louder now, her heart beginning to pound. Should she return, and fetch help? No, she told herself, he might simply be sleeping soundly, and it was obviously sensible to find out first.

She mounted the stairs, calling as she went. Both doors at the head of the stairs were shut, but she knew that the old soldier's room was on the right-hand side, his wall adjoining their own house.

She rapped on the door, and stood listening, head on one side. There was no sound.

She rapped again, rather more loudly, and now there was the squeak of bed springs, and grunting noises.

'Can I come in?'

'Who's there?'

'Diana Hale. Are you all right?'

'What d'yer want?'

The voice was surly, but not unfriendly. Emboldened, Diana pushed open the door.

The old man's bristly face peered suspiciously over the bed clothes. The room was stuffy, and the bed looked as though it had been used for two or three days without being made afresh.

'I was rather worried about you,' said Diana. 'We haven't seen you about and I wondered if you were ill.'

'I bin a bit rough,' admitted the old man. He looked thinner and his yellow face sagged. The fierce moustaches were down-bent, giving him an unusually depressed appearance.

'Let me get you a drink,' said Diana. 'What would you like? Hot milk, or tea, or something stronger?'

'I thought I had some tea,' said Sergeant Burnaby, looking about vaguely.

Diana took the empty cup from his bedside table. It was dry and stained, and had obviously been there for a day or two.

'I'll make you a fresh cup. When did you drink this?'

'Last night, I think. What's today?'

Diana told him. He looked disbelieving and slightly affronted.

'I come up here Monday night. Just after "Z Cars". Felt a bit rough with me chest.'

'I think you've been here ever since,' Diana said.

He put a hand to his ribs and winced.

'Got a sharpish pain here. Better sit up.'

She shook up the pillows and helped the old fellow upright. A spasm of coughing tore the man, and Diana was alarmed at the violence of the attack.

She waited until it had passed and he leant back upon the pillows exhausted.

'I'll get your drink,' she said, 'and then I think we must get the doctor to have a look at you.'

'Don't want no dam' doctor messin' me about,' wheezed the old man spasmodically.

Diana left him to make the tea. She could hear the sergeant's heavy breathing as she waited for the kettle to boil. She found a tin of biscuits and put them on the tray. There seemed to be remarkably little food in the pantry, but she did not like to pry too much. She resolved to bring him some home-made soup from home, and perhaps a boiled egg, if he could manage it.

He was grateful for the tea and drank it thirstily. Diana watched his trembling hands anxiously.

'Now, I'm going to pour you out a second cup, and while you drink it I'll ask the doctor to call on his rounds. Who do you have?'

'Young Barton at Springbourne. He's no good – like all of 'em. I tell you, I don't want nobody. I'll be all right if I rest.'

Diana said no more. She did not want to agitate him further, but she certainly intended to get help.

On her return to the cottage, she rang the surgery and was told that Dr Barton, though *excessively* busy, would call about twelve.

A little before midday, Diana went round again, bearing a light lunch. The old man was dozing, but woke at once and seemed almost pleased to see her.

She sat by the window and watched him eat. It would be best, she thought, to let him finish the meal before breaking the news of the doctor's impending visit.

When he had finished, she brought him a bowl of warm water, soap and sponge, spreading the towel which hung from the bed rail across the old man's lap.

'That's better,' he said, mopping the drops from his chin. 'You bin a good neighbour to me this morning.'

He smiled upon her and Diana took courage.

'You may not think so when I tell you that Dr Barton's calling.'

'You ain't rung 'im?' protested Sergeant Burnaby, his face clouding.

'I must,' replied Diana. 'You need an examination. It's the right thing to let your doctor have a look at you.'

'That's the worst of women,' said the old soldier viciously. 'Too dam' interfering.'

He tugged crossly at the bedclothes, and was smitten with another racking attack of coughing.

It was whilst this was in progress that the door opened and in walked the doctor.

★

Later, he came downstairs to where Diana was waiting.

'Are you a relative?'

'No, just a neighbour. The sergeant is our tenant.'

'He's pretty frail. Pleurisy and bronchitis, and his heart's not all it should be. What age is he?'

'Late seventies, I believe.'

The doctor nodded.

'Like most of these old people, he's underfed too. Can't be bothered to cook. All tea and biscuits. I'm sending the ambulance for him.'

Diana felt startled. She had not imagined that Sergeant Burnaby would need hospital treatment. The old man would be furious.

'Can you wait with him until it comes? I've several cases to attend to.'

'Of course.'

'Perhaps you could put a few things together for him? Pyjamas, soap – that sort of thing.'

He went out to his car, and Diana returned upstairs with some trepidation.

'Pleased with yerself?' asked Sergeant Burnaby nastily. 'Gets me out of the way, don't it?'

'Sergeant Burnaby!' protested Diana. Something in her face must have touched the old soldier's heart.

'All right, all right! Don't start piping yer eye. I've got enough to put up with without that. Give us a hand with me clothes, gal. If I've gotter go to the blasted hospital, I'd better go decent.'

16. Amy's Party

My friend Amy lives in the village of Bent, a few miles on the southern side of Caxley. I can take a roundabout route, through the lanes from Fairacre, and get there comfortably in half-an-hour.

The hedges were festooned with honeysuckle, the fragile trumpets giving out a wonderful scent in the warm evening air. Here and there, a late wild rose starred the greenery, and young fledglings squatted fearlessly among the grit in the road, and had to be warned of danger by a toot from the car's horn.

The corn was now golden, rustling in the light breeze which fanned the expanse, ruffling it like the wind across the sea. Soon the combines would be out, trundling round and round the acres like so many clumsy prehistoric beasts, while the farmers prayed for fine weather and freedom from mechanical breakdowns.

Nettled though I was by Amy's disparaging remarks about my perfectly good black dress, I had to admit that she had seen it a great many times, and perhaps a new one might be a good idea. Consequently, I was attired, not in red, but in an elegant affair of bottle-green, which I had bought at enormous expense in Caxley's leading store. The hole which this extravagance had made in my monthly budget was truly horrifying. I comforted myself with the thought that it was an investment, and that I could probably live on eggs, which were plentiful and cheap, and the perpetual spinach which was rioting in my vegetable plot. If the worst came to the worst I should have to borrow some money from the needlework Oxo tin, as I had done before in times of financial stress.

Aunt Clara's seed pearls did nothing to enhance my ensemble, I had decided, and had dug out a fat silver brooch from Mexico which looked rather splendid, I thought, after a brisk rubbing with Silvo at the last minute. If I had been richer I should have bought a stunning pair of shoes to match my frock, but in the circumstances I polished my old black patent ones and was quite content.

How nice it is to grow old, I mused, as I trundled along between the hedges. Twenty years earlier, I should have worried about the shoes. Now I didn't care a tinker's cuss that they were old. I really would not care if I were going barefoot, except on Amy's account. There is a limit to eccentricity, even between old friends.

There were several cars in the drive when I arrived. I was glad I was not the first, as I am so often.

'It looks as though you never have a square meal,' Amy scolded once. 'Bursting in on the dot, and sniffing the air like a Bisto Kid!'

'I like to be punctual,' I had replied, with dignity.

Amy's house was built in the thirties, and has a prosperous look about it with its wide eaves and pretty stonework. It looks across a valley, now golden with corn, towards distant hills to the south.

There were several people there whom I had met before and, surprisingly, the Mawnes from Fairacre. We greeted each other with unusual enthusiasm, meeting in a foreign part so unexpectedly.

'Let me present Mr Baker,' said Amy. 'Gerard Baker. Mrs Mawne and her husband, Henry Mawne. Miss Read. All from Fairacre, Gerard, and bursting with knowledge about Aloysius.'

I don't quite know what I had expected when Amy first told me about Gerard, but I was pleasantly surprised. Somehow, one does not expect a writer to look normal. If male, one half-expects a beard, or a mop of hair, or both, allied to a certain sallowness of complexion (burning midnight oil?) and either advanced emaciation because of failure to sell his work, or too much flesh because of unusual success.

Gerard Baker was neither thin nor fat, clean-shaven, with tidy fair hair and an air of cheerful competence. He would have made a reassuring dentist, or a reliable headmaster of a prep school.

All three of us explained hastily that we knew very little about the poet he was interested in, but I told him about Mr Willet's remarks, and he was eager to meet him.

'Aloysius sounds rather a trial,' he said. 'He's the sixth poet

I've tackled so far, and to be frank, they are all proving to be hopeless domestically.'

'But surely it's their work you're considering,' said Mrs Mawne.

'Yes, but the men too. I've come to the conclusion that life with a poet – and the more minor the worse – must have been uncommonly depressing for his family.'

At this moment, Vanessa was brought up to meet the great man. She looked tidier than usual, but still pale and unhappy. We drifted away as the movement of guests carried us, and let them converse.

Later, some of us wandered into the garden. Amy is splendidly up-to-the-minute with her garden. There are lots of shrubs and roses, and more foliage than flowers in her herbaceous border. As she is a keen flower-arranger, the place fairly bristles with hostas and dogwood, and lots of things with green flowers or catkins which are difficult to distinguish from the surrounding boskage.

A beautiful old lime tree scented the air, and I made a private bet with myself that not a branch entered Amy's house without being first denuded of its leaves. Did she still, I wondered, pop the young leaves against her mouth with a satisfying report? She had been a notable leaf-popper at college. Probably she had put such childish things behind her.

Whilst I mused, swinging my sherry in the glass, Gerard came to join me, and we went to sit on an elegant white wrought-iron seat which was much more comfortable than it looked.

'It's nice to be in the fresh air,' he confessed. 'Why do even the politest cocktail parties get so hot and noisy?'

I took this to be a rhetorical question and only smiled in reply.

'Do you know Vanessa well?' was his next question.

'Not very.'

'She seems such a charming child, but sad. Crossed in love I suppose. One always is at that age.'

I told him about the four times-married husband.

'But she looks better than she did,' I assured him. 'Amy tells me she's getting over it.'

'What a blessing it is to grow out of one's first youth,' said Gerard. 'Everything matters so terribly. So much to learn, so many mistakes to make. That line from *Gigi* – "Methuselah is my patron saint" – strikes a chord with me.'

'Me too,' I told him. 'I was thinking on much the same lines as I drove over here this evening.'

'Vanessa's staying here for a few days,' said Gerard. 'I wonder if she'd bring her aunt to lunch with me in Caxley? Do you think she'd find it boring?'

'Of course not. Ask her anyway. I'd say she'd be honoured.'

'Awful to be young,' he repeated, gazing across the valley. 'So vulnerable at that age – exposed to every blow, helpless, like a – like a – '

'Winkle without a shell?' I suggested, as he sought for words.

He threw back his head and roared with laughter.

'Exactly. I was searching for a much more poetic simile, but that hits the nail on the head.'

'We must go back and mingle,' I said. 'We've had our quota of fresh air.'

'I'll catch Amy now, before I go,' said Gerard, 'and ask about Vanessa.'

'Good luck,' I said, 'and if Amy can't come, I shouldn't let it worry you. After all, Vanessa is now legally an adult.'

As the guests drifted away, Amy took me to one side.

'Stop and help us eat up the bits, darling,' she begged. 'You won't have to wash up. Mrs Thingummy's come to help.'

'You misjudge me,' I said. 'I didn't think you wanted me to stay simply to do a bit of charring. And, yes please, I'd love to eat my way through those smoked salmon fripperies, not to mention the rolled asparagus tips.'

'It *is* useful to have a greedy friend,' exclaimed Amy.

Later, over enormous cups of coffee, Vanessa and I congratulated Amy on the success of the party.

'If only poor old James could have been here,' she said. 'He was called away this afternoon to some wretched meeting in Leicester.'

'Has he met Gerard Baker?'

'Yes, indeed. James introduced him to me. By the way, how did you get on?'

'Very well. I like his no-nonsense manner. He's not a bit as I imagined him.'

157

'He's invited Vanessa and me to lunch while he's in Caxley,' Amy said. 'Has he asked you, by any chance?'

'Alas, no. Any hopes you had of match-making, Amy, are in vain. Nice though he is, I doubt if Gerard is really interested in matrimony.'

Vanessa put down her cup with a crash, and sprang to her feet.

'How I do hate to hear people being picked over! I thought Mr Baker was the *kindest*, most *honest*, *sweetest* person I'd met for a long time. Not a bit like most grown-ups.'

She stalked to the door, slammed it behind her, and left us gazing at each other.

'Well!' I exclaimed.

Amy shrugged her shoulders and reached for another cigarette.

'The young', she said indulgently, 'are excessively trying.'

At Tyler's Row, Peter Hale was echoing Amy's thoughts. Before him stood a pile of school reports, for it was almost the end of term.

'Any news of the old chap next door?' asked Peter, pausing in his task.

'The hospital says he's comfortable,' replied Diana, looking up from her weekly letters to the boys.

'We all know what that means! Tubes stuck everywhere, a bed like rock, and being woken at five just when you've dropped off.'

'He's going to be there for a week or two,' she added. 'I'll go and see him one evening. I don't suppose he'll have many visitors.'

'What about things next door?'

'Mrs Willet's tidied up, and I've cancelled milk and papers and that sort of thing.'

'Not much more we can do then. It seems unnaturally quiet, doesn't it?'

Diana nodded. The windows were open, and only the sound of birds twittering, and a bee bumbling about the cotoneaster, could be heard.

Peter sighed.

'Well, can't sit here gossiping with these blasted reports waiting to be done. I often wonder what would happen if I put the literal truth. "The idlest boy I have ever met in over thirty years of teaching", for instance. Or "Is trying, in every sense of the word".'

'You would be assaulted and battered by enraged parents,' Diana told him.

'Or what about: "Needs a thorough caning for dumb insolence – and not always dumb".'

'Get on with them,' advised Diana, 'and keep those happy dreams to yourself.'

There was silence for a time while their pens worked steadily. Then Peter paused again.

'How's Mrs Fowler? She's remarkably quiet too. Is it because her old sparring partner's away?'

'Could be. She doesn't speak to me these days. But the dog's back, much to our Tom's annoyance.'

'Don't say he's starting a private war! I couldn't stand that.'

'Well, he goes through there quite often, and I should imagine he's sailing pretty near the wind. Mrs Fowler isn't above giving him a sly belting for trespass, particularly if he upsets her animal!'

'We must try and keep him in.'

'A cat? Impossible! He must just take his chance.'

They resumed their work, but Peter's mind wandered to other things. It was time Diana knew about the results of the doctor's tests. She had been wonderfully calm and cheerful during this waiting period, but if she were as worried as he was, then the suspense must be appalling. He could not bear to contemplate anything which would mar their happiness, or endanger Diana's health. Perhaps, he thought, they had been too lucky. Good health had always been theirs, and taken quite for granted. This shadow, which had fallen across them during the last few weeks, was something which a great many people lived under all their lives. It was a sobering thought.

'We must get away during the holidays,' he said suddenly.

Surprised, Diana looked up.

'But I thought we'd decided that it would be too expensive after the move? You know we've spent far more than we intended, and we've still got stage two of Bellamy's to face. That's bound to be even more crippling than stage one.'

'I know all that, but I still think we should get away for a few days. Somewhere not too far. We'll throw our stuff in the back of the car and push off to Wales or the Yorkshire Dales. Somewhere away from Tyler's Row, and the confounded neighbours.'

'If you feel like that, we will,' said Diana. 'I'd love it, of course. We seem to have had so many niggling little worries since we came here. It *would* do us good to go and forget them, and come back quite fresh.'

'Right. Towards the end of August perhaps. Or early September.'

He picked up his pen again and attacked the next report.

'Now here's a boy who works well, plays hard, ought to go to University, and is going to leave now, at sixteen.'

'Why?'

'Dad says he wants him in the shop. We've talked to him until our lungs have collapsed, but he's a proper mule-headed individual, so that's that. There are dozens of others who ought to leave at sixteen and get their teeth into a job of work, and they're just the chaps that have besotted parents who imagine them as future dons.'

'That's life,' said Diana. 'No justice, is there? I think it's much easier to be happy if you recognize that from the start. People always seem to think that they should get what they deserve, and it so rarely works out that way.'

'Now that's a dangerous outlook,' commented Peter. 'Do you mean to say that no matter how you behave the results are predestined? In that case, why have any rules, or any code of ethics at all?'

'Not *quite* that,' began Diana slowly, when the telephone bell rang, and she was spared the task of elucidation.

'I'll go,' she said.

Peter heard her making monosyllabic replies, and hoped to goodness she was not agreeing to take on more duties than she could manage at the moment. People seemed to be forever ringing her up wanting gifts for bring-and-buy coffee mornings, or asking Diana to sell raffle tickets, or collect for flag days.

Sometimes Peter felt like shooting these people who made such demands on his wife's time and energy. At the moment, particularly, he felt fiercely protective. He waited for her return, pen poised, but reports forgotten.

Diana appeared at the doorway. She looked perplexed and dazed.

'It was Doctor,' she said, and her voice trembled.

Peter's heart sank. He jumped to his feet, scattering the papers on the floor.

'He says everything's all right,' quavered Diana. 'No danger at all.'

Her face crumpled, and for the first time for years, Peter watched, with horror, his wife weeping.

17. *Speculation in Fairacre*

That night Diana slept without waking, the first full night's rest for many weeks. She awoke to such a feeling of relief and joyousness that she sang as she dressed, and felt as impatient as a child to get on with the wonderful business of living.

Peter was equally relieved.

'Thank God, it's all over,' he said.

'Well, not quite. I can have this ugly thing taken off my neck at any time. It's only a tiny operation, and I'd be glad to have it done. I'll fix up an appointment in the holidays, I think.'

'Today,' said Peter firmly, 'we're lunching out to celebrate.'

'And this evening I'll pop in and see poor old Burnaby.'

'Better ring first,' advised Peter.

The hospital said that visiting hours were from seven to eight-thirty sharp, only two visitors at a time, and the side door only was to be used as the decorators were in, and Sergeant Burnaby was – as ever – comfortable.

'Welcoming lot,' commented Diana, as the receiver was replaced briskly at the other end before she had time for further inquiries. 'I was going to ask if I could take him a bottle of something.'

'You take it,' said Peter. 'If there's any place you need a drop of the hard stuff, it's in a hospital bed.'

'You don't know anything about hospital beds! You've never been in one in your life.'

'I had my tonsils out at six, I'll have you know.'

'But no hard stuff in the locker then.'

'Well, no. But I had enough ice-cream to make an igloo. Absolutely delicious, except it hurt like hell to swallow anyway.'

'I shall take him some Burgundy,' Diana decided. 'And some Lucozade.'

'So that he can make a cocktail?' asked Peter, grimacing at the thought.

'In case he's not allowed to drink alcohol.'

162

'You shove it in his locker anyway. He'll find a use for it. No doubt the nurses could do with a glass. Make a change from nips of surgical spirit.'

'I'm quite sure,' said Diana, 'that the staff of Caxley Cottage Hospital is above reproach. Nips of surgical spirit indeed!'

'You don't want me to come too?'

Peter looked apprehensive. He had a horror of hospitals, Diana knew. She felt she would sooner face the visit on her own, and said so. The relief on Peter's face made her laugh.

'You can go next time,' she teased him.

They drove for lunch to a riverside pub, where the swans and ducks scattered bright drops of water as they scurried to collect the largesse thrown to them by children on the green bank. The willows trailed in the current, and now and again a punt floated by, its occupants wearing that vague glassy-eyed expression of bliss, which moving water evokes. Nearby, a weir tossed its frothing waters in roaring cascades, in contrast to the quiet main stream.

For Diana, her senses sharpened by happiness and escape from months of tension, the scene was unforgettable. It was, she decided, one of the most perfect moments of her time with Peter.

The side door of Caxley Cottage Hospital led into a corridor redolent of floor polish and disinfectant. Diana, bearing her two bottles, followed the dozen or so visitors along the passage-way to a central hall which had a signpost standing in the centre.

She seemed to be the only one going to the Men's Ward, and she wondered, idiotically, if Sergeant Burnaby could be the sole inmate. The ward was not very large, probably less than twenty beds altogether, Diana guessed, at her first quick glance, and Sergeant Burnaby, propped up on snowy cushions which accentuated the habitual primrose hue of his face, was very close to the door.

He caught sight of her and smiled delightedly, but to Diana's dismay she saw that an elderly couple were sitting one each side of the bed. Mindful of the stern warning that only two visitors were allowed at a time, she began to retreat, but Sergeant Burnaby hailed her with all his usual vigour.

'Come on in, ma'am! Come on in!'

Diana did as she was told.

'I thought I'd better wait outside,' she said. 'Surely you are only allowed two visitors?'

'Lot of nonsense!' declared the old man. 'Don't take no notice of it. Nobody else does.'

He waved a hand round the ward, and certainly there seemed to be plenty of patients with a number of friends and relatives around them, nibbling grapes, distributing clean pyjamas, and admiring the banks of flowers.

'My old friends,' said Sergeant Burnaby, by way of introduction. 'My old comrade Jim Bennett and Alice his sister. I forgot, Jim, you didn't know this was the lady as bought Tyler's Row off of you.'

'And very nice it is,' said Diana. 'When are you coming back there?' she asked the patient.

'Can't get no sense out of 'em. Might be another two weeks or even longer. It's me chest, see. I'm fine otherwise.'

'He won't be long in here,' Jim Bennett assured Diana. 'He's a tough old bird.'

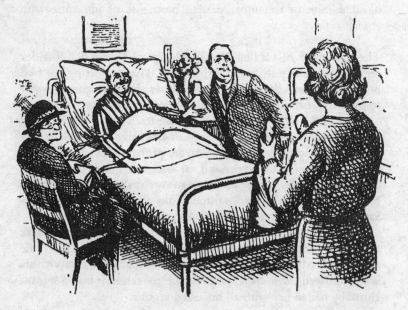

'Have to be,' commented Alice, 'to stand up to life in hospital.'

Diana took to this calm, fresh-faced countrywoman with her dry wit. She looked the sort of person who could cope with life perfectly, in hospital, or anywhere else.

'Have you had far to come?'

'Beech Green. There's a handy bus in.'

'I go through Beech Green – but, of course, you know,' said Diana. 'Would you like a lift back?'

'Very much indeed. There's only one bus back, and that's at nine-twenty. We're thinking of bed by then, Jim and me.'

'I've known old Jim,' remarked Sergeant Burnaby, struggling to sit upright, 'for nigh on sixty years. We've bin through plenty together haven't us, eh? Remember that estaminet near Poperinghe?'

He began to chuckle at their private joke, and started a fit of coughing. It was so violent that Diana wondered if she should summon a nurse, but Alice Bennett propped pillows at his back, and offered some water, and the old man was quiet again in a minute.

'Have you been a nurse?' asked Diana, full of admiration for such competence.

'Done a bit with our parents. They was bedridden for several years, poor souls, but I haven't been trained. Wish I had. It's the life I'd have liked.'

'Tell us about the village,' wheezed Sergeant Burnaby. 'Any gossip? Any births, deaths or marriages? And what about that old faggot, Mrs Fowler? She dropped dead, yet?'

Diana did her best to make a diplomatic reply. She told him that Mrs Willet had tidied the cottage ready for his return, that their gardens were full of roses, and various other innocent topics, leaving out Mrs Fowler's name carefully from her account.

'Pity about me brass,' said the old man. 'I does it every Saturday. It'll be a real mess by now.'

'Mrs Willet will be pleased to do it I know,' said Diana swiftly. 'If you'll let her, that is.'

'May as well,' Sergeant Burnaby said. His tone was grudging. Clearly, he did not trust anyone to cherish his brass as he did himself.

A sister appeared, impressive in her dark blue and white. Diana felt guilty, as though she were a youthful wrong-doer.

'I think I'd better go, and leave you to talk for a little. I'll be in the car. There's no hurry.'

She put the two bottles on Sergeant Burnaby's bedside locker.

'Now, that's handsome of you, ma'am,' said Sergeant Burnaby. His moustaches seemed to tilt up another degree or two.

'Hope you enjoy it,' responded Diana. 'My husband may call in to see you if you have to stay some time.'

'Very welcome. Very welcome,' replied the old man. Diana thought he was beginning to look tired, made her farewells, and walked rapidly from the ward before the sister took her name for detention.

It was very peaceful waiting in the car, and Diana thought how fascinating it was to sit there, virtually unseen, and watch people going about their affairs. A child, left in the next car, whilst its parents were inside the hospital, was blissfully unaware of Diana, not six yards away, and was systematically licking the side window, her pink tongue working from top to bottom making wavering stripes of relative cleanliness.

An old man, cap set dead straight upon his ancient head and a camel-hair muffler making a neat V at his withered throat, was beating time incongruously, presumably to the music of a transistor set inside the car. How odd people were on their own, thought Diana, and wondered if she too was equally enthralling to some other unseen watcher nearby.

Jim and Alice Bennett soon emerged. Alice took a back seat, and Jim settled with a gratified sigh by Diana.

'How does he seem, do you think?' asked Diana.

'Not too good. We managed to get a word with the duty sister on our way out. They won't let him out until he has someone to take responsibility for him. Not fit to live alone again evidently.'

Diana had a brief vision of trying to look after the old soldier herself with the help of the district nurse. Could she possibly cope? For a week or two, no doubt. Permanently, it would be impossible.

'Any chance of an old people's home?'

'He'd hate that,' said Jim. 'No, Alice and I've talked this over in the last few days, and we don't see why he shouldn't come to us.'

'It's extremely generous of you,' said Diana, trying to keep the relief from her voice.

'No more'n he'd do for us. We've been through a lot together: I couldn't see him in want, and we've got a good spare room downstairs we can fit up for him with his own bits and pieces.'

'It's a lot for your sister to take on,' said Diana, stepping on the brakes. A short-skirted mother, giggling with a friend, had pushed her pram well out into the road without bothering to look either way, oblivious of the possible outcome to her helpless baby.

'Me?' Alice Bennett sounded surprised. 'Lor, I shan't mind! We can all get along together – three old folk can help each other a lot, and I've always been fond of the old boy. He won't be any trouble.'

She spoke with such calm cheerfulness, almost as though she welcomed the extra responsibility, that Diana felt ashamed of her own relief. How mean-spirited she was compared with this generous woman! Here was someone who really did love her neighbour as herself, and was happy to serve him, despite the fact that she herself was getting on in years, her house was small, and there could not be much money to spare.

She dropped the couple at Beech Green. It was beginning to get dark, and as she wound her way back to Fairacre along the shadowy lanes, Diana felt chastened by the difference in her own attitude to Sergeant Burnaby's future, compared with his old friends'.

Peter's reaction to the news was much more practical.

'Well, this brings stage two of Bellamy's plan a step nearer.'

'Do you know,' said Diana, 'I never thought of that.'

'Savour the situation now,' advised Peter. 'It's an ill wind that blows nobody any good.'

Rumours flew swiftly about Fairacre. Sergeant Burnaby's condition gave rise to considerable speculation, and the news that he would not be returning to Tyler's Row caused even more.

'Whatever the doctors say,' Mrs Willet told Diana, 'I reckon the poor old man's suffering from yellow jaundice. It's plain from his looks. My niece looked just the same some years ago, and Dr Martin had to come six or seven times to get her over it.'

'I don't think it's that,' ventured Diana. But Mrs Willet, busily polishing windows, was intent on her own theories.

'My sister knew what it was at once, and as soon as Dr Martin put his head in the door she told him. Proper cross, he was. He can be pretty sharp when he likes. "And how do you know?" he says to her, sarcastic. "It don't need much learning to see what she's got," my sister said. "She's yellow as a guinea." "I'll do my own diagnosing," he told her, and examined the child. "Well?" says my sister. "Yellow jaundice," he said, and was fair nettled when my sister laughed.'

At the meeting of the Women's Institute, held in the garden of the vicarage, by kind permission of Mrs Partridge, Diana heard more theories put forward.

'Malaria,' boomed Mrs Pringle, resplendent in a navy blue straw hat decorated with a white duck's wing on the brim. 'It comes of visiting foreign parts. Mind you, Sergeant Burnaby was bound to go, being a soldier and under orders, but when I see the risks people run taking these holidays abroad among the foreigners and the germs and the water-not-fit-to-drink, I fairly trembles for them. And paying good money too to ruin their health!'

Mrs Mawne had heard, she told Diana over the teacups, that he was not expected to live. Pneumonia, wasn't it, and some virulent infection of the lungs? And what, if it wasn't being too premature, did the Hales propose to do about the cottage? If they were going to let it, until Mrs Fowler's became vacant too, she knew of a delightful couple, very musical, one with the flute and the other with the trumpet, who would make charming neighbours.

Mrs Johnson, hovering on the verge of the conversation, said that her husband knew of several young men, working with him at the atomic power station, who would be glad to rent a little place, no matter how primitive and inconvenient, until they could find better accommodation.

And the vicar too, amazingly enough, took Diana to admire his yellow roses, and in comparative privacy, away from the crowd of women, broached the subject of Sergeant Burnaby and his home.

'It sounds as though the poor fellow will be called to higher things before long,' he began, and before Diana could refute this statement, he continued.

'You may know that our infants' teacher at the village school has had to retire. Of course, the advertisement is in the *Teachers' World* and *The Times Educational Supplement*, and we hope to have a number of applicants. Accommodation is always such a problem for these young single women. In the old days, one could count on lodgings here and there, but there is *no one*, simply *no one*, who will board a girl in the village. Anyway, most of the young people seem to want to do for themselves, and Sergeant Burnaby's little place would be absolutely suitable, if you decide to let.'

'There is no question of it,' said Diana, with unaccustomed vigour. 'There is still a chance of the sergeant returning. As far as I know, he will be discharged from hospital in the next week or two. Friends are going to offer to have him with them, I believe, but he is an independent old man, as you know, and if he wants to return, then of course he must. In any case, at some time in the future we hope to incorporate the two end cottages into our own house.'

The vicar looked crest-fallen.

'Quite, quite! I felt I must mention the matter to you, as we shall be holding our interviews before long, and a little cottage, such as yours, would be an added attraction to the post.'

Two more people approached Diana, before the meeting ended, to inquire about Sergeant Burnaby and to broach the subject of renting his cottage. Diana began to feel hunted, and was relieved when she could get away, and walk though the village to Tyler's Row.

On her way, she called at the post office. A woman, whom she had not seen before, was chattering to Mr Lamb.

'Poor old soul,' she was saying, 'and to think those new folk have driven him out of his own home! Want to add it to their own, I hear. Can you believe it? The way some people –'

Mr Lamb, getting rosier in the face every minute, broke in upon the torrent of words.

'This is the lady who lives at Tyler's Row now, Mrs Strong.'

The woman had the grace to look abashed, but her ready tongue continued its work.

'We lived there for a time as children, me and my brothers. I was talking over old times with Mr Lamb here.'

Diana nodded, not trusting herself to speak.

'Well, I must be off. Takes a good twenty minutes over the hill to Springbourne.'

Mr Lamb and Diana watched her depart in silence. It was plain to the postmaster that Diana had heard every word. He spoke comfortingly.

'I shouldn't take any notice of what Effie Strong says, ma'am. She's got a tongue as reaches from here to Caxley.'

'I only hope that other people aren't thinking as she is. My husband and I are fond of Sergeant Burnaby, and hope he will soon be fit enough to come home. You may tell anyone this who is spreading such dreadful rumours.'

'There won't be any need,' Mr Lamb assured her. 'Fairacre's a shockin' place for gossip, but in their hearts people know the truth.'

And with this crumb of comfort, Diana had to be content.

Peter's comments were much the same.

'Let 'em tittle-tattle. We know we've nothing to reproach ourselves about. Dammit, the old boy might have snuffed it, if you hadn't gone to the rescue! If he's pining to come back and can manage on his own again, then he must have the place, of course.'

He paused to sneeze, fifteen times in quick succession.

'Those blasted pinks!' he gasped. 'But let's hope,' he continued, 'that Fate protects us from him after all.'

Honesty was one of Peter Hale's strongest virtues.

18. End of Term

Fairacre School said good-bye to Mrs Bonny with genuine regret.

The last few days of term had been over-shadowed by the problem of what to buy for her leaving present. All negotiations had to be conducted in secrecy, and many a sibilant whispering in my ear had driven me close to hysterics-by-tickling.

Ernest had suggested a silver tea-service. Someone had received such a gift after fifty years in the Caxley Borough offices, and no doubt the photograph in the *Caxley Chronicle* inspired Ernest's suggestion. When I pointed out the probable price, it was generally agreed that such richness was beyond our resources.

Joseph Coggs nobly offered a pair of rabbits, as his doe had just had a litter of eight, and was willing to make a hutch to house them if he could get a wooden box from the stores. I was much touched by this generous offer, but felt that Mrs Bonny might find it embarrassing. Joseph and I discussed the matter solemnly, and he agreed that transporting them would be exceedingly difficult, and that the sea air might not agree with country bred rabbits. Regretfully, the children turned down Joseph's suggestion, though there were plenty of offers to have any surplus rabbits for themselves, if Joseph wanted homes.

The girls' suggestions were rather uninspired, running to such things as scent, handkerchiefs and boxes of chocolates. The boys were outspokenly scornful.

'Has them for Christmas!'

'Scent! Proper soppy!'

'She don't eat chocolate. I know, 'cos she didn't want a bite off my Mars bar Thursday.'

'We wants to give her summat that'll last,' said Patrick. 'Like a tray.'

This inspired suggestion was greeted in respectful silence. It was Joseph Coggs who broke it.

'A tray'd be just right. We could get a little 'un for by her bed, or a big 'un for carrying out the washing up.'

I thought Patrick's idea was quite the best we had heard, and promised to go shopping in Caxley on Saturday on their behalf.

'Two-eighty us 'as got,' Ernest impressed upon me. 'Should get a good 'un for that. I suppose if you saw a real smasher for three pounds us might put a bit more towards it.'

I said I would be happy to add a little extra, but Ernest, brought up in a strict evangelical home, would have none of it.

'No, no! That's not right. You got enough to do with your money. It's the school's present, this is.'

Has he, I wondered, ever seen me rifling the Oxo tin when hard pressed? In any case, I admired his honourable outlook, and said I would do my best with the resources available.

That settled, we were able to cope with end-of-term activities such as Sports Day – refreshment tent under the kind supervision of the Parent–Teacher Association – clearing out cupboards, dismantling the nature table, writing reports, checking stock and so on.

Mrs Bonny was delighted, on the last afternoon, with her present of a sturdy carved oak tray, responded charmingly to the vicar's little speech, and invited us all to visit her whenever we were in her area.

Fairacre School broke up in a clamour of well-wishing, and the children streamed down the lane, shouting with exhilaration at the prospect of almost seven weeks of freedom.

Those mothers who had come to collect their offspring looked rather less joyous, I noticed.

One morning, in the early part of the holidays, I was wandering happily round the garden enjoying the morning sunshine. There is something wonderful about being free and outdoors at ten o'clock in the morning, when normally one is facing decimals or life in Anglo-Saxon England.

I was admiring my sweet williams and trying to persuade myself that they would do another year without splitting them when a car drew up, and out leapt Gerard Baker.

The passenger's door opened, and to my surprise, Vanessa emerged. She was actually smiling.

'Hello,' shouted Gerard. 'I'm Aloysius-hunting.'

'Well, he's not here,' I told him, 'but how lovely to see you both. Come and sit in the sun.'

'I came along for the ride,' said Vanessa, by way of explanation. 'Gerard brought Aunt Amy a book this morning, and offered me a lift. I feel rather a fraud. I'm sure I should never be able to do research on anything at all.'

She looked with open admiration at Gerard. This was the longest speech I had ever heard Vanessa utter. Gerard Baker certainly seemed to work miracles.

'Rubbish!' said Gerard. 'You've a very good brain. I'm going to ask you to make notes on this morning's discoveries. I'm sure you'll do it beautifully.'

He spoke briskly, like a kindly schoolmaster to a dim but striving pupil. I had to admit that the treatment seemed to be working.

'We've really called for directions. Can you tell us where Tyler's Row is? And do you think the people there will let us look at the cottage?'

I told him about Sergeant Burnaby's illness, and about the Hales who would be next door.

'But you simply must visit Mr Willet in the village before you go,' I said. 'He's the real authority on Loyshus. He had to sit through hours of his poem-readings. A real case of "And did you once see Shelley plain?"'

'Does Shelley come into it?' asked Vanessa.

'A quotation,' explained Gerard. 'Shelley lived some time before Aloysius.'

'And wrote rather better poetry,' I added. 'Have some coffee.'

'Now, that's *real* poetry,' said Gerard. 'I didn't have breakfast this morning.'

'Why ever not?' demanded Vanessa, looking protective. 'It's very wrong to miss breakfast. It sets you up for the day, and burns up all sorts of toxic whatnots.'

'You,' I said accusingly, 'have been listening to Aunt Amy. I bet she's on another dieting bout.'

'She is.'

They followed me into the kitchen, Gerard giving little grunts of appreciation as he came.

'This Victorian Gothic period is really due for a come-back. The windows of your school are perfect, and I love that pointed doorway.'

'Draughty,' I told him.

'And this house! A perfect period piece. What lovely wide window sills!'

'I had those put in ten years ago.'

Gerard was unabashed, and peered round the kitchen door interestedly.

'Oh, but you've modernized this! What a pity!'

'The Beatrice stove wore out,' I said, 'and the kitchen range needed to be burnished daily with emery paper, and black-leaded as well. Life wasn't long enough. Filling oil lamps, and trimming wicks, took more time than I could spare too.'

'Yes, I suppose so. No doubt, electricity does make things simpler.'

But he sounded disappointed nevertheless.

Over coffee, Vanessa told us that she was hoping to get a post at a hotel in Scotland in the early autumn.

'More fun than an office, and I can use my typing and book-keeping, as well as meeting lots of people, and helping to look after them. Meanwhile, Aunt Amy says I can stay at Bent as long as I like, or I can go home. I feel terribly lazy, but better in health since I've been here.'

And in spirits, was my unspoken comment. Clearly, the middle-aged philanderer was fast being forgotten.

'You just want to find as many interests as possible,' advised Gerard, 'until you get snapped up in matrimony in about six months' time.'

Vanessa turned great soulful eyes upon him.

'I shall never marry,' she told him earnestly. 'Never.'

'Don't you believe it,' was the robust reply. 'If you aren't the adored wife of some nice young man, with a baby in a pram on the lawn, within two years, I'll eat my new Irish tweed deer-stalker.'

Vanessa shook her dark head sadly.

'Come on, my dear,' said Gerard, jumping up. 'Work to do. The notebook's waiting for you in the car, and we must be off to Tyler's Row and Mr Willet.'

'Good luck with Loyshus!' I called after them, as they proceeded, with a series of alarming reports from the exhaust, towards the village.

A day or two later, I met Mr Willet as I went to buy my groceries.

'Very nice couple you sent me,' he said, leaning over his gate. 'They thinking of gettin' wed?'

'I shouldn't think so.'

'Ah well! Might be a case of May and December, though he's a *clever* man there's no denying.'

'I'm sure you were able to tell him quite a lot about Aloysius.'

'A tidy bit. He wanted to know what he looked like. "Proper mess," I told him. "Gravy stains all down 'is front, and none too fragrant behind the ears." 'E never 'ad a bath, you know, Miss Read, not for months and months towards the end.'

'He might have done if he'd had a bathroom.'

'A bathroom!' echoed Mr Willet, with scorn. 'None of us had no bathrooms, but we all kep' clean. We heaved the old tub in afore the kitchen fire of a Saturday night, and got out the scrubbing brush, and a chunk of yellow soap chopped off of the bar with the coal shovel, and we fair went to town. But not ol' Loyshus, not him!'

'Did Mr Baker see his cottage, do you know?'

'Yes, Mrs Hale took him in herself. That gal of his took a shine to it. Said she'd like to live there herself.'

'I wonder.'

'Tell you what, though,' said Mr Willet, lowering his voice. 'That Mr Baker don't know a thing about gardening. I was takin' him round the vegetables, and he never knew peas from carrots. What's more, when I was talking about my Kelvedon Wonder he kept looking across at my border and saying: "Which flowers are they?" It shook me, I can tell you. Been to school, and college too, I hear, and don't recognize Kelvedon Wonder. Makes you think about raisin' the school leavin' age, don't it? I mean, if a boy don't know about Kelvedon Wonder by fifteen, when's he going to?'

I thought the subject should be changed swiftly, as I was not too sure about Kelvedon Wonder myself, and asked him to come and have a look at the school skylight some time before term started.

'I'll do that,' he assured me, 'though you knows as well as I do that that damn' skylight's let water in for nigh on a hundred years, and ain't likely to stop now, unless we takes the bull by the horns one day and boards it over. That'd settle it!'

His eye brightened at the thought of vanquishing his old enemy, and I left him to his dreams.

Diana Hale was weeding the herbaceous border which ran down the garden, against the hedge which divided Mrs Fowler's garden from her own. On the whole, it had recovered very well from the onslaught of Mr Roberts' cows, and certainly the front of the border flourished.

But Diana was puzzled about the plants at the back. The tall delphiniums and lupins, the red-hot pokers and lofty Michaelmas daisies were looking decidedly peaky, and the leaves were turning brown. No doubt, Diana told herself, the old hawthorn hedge which had been there for so many years was the culprit, taking nourishment from the soil to the detriment of the newcomers. Nevertheless, it was perplexing.

As she pondered on the problem, Tom strolled through from Mrs Fowler's garden. Mrs Fowler appeared too, looking grim. Diana thought it might be a propitious time for extending the olive branch, and greeted her cheerfully.

'Lovely morning, Mrs Fowler. Are you well?'

'Mustn't grumble, I suppose,' said she, doing just that, from her tone.

'I do apologize for Tom. I hope he's not a nuisance to you. It's so difficult keeping a cat on his own premises.'

'Those of us with dogs has to,' commented Mrs Fowler tartly, 'or they gets criticized.'

She whisked indoors, and Diana resumed her weeding, very conscious that her olive branch had been thrown in her face.

Some days later, Tom was sick.

'What's he had for breakfast?' asked Peter, holding the shovel, a look of intense distaste on his face.

'Some new stuff, Pussi-luvs.'

'Well, ours doesn't obviously. I should throw the tin away. We don't get this trouble very often, thank God. The old boy's got a digestion like an ostrich's.'

A few days after this, Tom was sick again, and Diana was perturbed.

'Shall we get the vet?'

'No, don't bother him. He's obviously all right as soon as the stuff's out of the poor old chap. Has he had that rubbish again?'

'Pussi-luvs? No, just a morsel of liver this morning. He likes that normally.'

Tom's spirits certainly recovered quickly after the mishap, and nothing more occurred in the day or two before the Hales were due to set off on their brief holiday.

Kitty, their former neighbour in Caxley, was having Tom for the duration. He and Charlie could renew their friendship and their suburban hunting together.

Diana told Kitty about the mysterious attacks, but Kitty was reassuring.

'I'll watch his diet, don't worry. He probably picked up some mouse or shrew that had been sprayed with an insecticide –

something of that nature. You two go off and enjoy your break. Tom will be happy enough here.'

Diana was unusually silent as they drove back to Tyler's Row. Kitty's remark about picking up something poisonous had started an alarming train of thought. Those flowers against the dividing hedge, the implacable malice with which her greetings were returned, could they really be clues to something sinister which was going on? Could anyone, even someone so spiteful as Mrs Fowler obviously was, set out to hurt an unsuspecting animal, simply because it trespassed?

Diana told herself the whole idea was farfetched, and said nothing about her fears to Peter. Tomorrow they would be off on their travels, and heaven alone knew they both needed a rest. She welcomed the thought of leaving Tyler's Row and its troubles for a few days. What a relief it would be!

Nevertheless, the doubts remained at the back of her mind, and she wondered what the future might hold on their return.

19. *The Last Battle*

The Hales returned much refreshed from their few days' break. They had headed north, explored the Yorkshire Dales, and visited some of the fine towns for the first time. Richmond, in particular, delighted them, and they promised themselves a return trip one day.

It was a golden August evening as they drove down the slope of the hills which sheltered Fairacre. Already some of the fields had been harvested, neat bales of straw standing among the bright stubble, waiting to be collected.

Dahlias were out in the cottage gardens, and some tall chrysanthemums, their heads shrouded in paper bags, reminded passers-by of the Caxley Chrysanthemum Show to come before long.

'It looks autumnal already,' sighed Diana. 'I wonder how our garden's looking?'

'Grass up to our hocks, I expect,' replied Peter. 'It always grows twice as fast if you go away.'

They turned into the garage, and surveyed Tyler's Row with satisfaction. The thatch glowed warmly in the rays of the sinking sun. Sergeant Burnaby's yellow rose was in full flower for the second time, and the scent of mignonette and jasmine filled the garden.

'We've seen some heavenly places,' said Diana, walking up the path, 'but this beats the lot.'

'"Every prospect pleases",' quoted Peter, 'and only the neighbours are vile.'

'Which reminds me,' said Diana. 'I must find out about Sergeant Burnaby's plans.'

They spent the next hour or so unpacking, eating poached eggs on toast, and ringing Kitty to let her know they were back.

'By the way,' Kitty said, 'Tom's in great heart. No sickness, enormous appetite, polite to Charlie – in fact, the perfect guest. Leave him here any time you want to.'

They arranged to fetch him the next day, and Diana took a final walk round the garden before it grew too dark to see.

The plants at the back of the border looked as unhealthy as ever. What could cause their malaise? Could Mrs Fowler really be attacking them? Surely, no one would be so childish, thought Diana.

She looked towards her neighbour's cottage, and was amazed to see that two large white shells, which had once stood on each side of Sergeant Burnaby's doorstep, now flanked Mrs Fowler's. Above them, swinging from the thatch, was a hanging basket which the old soldier had kept filled with scraps for the birds.

Nonplussed, Diana went to the other hedge to check that Sergeant Burnaby's possessions had been moved. As she had suspected, the shells and basket had gone and, even more alarming, a number of holes in the garden gave evidence of plants having been dug up. No doubt, those too had found a home on Mrs Fowler's side of the hedge.

Diana told Peter about these matters as they prepared for bed.

'I had my suspicions about our border before we went away. This seems to prove that she is quite unscrupulous.'

'We'll go and have a good look round in daylight tomorrow,' said Peter, 'and that old besom is being faced with this. It's the last straw.'

'She'll think we want to turn her out so that we can get on with the conversion,' said Diana, remembering the conversation she had overheard in the post office.

'She knows perfectly well we can't give her notice to quit, but she's a constant menace. We've stood enough. This pilfering and damage is going too far.'

After breakfast the next morning, Diana and Peter took the key, and inspected the premises next door. Mrs Willet had done a thorough job of cleaning and tidying. Sergeant Burnaby would have approved. The precious odds and ends of brass shone like gold, the leaded panes gleamed, and only the faintest hint of dust lay across the polished surfaces of the old man's furniture.

Diana stood still and looked about her. As far as she could see, nothing in here had been taken. Mrs Fowler had not been able to gain an entry obviously. The first things to have gone would have been the brass ornaments, Diana felt sure. Human magpie that she was, Mrs Fowler would have been unable to resist them.

They went upstairs, and all looked exactly as Diana remembered it. The old man's counterpane was neatly spread, a pair of shoes stood side by side on the thin mat beside the bed. There was water in the flowered ewer standing in its matching basin on the old-fashioned washstand. It all looked so expectant, thought Diana, awaiting the master of the house. Would he ever come back to bring these things to life again? The whole house was forlorn in its silence, and she longed for voices, music, a fire, a kettle singing, even a fly buzzing against the window – anything to chase away the pathetic stillness of the waiting rooms.

'Nothing seems to be missing,' she said at last. They returned to the garden, locking the door behind them.

The old man's weatherbeaten wooden armchair still stood beneath the thatch by the back door, but something had gone. Diana wrinkled her brow with concentration.

'That rustic table,' said Peter. 'Used to stand here for his pipe and baccy, and his glass of beer.'

Diana nodded.

'And the antlers,' she added. These had been fastened to the wall. Bleached bone-white by years of Fairacre weather they had given no pleasure to Diana's eye, but had obviously been treasured by the old soldier. The shield-shaped mount had left a clear mark on the brickwork.

By daylight, they could see even more. Tell-tale holes where plants had been removed were numerous. It was difficult to remember the garden in detail, but they had seen enough to know that a marauder had been at work. Now all that was needed was to trace the stolen goods to Mrs Fowler's.

'We'll go round straight away,' said Peter, making for the gate.

'Wouldn't it be better if I called first?' said Diana, dreading a scene.

'*Straight away*,' repeated Peter, in a voice which brooked no argument.

Fearfully, Diana followed him as he strode towards Mrs Fowler's.

*

181

As so often happens, when one is girded for the fray, the enemy was not forthcoming. Mrs Fowler's cottage was as empty as Sergeant Burnaby's. Even the dog was absent.

They stood on the lady's doorstep and looked about them. The white shells gleamed from each side of the step. The rustic table was by the hedge, bearing a stone squirrel upon it. Several newly-planted clumps of flowers were apparent in Mrs Fowler's border, and a shallow slate sink, which Diana now remembered seeing in the old soldier's garden, stood by the house wall, strategically placed to catch any rain which ran down from the thatch, and so provide a bath for the birds. Beyond it, propped against the wall, were the antlers, awaiting their allotted place.

Here was evidence enough; the only thing missing was the accused.

'Blast!' said Peter. 'I was raring for a fight. Where d'you think she's gone?'

'Caxley,' said Diana. 'I've just remembered, it's market day. Let's go and fetch Tom, while our tempers cool.'

As one might expect, Tom was not present at Kitty's when the Hales arrived.

After eating his own and then Charlie's breakfast, he had made off into a distant garden.

'I'll bring him over when he appears,' promised Kitty, and went to brew coffee. Just as they were about to go, the Hales saw Tom reappearing through the hedge, and Diana ran towards him with a cry of pleasure. Tom glared stonily at her. He was not going to be placated so easily. Besides, he had seen that confounded cat basket in the car.

He turned to escape, but Peter was too quick for him. Defeated, Tom allowed himself to be placed in the hated basket where he set up a dreadful banshee wailing which he managed to sustain all the way to Fairacre.

'He certainly looks magnificent,' said Diana, when at last he was released, and was stalking about the house inspecting things. 'I wonder what upset him before we went away?'

'Too much grub,' said Peter, dismissing the subject. Diana could see that he was alert for any small sound next door which might mean that Mrs Fowler had returned, and that he could engage the enemy.

But it was many hours later when their neighbour came home. Peter and Diana had gone to bed early, and it must have been midnight when they heard the familiar clatter of Mrs Fowler's nephew's van outside in the lane.

The door of the van clanged, farewells were shouted, the van chugged away, and the sound of Mrs Fowler's footsteps could be heard on the brick path. Snuffling and whining betokened the presence of the dog.

Suddenly, the whining changed to furious barking, and the enraged squawking and spitting of Tom. The two old foes had met again.

'So *you're* back, are you?' they heard Mrs Fowler say ominously. 'We'll have to see about you, my boy.'

Her door slammed, and silence once more enveloped Tyler's Row.

The next day, much to Peter's annoyance, he was called into school unexpectedly by the headmaster. Two members of staff, newly appointed, were unable to start after the holidays, and this threw the time-table into unbelievable tangles. His visit to Mrs Fowler had to be postponed until the evening, and once again, she was out.

'Her niece and nephew fetched her in the van,' said Diana. 'They seem unusually attentive at the moment.'

Peter contented himself with mowing the grass while Diana set off to visit Sergeant Burnaby, who was still in Caxley Cottage Hospital.

As she approached the hospital, she overtook Jim and Alice Bennett walking up the hill from the bus station, and stopped to give them a lift.

'He's doing fine,' said Jim, replying to Diana's inquiries. 'They're letting him out next Wednesday. We've got his room ready. We went over to the cottage to collect some of his clothes while you were away.'

'It all looked very spick and span,' said Alice. 'Mrs Willet's got a good hand with housework. We're going to see what he wants in the way of his furniture. Jim's mate at the local said he'd fetch anything in the van.'

'Won't he want to come back himself to sort things out?'

'No. He's dead against it. It's that Mrs Fowler he can't stick. It's my belief, Mrs Hale, that he wouldn't go back there even if he was fit. She's poisoned Tyler's Row for the poor old chap – that she has!'

And not only for the poor old chap, thought Diana, drawing into the car park.

'Well, all I can say is Sergeant Burnaby's a lucky man to have such good friends,' said Diana.

'He's welcome,' replied Jim Bennett simply. The two words summed up the situation perfectly, thought Diana.

They found the old soldier sitting on a chair beside his bed, looking very much stronger and with a complexion faintly tinged with pink, for the first time in Diana's experience.

He was obviously excited at the thought of his new abode, and was full of plans.

'And what can I pack for you from the cottage?' offered Diana.

'I don't want much. Jim's fetched me clothes, and I'd better have me own china and eating irons. And me bits of brass! Must have them, and Jim says I can put me old chair in the garden in his arbour, so that'll have to come aboard.'

'Anything else?'

The old man ruminated.

'Them old shells by the door. I'd like them. Got 'em in India. They come off of some island in the Indian Ocean. I'm partial to them.'

'You shall have them,' promised Diana, determined to wrest them from Mrs Fowler by sheer force, if need be.

'Are you sure you don't want to have a look round for yourself?' she continued. 'We could fetch you one afternoon.'

The old man's expression grew mutinous.

'Not while that ol' cat's there. She curdles me. I feels the bile rising when I see her vinegar-face over the hedge. I don't want to see Tyler's Row again while she poisons the air.'

He looked up at Diana sharply.

'She pinched much? Out of the house?'

'Nothing from the house. It was securely locked.'

Luckily, Jim put a question at this point, and Diana was spared the embarrassment of further examination by Sergeant Burnaby.

It was good to see him so forward-looking. Obviously, he was leaving Tyler's Row with relief, which made things easier for the Hales. Diana left the three to make their plans for the next Wednesday, and waited as before, to give the couple a lift back to Beech Green.

It was beginning to get dark as she drove into her garage, and the lights were on in the house.

Peter met her at the door, looking worried.

'Better get the car out again. Tom's pretty ill. The vet says he'll see him immediately, if we take him in.'

They put the comatose cat into his basket. Tom was too weak to make his usual demurs, but occasionally gave a little whine of complaint which wrung Diana's heart.

The vet held Tom on the table. The cat's back arched and he was horribly sick. The vet studied the mess with an expert eye, examined Tom briefly, and spoke.

'He's been poisoned,' he said.

'Will he die?' cried Diana.

'No. He's practically cured himself by rejecting this lot, but I'll make sure with an injection.'

He went to work, and within ten minutes Tom was back in the car, and heading for home and convalescence.

'You know who's responsible?' Peter's tone was savage.

'I have my suspicions.'

'That woman', said Peter, 'doesn't know what's coming to her.'

It was, perhaps, fortunate for all concerned that Mrs Fowler's cottage was in darkness when the Hales returned. Once again, they were in bed when their neighbour returned in the ramshackle van. Muttering vengeance, Peter tossed in his bed as he heard the lady enter her home.

At eight-thirty the next morning he strode next door. Diana's presence, he told her, was not necessary.

'I'll do a better job alone,' he told her. 'You'll be too soft-hearted. I'm threatening the old hag with the police, and if she pipes her eye, all the better. If you're there you'll let her off with an invitation to tea.'

Diana watched him go with mixed feelings. She was relieved to be spared the encounter, but apprehensive about Peter's force. He had been so furious about poor Tom, he might even strike Mrs Fowler. The thought led Diana immediately to a court scene, with Peter in the dock facing a row of ferocious-looking magistrates, all bent on sending him forward to Assizes or Quarter Sessions or Crown Court, or whatever its new-fangled name was, with a recommendation for deportation, probably in iron gyves like Eugene Aram.

Diana contemplated this flight of fancy for some minutes, and then carried the breakfast things to the sink, and returned to earth.

It was ominously quiet next door – no raised voices, no crashing of china, no heavy thuds of close-in fighting. Perhaps Peter had felled her with one blow, as she opened the door? How long, Diana wondered, coffee pot in hand, did one get for Grievous Bodily Harm? She began her washing-up, ears strained to hear any significant sound from next door.

There, standing facing each other across the table were the two adversaries. A fine geranium in a pot stood centrally upon a plastic tablecloth which was decorated hideously with improbable scarlet flowers upon a sky-blue trellis work. Peter refused to let this monstrosity distract him from the task in hand. He spoke sternly.

'I've come about a serious matter. Can you tell me why Sergeant Burnaby's property is now on your premises?'

'Such as?' queried Mrs Fowler, with cool insolence.

'The two ornamental shells, the antlers, that little table by the hedge, the bird basket, and – I strongly suspect – a great many of the new plants in your garden there.'

'It so happens,' said Mrs Fowler, 'that I bought those odds and ends in here for safe keeping, until the old man got back from hospital. You should know there's thieves in Fairacre. You had plenty took afore you moved in.'

'And the plants?'

'Who said I took any plants?' She leant across the table menacingly. 'You come in here, accusing me. Well, prove it.'

There was certainly plenty of fight in Peter's enemy. She was going to be a tougher nut to crack than he had first thought.

'You can tell what tale you like,' he told her. 'Frankly, I don't believe any of it. This could be a case for police investigation, you know.'

'Police!' Mrs Fowler spat out the word. 'I know your sort. You've been angling to get me and the sergeant out of Tyler's Row ever since you set eyes on it. Well, you've got your way with the old boy. Now it's my turn, I suppose. Let me tell you, Mr Toffee-nose, I'll go when it suits me. You can't turn me out.'

Peter, ignoring this bitter truth, continued steadily.

'There are other matters too. I suspect that you have been doing your best to poison the plants in our border, and have made some attempt to do the same to our cat.'

'What that cat picks up when he's trespassing's no business of mine. You should keep him home, like I have to do my dog.'

'There's such an offence as malicious damage, as well as stealing,' warned Peter. 'Now, you understand, this sort of thing just won't be tolerated. You will have to change your ways if we are to remain neighbours.'

'You can keep your threats,' sneered Mrs Fowler. Her eyes were glittering strangely. A red flush had crept up her withered neck into her face. She came round the table, and Peter half-expected a blow in the face.

'Listen here, you. I know when I'm not wanted. I'm giving *you* notice. I wouldn't stay in this place another winter, if you paid me to. I've made me plans already, and I'll be shot of you by the end of the month. My niece and nephew want me, if *you* don't. They've bought a little shop, see? With a flat over it, where I can live in a bit of peace, and keep an eye on things at nights with the dog here. We've been planning this for the last two months – so you don't frighten me with your high and mighty air, and your policemen. I'm glad to see the back of you.'

The venom with which this was said made Peter wonder if his neighbour were mentally unhinged. It certainly gave him some idea of the wicked malice of the woman.

'I'm glad to hear you are going. It's the best way for all of us. The sooner you can go the better, Mrs Fowler. Meanwhile, I expect you to return the sergeant's property today. If there's any hanky-panky, I fully intend to inform the police, and they can make further inquiries.'

He made his way towards the door, feeling that, although he may have had the last word, Mrs Fowler had come out of the conflict with considerable success.

But any slight chagrin was overwhelmed by the flood of relief which this news brought. She was going! The cottage would be empty!

Tyler's Row, at long last, would be all their own.

20. Double Victory

The school holidays, as always, sped past at twice the speed of term time, and it was with horrible shock that I realized that only one week remained of freedom.

Two applicants only had appeared for the advertised post of infants' teacher, and both had failed to get the job. I was beginning to brace myself for tackling the whole school single-handed next term, when the vicar called.

'Good news!' were his first words. 'I've just been to see Mrs Annett, who has agreed to come for the whole of next term, unless we can get someone. Isn't that splendid?'

I agreed wholeheartedly.

Mrs Annett taught at Fairacre School before her marriage to a neighbouring headmaster. She was a first-class infants' teacher, knew the families, and we had always got on well together.

'Such a pity we could not make an appointment,' went on the vicar, looking distressed. 'But they were both *hopelessly unsuitable*. One was not a Christian, in fact, she *boasted*, there is no other word for it, about being an atheist! "Why apply for a post in a church school?" I asked her. And she had the impertinence to say that even atheists had to live.'

'What about the other one?'

'A most admirable character, but she had an invalid husband, a mother of ninety-two living with her, and six children, some quite young. We were much touched by her case, but in fairness to the children at Fairacre School, and to you too, Miss Read, we felt we could not possibly appoint someone with so many commitments already. We feared that there were bound to be periods when she could not get to school. A sad case, a very sad case. I made it my business to get in touch with her parish priest – a new fellow evidently. I think he may be able to help.'

I had no doubt that our good Mr Partridge had already sent help via the said parish priest. His stipend is small, for the living of Fairacre is not a rich one, but those in need never go away

189

from the vicarage empty-handed. The poor woman may not have secured the post, but she had made a staunch friend in our vicar, and some lightening of her burden would assuredly be forthcoming.

'I wondered whether to call on Miss Clare yet again,' went on the vicar, 'but she is really so frail, particularly since dear Emily's death, that it seemed hardly fair to suggest it. But Mrs Annett was a brainwave of my own!'

He looked as pleased as a child who has put the last piece into an intricate jig-saw puzzle. I congratulated him warmly.

'Well, there it is,' he said happily, collecting his things together. 'That's all settled. Mrs Annett can be here for a whole term, if need be.'

'But only for a term,' I pointed out. 'We must still advertise for a permanent teacher.'

His face puckered with dismay.

'Yes, yes. Of course we must. I suppose we *shall* get some-one?'

'We'll live in hope,' I said firmly, leading him to the gate.

That evening Amy called to deliver some plants.

'I promised you these,' she told me, depositing several large, damp newspaper parcels on my nicely scrubbed kitchen table.

'What are they?'

Amy swiftly poured out a torrent of dog Latin which meant nothing to me, and I said so.

'What sort of flowers do they have?'

'Fairly insignificant. It's the *foliage* which is the chief attrac-tion.'

'No real flowers?' I cried in dismay. 'I like nice, bright things like nasturtiums and marigolds.'

'So anyone can see from your primitive flower garden,' said Amy. 'You really haven't progressed from the mustard-and-cress stage of horticulture.'

'Well, thank you anyway,' I said nobly, remembering my manners. 'I'll put them in before I go to bed.'

'James and I are going off for a week in Scotland,' Amy said, lighting a cigarette from an exquisite gold lighter. 'Vanessa's up there already, incidentally. A friend of her mother's runs a hotel near Aberdeen, and she's gone up to help. I must say, she's a changed girl. I tell Gerard it was largely his doing.'

'How's the Bolivian heart-throb?'

'In prison, I hope. Thank God that phase is over. In fact, she's met a Scotch – or is it Scots or Scottish? – boy, who is being very attentive. He's very handsome, according to Vanessa, and wears the kilt. Now, why THE kilt? It sounds as though the whole male population only owns one garment between the lot of them, doesn't it?'

'Do you think she might be serious?'

'Well, she's sent a photograph of him, and he has quite beautiful knees above those long woolly socks with tags sticking out at the top. And he's six-foot-three, and sturdily built. "Braw", I suppose, is the word. I must say he's a very personable young man, and has some money too, which always helps.'

'I hope something comes of it. She looked ripe for matrimony, to my eye.'

Amy looked at me speculatively.

'You don't feel drawn that way yourself?'

'No, Amy dear, I don't. I'm really too busy to get married, even if anyone wanted me.'

'It was a pity about Gerard –' began Amy.

'No, it wasn't,' I broke in. 'Gerard Baker no more wants to marry than I do. If only people like you would face the fact that there are marrying folk and non-marrying folk, the world would be a much simpler place.'

'I suppose so,' admitted Amy. She blew a smoke ring, and watched it float through the French window and across the despised marigolds outside.

'He has a rather interesting bachelor friend –' she began dreamily.

'*Amy!*' I shouted. 'You are absolutely incorrigible! Have some coffee?'

'An excellent idea!' said Amy, swiftly abandoning her matchmaking.

Mr Willet came up to the school to mend the refractory skylight.

'Love's labour lost,' he commented, gazing up at it. 'It's the one job in this 'ere village as gives no satisfaction. Gardening, cuttin' hedges, diggin' a grave, painting the house – they all gives you some reward, but this 'ere skylight leaks again as soon as it's done. Still, 'ere goes!'

He began to climb the ladder, but paused on the third rung.

'Heard the news from Tyler's Row? That Mrs Fowler's leaving. Goin' to live with her niece and nephew at Caxley, she says. Makes out it was all arranged afore the fuss about old Burnaby's things, but I bet that's all my eye and Betty Martin.'

'So both cottages are empty then?'

'That's right. Sergeant Burnaby's bits and pieces went over to Beech-Green the day before yesterday. He'll be a sight better off with the Bennetts than scratching along on his own, poor old fellow, and I bet the Hales will be glad to get the place to theirselves at last. They done wonders with the middle bit, my wife says. Be a treat to see that place pulled up together. It's years since anyone took an interest in it.'

'Maybe it will become a shrine for Loyshus when Mr Baker's book comes out.'

'Been plenty of other funny souls dwellin' under that roof,' commented Mr Willet. 'Remember Sally Gray, as took to flying? I told you about her one day. Got a nice headstone, Sally has, in the churchyard. Don't make 'em like that any more.'

He climbed up two rungs and looked towards the village.

'Here comes that Mrs Johnson. I'll get started.'

He scampered up the ladder with the agility of a ten-year-old, and left me to face my visitor alone.

'I come on a sad errand,' began Mrs Johnson, looking anything but sad I thought.

'Not the children? They are well, I hope?'

'Perfectly, thank you, and out on their Holiday Project at the moment.'

'What's that?'

'"The Conditions of the Rural Poor. Are we still Two Nations?" It involves a certain amount of calling at the cottages, of course, and asking people about their incomes, and how they manage their housekeeping, and so on.'

I was staggered. The thought of the three Johnson children

laying themselves open to lashing tongues and well-aimed cuffs appalled me.

'People have been so cooperative,' went on Mrs Johnson. 'It's amazing how wages differ, and some of the men spend over five pounds on beer, and their wives often buy steak and oysters.'

This was so patently outrageous that I saw that Fairacre was positively enjoying its leg-pulling. Trust a countryman to have the last laugh.

The wind began to blow fragments of old paint and splinters of wood from Mr Willet's handiwork.

'Come inside,' I said, 'out of the mess.'

The school had its chilly holiday stillness about it, the smell of Mrs Pringle's yellow soap and black-lead. The nature table, the cupboard tops, the window sills were all uncannily bare. The whole place seemed derelict despite its tidiness. For one moment – a very brief one – I longed for the beginning of term, for voices and laughter and the school bell ringing high above.

'The fact is, Miss Read,' said Mrs Johnson, seating herself on a desk lid, 'we are moving back to London. It's promotion for my husband, and frankly we shall all be glad to get back to civilization. It's been an interesting interlude in our lives – I don't think any of us quite realized how *primitive* conditions still were in some parts of this country, but we shall be glad to get back to some *intelligent* and *cultured* society.'

'Of course,' I said politely.

'I do regret having to give up my part in the Parent–Teacher Association, but it's nice that the good work will go on.'

'I suppose so,' I replied, trying not to sound regretful.

'Mrs Mawne has been briefed, and I think the autumn programmes I have sketched out will carry you through until you can manage for yourselves.'

At this moment, I was spared replying by the advent of Mrs Pringle, who entered carrying an interesting-looking parcel wrapped in a snowy teacloth.

'Brought you a fowl. It's one of my brother's, and I've got it ready for the table, knowing you. I'd be ashamed to admit I couldn't draw a bird and dress it for the table, but there it is – If you can't, you can't.'

I thanked her sincerely, and said I would go and get my purse.

'I would've left it in the porch but for that cat of yourn. I didn't know you was busy.'

She cast a dour glance upon Mrs Johnson.

'Those desks,' she said heavily, 'have been polished.'

Mrs Johnson rose hastily, and followed me to the door. Mrs Pringle brought up the rear.

I was about to go across to the house when Mr Willet called me. The next few minutes were spent in shouting to each other about the skylight, but I could hear Mrs Johnson's and Mrs Pringle's conversation much more clearly than our own.

'I must say,' said Mrs Johnson, after explaining that her family were moving, 'it will be a relief to get the children into proper schools again. With the help we've been able to give them at home, they have *just* kept their heads above water in this backward place. But it's certainly been a great struggle.'

Mrs Pringle's face was as red as a turkey-cock's. She seemed to have swollen to twice her size. I began to tremble for Mrs Johnson's safety.

'Let me tell you,' boomed Mrs Pringle, prodding Mrs Johnson's chest with a fore-finger like a pork sausage, 'that you won't find a better school than this one in the length and breadth of the land! Nor a better teacher'n our Miss Read. I've seen plenty of teachers come and go over the years, and though she may not be *Tidy*, she can learn them children better'n any of 'em. I won't hear a word against her.'

I clung to Mr Willet's ladder with shock. Feeling the tremor he looked down at me anxiously.

'You all right? You gone a bit pale.'

'I'm fine,' I croaked. And I felt it.

Mrs Johnson set off in silence, away from her adversary, and I found my voice in time to shout after her.

'Goodbye, Mrs Johnson. Good luck!'

She acknowledged my farewells with a stiff nod, and vanished round the corner of the lane. Mrs Pringle, still bearing the snowy parcel, accompanied me across the playground to the school house.

'Cheek!' she muttered under her breath, still smouldering. 'The sauce! The upstart! Good riddance to bad rubbish! London, indeed! It's welcome to her!'

I fetched my purse and put money into her hand. Her face was still rosy with wrath.

'Thank you, Mrs Pringle,' I said. 'Thank you for everything.'

Mrs Fowler moved out of Tyler's Row three days before Peter returned to school. The shabby van made several trips to Caxley. Sergeant Burnaby's treasures had been returned, and were now with their rightful owner at Beech Green.

Mrs Fowler left the cottage spotlessly clean. Nothing which she had bought was left in place. Even the electric light bulbs had been taken.

Diana was the last person to see her. Mrs Fowler brought the key, and was about to slip it through the letter box and depart, but Diana, who felt that she could not let the old lady go in such a mood, opened the door and spoke to her.

'Goodbye, Mrs Fowler. I hope you'll be happy in Caxley.'

'A fat lot happier than I've been here,' replied Mrs Fowler viciously. 'I'm glad to see the back of Tyler's Row.'

She thrust the key at Diana, and stalked away to the waiting

van, her back as straight as a ramrod, registering malice to the last.

'She enjoys it, my dear,' Peter said when Diana told him later. 'What you don't understand is that some people thoroughly enjoy a fight. They're hawks by nature. You're a dove, and a particularly soft-hearted one. Rather a rare bird, in fact.'

He smiled affectionately at his wife.

'Shall we go out and celebrate our freedom?'

'No, I'd sooner stay here and enjoy the wonderful feeling of peace,' said Diana. 'I can't really believe that at last Tyler's Row is our own.'

'Not for long,' Peter warned her. 'Soon it will all begin again – the bricklayers, the plumbers, the electricians, the painters, the plasterers. Cups of coffee for old Fairbrother and those transistor-mad maniacs of his. Chaos all over again!'

'I can face it,' said Diana. 'I can face anything at the moment.'

Later that evening she went into the garden to pick some mint. Darkness was falling, and a light mist veiled the downs. Autumn was in the air. Soon it would be time to light bonfires, to stack logs and to prepare for their first winter at Tyler's Row.

Holding the cool stalks of the mint, she looked at their home. There it stood, as it had done for generations, silvery thatched, ancient and snug, melting into the shadowy background of trees and downland. How many men and women who had lived there, thought Diana, had stood as she did now, looking upon their home, and finding it good?

The windows glowed from the dark bulk of the building. Diana, shivering with the first chill touch of autumn, went thankfully towards the warm haven of Tyler's Row.

Peter was telephoning when she opened the door. There was a look of utter contentment on his face.

'Any time you like, Bellamy,' he was saying. 'Any time.'

He held out his free hand to Diana, and they stood there, hand in hand like two children. His voice became triumphant.

'Stage Two can begin!'

Farther Afield

*For Audrey and Jack
with love*

CONTENTS

PART ONE

A Visit to Bent

1. *End of Term*

'When do we come back?' said Joseph Coggs.

He stood close by my chair, rubbing the crepe sole of his sandal up and down the leg. A rhythmic squeaking, as of mice being tortured, had already turned my teeth to chalk. I turned to answer the child, anxious to put us both at ease, but again I was interrupted.

In the midst of the hubbub caused by end-of-term clearing-up, Patrick and Ernest had come to grips, and were fighting a silent, but vicious, battle.

Without a word, I left Joseph, moved swiftly into the arena, and plucked the two opponents apart with a practised hand. With a counter-movement I flung them into their desk seats where they sat panting and glowering at each other.

Despite all the modern advice by the pundits about irreparable damage to the child's ego, I continue to use out-dated but practical methods on an occasion like this, and find they work excellently. Sweet reasoning will not be any more effective with two young males in conflict than it will with a dog-fight on one's hands. The first objective is to part them; the second to find out why it happened.

In this case, a revoltingly dirty lump of bubblegum had been prised from under a desk, and both boys laid claim to it.

Both are well-nourished children, from decent homes, whose mothers would have been as disgusted as I was by this filthy and aged sweetmeat finding its way into their hands, let alone their mouths.

I held out my hand, and Patrick put the clammy object into it. For once, it landed in the waste-paper basket without mishap, and the incident was closed.

Patrick and Ernest returned to their desk-polishing, much refreshed by the tussle, and at last I found time to answer Joseph Coggs.

'Term begins on 5 September,' I told him.

He sighed.

'It's a long time,' he said mournfully.

'A *very* long time,' I agreed, beaming upon him.

No matter how devoted, dedicated, conscientious and altogether *noble*, a teacher is, I feel pretty sure that each and everyone feels the same sense of freedom and relief from her chains when the end-of-term arrives.

And of all end-of-terms, the most blissful is the end of the summer term, when six weeks or more stretch ahead, free of time-tables, bells, children and their parents. Six weeks in which to call your soul your own, to enjoy the garden, to think about next year's border plants, and of stocking up the log shed, even, perhaps, a little house decoration and tidying cupboards, although the thought of Mrs Pringle over-seeing the latter operation cast a cloud upon the sunny scene.

Mrs Pringle, school cleaner and general factotum to Fairacre School, sometimes obliges by giving me an extra hour or two on Wednesdays. I greet her offers with mixed feelings. On the one hand, the house certainly benefits from her ministrations, but her gloomy forebodings and her eloquent dissertations on the deplorable way I manage my house-keeping affairs are enough to dash the stoutest heart.

I had already determined to assist Mrs Pringle in her 'bottoming', as she terms a thorough cleaning, and to behave in as kind and Christian a manner as was possible under extreme provocation. If, as I knew from experience, Mrs Pringle's needling became intolerable, I could always put some cheese, biscuits and fruit in the car, with the current book and that day's crossword puzzle to solve, and drive to one of the nearby peaceful spots far from Mrs Pringle's nagging tongue and the reek of unnecessarily strong disinfectant.

'After all,' I told myself, 'I can take quite a lot of Mrs P. It's when Mrs Hope is dragged up and flaunted before me that I crack.'

Mrs Hope was the wife of a former headmaster, and had lived in the school house as I do now. She must have had a dog's life, for her husband drank, and she found solace in unceasing work in the little house.

'From dawn to dusk, from morning till night,' Mrs Pringle has told me, far too often, 'Mrs Hope kept at it. Never without a duster in her hand, and anybody invited to tea was met on the doorstep, and offered a clothes brush and a pair of slippers so as not to soil the place.'

'I shouldn't think many returned.'

'No, that's true,' said Mrs Pringle thoughtfully. 'But then Mrs Hope was *very* particular who came to the house.'

This was a side-swipe at me whose door stands open for all to enter.

Mrs Hope, so I am told, was always at the wash-tub before seven, twice a week, and even scrubbed out the laundry basket each time. Like Mrs Tiggywinkle she was 'an excellent clear-starcher', and naturally *nothing*, not even heavy bed-spreads and curtains, was ever sent to the laundry.

'Mrs Hope would have scorned such a thing, and anyway laundries don't get the linen really clean. And, what's more they use *chemicals!*'

If she had said that the dirty linen was prodded by devils with pitchforks, she could not have sounded more scandalized.

The introduction of Mrs Hope into any conversation was usually breaking point for me, and I could foresee many alfresco meals whilst Mrs Pringle was obliging.

There are many places within a quarter of an hour's drive from Fairacre which make glorious picnic spots. There are hollows in the downs, sheltered from the winds, where the views are breathtaking, and the clouds throw little shadows like scurrying sheep on the green flanks of the hills.

There are copses murmurous with cooing wood pigeons, and fragrant with damp moss and aromatic woodland flowers. But my favourite spot is by the upper reaches of the River Cax, before it wanders into Caxley, and threads be-tween the rosy houses to find its way eastward into the Thames.

Here the wild cresses grow in the shallows, their white flowers dazzling against the darker water. Little water-voles splash from the bank into the stream, stopping occasionally to nibble a succulent shoot, or to chase another of their kind.

And here too a heron can be seen upstream, standing like some shabby furled umbrella, dark, gaunt and motionless upon the bank.

It is here, particularly on a sunny day, that its magic works most strongly. It is the 'balm of hurt minds'. No human being is in sight. No human habitation distracts the eye. The slow-moving water flows at the same pace as it has always done, sheltering and giving life to fish, plants and insects. Thirsty bees cling to the muddy brink. Dragon-flies dart, shimmering, across the surface, and the swallows swoop to drink. Below, in the murk, among the drifting water weeds, the dappled trout lie motionless. Life, in its infinite forms, pursues its unchanging course, timeless and unhurried, and a man's cares fall from him as the things that matter – sunshine, moving water, birds and small beasts – combine to cast their spell upon him.

I was snatched from my reverie by Linda Moffat's voice.

Where, she was demanding, should she put the two dozen or so fish-paste jars she had just collected and washed 'off of the nature table?'

'Never use "off of",' I replied mechanically, for the two thousandth time that term. A losing battle this, I thought resignedly, but one must soldier on. 'Having a lend of' or 'a borrow of' is a similar enemy, while 'she never learnt me nothing' or 'I never got teached proper', pose particular problems to those attempting to explain the niceties of English usage.

'Try the map cupboard,' I suggested, watching the child transferring a black smear from her hand to a freshly-starched linen skirt. Poor Mrs Moffat, I thought compassionately, and the child at home for six weeks!

'Miss,' shouted Ernest, above the din, 'it's home time.'

'Two minutes to finish clearing up,' I directed, fortissimo.

Within three, they rose for prayers. The class-room was bare, ready for Mrs Pringle's ministrations during the coming week, and the wastepaper basket was overflowing.

'Hands together, eyes closed.'

I waited until the seats had stopped banging upright, and the fidgeting had stopped.

'Lord, keep us safe this night,
Secure from all our fears
May angels guard us while we sleep,
Till morning light appears.
                    Amen.'

If this was taken at a more spanking pace than usual, why not? Ahead stretched freedom, fresh air, bathing and fishing in the infant Cax, wrestling and jumping, rejoicing in growing strength, and, no doubt, eating all day long – ice-cream, potato crisps, biscuits and loathsome bubblegum, in an endless stream.

'Make sure you take *everything* home, and enjoy your holidays. When do you come back?'

'September the fifth, miss,' they chanted.

'Very well. Good afternoon, children.'

And then began the stampede to get out into the real world which was theirs for six whole weeks.

I remained behind for a few minutes, locking drawers and cupboards, and retrieving a few stray papers to add to the load in the wastepaper basket.

I locked the Victorian piano. How much longer would it hang together, I wondered? The tortoise stove stood cold and dusty now, but Mrs Pringle's hand of plenty of black lead would prepare it for the autumn term. There would be the familiar battle I supposed, about '*the right day*' to light it, Mrs Pringle playing for time, whilst I pleaded, cajoled, and finally ordered, the stove to be lit.

But what did that matter now? 'Seize the moments as they pass,' said the poet; I intended to follow his sound advice, and locking the school door, emerged into the sunshine.

There was a welcoming chirrup from Tibby as I entered the front door of the school house. She was at the top of the stairs, yawning widely, her claws gripping the carpet rhythmically as she stretched.

Plain Wilton carpet costs an enormous amount of money, as I discovered when I was driven to replace the threadbare stair carpet last year. Tibby has seen to it that the top and bottom stair are generously tufted, much to the horror of Mrs Pringle, and to my lesser sorrow.

It is sad, I know, to see such maltreatment of one's furnish-

ings, but one must look realistically at life. Either one has no cat and plain Wilton, or one has a cat and tufted Wilton. I prefer the latter.

Tibby, I knew, had just risen from her resting place on my eiderdown – another habit which Mrs Pringle deplores.

'Cats' fleas cause cholera,' she told me once with such conviction that I almost believed her. She followed up the attack with a vivid account of someone she knew who had allowed their child – or maybe it was their second cousin's child – to bite the skin of a banana. The result was a rash, diagnosed on the spot by the doctor as leprosy, and the child was never seen again by the family.

Although I did not believe a word of this cautionary tale at the time, so downright was Mrs Pringle's manner whilst telling it, that I still find myself opening a banana with careful fingers and making sure that the children do the same. The cholera I have decided to ignore. A school teacher's life is too busy to follow up every precaution suggested, and in any case, Tibby, I tell Mrs P. robustly, has no fleas.

The cat sprang down the stairs and accompanied me into the kitchen, watching the kettle being filled, the tray being set, and all the familiar routine leading to a few drops of milk in a saucer for her, as I drank my tea.

A quarter of an hour later, my second cup steaming beside me, I watched her as she lapped. Eyes half-closed in bliss, her pink tongue made short work of the milk.

'We've broken up, Tib,' I told her. 'Broken up at last.'

I leant back and thought idly about the hundred and one domestic affairs I must see to. There was Mr Willet to consult about a load of logs. And then I promised the vicar I would play the organ whilst the regular organist, Mr Annett, had his annual holiday. I must check the dates. And the sitting room curtains were in need of attention. Ever since their return from the cleaners, the lining had hung down a good three inches, so that even I had been irritated by their slip-shod appearance.

Then I really ought to tidy all the drawers in the house. The kitchen table drawer jammed itself stubbornly on the fish-slice every time it was opened. But where could the fish-slice go? And the paper-bag drawer had so many stuffed into it that half of them had fallen over the back into the bottling jar cupboard below.

Never mind, I told myself bravely, with all this time before me the place would soon be in apple-pie order. Why, I might even get round to labelling all those holiday prints of yesteryear before I clean forget the names of the places.

It was pleasant lying back in the armchair reviewing all the jobs waiting to be done, confident that all would be accomplished in the golden weeks that lay ahead. I should tackle them methodically and fairly soon, I told myself, stretching as luxuriously as Tibby. No need to rush. And later on I should take myself for a short holiday somewhere pleasant – Wales, perhaps, or Northumberland, or the Peak District. Or what about Dorset? Very attractive, Dorset, they said . . .

Near to slumber, I basked in my complacency. The teapot cooled, the cat purred and a bumble bee meandered murmurously up and down the lavender hedge outside.

Months later, looking back, I realized that that blissful hour was the high-light of the entire summer holiday.

2. *Struck Down*

Dawn breaks with particular beauty on the first day of the holidays, no matter what the weather. On this occasion, the sun fairly gilded the lily, rousing me with its beams, and dappling the dewy garden with light and shade.

I took my coffee cup outside, and sniffed the pinks in the border. This was the life! Even the thought of Mrs Pringle, due to arrive at 9.30 for a 'bottoming' session, failed to quench my spirits.

Across the empty playground stood the silent school. No bell would toll today in that little bell-tower. No jarring foot would jangle the metal door scraper. No yells, no screams, no infant wailings would make the air hideous. Fairacre School was as peaceful as the graveyard nearby – a place of hushed rest, of gathering dust, given over to the little lives of spiders and curious field mice.

Not for long, of course. Within a few days Mrs Pringle would begin her onslaught. Buckets, scrubbing brushes, sacking aprons, kneelers, and a lump of tough yellow soap prised from the long bar with a shovel, with an array of bottles containing disinfectant, linseed oil and vinegar, and other potions of cleanliness, would assault the peaceful building under the whirlwind direction of Mrs Pringle herself. Woe betide any stray beetle or ladybird lurking behind cupboards or skirting boards! By the time Mrs Pringle's ministrations were over, the place would be as antiseptic as a newly-scrubbed hospital ward.

In the far distance I could hear sheep bleating and a tractor chugging about its business. A car hooted, a man shouted, a dog barked. The life of the village went on as usual. The baker set out his new loaves, the butcher festooned his window with sausages, the housewife banged her mats against the wall, and the liberated children beset them all.

Only I, it seemed, was idle, glorying in my inactivity as

happily as the small ruffled robin who sat sunning himself on a hawthorn twig nearby. But such pleasant detachment could not last.

St Patrick's had long ago struck nine o'clock, and the crunch of gravel under foot now told of Mrs Pringle's arrival.

I sighed and went to greet her.

Mrs Pringle's black oil-cloth bag, in which she carries her cretonne apron and any shopping she has done on the way, was topped this morning by a magnificent crisp lettuce, the size of a football.

'Thought you could do with it,' she said, presenting it to me. 'I know you don't bother to cook in the holidays, and I noticed all yourn had bolted. Willet said you was to pull 'em up unless you wanted to be over run with earrywigs.'

I thanked her sincerely for the present, and the second-hand advice.

'Tell you what,' went on the lady, struggling into her overall, 'if you pull them up just before I go, I can throw them to my chickens. They can do with a bit of fresh green.'

I promised to do so.

'Well, now,' said Mrs Pringle, rolling up her sleeves for battle, 'what about them kitchen cupboards?'

'Very well,' I replied meekly. 'Which shall we start on?'

Mrs Pringle cast a malevolent eye upon the cupboards under the sink, those on the wall holding food, and the truly dreadful one which houses casseroles, pie-dishes, lemon-squeezers and ovenware of every shape and size, liable to cascade from their confines every time the door opens.

'We start at the top,' Mrs Pringle told me, 'and work down.' She sounded like a competent general issuing orders for the day to a remarkably inefficient lieutenant.

I watched her mount the kitchen chair, fortunately a well-built piece of furniture capable of carrying Mrs Pringle's fourteen stone.

'Get a tray,' directed the lady, 'and pack it with all this rubbish as I hand it down. We'll have to have a proper sort-out of this lot.'

Obediently, I stacked packets of gravy powder, gelatine,

haricot beans, semolina and a collection of other cereals and dry goods which I had no idea I was housing.

'Now, why should I have three packets of arrowroot?' I wondered aloud.

'Bad management,' snorted Mrs P. There seemed no answer to that.

'And half this stuff,' she continued, 'should have been used months ago. It's a wonder to me you haven't got Weevils or Mice. I wouldn't care to use this curry myself. That firm went out of business just after the war.'

I threw the offending packet into the rubbish box – a sop to Cerberus.

'Ah!' said Mrs Pringle darkly, 'there'll be plenty more to add to that by the time we've done.'

It took us almost an hour to clear all three shelves. Mrs Pringle was in her element, wrestling with dirt and disorder, and glorying in the fact that she had me there, under her thumb, to crow over. I can't say that I minded very much.

Mrs Pringle's slings and arrows hardly dented my armour at all, and it was pleasant to come across long lost commodities again.

'I've been looking everywhere for those vanilla pods,' I cried, snatching the long glass tube from Mrs Pringle's hand. 'And that bottle of anchovy essence.'

'It's as dry as a bone,' replied Mrs Pringle with satisfaction, 'and so's this almond essence bottle, and the capers. What a wicked waste! If my mother could see this she would turn in her grave! Every week the cupboards were turned out regular, and everything in use brought forward and the new put to the back. "Method!", she used to say. "That's all that's needed, my girl. Method!", and it's thanks to her that I'm as tidy as I am today,' said my slave-driver smugly.

'My mother,' I replied, 'died when I was in my late teens.'

But if I imagined that this body blow would affect my sparring partner, I was to be disappointed.

'It's the early years that count,' snapped Mrs Pringle, throwing a box of chocolate vermicelli at my head.

I gave up, and we continued in silence until the cupboard was bare. Then I was allowed to retreat upstairs to dust the bedrooms whilst Mrs Pringle attacked the shelves with the most efficacious detergent known to man.

A little later, over coffee, Mrs Pringle gave me up-to-date news of the village.

'You've heard about the Flower Show, I suppose?' she began.

I confessed that I had not attended this Fairacre event on the previous Saturday.

'A good thing. There's trouble brewing. Mr Willet says he's writing to the paper about it.'

'Why? What happened?'

'You may well ask. Mr Roberts won first prize for the best kept garden.'

This did not seem surprising to me. Our local farmer always keeps a fine display of flowers and vegetables.

'What about it?'

Mrs Pringle took a deep breath, so that her corsets creaked.

'Mr Roberts,' she said, with dreadful emphasis, 'has Tom Banks working in that garden three days a week – if working you can call it. And, what's more, he had all the farmyard manure at his beck and call. How can us cottagers compete with that?'

I saw her point.

'The Flower Show's never been the same,' said Mrs Pringle, 'since that fellow that worked up the Atomic got on the committee. Good thing he's been posted elsewhere, but the trouble still remains. All this Jack's-as-good-as-his-master nonsense! Don't you remember the outcry when he wiped out the cottager classes? Said it was degrading to have two types of entry. As though we bothered! If you does your own digging and planting, you're a cottager. If you get help, you're not. I never could see why that man was allowed to question the ways of the Almighty. "The rich man in his castle, the poor man at his gate" says the hymn. And what's wrong with that, I'd like to know? If there'd been a cottager's class, as there always used to be, then Mr Willet would have come first, and rightly so. He's drafting a fair knock-out of a letter to the Caxley.'

I said I should look forward to reading it in next week's *Caxley Chronicle*.

'Oh, I don't say it will be in that early,' said Mrs Pringle, stacking our cups. 'So far it's only got as far as the first draft on a page of Alice Willet's laundry book. But he's keeping at it.'

She replaced the lid of the biscuit tin.

'Mrs Partridge's niece goes back to London today. I should think she and the vicar will be downright thankful. As far as I can hear, the girl's done nothing but wash her hair and walk about with one of those horrible transistors all day.'

'She's supposed to be a very clever girl,' I said rising to the absent one's defence.

'Being clever don't get you far,' sniffed Mrs Pringle. 'There's some, not a hundred miles from here, who's passed examinations and that, but don't know no more than that cat what's in their cupboards.'

Reminded of her duties, she rose and removed the tray from the kitchen table to the draining board.

'You'd be least bother to me,' she told me, 'if you made yourself scarce while I tackle that china cupboard. I don't trust myself to keep a civil tongue in my head whiles that's being bottomed, and I've never been one to speak out of place, I hope.'

She glanced at me sharply.

'I suppose you wouldn't have such a thing as some white paper for lining the shelves when I've washed them?'

'As a matter of fact,' I told her with some pride, 'there's a roll of lining paper upstairs. I'll run up and get it.'

It was pleasant to dazzle Mrs Pringle with my efficiency for once, and I rooted about in the landing cupboard among boxes of stationery, stored Christmas tree decorations, and a mound of yellowing cuttings from magazines which I tried to deceive myself into calling 'Reference Material' although, in my honest moments, I knew full well I should never refer to them.

The roll of lining paper had managed to work its way to the very bottom of the cupboard, and right to the back behind a pile of box files dusty with age, and bearing such labels as 'Infant Handwork Ideas', 'Historical Costumes', and the like. I wouldn't mind betting that most teachers have just such a collection of junk tucked away, carefully garnered as an insurance against the future, and looked at only once in a blue moon, or else forgotten completely.

The cupboard was a deep one and by the time I had wriggled the slippery roll from behind the boxes, I was hot and dusty and had laddered one stocking. I struggled to my feet feeling quite giddy with my exertions.

I hoisted one of the dusty files under one arm. It contained, if I remembered rightly, some patterns for making simple lamp shades, and these might prove useful for handwork next term. I would go through the box at my leisure.

Mrs Pringle's lining paper began to behave like a telescope, the inside sliding out at remarkable speed. From being eighteen inches in length, the roll rapidly became thirty, and caught itself in the banisters as I took the first unsteady step downwards.

Everything happened at once. The heavy file slipped, the

lining paper jammed, my ankle turned over with a crack, and the hall carpet rushed upwards to meet me amidst whirling darkness lit with stars. The latter moved into a circle, as though about to embark on 'Gathering Peascods'. Suddenly, they vanished altogether, and I wondered why so many bells were ringing.

When I came round I was sitting on the bottom stair with my face against Mrs Pringle's bosom.

It was enough to bring me rapidly to full consciousness.

'You bin and fell down,' said that lady reproachfully.

There seemed nothing to add.

Five minutes later, on the sofa, I found myself trying to control my chattering teeth and to assess the damage done.

Mrs Pringle, who had collected the papers strewn all over the hall, now surveyed me lugubriously.

'Well, you've made a proper job of it,' she told me, with some satisfaction. 'If you don't have a black eye by morning, I'll eat my hat. And something's not right with that ankle.'

'Sprained,' I said. 'Nothing more, but my arm feels strange.'

It hung down at approximately its usual angle, but felt queerly heavy.

'Could be broken,' Mrs Pringle suggested, about to investigate.

'Don't touch it,' I squealed. I lifted it carefully.

'I don't think it can be broken,' I said. 'I mean there aren't any bones sticking through the flesh, and it isn't a funny shape, is it?'

'Could still be broken,' replied Mrs Pringle, with conviction. 'You don't know much about it, do you?'

I admitted that I was entirely ignorant when it came to anatomy. All I knew was that I was shaking and cold and for two pins would have howled like a dog.

'I should like some brandy,' I said. 'It's in the sideboard.'

Leaning back, I closed my eyes and gave myself over to being a casualty. Hell, how that ankle hurt! It would be swollen to twice the size in an hour, that was sure, and heaven alone knew what was the matter with my right arm.

I took the proffered glass in my left hand and sipped the fire-water.

'Where's Dr Martin this morning?' I asked. 'He'd better look me over, I suppose.'

'Wednesday,' said Mrs Pringle, seating herself heavily on the end of the sofa, far too close to my damaged ankle for my peace of mind. 'Wednesdays he's in Fairacre. He'll be looking at Margaret Waters sometime this morning, having a look at her bad leg. What a bit of luck!'

'Who for?' I said crossly. 'Oh, never mind, never mind. I'll ring there and leave a message.'

I struggled to my feet, screamed, and fell back on to the sofa again.

'It's The Drink,' said Mrs Pringle, in a voice of doom. I remembered that the blood of dozens of Blue-Ribboners beat in her veins, and regretted that I had allowed her to administer brandy to me, even for purely restorative reasons.

'No,' I managed to say, 'it's the ankle. Perhaps you would ring Miss Waters and ask her to see if Dr Martin could call.'

She went into the hall, and I swallowed the rest of the brandy. It was such a solace in the midst of my increasing discomfort that, for the first time in my life, I began to understand why people took to the bottle.

I lay back and surveyed the room through half-closed eyes. A bump over my right eye was coming up at an alarming rate. Would it be the size of a pigeon's egg by the time the doctor arrived, I wondered? And why a *pigeon's* egg? Why not a hen's or a bantam's egg?

Objects in the room had a tendency to shift to the left when I looked at them, and the curtains swayed in a highly distracting fashion. The clock on the mantel-piece grew large and then small in a rhythmic manner, and I began to feel as though the sofa had floated out to sea and we had run into a heavy swell.

Above the rushing noise in my head, I heard Mrs Pringle's boom from the hall.

'I'll tell her, Miss Waters. We'll be glad to see him. She looks very poorly to me – very poorly indeed. Oh, no doubt it'll be hospital with these injuries! Yes, I'll let you know.'

'*I'm not going to hospital!*' I shouted to the open door. Something crashed inside my head and, groaning, I turned my face into the sofa, giving the bump a second wallop.

Mrs Pringle appeared in the doorway.

'It's a good thing it's the first day of the holidays,' she said smugly. 'Give you plenty of time to get over it, won't it, dear?'

I drew in my breath painfully.

'Mrs Pringle,' I said, very quietly and carefully, 'I could do with a little more brandy.'

3. *Medical Matters*

Extreme pain, it seems, has a curiously numbing effect on one's normal reactions. Pre-occupied as I was with my afflictions, Mrs Pringle's deplorable remark, which ordinarily would have aroused my fury, now simply appeared to be unhappy but true.

It certainly looked as though a week at least would be needed to put me back into fighting trim. Nursing my arm I began to mourn those blissfully planned picnics, the efficient tidying-up and the trips to distant places.

'Can't see you doing much in the next week or two,' announced Mrs Pringle, as if divining my melancholy thoughts. 'When my John sprained his ankle at football it was all of three months before he could put his weight on it – and him a *young* man, of course.'

Still cocooned, in my pain, from these barbs, I nodded agreement.

'Tell you what,' said the lady. 'I could come in each morning for an hour or so, seeing as it's holiday time. Get you an egg, say, or some soup to keep you going.'

This was a kind thought and I did my best to register gratitude. By now my arm was beginning to swell, and hurt badly. Would Dr Martin be able to get my sleeve rolled up? Would it have to be cut from the frock?

Alarmed now, I sat up and begged Mrs Pringle to help in my undressing.

'Before the doctor comes?' she asked scandalized.

I explained my fears.

'If that's all, I can slit it up now with the kitchen scissors,' she volunteered, making for the door.

'But I don't want it slit,' I wailed. 'I like this frock! If we can get it off now before this blasted arm gets more and more like a bolster, I can put on a dressing gown.'

'That would look decent enough,' conceded Mrs Pringle,

'and of course I'll stay in the room while he's here. It's only proper.'

She went stumping up the stairs, leaving me to wonder if Dr Martin, now somewhere around seventy, was in any great danger from a plain middle-aged school teacher temporarily one-legged and one-armed.

I could hear Mrs Pringle opening doors above. The room still pitched about, though the swell was not quite as severe as at first.

Closing my eyes, I let myself float gently out to sea upon the sofa.

'Well,' said a man's voice. 'You lost that fight, as far as I can see.'

I opened my eyes and saw Dr Martin surveying me. Mrs Pringle stood beside him.

He pulled up a chair and began to examine the bump on my temple.

'Any pain?'

'Of course there is,' I said, wincing from the pressure of his ice-cold fingers. I explained the symptoms of rocking motions and the movement of furniture in the room.

'Humph!' He felt my skull gently.

'Any pain in the ox-foot?'

'In the *what*?'

'The ox-foot.'

I looked blankly at him.

'The *occiput*, the back of the head, woman!'

'Oh, no, no! None at all,' I assured him. 'Just this bang on the forehead.'

I began to feel rather cross. Why do medical men expect people to know all the Latin terms?

Most patients, I suspect, are as ignorant of anatomy as I am.

My doctor gets a plain statement in basic English from me, and I can't think why his reply cannot be expressed in the same vein.

If I tell him that the bony bump on my wrist hurts, what sort of answer do I get?

It is usually some glib explanation about the action of the lower lobelia on the gloxinia, which may well affect the ageratum and so lead to total tormentilla. Bewildered by all this mumbo-jumbo the patient's normal reaction is to go straight home, apply witch hazel and make a cup of tea.

Dr Martin opened his black bag, moistened some cotton wool and dabbed my forehead.

'You'll survive,' he assured me, as I flinched. He looked across at the brandy bottle.

'Being drinking?'

'Purely for medicinal purposes,' I told him with dignity.

There was a sniff from Mrs Pringle.

'No need to keep you from your work,' said Dr Martin.

Mrs Pringle left the room reluctantly.

'Now let's look at the arm.'

He felt it and I screamed.

'Can you bend it here?'

'*No!*' I shouted fortissimo. He nodded with evident satisfaction.

'Radial trouble, I think,' he said. 'Have to get it X-rayed.'

At that moment the telephone shrilled, and I heard Mrs Pringle lift the receiver.

By this time, the doctor had produced a calico sling from his bag and was folding it deftly. It smelt horribly of dog biscuits and was very rough when tied round my neck.

'Must keep it still and supported,' he told me. 'You're bound to have a good deal of pain with an elbow injury.'

No one could be kinder than dear Dr Martin, and normally I count him among my most respected friends at Fairacre, but the evident relish with which he imparted this information was hard to bear.

I lay back, exhausted, on the sofa. The pain had frightened me, and I was very careful to keep the arm quite still.

Dr Martin now turned his attention to the ankle. I had taken off my stockings and shoes, and looked morosely at the swelling of my left ankle.

He began to wriggle the toes this way and that, and Mrs Pringle came into the room.

'Mrs Garfield on the phone,' she told us. This was Amy, my old college friend, and it was welcome news. Perhaps she could come to my aid?

'I must speak to her,' I told Dr Martin. 'She might be able to take me into Caxley if I have to go to be X-rayed.'

'Caxley? That's no good to you, my girl. There's no casualty department there now.'

I looked at him in horror.

'Do you mean I've got to be jogged all the way to Norchester?'

'That's right, my dear. And if your friend can take you, the sooner the better.'

The thought of travelling over fifteen miles to our county town appalled me. I lowered my bare legs gingerly to the ground, clutching my wounded arm tenderly the while.

Dr Martin came to my aid, and leaning heavily on his shoulder I hopped to the telephone.

'I've told her you're suffering from an accident,' Mrs Pringle said importantly, as I stood on one foot holding the receiver.

'What's happened?' asked Amy.

I told her.

'I'll be over in half an hour,' she promised. 'Get ready for the hospital and I'll take you straight there.'

My cries of gratitude were cut short by a click and the line going dead.

Amy had gone into action.

By the time she arrived, Dr Martin had departed on his rounds, and I was lying on the sofa, dressed by Mrs Pringle ready for the journey.

It had not been an easy preparation. Fastening stockings to suspenders I now found quite impossible with one hand, and I was obliged to Mrs Pringle for her assistance.

It was equally impossible to put on a coat, and this was draped round my shoulders, insecurely. The sling was like emery paper round the back of my neck, until Mrs Pringle managed to insert a silk scarf between it and my scarlet flesh. The ankle had been wrapped in yards of crepe bandage, and I felt as swaddled as an Egyptian mummy.

'You'll be a lot worse before you're better,' Mrs Pringle warned me.

The cupboards had been abandoned since my fall, and I could see she was torn between returning to her duties and tending the fractious sick.

'I'll be all right,' I told her, 'if you like to get on with the work.'

Before she had time to make her decision, the door opened and in walked Amy, looking as elegant as ever in a cream silk suit.

'Poor old love,' she said, in a voice of such warm sympathy, that only Mrs Pringle's presence kept me from shameful weeping.

'What do you need?' she asked more briskly.

'Only this chit from Dr Martin, I think.'

'Then let's ease you into the car and trundle on our way.'

Together, they helped me to hop to Amy's waiting limousine.

'Take the lettuces,' I shouted to Mrs Pringle through the window, 'and your money, and a thousand thanks.'

I finished on a high-pitched yelp as Amy let in the clutch and my elbow moved a millimetre.

'Sorry,' said Amy, looking anxious.

With infinite caution we began our journey.

Amy and I have known each other ever since our college days. She was one of that establishment's brighter stars, excelling in sport as well as work, and would have made a splendid headmistress of some lucky school had she not married within three years of leaving college.

It was quite apparent that James would succeed in anything he took up. He was a dark-eyed charmer, with boundless energy and an effervescent sense of humour. He loved parties and social occasions of all kinds, going to great lengths to arrange outings which would please his friends, and always generous with his time and money.

He was, as the saying goes, 'good with children', and I know it was a blow to both of them that they had no family of their own. Nephews and nieces were frequent visitors to the house, and I think that Amy's spells of supply teaching gave her much-needed contact with children.

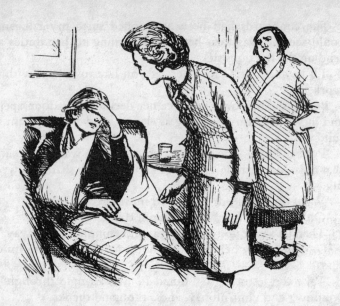

These spells grew more frequent as James advanced in his career and was more and more away from home. At this time he was a director of a cosmetic firm, and his work took him abroad several times a year. There were also a great many meetings in the United Kingdom to attend, and Amy was often alone at the lovely house in Bent, the village not far from Caxley and Fairacre, where they lived.

I must confess that I had my suspicions about James's fidelity. He was a warm-hearted gay fellow, as appreciative of pretty women as he was of the other attractive things in life. His frequent absences from home gave him ample opportunities for dalliance, and although I never doubted his love for Amy, some of his absences seemed unusually protracted to me. Added to that, his home-coming presents to Amy were so magnificent, that I personally should have viewed them with some suspicion, even from such a generous man as James.

Amy, however, was completely loyal and discreet. Secretly I had no doubt that she shared my feelings – she was far too astute to be deceived. Nevertheless, nothing had ever been said between us, and our affection increased over the years.

Certainly, Amy tends to be bossy, and is always attempting to reform me in one way or another, but I am wonderfully resistant to pressure, as Mrs Pringle knows, and Amy's failure to improve me had not altered the very warm regard which we feel for each other.

This immediate response to my cry for help was typical of her, and I tried to tell her so, as we turned into the hospital grounds.

Still clutching my piece of paper from Dr Martin, I was ushered into the waiting room of the casualty department, with Amy in attendance.

There were about fifteen of us unfortunates gathered there, some looking, to my inexperienced eye, at the point of death. There were also several children, all of whom appeared to be in excellent spirits.

'Sit down, dear,' said a nurse briskly, pushing up a wheel chair. It struck me smartly behind the knees, so that any modest refusal was cut short as I sat down abruptly.

A lively six-year-old pranced up to make my acquaintance.

'Are you very bad?'

'No,' I said bravely. 'Just my arm and leg are hurt.'

'My sister's bitten her tongue in half,' he said indicating a screen in the middle distance. 'She won't let them put the stitches in.'

I began to hope that the child would be called away. I had quite enough to bear without all this extra harrowing.

'D'you know what that's for?' he asked, indicating a small scoop about the size of an ash tray, on the arm of my chair.

'No,' I said faintly. Hadn't this horrible child got a mother somewhere?

'It's to be sick in,' he told me.

'Here,' said Amy severely, 'you run away and find a book to read. This lady doesn't want to be bothered with you.'

'I don't want to be bothered with *her* either,' said the horror, moving towards the end of the room, where a battered cardboard box housed a collection of even more battered toys.

He selected a fiendish mechanical car which needed to be run over the tiled floor to make it work. The noise was hideous, but infinitely preferable to the child's company.

He was still at it when I was summoned to be examined by a doctor young enough to be my son. Used as I am to Dr Martin's venerable aspect, I had some qualms, but he was quick and competent and I was dispatched to the X-ray department with yet another piece of paper.

Amy waited in the first room and smiled cheerfully at me as I passed to be wheeled down a long corridor. There is nothing, I decided, as we steered an erratic course down the shiny passage, quite so demoralising as being obliged to sit in a push chair.

By now the elbow was torturing me, and no matter how carefully the nurse arranged my arm for the camera I yelped frequently.

'One of the most painful injuries,' she told me, echoing Dr Martin, 'and of course it can't be put in plaster.'

I heard this with mixed feelings.

'The sling will be a great help,' she assured me, seeing my consternation.

'This one won't,' I told her. 'It's as rough as emery paper.'

'I'll change it,' she promised me. 'This does seem rather antique. Must be war issue.'

She set me up with one rather less scratchy, and I begged her to accept Dr Martin's.

'Dear me, no,' she replied, folding it up briskly. 'Take it home as a spare. After it's been boiled a few times it will be quite comfortable.'

We returned in the push chair to the waiting Amy. The horrible boy had been joined by another, slightly larger, and they were engaged in sticking out their tongues at each other.

'I'm glad you've found a *quieter* game,' said Amy kindly to them.

We waited yet again. At last, my X-ray photographs were displayed on a screen.

'A nasty crack across the radius,' I was told. 'Don't move it for three weeks, and we'll see you then.'

Don't move it, I thought rebelliously! What a hope!

I shuffled crossly towards the door, with Amy in attendance.

'Goodbye, Auntie Hopalong,' shouted the rude boy.

★

I think you'd better come straight home with me,' said Amy, as we left the town behind us, 'you can't be alone like this. You're practically helpless, and there are some knock-out pills which I see Dr Martin left on the mantelpiece which you are supposed to take before you go to bed. Lord knows what they'll do!'

'It's terribly good of you, Amy, but I really can't be such a nuisance to you. Besides there are all sorts of things to see to. Tibby, for instance, and the laundry hasn't been sorted, and the groceries arrive tomorrow, and I'll have to make some plans with Mrs Pringle.'

'Then I'll come and stay with you tonight,' said Amy firmly. 'James is away. There's nothing to worry about, and you're not staying alone in the house. So, no arguing.'

I was deeply grateful. If only I could go to sleep, I felt that I would face anything when I woke up. Now all that I craved for was oblivion, and no doubt the pills would help there.

The journey seemed endless, but at last the school house was in sight. I edged my way painfully from the car, and was glad to gain the sitting room.

'Good heavens,' I said, catching sight of the clock. 'It's only half past two! I feel as if I'd been away for a fortnight.'

'I'm going to heat some soup,' said Amy, 'then make up a bed for you on the couch here. Mrs Pringle's left you a note.'

She handed it to me and then vanished into the kitchen.

It said:

'Have put all to rights and fed the cat. Will come up this evening. Can live in if needed.'

Amy reappeared in the doorway.

'I take back all I've ever said about Mrs Pringle,' I told her, giving her the note to read.

'A handsome offer,' agreed Amy.

'Downright noble,' I said warmly.

'And how long,' said Amy, 'do you think you two could rub along together?'

'Well −' I began, and was cut short by Amy's laughter.

4. Amy Takes Command

Those of us who are lucky enough to live in a village, face the fact that our lives are an open book. Those dreadful stories of town-dwellers found dead in their beds, having been there for months, and even years sometimes are not likely to be echoed in smaller communities.

Here, in Fairacre, villagers tardy in bringing in their milk bottles run the risk of well-meaning neighbours popping round 'to see if they are all right'.

There are times when this concern for each other seems downright irritating. On the other hand, how comforting it is to know that people care about one's welfare!

Mrs Pringle, of course, had not been able to resist telling several of her friends about the drama in which she had taken part that morning.

Thanks to one of Dr Martin's pills I knew nothing from three o'clock that afternoon until I woke at ten that night, but Amy evidently had a succession of visitors during that time, and was very touched by their sympathy and their practical offers of help.

'The vicar's wife brought those roses,' she told me, waving towards a mixed bouquet which smelt heavenly on the bedside table.

'And she says you are not to worry about the organ on Sunday, as she is quite able to cope if she transposes everything into the key of C, and they cut out the anthem.'

I clutched my aching head with my sound hand.

'I'd forgotten all about that!'

'Well, keep on forgetting,' Amy advised me. 'You'll have to get used to the brutal fact that no one is indispensable.'

I nodded meekly, and wished I hadn't. Those pills were dynamite.

'And Mrs Willet's sent six gorgeous eggs and some tomatoes, and will do any washing while your arm's useless.'

'That woman's an angel. Luckily, her husband recognizes it.'

'Someone from the farm – I didn't catch the name –'

'Mrs Roberts.'

'That's it. She'll help in any way you like. Shopping, bringing you a midday meal. Anything!'

'People *are* kind.'

'They most certainly are,' agreed Amy, 'and I am absolutely flabbergasted at the way they're all rallying around you.'

I felt slightly nettled. Anyone would think that I am normally such a monster that I do not deserve any consideration. I was deeply grateful for all this concern, but Amy's astonishment was hard to bear.

'It isn't as though they have children at the school,' went on Amy, musing to herself.

'Even Mrs Pringle,' she continued thoughtfully, 'called this evening to see how you were.'

She sighed, then jumped up to straighten the counterpane.

'Ah well! People are odd,' she said, dismissing the subject.

But by this time, my irritation was waning, for Dr Martin's blue pill was wafting me once more into oblivion.

The sun was warm upon the bed when I awoke. It shone through the petals of the roses, and sent their fragrance through the room.

Amy was gazing at me anxiously.

'Thank God, you've woken up! I was beginning to wonder if you'd ever come to.'

'Why, what's the time?'

'Ten o'clock.'

'No! I must have had about sixteen hours' sleep.'

'How do you feel?'

'Marvellous, if I don't move.'

'Could you manage an egg?'

I sat up cautiously.

'I could manage an egg and toast and marmalade and butter and lashings of coffee and perhaps an apple.'

Amy laughed.

'You've recovered. Do you ever lose your appetite?'

'It improves in a crisis,' I assured her. 'When war broke out, I ate with enormous gusto. The more sensitive types on the staff of the school I was at then, couldn't touch a morsel – or so they said – but I had the feeling each meal might be my last, so I made the most of it.'

Amy laughed, and went to the kitchen.

I could hear her moving china and saucepans, and lay back feeling one part guilty and nine parts relieved. How pleasant it was to be waited on! I tried to remember the last time I had lain in bed while someone else cooked my breakfast, and found it beyond my powers.

Tibby came undulating into the room giving little chirrups of pleasure at having found me at last. She jumped elegantly on to the bed, missing my damaged ankle by a millimetre. I clasped my poor arm in trepidation. Tibby's affectionate attention was a mixed blessing this morning.

Before she could do much damage, Amy appeared with the tray.

'I've cut your toast into fingers, my dear, and I'll spread your marmalade when you want it.'

'I feel about three years old,' I told her, 'and backward at that.'

Eating a boiled egg left-handed is no easy task, and I should certainly have gone without butter and marmalade if Amy had not been there to help me. Suddenly, I realized how horribly helpless I was. It was frightening.

'Now, about plans,' said Amy, putting down the knife.

'With all these offers of help from kind neighbours, I should be fine,' I said.

She looked at me quizzically.

'You haven't tried walking yet, or washing, or doing your hair or dressing.'

'No,' I agreed sadly.

'And let's face it, you can't possibly negotiate the stairs even with that ankle strapped.'

I knew this was the plain truth.

'I've thought it all out. You're coming back to Bent with me. There's plenty of room. I shall be glad of your company, and it will do you good to have a change of scene. So say no more.'

'It's more than generous of you, Amy, but –'

'It's no use arguing. I know what you are going to say. Well, Tibby can come too, or Mrs Pringle has offered to come in to feed her, so that's that. We can shut up the house and give Mrs P. the key. Mr Willet says he'll keep an eye on the garden and mow the grass.'

'But Dr Martin . . .?'

'Dr Martin can be kept informed of your progress by telephone, and is welcome to visit you at my house.'

I looked at Amy with admiration.

'You've worked it all out to the last detail, I see.'

'I had plenty of time yesterday – and lots of offers from others, don't forget.'

I nodded in silence.

'Let's get you along to the bath.'

Bracing my arm stiffly, for I dreaded the pain when it was moved, I struggled to get my legs to the floor. Once they were there it was obvious that only the right one could bear any weight. Amy was quite right, I was helpless.

She was looking at me with some amusement.

'Well?'

'You win, you lovely girl. I'll come thankfully, bless you.'

One arm round her shoulders, I shimmied my way to the bathroom.

We were seen off that afternoon by a number of friends and well-wishers. I began to feel rather a fraud. After all, no one could say I was seriously ill.

Nevertheless, it was delightful to receive as much sympathy and attention.

'The vicar and I will visit you next week,' promised Mrs Partridge.

'I've taken the dirty clothes,' called Mrs Willet.

'And I'll give the place a proper bottoming, cupboards and all, before you're back,' said Mrs Pringle, in a tone which sounded more like a threat than a promise.

We moved off, waving like royalty, to the accompaniment of Tibby's yowling from a cat-basket borrowed from Mr Roberts.

It is only about half an hour's run to Bent but I was mighty glad to arrive at Amy's house and to be ensconced in the spare room. Some wise person in the past had made sure that the window sills in the bedroom were low enough for the bedridden to admire the view, for which I was truly grateful.

Beyond Amy's immaculate garden, bright with lilies and roses, stretched rolling, agricultural land. The crops were already ripening, and no doubt the combines would be out in the fields long before my beastly arm was fit to use. In the middle distance, a blue tractor trundled between the hedges on its way to the fields, and near at hand, on Amy's bird table, tits and starlings squabbled over food.

There would be plenty here to amuse me. How good Amy was! She had made light of taking me on, useless as I was, but I knew how much extra work I should be making, and determined to get downstairs as soon as possible.

Tibby, released from the hated basket, was roaming cautiously about the room, sniffing at Amy's rose and cream decor with the greatest suspicion and dislike. She had deigned to drink a little milk, but was clearly going to take some time to settle down.

'You are an ungrateful cat,' I told her. 'You might well have been left behind with Mrs Pringle, and she would have bottomed you with the rest of the house.'

Amy entered with the tea tray.

'I imagine heaven's like this,' I said. 'Perfect surroundings, and angels wafting in with the tea.'

'But this one's going to watch you spread your own jam this time,' she warned me.

Later that evening, as the summer dusk fell and the scent of the lime flowers hung on the air, Amy sat by the lamp and stitched away at her tapestry. A moth fluttered round the light, tapping a staccato tattoo on the shade, but Amy did not seem aware of it.

It was very quiet in the room. It seemed to me that Amy was unusually pensive, and although she had enough to think of, in all conscience, with me on her hands, somehow I felt her thoughts were elsewhere.

'Amy,' I began, 'you know I can't thank you enough for all you're doing, but won't I be even more of a burden when James comes home?'

'It won't be for several days,' said Amy, snipping a thread. 'It may be even longer. There was some possibility of going straight on to Scotland, if he can arrange things with somebody at the office to attend to that end and save him coming back again.'

There was something in Amy's tone which disquieted me. Despondency? Resignation? Hopelessness?

I had never seen Amy in this mood, and wondered what was the cause.

'I don't think I shall need a blue pill tonight,' I said, changing the subject. 'I can hardly keep awake as it is.'

'I'm horribly sleepy too,' confessed Amy. She began to roll up her work, and glanced at the clock.

'James usually rings about eight, but something must have stopped him. No doubt there will be a letter in the post in the morning. I shan't wait up any longer.'

She rose, and came close to the bed.

'Have you got all you need? I've left this little bell to ring if you need me in the night, and I shall prop my door ajar. Tibby's settled in the kitchen, so there's nothing for you to worry about.'

She bent to give me a rare kiss on the forehead.

'Sleep well. I'll see you in the morning.'

After Amy had gone, I turned out the light and slid carefully down the bed. Tired though I was, I could not sleep.

It grieved me to see Amy so unhappy. Something more than my problems was eating at her heart. I had not know Amy for over thirty years without being able to measure her moods.

That James was at the bottom of it all, I had no doubt. Was the rapscallion more than usually entangled this time? Was their marriage seriously threatened by the present philanderings?

It is at times like this that a spinster counts her blessings. Her troubles are of her own making, and can be tackled straight-forwardly. She is independent, both monetarily and in spirit. Her life is wonderfully simple, compared with that of her married sister. And she cannot be hurt, quite so cruelly, as a woman can be by her husband.

Conversely, she has no-one with whom to share her troubles and doubts. She must bear alone the consequence of all her actions and, coming down to brass tacks, she must be able to support herself financially, physically and emotionally.

I know all this from first-hand experience. I know too that there are some people who view my life as narrow and self-centred. Some, even, find a middle-aged single woman pitiable, if not faintly ridiculous. This, I have always felt, is to rate the value of men too highly, although I recognize that a truly happy marriage is probably the highest state of contentment attainable by either partner.

But how often something mars the partnership! Jealousy, indolence, illness, family difficulties, money troubles – so much can go wrong when two lives are joined.

Outside, in the darkness, a screech owl gave its bloodcurdling cry. A shadow crept over the moon, and turning my face into the comfort of a pillow – supplied by James – I decided that it was time for sleep.

5. Recovery at Bent

The days passed very agreeably at Amy's. Time hangs heavily, some people say, when there is nothing to do, but I found, in my enforced idleness, that the hours flew by.

The weather had changed from its earlier brilliance. The sky was overcast, the air was still. There was something curiously restful about these soft grey days. The air was mild and I sat in the garden a great deal, nursing my arm and propping my battered ankle on a foot-rest.

Amy had a small pond with a tinkling fountain in her garden, and the sound of the splashing water was often the only noise to be heard. I felt stronger daily, and began to get very clever at using my left hand. I was more and more conscious how much I owed Amy's generosity of spirit. Without her care and companionship these early days of progress would have been much slower.

During these quiet days I had the opportunity of observing Amy as she went about her tasks. She dealt with her domestic routine with great efficiency, and I began to realize, at the end of a week, that without the method with which she approached each chore, I should have been alone far more often. As it was, she had time to sit and talk to me, or simply to sit beside me and read, or work at her tapestry. I think we grew closer together, in those few days, than we had ever been before.

Very little mention was made of James, although Amy did say one evening that he had telephoned to say that he was in Scotland and would not be returning for a week or so. The determinedly gay manner in which she told me this, confirmed my fears that Amy herself was a very worried woman. It made her kindness to me doubly dear.

One morning I was taking my cautious walk in the garden, leaning heavily upon a fine ebony stick of James's, when I was horrified to see the corpse of a hedgehog floating in the pond. Obviously, it had tried to reach the water, toppled in, and been unable to scramble out again. It was a pathetic sight, and I was wondering how I could get it out when Amy called from the house, and emerged with one of her friends, Gerard Baker.

I had met him first at one of Amy's parties, and several times since then. He had been collecting material for a book about minor Victorian poets, and visited Fairacre once or twice to learn more about our one poet Aloysius Stone.

We, in Fairacre, are rather proud of Aloysius, who lived in one of the cottages in Tyler's Row, and was somewhat of a trial at village concerts in the early part of the century. He loved the opportunity of reciting his poems, and was apt to go on for far longer than his allotted time, much to the consternation of the programme organizers and the outspokenness of his audience.

'This is a great day,' said Amy after we had exchanged greetings, and Gerard had commiserated with me about my battered condition. She held up a book.

'Not *The Book*?' I said.

'The very same,' said Gerard. 'Came out last month.'

'Well! And I didn't hear a thing.'

'I'm not surprised. I shouldn't think a book ever crept out into the world with as little notice as this one had.'

'But surely it will be reviewed? After all your hard work you're bound to have some recognition.'

'I doubt it. I'm not carping. There aren't exactly queues at the bookshop doors for *any* book, and one about Victorian poets won't set the Thames on fire. If it covers the costs I'll be content, and so will the publishers.'

By this time, Amy had walked across to the pond, and was studying the floating corpse with some distaste.

'Give me the rake,' said Gerard, approaching, 'and I'll fish the poor thing out for you.'

We surveyed the pathetic body, the shiny black snout, the brindled prickles, the scaly black legs.

Amy returned with the rake.

'It's really dead, I suppose?' she asked, bending closer to examine the corpse.

'Well, I can tell you flat,' said Gerard, casting his rake, 'that

I'm not volunteering to give it the kiss of life! There are limits to the milk of human kindness.'

He fished the body to the edge and lifted it out.

'I think a distant patch of nettles, or some rough cover, would be his best shroud. You aren't proposing burial? I'm no great shakes with a spade.'

'Good heavens, no, Gerard dear!' exclaimed Amy. 'Follow me, and we'll put him over the hedge into the ditch in the cornfield, poor little sweet.'

'"Sweet",' said Gerard, his nose wrinkled, 'is not quite the word for it.'

He followed Amy towards the end of the garden, balancing the dripping victim precariously on the rake. I watched the funeral cortege from my chair with some amusement. The more I saw of Gerard Baker, the more I liked him.

He was clever but unaffected, sympathetic but not mawkish, and had a cheerful practical approach to problems – such as this present one – which I found wholly admirable. No wonder Amy welcomed him.

'What about a restorative?' she said when they returned. 'Gin, sherry?'

'Could it be coffee?' asked Gerard.

'Of course.' She went into the house.

'What a marvel she is!' exclaimed Gerard.

'I'll endorse that,' I said, and told him how wonderfully she had coped with me.

'Typical,' said Gerard. 'I was full of admiration for the way in which she coped with that lovelorn niece of hers, Vanessa.'

'I believe we may see something of her before long,' I told him. 'Evidently she's quite got over that infatuation. You know she's in Scotland? Working in a hotel?'

Gerard, to my surprise, looked somewhat embarrassed.

'Yes, I did know. As a matter of fact, I happened to call at the hotel a week or two ago. She seemed in great spirits.'

'Did you hear that, Amy?' I cried, as she put down the tray. 'Gerard has seen Vanessa, and she's very well.'

Amy shot a lightning glance at Gerard's face, and looked away quickly. He was endeavouring to look nonchalant, and not succeeding very well.

'I was in the district. I'm collecting material for a book about Scottish poets – a companion volume to the Victorian one, I hope – and I remembered the name of the hotel.'

'How nice! Is she flourishing?'

'In very good spirits. She said something about a holiday soon, and I gather she may come and see you.'

'That's right,' agreed Amy. She poured the coffee.

'Any news of the young Scotsman who was being so attentive?' she asked. Her tone was polite, but I detected a hint of mischief in her face.

Gerard had recovered his composure.

'I didn't hear anything about him. No doubt there are a number of attentive young Scotsmen. Vanessa's looking very attractive these days. Quite a change of aspect from the time when she was mourning the Chilean.'

'Bolivian!' said Amy and I together.

We sipped our coffee, relaxed and happy. A red admiral butterfly flitted decoratively from flower to flower in the herbaceous border, and I remembered the pale unhappy Vanessa whose passion for a four-times-married foreigner had blinded her to all summer delights on the first occasion of our meeting. She had spent a week with Amy then, and I don't quite think I had ever seen my normally resilient friend quite so exhausted.

'And how's Fairacre?' inquired Gerard. 'What of my friend Mr Willet?'

I gave him a brief account of village affairs to date, and conversation grew general. It was half-past eleven before he leapt to his feet, protesting that he must be off.

'I've an aunt living not far from here, and I'm taking her out to lunch. She's eighty-five and a demon for exercise. Think of me at about two-thirty, walking my legs off along some cart track.'

'Come again,' said Amy.

'I will,' he promised. 'But no corpses next time, please.'

That afternoon I broached the subject of my return home to Amy. I had been with her for well over a week, looked after as never before, and felt that I could not impose upon her much longer.

'But I love to have you,' she assured me.

'You're too kind. There are lots of things you must be neglecting, and surely there's a holiday cropping up soon?'

I remember that she had discussed a visit to Crete earlier in the year. Nothing had been said about it while I had been staying at Bent, and it occurred to me that perhaps the plans had fallen through.

'That's nearly a fortnight away,' said Amy.

'You'll probably need to go shopping.'

'That doesn't mean that you've got to go back to Fairacre.'

I pointed out that there were a number of matters to attend to at home. There were some school forms to be filled up, and a certain amount of organization for next term. My domestic arrangements also needed some attention, though no doubt Mrs Pringle's bottoming would be almost finished.

'I'm mobile now,' I said, stretching out my lumpy ankle. 'Why, I can even dress myself if I keep to button-down-the-front things, and remember to thread the bad arm through the sleeve first!'

'You're getting above yourself,' Amy smiled. 'I really think you *are* getting better.'

She surveyed me with her head on one side.

'I can see you're really bent on going. Tell you what. Let's drive over tomorrow afternoon and get the place ready, and see if you can manage the stairs and so on. If so, I'll install you in the day after.'

And so it was agreed.

Amy took up her tapestry and I turned the pages of a magazine.

The thought of going home excited me. I should never cease to be grateful to my old friend, but I longed to potter about my own home, to get back to my books and my garden, to see the familiar birds on the bird table, and to smell the pinks in my border again. Tibby, too, would welcome the return.

Beyond Amy's window the rain was falling. Grey veils drifted across the fields, blotting the distant hills from view. It made the drawing-room seem doubly snug.

'I wonder how long it will be before I can do without this

confounded sling,' I mused aloud. 'I can wriggle my fingers quiet well. How long does a bone take to mend?'

Amy looked at me thoughtfully.

'Weeks at our age, I imagine.'

'I'm not decrepit, and I don't feel old.'

'I do now and again,' said Amy, with such a vigour that belied her words. 'I find myself behaving like an old lady sometimes. You know, never walking up escalators, and not minding if young things like Vanessa stand up when I enter a room.'

'I haven't got quite to that stage yet.'

'But when I start pinning brooches on my hats,' said Amy, resuming her stitching, 'I shall know I'm *really* old.'

There was a companionable silence for a while. Outside, the rain grew heavier, and began to patter at the windows.

'Of course, I think about dying now and again,' I said.

'Who doesn't?'

'What do you do about it?'

'Well,' said Amy, snipping a thread, 'I make sure I'm wearing respectable corsets – not my comfortable ones with the elastic stretched and speckled with rubber bits – and I pay up outstanding bills and, frankly, there's not much else one can do, is there, dear?'

'But hope,' I finished for her.

'But hope,' she echoed.

She turned her gaze upon the rain-swept view through the window. There had been a dying fall in those last two words.

It was plain that it was the sadness of living, not of dying, which preoccupied my friend's thoughts.

And my heart grieved for her.

The next afternoon we drove from Bent to Fairacre. The rain had ceased, leaving everything fresh and fragrant. The sun shone, striking rainbows from the droplets on the hedges, and in its summer strength drawing steam from the damp roads. Sprays of wild roses arched towards the ground, weighted with the water which trembled in their shell-pink cups, and everywhere the scent of honeysuckle hung upon the air.

In the lush fields the cattle steamed as they fed, and birds splashed joyously in their wayside baths. Everywhere one looked there was rejoicing in the sunshine after the rain, and my spirits rose accordingly.

As Fairacre drew nearer I grew happier and happier, until I broke into singing.

Amy began to laugh.

'What an incorrigible home-bird you are! You remind me of Timmy Willie.'

'When he was asked what he did when it rained in the country?' I inquired.

'"I sit in my little sandy burrow and shell corn and seeds."'

'"And when the sun comes out again,"' I finished for her, '"You should see my garden and the flowers – roses and pinks and pansies."'

'I'm sorry for children who aren't brought up on Beatrix Potter,' said Amy. 'Look! There's St Patrick's spire ahead. You'll be back in your burrow in two shakes.'

The lane to the school was empty, and we arrived unseen by the neighbours. It was very quiet, the village sunk in the somnolence of early afternoon.

Inside the school house everything was unusually tidy. A few fallen petals from the geranium on the window sill made it look more like home, however, counteracting the symmetrically draped tea-cloths on the airer, and the 'Vim', washing up liquid and so on, which were arrayed with military precision in order of height on the draining board. Every polished surface winked with cleanliness. Never had the stove flashed so magnificently. Never had the windows been so clear. Even the doormat looked as if it had been brushed and combed.

'Well,' said Amy, gazing round. 'Mrs Pringle's had a field day here.'

Awe-struck, we went into the sitting room. Here, the same unnatural tidiness was apparent.

'I feel as though I ought to take off my shoes,' I said. 'It's positively holy with cleanliness.'

The coffee pot on the dresser, behind which I stuff all the letters needing an answer, now stood at the extreme side of the board. There was nothing – not even a single sheet of paper – behind it.

'Save us!' I cried. 'Where on earth is all my correspondence?'

'Gone to heaven on a bonfire,' Amy replied.

'But I *must* have it,' I began in bewilderment.

'Calm down,' said Amy, 'or you'll break your arm again.'

This idiotic remark had the effect of calming us both. We sat down, somewhat nervously, on the newly washed chair covers.

'She's washed every blessed thing in sight,' I said wonderingly, 'and I declare she's oiled the beams too. Look at the fire-irons! And the candlesticks! And the lamp shades! It's positively uncanny. I shall never be able to live up to this standard.'

'Don't worry,' said Amy comfortingly. 'By the time you've had twenty-four hours here, it will look as though a tornado has hit it, and it will be just like home again.'

It was one of those remarks which could have been more delicately expressed, or, better still, left unsaid. In normal circumstances I might have made some sharp retort, but Amy's kindness over the past week or so enabled me to hold my tongue.

We sat for a few minutes, resting and marvelling at Mrs Pringle's handiwork before embarking on a tour of the whole house. It was a relief to find that I could negotiate the stairs if I attacked them like a toddler, bringing both feet to one stair before essaying the next. I could have wished the banister had been placed on the left hand side instead of the right, but by assuming a crab-like motion I could get up and down very well and was suitably smug about it.

'And what about getting in and out of the bath?' asked Amy, deflating me.

'I'm going to get one of those rubber mats, so that I don't slip,' I told her. 'And I shall *kneel* down to bath, so that I can get up again easily.'

Amy laughed.

'You win, my love. If the worst comes to the worst, you can always ring me, and I'll nip over to scrub your back.'

We checked the goods in the larder, and made out a shopping list, and then went to inspect the garden. As well as

Timmy Willie's roses and pinks and pansies, the purple clematis had come out, the velvety flowers glorious against the old bricks of the house.

We sat together on the rustic seat warmed by the sun, and tilted up our faces to the blaze as thankfully as the daisies on the grass.

Tomorrow, I thought, I shall be back for good. As if reading my thoughts, Amy spoke.

'No place like home, eh?'

She sounded relaxed and slightly amused at my happiness.

'None,' I said fervently.

244

6. Amy Needs Help

I woke next morning in jubilant spirits. Through the bedroom window I could see two men examining the standing corn. No doubt the farmer was hoping to start cutting later in the day when the dew had vanished. I should not be there to see it, I thought happily.

The harvest fields of Bent would be far distant. I should be watching Mr Roberts, our local farmer, trundling the combine round our Fairacre fields. but that would be a week or so later, for our uplands are colder than the southward slopes of Amy's countryside, and all our crops are a little later.

Amy and I lingered over our coffee cups. I was looking hopefully among the newspaper columns for some crumb of cheer among the warfare, murders, rapes and attacks upon old men and women for any small change they might have had upon them, without – as usual – much success. Amy was busy with her letters.

She had left until last a bulky envelope addressed in James's unmistakable hand. She slit it open, her face grave, and gave the pages her close attention. I refilled her coffee cup and my own, in the silence, and turned to an absorbing account of a woman with nine children and a tenth on the way, who had struck her husband over the head with a handy frying pan, after some little difference about methods of birth control.

She was reported as saying that 'he didn't like interfering with Nature,' and I was glad to see that her solicitor was putting up a spirited defence. I wished her luck. Really, marriage was no bed of roses for some women, I thought, congratulating myself, yet again, on my single state.

The rustling of paper brought me back to the present. Amy was stuffing the letter back into the envelope. Her mouth was set grimly, and I looked hastily at the newspaper again.

I was conscious that Amy was staring blindly across the cornfields. I finished my coffee and rose.

'If you'll excuse me,' I said, 'I'll go and finish packing.'

There was no reply from Amy. Still as a statue, she stared stonily before her, as I crept away.

An hour or so later, we packed up the car together. Amy seemed to have recovered her good humour, and we laughed about the amount of luggage I seemed to have accumulated.

Tibby's basket took up a goodly part of the back seat. An old mackintosh had been folded and placed strategically beneath it. We had had trouble before, and were determined to prevent Amy's lovely car 'smelling like a civet's paradise', to quote Mr Willet, referring to the poet Aloysius Stone's noisome house long ago.

Two cases, a pile of books, a bulky dressing gown and a basket of vegetables and flowers from Amy's garden, filled the rest of the back seat and the boot, and we still had a box of groceries to collect from Bent's village stores.

'Anyone would think we were off for a fortnight's holiday,' observed Amy, surveying the luggage.

'Well, you will be soon,' I said.

Amy's smile vanished, and I cursed myself for clumsiness.

'Let's hope so,' she said soberly.

I edged myself into the passenger seat while Amy returned to the house to lock up. How I wished I could help her! She had been so good to me, so completely selfless and welcoming, that it was doubly hard to see her unhappy.

But nothing could be done if she preferred to keep her troubles to herself. I respected her reticence. Too often I have been the unwilling recipient of confidences, knowing full well that, later, the impulsive babbler would regret her disclosures as much as I regretted hearing them. 'Least said, soonest mended', is an old adage which reflects much wisdom. I could only admire Amy's stoicism, and hope that one day, somehow, I should be able to help her.

We set off for Fairacre, stopping only once to pick up the groceries. Our pace was sedate, for the faster we went the shriller grew Tibby's wails of protest from the wicker basket. Even at thirty-five miles an hour the noise was ear-splitting.

'I meant to have told you,' shouted Amy above the racket,

'that I had a letter from Vanessa this morning. She's coming down for a day next week. She's on holiday, I gather.'

'Bring her over if she can spare the time,' I shouted back.

Amy nodded.

'Funny thing about Gerard, wasn't it?' she said at last. 'Do you smell a romance?'

'What? Between Gerard and Vanessa?'

'Yes. I thought he looked remarkably like a cat that has got at the cream when he spoke of her.'

I digested this unwillingly.

'No, I don't think so,' I said finally. 'He's years older.'

'A mature man,' began Amy, in what I recognized as her experienced-woman-of-the-world voice, 'is often *exactly* what a young thing like Vanessa *needs*. She probably knows this subconsciously. She's very intelligent really underneath all that dreadful clothing and flowing hair. I shall do my best to encourage it.'

I began to feel alarmed for both innocent parties. Amy, on match-making bent, has a flinty ruthlessness, as I know to my cost. On this occasion, however, I decided to keep silent.

An ominous pattering sound, as of water upon newspaper distracted our attention from Vanessa and Gerard, and directed it upon Tibby.

'Thank God for the mackintosh!' exclaimed Amy, accelerating slightly.

We drew up with a flourish at the school house, and let the cat escape into the kitchen, where she stalked about, sniffing at the unusual cleanliness with much the same expression of amazement which Amy and I had worn.

We unpacked, and Amy insisted on putting a hot water bottle into my bed, despite the bright sunshine. We made coffee, and I asked Amy to stay to lunch.

'Scrambled egg,' I said, 'I can whip up eggs with my left hand beautifully.'

'I mustn't my dear,' she said rising. 'James comes home tonight, and there's a lot to do.'

'Then I won't keep you,' I said, and went on to try and thank her once again for all she had done. She brushed my efforts aside.

'It was good to have company,' she said.

'Well, you'll have James now.'

'Only for a day or so. We've a lot to discuss before the holiday. Some of it, I fear, not very agreeable.'

She climbed into the car and waved good-bye, leaving me to savour her last sentence.

It was, I discovered later, the biggest understatement of Amy's life.

During the afternoon, Mrs Pringle called.

I invited her in, and thanked her from my heart for all she had done.

'The house,' I told her, 'is absolutely transfigured. You must have spent hours here.'

A rare smile curved Mrs Pringle's lips. Her mouth normally turns down, giving her a somewhat reptilian look. Turned upwards, it had the strange effect as if a frog had smiled.

'Well, it needed it,' said Mrs Pringle. 'What I found in them chair covers when I pulled them out is nobody's business. Pencils, knitting needles, nuts, buts of paper, and there was even a boiled sweet.'

'No!' I cried. 'What, all sticky?'

Slattern though I am, I could not believe that a sucked sweet would turn up in the debris.

'Luckily it was wrapped in a bit of cellophane,' conceded Mrs Pringle. 'But it is not what anyone'd have found when Mrs Hope was here.'

'Have a cup of tea?' I asked, changing the subject abruptly. Mrs Hope's example leads to dangerous ground. Over the tea cups, Mrs Pringle brought me up to date with village news. The Scouts were having a mammoth jumble sale. (All our village jumble sales are 'mammoth'.) The Caxley bus was now an hour earlier on market day, and a dratted nuisance everybody found it. The new people at Tyler's Row had bought a puppy, and Mr Mawne had seen a pair of waxworks in the garden.

I must admit that this last snippet of news took me aback, until I remembered that Henry Mawne's hobby is ornithology and Mrs Pringle was probably referring to wax-wings.

'I thought they came in the winter,' I hazarded.

'Maybe they do,' agreed Mrs Pringle. 'But that garden of the Mawnes is always perishing cold. It may have confused the waxworks.'

Privately, I thought that they were not the only ones to be confused, and we let the matter drop.

'While your arm's mending,' said Mrs Pringle, 'I'll be in each morning for an hour.' I thanked her.

She rose to go, looking with pride at the tidiness around her.

'Don't want to see this slide back into the usual mess,' she said, echoing Amy, and departed.

The next two or three days passed pleasurably, and I gloried in my growing accomplishments. I found that I could lift my right arm, if I held it at exactly the correct angle, and even began to comb the hair on my *occiput* with my right hand. I became quite nimble at mounting and descending the stairs, and each small triumph cheered me greatly.

One morning Amy rang me.

'Vanessa is with me. May we come over?'

I expressed my delight.

'And another thing,' said Amy, and stopped.

'Yes?'

'Perhaps I should wait until I see you.'

It was most unlike Amy to shilly-shally like this.

'What's it about?'

'Crete.'

'Crete? I don't know a thing about it! Do you want to borrow a map or something?'

'No. I want you to consider visiting it with me, as my guest of course.'

I was struck dumb.

'Are you still there?'

'Partially.'

'Well, think about it. James can't come, but wants me to go ahead with the holiday. We'll talk about it later.'

There was a click and the line went dead.

Dazed by this thunderbolt, I wandered vaguely through

the open French window, caught my poor arm on the latch and, cursing, returned to earth again.

The two arrived soon after lunch, and in the meantime I had turned over this truly wonderful invitation in my mind. Of course, I should love to go, and so much better was I, that my disabilities would not hold up proceedings in any way. We should be back several days before term began. Mrs Pringle, no doubt, would be only too glad to have charge of the house again, and the local kennels would look after Tibby – not, of course, to the cat's complete satisfaction – but perfectly well.

On the other hand, I had accepted so much from Amy already that I hardly liked to take an expensive holiday as well. My bank balance would certainly not stand the expense of paying my share, which would be the right thing to do, and so I felt that I really should refuse, sad though it was.

It was good to see Vanessa again. She was dressed in a white trouser suit with a scarlet blouse, unbuttoned to the waist, under which she wore nothing. I was rather perplexed about this. Did she know that she was unbuttoned? Should she be told? I decided to say nothing, but felt rather relieved that no men were in the party.

On her feet were two bright red shoes, so clumsy and stubtoed that they might have been football boots, and in her hand was a minute bag of silver mesh of the kind that my grandmother carried at evening parties.

But her long hair was as lustrous as ever, and her looks much improved since the overthrow of the Bolivian Roderick who had so fascinated the poor child when last she was in Fairacre.

On her first visit to the school house she had said practically nothing. Today she rattled on, with much animation, about Scotland and her work at the hotel.

'And you saw Gerard?' I could not resist saying.

Her face lit up.

'Wasn't it lucky? He happened to be nearby. I can't tell you how lovely it was to see him again. We write sometimes, but it's not the same thing as meeting.'

She clapped a hand to her brow, and looked anxiously at Amy.

'The book! Did we bring it?'

'In the car,' said Amy. 'It's for Mr Willet,' she explained. 'Gerard asked Vanessa if she would deliver it as he knew we were coming to Fairacre.'

'I'll walk down,' said Vanessa, scrambling to her feet. She surveyed the red football boots proudly. 'These are real waling shoes, the girl in the shop told me. But, of course, I mustn't get them wet.'

'Why not?' I asked. 'Surely shoes are worn for the purpose of keeping the feet dry.'

'Not these days,' Vanessa assured me pityingly. 'That's a very old-fashioned idea. Today the shoes have a label on saying that they mustn't be used in the wet.'

She smiled upon me kindly, and went off for the book.

Now that we were alone, Amy turned directly to the subject which was uppermost in our minds.

'Well? What do you think? Would you like to see Crete?'

'I'd love to –' I began.

'It won't be quite as lovely as it was when I first saw it one April. It's bound to be drier and hotter, but the air in the mountains is delicious, and there is plenty of shade at the hotel.'

'But, Amy,' I persisted. 'I really can't accept a holiday like this.'

'Why not, for heaven's sake? It's all paid for and arranged. You'd simply be taking over the plane seat and James's bed and board. Perfectly straightforward.'

'But I can't afford it, my dear.'

'No one wants you to afford it. I told you that, so put that out of your dear, upright, puritanical mind. I should be most grateful for your company. It would be a kindness from *you* to *me*. Not the other way round.'

'You've done so much already,' I said, weakening.

'Right,' said Amy briskly. 'Return the compliment, and help me out.'

She jumped up suddenly and went to the window. Her back towards me, she spoke quickly.

'Things are very rough between James and me at the

moment. I'm quite used to seeing him make a minor ass of himself over a pretty face, now and again, but this time I'm frightened. He's deadly serious about some young thing about Vanessa's age. I've never seen him so determined, so ruthless –.'

Her voice broke, and I moved swiftly to comfort her. She shook her head violently.

'Don't be kind to me, or sympathize, or I shall sob my heart out, and have eyes like red gooseberries.'

She fought for control, and then continued.

'He wants me to give him a divorce. I've refused to consider such a step, until we've both had time to think things over. We shall stay apart for a few weeks, and he wants me to go to Crete as arranged and have a break. Apart from this terrifying singleness of purpose about the girl, he's as considerate as ever. It makes it all the more incredible.'

She turned to face me. Her poor face was crumpled and her eyes were wet.

'Now will you come with me?' she pleaded.

'Yes, please,' I said, with no more hesitation.

7. *Flying Away*

Fairacre's reaction to my proposed foreign jaunt was swift and varied.

The first person to be told was Mrs Pringle, of course, when she arrived the next morning to repair any havoc I might have caused overnight. Her response was typical.

'If you ask for my opinion,' she began heavily (I hadn't, but was obviously going to get it), 'then I should say you was very unwise indeed!'

She folded her arms across her cretonne-clad bosom, and settled down to a good gossip.

'I take it this place is in the Mediterranean?'

I said that it was.

'Then don't touch the fish,' said Mrs Pringle, warming to her subject. 'The pollution out there's something chronic, and the fish don't stand a dog's chance, if you follow me.'

I nodded.

'And keep the water off of that arm of yours – no bathing or any of that lark, or you'll be writhing in agony from *germs.*'

'Oh really –!' I began to expostulate.

'Furthermore,' went on Mrs Pringle ruthlessly, 'lay off the fruit and veg. unless they've been cooked. An aunt of mine had a very nasty rash from eating raw fruit in Malta. Disfiguring, as well as irritating. Never looked the same after, and she had been a nice looking woman when made up.'

I said that I should take all reasonable precautions, and rose, hoping that Mrs Pringle would take the hint.

'And another thing,' said she, not budging, 'You'll be flying, I take it?'

'Yes. It only takes four hours or so.'

Mrs Pringle gave a short bark of a laugh.

'If you're lucky! This aunt I told you of, spent eight hours getting to Malta. First, the aeroplane needed mending, and

253

when they started off two hours late, they found something else wrong, no petrol or one wing off – something of that – so they landed again for another two hours.'

'There's often some delay –,' I began, but was brushed aside.

'Mind you,' said Mrs Pringle fairly, 'they give 'em something to eat while they waited. Spam and sardine sandwich –'

'What? Mixed?' I exclaimed in horror.

'That I couldn't say,' responded Mrs Pringle heavily, after thought, 'but they didn't have to pay a penny for it.'

She now made a belated foray to the dresser drawer to find a duster. Her face brightened.

'It'll keep this place tidy for a bit longer, won't it, having you away?'

Happiness comes in many guises, I thought.

Mrs Partridge, the vicar's wife, was more enthusiastic, and told me not to miss Knossos on any account – she would look out a book they had about it – and would I please take plenty of pictures so that I could give a talk or, better still, a *series* of talks to the Women's Institute when I returned.

Mr Mawne said that there was a particularly rare hawk indigenous to Crete, though he doubted if I should see one, as the Cretans probably shot every bird in sight like the blasted Italians. Strange, he mused, that such warm-hearted people, positively *sloppy* about their children and so on, should be so callous in their treatment of animals. Anyway, he hoped I should enjoy myself, and if I were lucky enough to catch sight of the hawk then of course a few close-up photographs would be invaluable.

Mr Willet said it would do me the world of good to have some sea air and sunshine, although Barrisford would have been a sight nearer and less expensive. His cousin had been in Crete during the last war, but hadn't cared for it much as the Germans overran it while he was there and his foot was shot off in the upset.

'Still,' he added cheerfully, 'it should be nicer now the fighting's over. I don't doubt you'll have a very good time out there.'

'Crete,' mused Mr Lamb at the Post Office. 'Now would that be the one up in the right-hand corner, shaped like a whelk?'

'Cyprus,' I said.

'Ah, then it's the one with the famous harbour, Valetta!'

'Malta,' I said.

'That so? Well, I must be getting nearer. It's not that triangular one off the toe of Italy, is it?'

'Sicily,' I said.

'Don't tell me,' begged Mr Lamb, 'I'll get it in the end. It's not one of that lot like a hatful of crabs hanging off the bottom of Greece?'

'You're getting nearer.'

'It's the long thin one,' he shouted triumphantly. 'Am I right? With some old city a chap called Sir Arthur Evans dug up with his bare hands? Our scout master told us all about it one wet evening when the cross-country run was washed out.'

'I don't know about the bare hands,' I told him, 'but the rest is right enough.'

Mrs Coggs, who had been waiting patiently to collect her family allowance, while this exchange was going on, hoped I'd have a lovely time and come back sunburnt.

Joseph, who was with her, looked alarmed.

'You *are* coming back?' he asked.

'Joseph,' I assured him, 'I'll be back.'

The next few days passed in a flurry of preparations. Amy
fetched me one afternoon for a last-minute shopping spree in
Caxley, as I was still unable to drive my car.

She had a wan, subdued look about her, so unlike her usual
energetic manner that my heart was wrung for her. She
mentioned James only once, and then simply to say that they
had seen each other once or twice, and now proposed to
think things over and have a discussion after the holiday.

'At least, I'm supposed to think things over,' said Amy
bitterly. 'As far as I can see, his mind is made up. How this
chit of a girl could have managed to get such a hold on
someone as intelligent as James, I simply can't imagine!'

We were flying from Heathrow at a little after eleven in
the morning, so that we did not have to make one of those
dreadful journeys by car in the small hours which so often
add to the traveller's discomfort.

It was one of those cold grey summer days when Amy
came to collect me. A chilly wind whipped round corners,
scattering a few dead leaves and wreaking havoc with our
newly-arranged hair.

'I've got one of those net things with little bows all over
it,' confessed Amy when we had finally stowed our baggage
in the boot, and checked, yet again, passports and other
documents. 'But I look like a culture-vulture from the mid-
west in it, and am too vain to wear it, although it does keep
one's hair tidy.'

I said I had a silk scarf if the wind became too boisterous,
but I looked more like little Mother Russia in my headgear.

'Besides,' I said, 'it grieves me to pay a pound to have my
hair fluffed out and then to see it flattened in five minutes.'

Rain began to fall as we approached the airport.

'Won't it be marvellous to leave all this murk behind?'
crowed Amy. 'Just think of the blue skies waiting for us, and
all that lovely sunshine.'

Our spirits rose, and remained high throughout the leaving

256

of the car, the taxi ride through the tunnel, and the slow shuffle through to the departure lounge.

We found a seat, disposed our hand luggage around us, and settled down to watch our fellow travellers, and to look at the magazines we had brought to pass the time.

It was while we were thus engaged, that it suddenly dawned upon me that Amy was looking uncommonly nervous. It was the first inkling I had that she might suffer from the fear of flying.

'Do you mind flying?' I ventured.

'I loathe it,' replied Amy with some of her old energy. 'In the first place, it's dead against nature to have that great lump of metal suspended in mid-air, and no amount of sweet reasoning is going to budge that basic fact from my suspicious mind.'

'But think of the thousands and thousands of people who fly all over the place daily.'

'Lucky to be alive,' said Amy firmly. 'And think of all the hundreds who died in air crashes. I always do.'

'You shouldn't dwell on such things.'

'If you hate flying you can't help dwelling on such things! Then think of all the thousands of screws and bolts and rivets and so on, supposed to keep the bits together. How can you be sure every one of them is reliable? And what about all-over metal fatigue? Not to mention having so little time, or enough mechanics, to service the thing properly between flights.'

Amy, warming to her theme, was much more her usual forthright self, and I was pleased to see that, for a time anyway, James was forgotten.

'And then there's fire. I don't feel at all happy about all that petrol being pumped into the thing before you start off.'

'Better than forgetting it,' I pointed out. Amy ignored me.

'How does one know that there is not some ass with a cigarette drifting about nearby, and we won't all be burnt to a cinder on the tarmac?'

'There are fire tenders.'

'I daresay. With the crews in the canteen swilling coffee, and you frizzled before they can stick their axes in their belts.'

At this point, a confused noise came from the loud speakers. Someone with his head in a blanket was evidently honking down a drain-pipe. The message was quite incomprehensible to my ears, but an alert young man nearby spoke to us.

'Gate Nine, evidently.'

We collected our baggage and joined the queue.

'Well, here we go,' said Amy resignedly. 'I wonder if the pilot is a dipsomaniac?'

We settled into our seats, Amy insisting that I took the one by the window. Through it I had a view of the rear side of the wing, and beyond that the grey expanse of the airport with only the brightly coloured tankers and aeroplanes to enliven the scene.

'Thank heaven it's daylight,' said Amy, 'and we shan't be able to see the flames shooting out of the exhausts! I face death every time I get into a blasted plane.'

'It's a quick one, I believe.'

'I wonder. I always imagine twirling round and round like a sycamore key, with one wing off.'

'Caught in the enemy's search-lights, I suppose? Amy, you've been watching too many old war films on television. Have a barley sugar, and think of Crete.'

The engines began to roar, and the aeroplane began its interminable trundling round the airport, bumping and bumbling along like some clumsy half-blind creature looking for its home.

Amy had closed her eyes, and both hands were clenched in her lap, resting on the glossy cover of a magazine which had blazoned across its corner: 'Australia: Only A Day's Flight Away.'

Suddenly, the pace of the engines altered, the roaring was terrifying, and we started to set off along what one sincerely hoped was the correct runway, and the path to Crete.

Buildings rushed past in the distance, the grass dropped away, the wing of the aeroplane dipped steeply, and far below us, tipped at an absurd angle, the streets and parks, the reservoirs and rivers of Middlesex hung like a stage back-cloth.

Excitement welled in me. Amy opened her eyes and smiled.

'Well, we're off at last,' she said, with infinite relief in her voice. 'Now we can enjoy ourselves.'

The adventure had begun.

PART TWO

Farther Afield

8. In Crete

Our first glimpse of Crete was in the golden light of early
evening for we had been delayed at Athens airport. It would
have given Mrs Pringle some satisfaction.

If we had known how long we should have to wait for the
aeroplane to Heraklion we could have taken a taxi into
Athens and enjoyed a sight-seeing tour. As it was, we were
told at half-hourly intervals that the mechanical fault was
almost repaired and we should be going aboard within minutes. Consequently, we were obliged to wait, while Amy and
her fellow-sufferers grew more and more nervous, and even
such phlegmatic travellers as myself grew heartily sick of cups
of tepid coffee, and the appalling noise and dust made by a
gang of workmen who were laying a marble floor. It was
infuriating to be so near the cradle of western civilization and
yet unable to visit it, tethered as we were by the bonds of
modern technology, and a pretty imperfect technology at
that.

But our view of Crete from the air dispelled our irritation.
There it lay, long, green and beautiful in a sea so deeply blue,
that the epithet 'wine-dark' which one had accepted somewhat
sceptically, was suddenly proved to be true.

Below us, like toys, small boats were crossing to and from
the mainland, their white wakes echoed by the white vapour
trails of an aeroplane in the blue above.

We circled lower and lower, and now we could see a white
frill of waves round the bays, and white houses clustered on
the green flanks of the hills. Away to the west the mountains
were amethyst-coloured in the thickening light, with Mount
Ida plainly to be seen.

By the time we had gone through customs, and boarded a
coach, it was almost dark, and we set off eastwards along the
coast road to our destination.

It was a hair-raising ride. The surface of the road – probably one of the best in the island – was remarkably rough. The coach which had met us rattled and swayed. Seats squeaked, metal jangled, windows clattered, and the driver kept up a loud conversation with our guide, only breaking off to curse any other vehicle driver foolish enough to cross his path.

We soon realized how mountainous Crete is. The main ridge of mountains runs along the central spine of the island, but the coast road too boasted some alarming ascents and descents. Part of our journey was along a newly built road, but there was still much to be done, and we followed the path used by generations of travellers from Heraklion to Aghios Nikolaos for most of the way.

The last part of the journey took place in darkness. The headlights lit up the white villages through which we either hurtled down or laboured up. Occasionally, we saw a tethered goat cropping busily beneath the brilliant stars, or a pony clopping along at the side of the road, its rider muffled in a rough cloak.

Every now and again the coach shuddered to a halt, and a few passengers descended, laden with luggage, to find their hotel.

'I wouldn't mind betting,' said Amy, with a yawn, 'that we are the last to be put down.'

She would have lost her bet, but only just, for we were the penultimate group to be dropped. Two middle-aged couples, and a family of five struggled from the coach with us and we made our way through a courtyard to the doorway.

We were all stiff and tired for we had been travelling since morning. A delicious aroma was floating about the entrance hall. It was as welcome as the smiles of the men behind the desk.

'Grub!' sighed one of our fellow-travellers longingly.

He echoed the feelings of us all.

School teachers do not usually stay in expensive hotels, so that I was all the more impressed with the beauty and efficiency of the one we now inhabited.

The gardens were extensive and followed the curve of the bay. Evergreen trees and flowering shrubs scented the air, lilies and cannas and orange blossom adding their perfume. And everywhere water trickled, irrigating the thirsty ground, and adding its own rustling music to that of the sea which splashed only a few yards from our door.

Amy and I shared a little whitewashed stone house, comprising one large room with two beds and some simple wooden furniture, a bathroom and a spacious verandah where we had breakfast each morning. The rest of the meals were taken in the main part of the hotel to which we walked along brick paths, sniffing so rapturously at all the plants that Amy said I looked like Ferdinand the bull.

'Heavens! That dates us.' I said. 'I haven't thought of Ferdinand for about thirty years!'

'Must be more than that,' said Amy. 'It was before the war. Isn't it strange how one's life is divided into before and after wars? I used to get so mad with my parents telling me about all the wonderful things they could buy for two and eleven-three before 1914 that I swore I would never do the same thing, but I do. I heard myself telling Vanessa, only the other day, what a hard-wearing winter coat I had brought for thirty shillings *before the war*. She didn't seem to believe me, I must say.'

'It's at times like Christmas that I hark back,' I confessed. 'I used to reckon to buy eight presents for college friends for a pound. Dash it all, you could get a silk scarf or a real leather purse for half a crown in those days.'

'And a swansdown powder puff sewn into a beautiful square of crêpe-de-chine,' sighed Amy. 'Ah, well! No good living in the past. I must say the present suits me very well. Do you think I'm burning?'

We were lying by the swimming pool after breakfast. Already the sun was hot. By eleven it would be too hot to sun-bathe, and we should find a shady place under the trees or on our own verandah, listening to the lazy splashing of the waves on the rocks.

On the terrace above us four gardeners were tending two minute patches of coarse grass. A sprinkler played upon these tiny lawns for most of the day. Sometimes an old-fashioned lawn-mower would be run over them, with infinite care. The love which was lavished upon these two shaggy patches should have produced something as splendidly elegant as the lawns at the Backs in Cambridge, one felt, but to Cretan eyes, no doubt, the result was as satisfying.

For the first two or three days we were content to loll in the sun, to bathe in the hotel pool, and to potter about the enchanting town of Aghios Nikolaos. We were both tired. My arm was still in a sling for most of the time, and pained me occasionally if I moved it at an awkward angle. Amy's troubles were far harder to bear, and I marvelled at her courage in thrusting them out of sight. We were both anxious that the other should benefit from the holiday, and as we both liked the same things we were in perfect accord.

'We'll hire a car,' Amy said, 'for the rest of the holiday. There are so many lovely things to see. First trip to Knossos, and I think we'll make an early start on that day. It was hot enough there when I went in April. Heaven knows what it will be like in August!'

Meanwhile, we slept and ate and bathed and read, glorying in the sunshine, and shimmering heat, the blue, blue sea and the sheer joy of being somewhere different.

Now and again I felt a pang of remorse as I thought of Tibby in her hygienic surroundings at the super-kennels to which I had taken her. No doubt she loathed the comfortable bed provided, the dried cat-food, the fresh water, and the concrete run thoughtfully washed out daily with weak disinfectant by her kind warders.

Where, she would be wondering, is the garden, and my lilac tree scratching post? Where is the grass I like to eat, and my comfortably dirty blanket, and the dishes of warm food put down by a doting owner?

It would not do Tibby any harm, I told myself, to have a little discipline for two weeks. She would appreciate her home comforts all the more keenly when we were reunited.

Our fellow guests seemed a respectable collection of folk. In the main, they were middle-aged, and enjoying themselves in much the same way as Amy and I were. There were one or two families with older children, but no babies to be seen. I assumed that there were a number of reasons for this lack of youth.

The hotel was expensive, and to take two or three children there for a fortnight or so would be beyond most families' purses. The natural bathing facilities were not ideal for youngsters. The coast was rocky, the beaches small and often shelving abruptly. The flight from England was fairly lengthy, and it was easy to see why there were very few small children about.

It suited me. I like children well enough, otherwise I should not be teaching, but enough is enough, and part of the pleasure of this particular holiday was the company of adults only.

We looked forward to a short time in the bar after dinner, talking to other guests and sometimes watching the Greek waiters who had been persuaded to dance. We loved the gravity of these local dances as, arms resting on each others' shoulders, the young men swooped in unison, legs swinging backwards and forwards, their dark faces solemn with concentration until, at last, they would finish with a neat acrobatic leap to face the other way, and their smiles would acknowledge our applause.

One of the middle-aged couples who had made the journey with us, often came to sit with us in the bar. Their stone house was near our own, and we often found ourselves walking to dinner together through the scented darkness.

She was small and neat, with prematurely white silky hair, worn in soft curls. Blue-eyed and fair-skinned she must have been enchanting as a girl, and even now, in middle-age, her elegance was outstanding. She dressed in white or blue, accentuating the colour of her hair and eyes, and wore a brooch and bracelet of sapphires and pearls which even I coveted.

Her husband looked much younger, with a shock of crisp dark hair, a slim bronzed figure, and a ready flow of conversation. We found them very good company.

'The Clarks,' Amy said to me one evening, as we dressed for dinner, 'remind me of the advertisement for pep pills. You know: "Where do they get their energy?" They seem so

267

wonderfully in tune too. I must say, it turns the knife in the wound at times,' she added, with a tight smile.

'Well, they're not likely to parade any secret clashes before other people staying here,' I pointed out reasonably.

'True enough,' agreed Amy. 'Half the fun of hotel life is speculating about one's neighbours. What do you think of the two who bill and coo at the table on our left?'

'Embarrassing,' I said emphatically. 'Must have been married for years, and still stroking hands while they wait for their soup. Talk about washing one's clean linen in public!'

'They may have been married for years,' said Amy, in what I have come to recognize as her worldly-woman voice, 'but was it to each other?'

'Miaow!' I intoned.

Amy laughed.

'You trail the innocence of Fairacre wherever you go,' she teased. 'And not a bad thing either.'

It was the morning after this conversation that I found myself dozing alone, frying nicely, under some trees near the pool. Amy was writing cards on the verandah, and was to join me later.

I heard footsteps approach, and opened my eyes to see Mrs Clark smiling at me.

'Can I share the shade?'

'Of course.' I shifted along obligingly, and Mrs Clark spread a rug and cushion, and arranged herself elegantly upon them.

'John's in the pool, but it does mess up one's hair so, that I thought I'd miss my dip today. How is your arm?'

I assured her that I was mending fast.

'It's all this lovely fresh air and sunshine,' she said. 'It's a heavenly climate. My husband would like to live here.'

'I can understand it.'

'So can I. He has more reason than most to like the Greek way of life. His grandmother was a Greek. She lived a few miles south of Athens, and John spent a number of holidays with her as a schoolboy.'

'Lucky fellow!'

'I suppose so.' She sounded sad, and I wondered what lay behind this disclosure.

'We visited her, as often as we could manage it, right up to her death about five or six years ago. A wonderful old lady. She had been a widow for years. In fact, I never met John's grandfather. He died when John was still at Marlborough.'

She sat up and anointed one slim leg with suntan lotion. Her expression was serious, as she worked away. I began to suspect, with some misgivings, that once again I was destined to hear someone's troubles.

'You see,' she went on, 'John retires from the Army next year, and he is set on coming here to live. He's even started house-hunting.'

'And what do you feel about it?'

She turned a defiant blue gaze upon me.

'I'm dead against it. I'm moving heaven and earth to try to get him to change his mind, and I intend to succeed. It's a dream he has lived with for years – first it was to live in Athens. Then in one or other of the Greek islands, and now its definitely whittled down to Crete. I've never seen him so ruthless.'

I thought of Amy who had used almost exactly the same words about James.

'Perhaps something will occur to make him change his mind,' I suggested.

'Never! He's thought of this kind of life wherever he's been, and I feel that he's been through so much that it is right in a way for him to have what he wants, now that he will have the leisure to enjoy it. But the thing is, I can't bear the thought of it. We should have to leave everything behind that we love, I tell him.'

She began to attack the other leg with ferocity.

'We live in Surrey. Over the years we saved enough to buy this rather nice house, with a big garden, and we've been lucky enough to live in it for the past seven years. Before that, of course, we were posted hear, there, and everywhere, but one expects that. I thought that John had given up the idea of settling out here. He's seemed so happy helping me in the garden, and making improvements to the house. Now I realize that he was looking upon the place as something valuable to sell to finance a home here. And the garden –'

She broke off, and bent low, ostensibly to examine her leg.

'Tell me about it,' I said.

'I've made a heavenly rockery. It slopes steeply, and you can get some very good terraces cut into the side of the hill. My gentians are doing so well, and lots of little Alpines. And three years ago I planted an autumn flowering prunus which had lots of blossom last October – so pretty. I simply *won't* leave it!'

'You could make a garden here I expect. My friend Amy tells me that when she was here last, in April, there were carnations and geraniums, and lilies of all sorts. Think of that!'

'And then there are the grandchildren,' she went on, as though she had not heard me. 'We have two girls, both married, who live quite near us, and we see the grandchildren several times a week. There are three, and a new baby due soon after we return. I'm going to keep house for Irene when she goes into hospital, and look after her husband and Bruce, the first boy.'

'You'll enjoy that, I expect,' I said, hoping to wean her from her unhappiness. I did not succeed.

'But just think of all those little things growing up miles away from us! Think of the fun we're going to miss, seeing them at all the different stages! I keep reminding John of this. And then there's Podge.'

'Podge?'

'Our spaniel. He's nearly twelve and far too old to settle overseas, in a hot climate. Irene has offered to have him, but he would grieve without us, and I should grieve too, I don't deny. No, it can't be done.'

She looked at me, and smiled.

'I really shouldn't be worrying you with my problems, but you have such a sympathetic face, you know.'

This is not the first time I have been told this. I cannot help feeling that my face works independently of my inner thoughts. It certainly seems to make me the repository of all kinds of unsolicited confidences, as I know to my cost.

'I'm quite sure,' she continued, screwing on the stopper of the lotion bottle, 'that my daughters wouldn't be putting up with this situation. For one thing, of course, they could be financially independent, a thing I've never been.'

'Even if you were,' I said cautiously, 'you wouldn't part from your husband surely?'

'No, I suppose not.' She sounded doubtful. 'There's been no choice, of course. I wasn't brought up to do a job of any kind, and I married fairly young. Now I suppose I am virtually unemployable. I must stay with John, or starve.'

She laughed, rather tremulously, and hastened to skate away from this thin ice. She spoke firmly.

'No, of course, I wouldn't leave him. We really are devoted to each other, and he is a wonderful husband. It's just this terrible problem . . .'

Her voice trailed away. Sighing, she lay down again, and stretched herself, enjoying the warm air, heavy with the scent of orange blossom.

Far away a gull cried, and water slapped rhythmically against a wooden boat moored by the little stone jetty. It seemed sad to me that such an earthly paradise should be spoilt for this poor woman by the cloud of worries which surrounded her.

One's first thought was how selfish her husband was to insist on disrupting her happy domesticity.

On the other hand he had served his country well presumably, had been uprooted time and time again in the course of his duties, and surely he was entitled to spend his retirement in the place he had always loved.

A pity they were married, I thought idly. Separately, they could have been so happy – she in Surrey, he in Crete. Or would they have been? Obviously, they loved each other. She would not be suffering so if she were not concerned for his happiness.

Ah well! There was a lot to be said for being single. One might miss a great deal, but at least one's life was singularly uncomplicated.

Side by side, spinster and spouse, we both slipped into slumber, as the sun climbed the Cretan sky.

9. At Knossos

The night before our trip to Knossos we had a thunderstorm, frightening in its intensity.

Normally, I enjoy a thunderstorm at night when the black sky is cracked with silver shafts, and sheet lightning illumines the downs with an eerie flickering. Nature at her most dramatic can be very exhilarating, but a Mediterranean storm was much more alarming, I discovered, than the Fairacre variety.

The sea had become turbulent by the time we undressed for bed. The usual gentle lapping sound was transmuted to noisy crashes. Our little stone house, so solidly built, seemed to shudder in the onslaught from the sea.

But soon the noise of the waves was lost in the din of the storm. Thunder rumbled and cracked like a whip overhead. The lightning seemed continuous, turning the bay into a grotesquely coloured stage-set, against which the moored boats jostled and dipped like drunken men trying to stay upright.

The rain came down like rods. Everything glistened, roofs, walls, trees and flowers. And everywhere there was the sound of running water. It poured from gutters, rushed down slopes, turning the brick paths to rivers, and washing the carefully garnered soil down to the sea below.

'You can't wonder,' shouted Amy, above the din, from her bed, 'that the Greeks made sacrifices to propitiate the gods when they thought they were responsible for all this racket. I wouldn't mind pouring out a libation myself, to stop the noise.'

'No oil or wine available,' I shouted back, 'unless you care for a saucerful of my suntan oil.'

'We may as well put on the light and read,' said Amy, sitting up. 'Sleep's impossible.'

Propped against our pillows we studied our books. At least, Amy did.

She was zealously preparing for tomorrow's trip by reading a guide to Knossos. Amy's powers of concentration far outstrip my own, and despite the ferocity of the storm outside, she was soon deeply engrossed.

Less dedicated, I turned the pages of one of the magazines we had brought with us, and wondered how Fairacre would react if, salary allowing, I appeared in some of the autumn outfits displayed. What about this rust-coloured woollen two-piece trimmed with red fox? Just the thing for writing on the blackboard. Or this elegant pearl-grey frock banded with chinchilla? The plasticine would settle in that beautifully.

'Do you imagine anyone ever buys these things?' I asked, yawning. 'Or do they all go to Marks and Spencer, and their local outfitter's as we do?'

Amy looked vaguely in my direction. One could see her mind gradually returning from 2000 BC to the present time.

'Of course someone wears them,' she replied. 'I've even had some myself when James has been feeling extra generous.'

She drew in her breath sharply. She was once again firmly in the present with all its hurts and its hopes. I cursed myself for disturbing her reading and its temporary comfort.

'Listen,' I said, 'the storm is going away.'

It was true. The rain had become a mere pattering. The thunder was a distant rumbling, the spouting of gutters diminished to a trickle.

Amy smiled and closed her book.

'That *silly* man,' she said lovingly. 'I wonder what he's doing?'

She slid down under the bedclothes and was asleep in three minutes, leaving me to marvel at the inconsistency of women.

The morning was brilliant. Everything glittered in its freshness after the storm, and the sea air was more than usually exhilarating.

We piled our belongings into the hired mini which was to carry us to Knossos, and a score of other places, during the rest of our stay. It was the cheapest vehicle we could hire, and privately I thought the sum asked was outrageous, but Amy did not turn a hair on being told the terms, and once again I was deeply conscious of her generosity to me.

'Let's lunch in Heraklion,' said Amy, 'and have a look at the museum first. Most of the things are of Minoan period. I must have another look at the ivory acrobat, and spend more time looking at the jewellery which is simply lovely. Last time, we spent far too long gazing at frescoes, and to my mind, it's the small things which are so fascinating.'

Her enthusiasm was catching, and we drove westward towards Crete's capital in high spirits. The mini coped well with the rough surfaces and the steep gradients, and I felt considerably safer with Amy at the wheel than I had with our first coach driver.

Heraklion teemed with traffic, but Amy found a car park, with her usual competence, not far from the museum, so that all was well.

It was a wonderful building, with exhibits well arranged, and everything bathed in that pellucid light which blesses the Greek islands. Amy and I started our tour together, but gradually drifted apart, enjoying the exquisite workmanship of almost four thousand years ago, at our own pace. I left her studying the jewellery while I went upstairs.

I could see why she and James had spent so long admiring the frescoes on their earlier visit. There was such pride and gaiety in the processions of men and women on the walls. Sport was depicted everywhere, vaulting, leaping, running, wrestling; and the famous bulls of Crete were shown in all their powerful splendour by the Minoan artists.

We spent two hours there, dazed and awed by so much magnificence.

'What we need,' said Amy, when we met again, 'is two or three months in this place.'

'But first of all, lunch,' I said.

We crossed the road to some shops and cafés which seemed to have tables set out on the pavement under shady awnings. We were met by three or four garrulous proprietors, each rubbing and clapping his hands, pointing out the superior quality of his own establishment, and the extreme pleasure which he would have in receiving our custom. The noise was deafening, and the constant stream of traffic made it worse.

We were practically tugged into one café and settled meekly at the paper-covered table. A large dark hand brushed the remains of someone else's lunch to the ground, and a menu was thrust before us.

'All sorts of salads,' observed Amy, studying it closely, 'or something called "Pork's Livers Roasted" and another one named "Chick's Rice Fried". Unless you fancy "Heart's Beefs Noodled".'

I said I would settle for shrimp salad. We had soon discovered that the shrimps in Crete are as succulent as prawns, and much the same size. We were fast becoming shrimp addicts.

'Me too,' said Amy, giving our order to the beaming proprietor.

An American couple were deposited suddenly in the two empty chairs opposite us. They looked apologetic, as their captor rushed away to rescue the menu.

'I hope you two ladies don't object to us being thrust upon you,' said the man earnestly. 'We didn't intend to have lunch here, but were kinda captured.'

We said we had been too.

'One comfort,' said Amy, 'the food looks very good.'

'I'm sure glad to hear that,' said the man. 'I can eat most anything, but Mrs Judd here has a highly sensitive stomach, and is a sufferer from gas. Ain't that so, Mother?' he said, bending solicitously towards his wife, who was studying our fellow diners' plates with deepest suspicion.

Mother, who must have weighed fourteen stone and had a mouth like Mrs Pringle's, with the corners turned down, was understood to say she couldn't relish anything in this joint, and how about pushing on?

Her husband consulted a large square watch on a hairy wrist, and surmised time was on the short side if they wanted to take in Knossos, and get back again for shopping, before meeting the Hyams for a drink at 6 o'clock. He guessed this place was as good as the next, and at least they were at the table, no lining up like that goddam place they went to yesterday, so why not make the best of it?

Mother pouted.

Of course, said her husband swiftly, if Mother was real set on going elsewhere, why, that was fine by him! Just whatever Mother wanted.

At that moment the menu arrived.

'Beefs very good. Porks very good. Chicks very good. Salads very good,' chanted the waiter, his eyes darting this way and that in quest for yet more clients.

'What you two girls having?' asked Mother grumpily.

'Shrimp salad,' we chorused.

'That'll do me, Abe,' she said, 'the tomaytoes are certainly fine in this country. You got tomaytoes?' she added anxiously.

'Plenty tomaytoes,' nodded the waiter. 'Tomaytoes very good, You like?'

'I'll have the same,' said Abe

The waiter vanished. Abe patted Mother's hand, and beamed upon her.

'You certainly know what you like,' he said proudly. If she had suddenly explained Einstein's theory he could not have been more respectful.

Our shrimp salads arrived, and Abe and Mother studied them as we ate. They were delicious, and soon a mound of heads and tails grew at the side of our enormous white plates.

A thin white cat weaved her way from the shop through the legs of the chairs, and sat close to us.

With thoughts of my incarcerated Tibby, I handed down a few shrimp heads. There was a rapid crunching, and the pavement was clear again. I repeated the process. So did the cat.

'Like a miniature Hoover,' commented Amy.

'Starving, poor thing,' said Mother. 'Or got some wasting disease maybe.'

'I haven't seen any animals looking hungry in Crete,' I said, coming to the defence of our hosts. 'Cats in hot climates often look thin to our eyes.'

'I was raised where cats were kept in their place,' said Mother. 'If us kids had fed our animals at the table, we'd have caught the rough side of our Pa's tongue.'

I forbore to comment.

'You ladies aiming at going to Knossos?' asked Abe, changing the subject with aplomb.

We said we were.

'You done the museum?'

We said we had.

'Some beautiful things there,' said Mother, 'but I didn't care for the ladies in the wall-paintings. Shocking to think they went topless like any disgusting modern girl. I sure was thankful our Pastor wasn't present. What did you think, Abe?'

Abe looked uncomfortable.

'Well, I thought they were proper handsome. Fine upstanding girls they looked to me.'

Mother gave him a stern look.

'After all,' said Abe pleadingly, 'it was a long time back. Maybe they didn't know any better.'

At that moment, their plates arrived, and we asked for our bill and paid it.

'See you at Knossos!' shouted Abe, as we said our farewells and walked away from the table.

'Do you take that as a threat or a promise,' asked Amy, when we were safely out of earshot.

As luck would have it, we did not come across our friends at Knossos, but Amy commented on them as we parked the car at the gates of the site of the ruined palace.

'I wonder how many English wives would be pandered to as Mother is,' she mused.

'Would they want it?'

'On the whole, no. On the other hand, it must be wonderfully encouraging to be deferred to so often. It might make one terribly selfish, of course. After all, it hasn't done Mother a lot of good – sulking like a spoilt child when things go wrong.'

'Perhaps they haven't any children,' I surmised. 'Couples without children often get over-possessive with each other.'

'Not all of them,' said Amy dryly. And I remembered – too late as usual – that she and James were childless. Whoever it was called the tongue an unruly member was certainly

277

right. Trying to control my own proves well-nigh impossible, and results in more self-reproach than I care to admit.

'Or perhaps,' I continued hastily, 'it's a case of arrested development, and Abe panders to her simply because she's so immature.'

'Immature? Mother?' snorted Amy, locking the car door with a decisive click. 'Mother's development has reached its highest peak, for what it's worth. She's got that man exactly where she wants him – under her thumb. Whether it makes her happy or not is another thing, but you see it over and over again in marriages. One must be boss; never an equal partnership.'

We made our way in the brilliant sunshine to the entrance to Knossos.

'You make marriage sound a hazardous proceeding,' I remarked. 'I don't think I could have succeeded in it.'

Amy shook her head at me.

'You don't know what you have missed, my girl. It has a bright side, believe me. I'll tell you all about it one day. I bet even Abe and Mother have a few happy times.'

'Well, let's hope they enjoyed their shrimp salads. I don't like to think of Mother suffering with gas while she's sight-seeing.'

We entered the grounds, and made our way through a shady avenue which led uphill to the site of the great palace, where men and women, some two thousand years BC, had faced, no doubt the same material problems at large today.

I had no idea, when reading about Knossos, how vast an area the whole concourse covered. As before, Amy and I started our tour together, but soon decided to meet, two hours hence, at the gate, for there was so much to see that one was better on one's own.

As always, it was the light that impressed me most. It was easy to see how such a happy civilization evolved. The clarity of light, the warmth of the sun and the embracing sea, combined to give an exhilaration of spirit. Fertile soil, many rivers and trees were an added blessing. Small wonder that the ancient Minoans had a spontaneous gaiety and energy which created such a wealth of superb architecture, paintings and sculpture.

They were practical people too, I was glad to see, with sensible plumbing, spacious bathrooms and plenty of storage space for their provisions. Many a twentieth-century builder in England, I thought, could have learnt a thing or two from the workmen of Minoan Crete.

The great staircases, supported by the massive red columns, smaller at the base than the top, led from one floor to another, and on each were things to stand and marvel at. A little crowd stood looking at King Minos' throne, reckoned to be the oldest in the world. But the object which gave me most pleasure was the fresco in the Queen's room showing dolphins at sport above the entrance. There they play, some four thousand years old, still bearing that particularly endearing expression of benignity which so enchants us when we see the fish today cavorting, for our delight, in water parks and zoos.

Their gaiety was echoed in the frescoes showing processions or feats of physical skill. Many we had seen in the museum, but replicas were here, and one could not help but be impressed with the physical beauty and elegance of the men and women. The topless gowns, so frowned upon by Mother, had beautiful bell-shaped skirts, and the stiff bodices, cut away to expose the breasts, supported them and were intricately adorned with gold and precious jewels. Their hair was long and wavy, their eyes made up as lavishly as Vanessa's. They were really the most decorative creatures, and not above helping in the acrobatic pursuits, as the pictures of them assisting their men-folk in the bull-vaulting escapades showed clearly.

Perhaps, I mused, this is what northerners lack. Our climate is against flimsy clothing, sea-bathing and outdoor sports. If we took more physical exercise, should we be more blithe and energetic? Would our lives become as creative and as happy as the Minoans' most certainly were? Should we be less introspective, less prone to self-pity, less critical of others?

The secret, I decided, was simply in the sun. Given that, given warmth and light, one was more than half-way to happiness.

I rose from my staircase seat looking out to sea, and made my way reluctantly to the outside world.

'But I shall come again,' I said aloud, stroking the ancient dust from a pillar as I passed. There was so much more to learn from the Minoans about the proper way to live.

10. *Amy Works Things Out*

'It is a truth universally acknowledged,' Jane Austen tells us, 'that a single man in possession of a good fortune must be in want of a wife.'

A lesser truth, universally acknowledged, is that the first week of a fortnight's holiday is twice as long as the second week. Why this should be so remains a mystery, but no doubt the theory of relativity might throw some light on the matter if one could only understand it.

'Of course,' say some people, trying to be rational, 'one *does* so much the first week. Trips here and there, friends to visit, new people to meet – it's bound to seem longer.'

But this theory did not apply to Amy and me. Apart from the trip to Knossos, and some blissful walks in the mountains after the main heat of the day had passed, we had done nothing but sleep, bathe, eat and converse in a languid fashion. True, we had roused ourselves to write a few post-cards, now and again, but on the whole the first week had seemed like two days, and here we were, embarking on our second week, with dozens of places as yet unvisited.

Aghios Nikolaos itself we quartered fairly thoroughly, for we had taken to shopping for our midday picnic, collecting a hot fragrant loaf from the bakery in a cobbled side street, choosing cheese and chocolate, but learning quickly to wait until we reached the villages to buy the famous tomatoes, for here, in the town's dusty streets, their freshness soon withered. We soon knew the most welcoming cafés, the newsagent who sold English newspapers, the shoe-maker who would make you a pair of leather sandals in next to no time, and the jewellers who displayed the beautiful gold filigree work which was beyond even Amy's purse.

But it was life in the country, in the small villages among the olive groves and the carob trees, which fascinated us.

Despite the splendid electric lights which hung in some of

the narrow streets, most of the houses seemed to have none indoors. The interiors were dark, and the families seemed to sit on their doorsteps as long as the light lasted.

We met them, during the day, and particularly in the early evening, on their way home. The little groups usually consisted of a man and wife, and perhaps one or two children. They would be accompanied by a mule or a donkey, sometimes both and two or three goats. Occasionally, a cow swaggered indolently with them, its full bag swaying from side to side. The animals were in fine condition, and the American, Mother, was quite wrong to accuse the Cretans of callousness. All those we saw were lovingly tended, and the sheepdogs that sometimes ran with the family were as lively as those at Fairacre.

Always there would be a great bundle of greenery, culled from the banks, for the beasts' evening fodder, and always too, a large bundle of kindling wood lodged across the front of the donkey's saddle, intended, no doubt, for cooking the evening meal.

The women were dressed in black, and the men in clothes of dark material. All acknowledged us when we met, and smiled in a friendly way, but it was quite apparent that they were busy. They were at work. They wished us well but would not dally. Here, the Biblical way of life still held − a day to day existence, charted by the hours of light and darkness, and by the swing of the seasons. There was a serenity about these people which we have lost it seems. Perhaps we have too many possession, look too far ahead, take 'too much thought for the morrow, what we shall eat, what we shall put on'. Amy and I would not have wanted to change to this style of living, even if we could, but it was balm to our spirits to see the simplicity and dignity of another way of life, and to learn from it.

We decided to visit the monastery of Toplou at the far eastern end of the island. We had soon realized that it was impossible to attempt to see the western half of Crete, for the hilly nature of the country and the surface of many of the roads made the going slow.

'We'll come again,' promised Amy, 'and we'll stay in Heraklion next time, and push westward from there.'

Meanwhile we intended to see as much as we could with Aghios Nikolaos as our very good centre. The coast road eastward, we soon discovered, on the morning we set off for Toplou, had its own hazards, for falls of rock had crashed into the road and gangs of workmen shook their heads and did their best to stop us.

Amy was at her most persuasive, and tried to explain that we should never be so foolhardy as to run into real danger, but surely, if they themselves were brave enough to be working on the road then our little car − driven with *infinite* care − could edge past?

They grimaced at us, poured forth a torrent of Greek to each other, held up their elbows and looked fearfully above them, miming the dangers we must expect if we persisted. We sat and smiled at them, nodding to show we understood, and at last, with a shrugging of shoulders, they beckoned us on. Their expressions showed clearly their feelings. On our own heads be it − and that might well be, literally, a ton or two of overhanging rock, made unsafe by the violent storm of a few nights before.

We survived. The sky was overcast that day, but the sea air lifted our hair, and we sat on short turf which smelt aromatically of thyme, to have our picnic.

'I wonder,' said Amy lazily, as we rested after lunch, 'what the outcome will be between the Clarks. She came round this morning, when you were up at the hotel, to borrow the Knossos guide book. Do you know, that wretched man thinks he's found a house! She's beside herself.'

'Where is the house?'

'Malia.'

I remembered it as one of the ancient sites on the road to Heraklion. I also remembered it as a dusty, somewhat sleazy, long street full of booths selling straw hats, and bags, and some pretty fearful souvenirs. I couldn't see Mrs Clark settling there after the green and pleasant purlieus of Surrey.

'What's her reaction?' I asked.

'Unusually forceful, which I think's a good thing. He's gone a little too far a little too quickly, and while she was really doing her best to meet him half-way a week ·ago, now she's beginning to get much tougher.'

'What a problem! I only hope they don't fall out permanently. They seem so fond of each other, that I can't see them getting too vicious over this affair.'

'I'm sure they'll find some solution. Evidently, she now stipulates that nothing is bought outright until they have lived in the place for a few months, and can see how they like it.'

'Seems sensible. So he's agreed to rent something?'

'I don't know. The difficulty is that people move step by step into awkward positions, and then won't swallow their pride and climb down.'

'Too true.'

'Look at James. I really can't believe that he wants to spend the rest of his life with this girl. She'll bore him to tears by the end of the year.'

'You know her then?' I was taken by surprise. Amy had said so little about the girl that I had jumped to the conclusion that James had met her somewhere on his travels.

'I've met her a few times in James's office. She's one of his typists. Perfectly nice child, I imagine, but should be flirting with some cheerful young man at her local tennis club or dramatic society – not ogling her boss.'

Amy stubbed out a cigarette viciously among the thymy grass.

'If this had happened twenty or thirty years ago,' she went on, 'I should have tackled it quite differently.'

'I keep remembering my Aunt Winifred who coped with much the same situation when she was my age. Did I ever tell you about it?'

'No,' I said, settling comfortably for a domestic saga. 'Tell on.'

'Well, soon after I left college I had a couple of years at a rather nice school near Highbury. As my Aunt Winifred lived close by, my parents, after much heart-searching, asked her if I might stay there as a PG.

'She was a game old girl, and had no children of her own, and said of course I must stay there, which I did, going home at weekends. Incidentally, she refused to take a penny in rent which made my upright parents most uncomfortable, but there it was.

'My uncle Peter was an accountant – perhaps book-keeper is nearer the mark – at one of the good London stores, Harrods or Jacksons, something of the sort. He caught the 8.10 train every morning and came into the house between 6.30 and 7 every evening. He was very sweet and gentle, and always brought us a cup of tea in bed in the mornings, and spent his spare time pottering about in his greenhouse.

'Imagine then, the horror when he calmly asked Aunt Winifred if she would kindly remove herself as he wished to bring home "*a very lady-like girl*" – I can hear my poor Aunt Win mimicking his tone to this day – whom he hoped to marry as soon as he and Aunt Winifred could get a divorce.

'I was not present, naturally, at this scene, but heard all about it from my aunt some time later.'

'What on earth did she do?'

'You'll be amazed. As amazed as I was, all those years ago, I expect. She told me this with a smile of such self-satisfaction on her face that I was rendered speechless at the time. It seems that she had been left a small legacy by a godfather not long before. Something in the region of two hundred pounds. When she was telling me this, I remember thinking: "Oh, what a good thing! She could make a start somewhere else!" But I realized that she was telling me that she decided to use the money "to win him back". She proposed to ignore his suggestion completely, but do you know what she did?'

'Bought him back with two hundred?'

'As near as! She blew the lot on having her hair dyed and restyled. She bought masses of new clothes. She had a face-lift and heaven knows what else. Then she calmly waited for him to fall in love with her all over again.'

'And did he?'

'I think not. He was even more subdued after that little escapade; but she did succeed as she intended to do.'

Amy sighed.

'You can imagine my feelings on hearing this tale. I was absolutely furious. At that age I thought I should have let the man have his way, and gone off myself, rejoicing in the two hundred which would keep me going until I found a suitable job. To crawl around trying to get him back was the last thing I should have done. I was so shocked by my aunt's attitude that I said nothing. Perhaps it was as well.'

'And how do you feel now about it?'

Amy looked at me steadily.

'I'm thirty years older and wiser. I know now how Aunt Winifred felt. To put it at its lowest level first – why should she give up her bed and board, and all the settled ways of a lifetime simply because he wanted to opt out of a solemn contract they had made? Why should she – the innocent party – shatter her own life simply because he wanted to be unfaithful?

'On a slightly less material plane, she realized, I know – and now that I'm facing the same problem I know how much it hurts – that one can't just destroy a shared life by walking away. The memories, the experiences, the influences one has had on the other, have simply made you what you are, and they can never be completely wiped out.'

Amy reached for a piece of grass and began to nibble it thoughtfully. Her voice was steady, her eyes dry. It seemed to me that this outpouring was the fruit of much suffering and tension. One could only hope it would give her relief, and I was glad to be able to play the role of passive friend.

'And then, of course, Aunt Winifred was a religious woman and took her marriage vows seriously. When she was told that God had joined them together and that no man, or woman should put them asunder, then she believed it without a shadow of doubt. I'm sure she stuck to Uncle Peter as she did because she felt sure he would be committing a mortal sin and must be saved from this truly wicked temptation. She told herself – as God knows I've told myself often enough – that this was a kind of madness which would pass if she could only hold on.'

Amy threw away her ruined grass stalk.

'And she did, and the marriage held, and I don't think she ever chided Uncle Peter about the affair. But for all that, it could never be quite the same again. You can't be hurt as much as that and get away without the scars.'

There was a little silence, broken only by the mewing of a seagull, balancing in the air nearby.

'And will you hold on?' I ventured.

Amy nodded slowly.

'I've learnt that much from Aunt Winifred. In the end, the outcome may not be the same, but I've more sense now, than I had thirty years ago, than to fling off in high independence and precipitate things.'

She turned to me suddenly and smiled.

'And another thing, I'm so awfully fond of the silly old man. We've shared too much and for too long to be pettish with each other. I'm not throwing that away lightly. That's the real stuff of marriage which you lucky old spinsters, with your nice uncomplicated lives, can't appreciate. It's an enrichment. It's fun. It's absorbing – more so, I imagine, if you have a family – and so you just don't destroy it, but nurture it.'

She sprang to her feet, took my one good hand in hers and heaved me upright.

287

'Come along, Nelson,' she said, as I adjusted my sling. 'Toplou is some way off. Think of those fortunate monks who have no such problems as mine!'

We piled the remains of our picnic into the basket, and picked our way back to the car.

Amy's spirits had recovered. She chanted as we headed east-ward:

'And miles to go before I sleep
And miles to go before I sleep.'

11. *Toplou*

The monastery of Toplou stood like a fortress silhouetted against the grey sky. We approached it by a tortuous road, snaking up the hillside.

The wind grew stronger as we ascended, and a fine drizzle of rain misted the windscreen. At the summit, we drove across bumpy grass into a deserted forecourt.

The wind buffeted us as we emerged from the car, and went towards the cliffs' edge. We stood on a headland, the dark sea hundreds of feet below us clawing with white foamy tentacles at the rocks below. Sea-birds screamed and wheeled, floating like scraps of paper in the eddies of wind. It was too rough to talk. The wind blew into our mouths, snatching words away, making us gasp with shock.

There was no one in sight. A disused mill, sails gone, and one salt-bleached door hanging awry, stood nearby. At its footings, a dozen or so scrawny chickens scratched and pecked, scurrying away with clucks of alarm, as we struggled by them.

It was more sheltered in the courtyard, but equally deserted. A verandah ran round the four sides, at first floor level, and large rusty tins were ranged at intervals. Once they had acted as window-boxes, it would seem, but now, rust-streaked and battered, only a few dead stock plants protruded from them.

Everywhere the paint was flaking, and the walls were streaked with the rain-trickles of many seasons. This famous Christian monastery, built by the Venetians 600 years earlier to withstand the assaults of the infidel Turks across the water, presented a pathetic sight close to, in contrast with the magnificence of its aspect when viewed from afar.

We approached a door and knocked. There was no sign of life. We looked about us as we waited. Someone, somewhere, lived in this sad place. A tattered tea towel flapped from a make-shift wire line, destined never to dry whilst the misty air encompassed all.

We knocked again, louder this time, but with the same result. Disconsolate, we began to explore further. A dark archway seemed to lead to another courtyard. A broom was propped against a wall. A bucket stood nearby. Were those potato peelings in its murky depths?

We tried another door. This time we began to open it gently after our preliminary knocks had brought no answer. The handle was rough and gritty to our touch, eroded by the salt air, clammy in our palms.

'May we come in?' we cried into the twilit room.

There was a responsive rumbling, and the sound of a chair being pushed back upon stones. A monk, in his black habit smiled a welcome. I suspect we had woken him from a nap.

He spoke little English. We had no Greek, but he nodded and smiled, and led the way across the courtyard to the chapel. He was obviously very proud of it. His face was lined and tired, I thought, although he could not have been much more than forty, but it lit up with happiness as he conducted us from one ikon to another and stood back to let us study them.

Truth to tell, the place was so dark, and the ikons so dimly lit that I am sure we saw less than half of the beauties with which he was familiar. But we admired them, and followed our guide on a further tour of inspection.

It was uncannily quiet. Our companion was the only living soul we saw. Could the other monks be away for the day, or locked somewhere in mediation or prayer? We did not like to inquire, and in any case could not possibly ask for enlightenment in the primitive sign language we were obliged to use for communication.

We followed him through a long room which reminded me so sharply of Fairacre's village hall that a pang of homesickness swept over me. Wooden chairs were ranged all round the walls. A billiard table took up the major part of the room, and photographs hung awry on the walls.

Everywhere lay dust. The smell of sea-damp clung about the rooms, and the banisters and rails were sticky with the all-pervading salty air.

Our host continued to smile and to point out objects of

interest – a framed text, incomprehensible of course, to us, an archway, a window. At last we came back to the door where we had met him. What, we wondered, did we do about alms-giving? We noticed a wooden platter on a low shelf, just inside the door, in which a few coins lay. We put our own upon them, looking questioningly at our guide, who nodded and smiled and bowed.

He held our hands in farewell. His were cold and bony, and with a rare maternal urge I wished suddenly that I could cook him a luscious meal and build a good fire, to keep out the desolation of the place.

We retraced our steps. I was chilled to the marrow, and would have been glad to climb back into the car, but Amy strode across to a white marble war memorial hard by the deserted mill, and I followed her.

The monastery itself had been forlorn enough, but here was the very essence of sadness. Against the foot of the cross was propped a wreath of brown dead laurel leaves. Above it, the inscription was streaked with brown stains. Dead grass shuddered in the wind from the sea, and nearby an old fruit cage, its wire broken and rusty, protected nothing but a jungle of tall grass bleached white by the salt winds, and rustling like the wings of a flock of birds.

Another chapel stood beyond it. It too was deserted, some of the windows broken and boarded. On this magnificent headland, in its proud position as one of the bastions of Christianity, it was infinitely sad to see this once-loved, splendid place, so desolate and forlorn.

We returned in silence to the car, too moved to speak, until we had wound our way down the great hill and reached the road again.

This experience had made us pensive, and I reflected, as we drove in silence, upon the life of the monk, living in chill discomfort, in that remote place high above the sea. For once, my smugness at contemplating the single life was shaken. I felt again the touch of the cold thin hand in mine, the gritty dampness of the surrounding walls, the dust, the darkness.

And, for a moment, I looked upon a lot which might well be mine and other solitary old people's in the future, where loneliness and bleakness stalked, and even the light of religious beliefs could do little to comfort.

I shivered, and Amy patted my knee with a warm hand.

Thank God for friends, I thought gratefully.

Our spirits rose as we took a roundabout route back to the hotel. The clouds lifted, and the blue Cretan sky was above us again.

We stopped in Kritsa, a village we had grown to love, a few miles from our hotel. It lay in the hills among olive and carob groves, and there were wonderful walks nearby, as we had discovered.

We sat on a log on the side of the hill, our feet in the damp grass. In the distance we could see a woman on her balcony busy spinning wool on a hand spindle. Nearer at hand, another woman dragged branches of carob tree towards three splendid white goats, who strained at their chains bleating madly. Their stubby tails flickered with excitement and anticipation, and as soon as the greenstuff was near enough they fell upon it, crunching the bean pods with every appearance of delight.

We walked down the hill and revisited the church. This was freshly whitewashed, and as spruce inside as out. Two dark-eyed children jostled each other as they rushed towards us, a bunch of wilting flowers in their hands, hoping for custom.

There were two letters for me when we returned, which I welcomed with cries of joy. Why is it that letters when away are so much more satisfying than those that drop through one's own letter box?

One was from the kennels assuring me that Tibby had settled down well, was eating everything put before her, including the dried food which is spurned at home, and seemed well content.

How typical of a cat, I thought sourly. At home, she will reject anything from a tin, and all forms of dried cat food. Rabbit, from *China* not *Australia*, is welcomed, preferably still warm from her personal casserole, raw meat cut very small, and occasionally poached fish. Her tastes are far too extravagant for a teacher's budget, but I weakly give in. Now, it seemed, she wolfed everything in sight, and made me appear an even bigger ass than I am.

The other letter was from Mrs Partridge, the vicar's wife, and I thought how uncommonly kind she was to take time from all her commitments to cover three pages to me with all the news of Fairacre.

Mrs Pringle's bad leg had flared up again and Dr Martin had been to see her. However, she was still at work, both in the school and the school house. (I could foresee that I should have to express my gratitude and admiration to the martyr, when I returned, in terms as fulsome as my conscience would permit.) The Mawnes had held a coffee party which raised twenty-eight pounds, and would no doubt have raised more but it rained, which damped things. (Not surprising.)

Mr Mawne had high hopes of my returning with plenty of pictures of the hawk. Had I had any luck? The Coggs twins had gone down with measles, but appeared to be playing with all and sundry, as recommended by modern medical men – such a mistake; it would never have been allowed in their own nursery – so no doubt my numbers at school would be much depleted when term began.

She ended with high hopes for my complete recovery and kind regards to Amy.

'I am to pass on Mrs Partridge's kind regards,' I said, turning to her. She was engrossed in a letter of her own, and did not reply for a minute or two.

'Very sweet of her,' she remarked absently, looking up at last. She waved her own letter.

'From Vanessa. She wants a silk scarf trimmed with little gold discs. You can wear it over your head, she says, and somebody called Bobo, or maybe Baba – the child's handwriting is appalling – Dawson, brought one home from Greece recently and looks "Fantastic" – spelt with a "k" – in it.'

Amy looked inquiringly at me.

'Have you seen such a thing?'

'There are lots in the hotel shop.'

'Must be white, black or a "yummy sort of raspberry pink",' said Amy, consulting the letter.

'I think I saw a black one.'

'Then we'll snap it up as soon as the shop opens,' said Amy decisively. 'I'm not trying to track down "a yummy sort of raspberry pink". By the way, Gerard's been up to Scotland again. It does look hopeful, doesn't it?'

'He's bound to be there quite a bit,' I pointed out reasonably, 'if he's doing this book on Scottish poets.'

Amy snorted.

'He's staying at Vanessa's hotel, and she sounds delighted to see him. I should say there's definitely something cooking there. Here, would you like to read her letter?'

'Read all about Fairacre in return,' I said, as we exchanged missives, and I settled back in the armchair to decipher Vanessa's sprawling hand. Amy certainly had the best of this bargain, I thought, remembering Mrs Partridge's immaculate copperplate.

'This Hattie May,' I said, struggling laboriously through the letter, 'she had tea with. Does she mean *the* Hattie May who was leading lady in all those musical comedies just after the war?'

'Must be, I suppose. She faded out after she married, I remember.'

'Well, Vanessa says that she is now a window – widow, presumably – and happily settled in a cottage near their hotel. I think I saw her in everything she did. What a dancer!'

'Come to think of it,' said Amy, putting down Mrs Partridge's letter, 'she mentioned her when she stayed with me last. Hattie May was living in the hotel then and looking for a permanent home. Nice of her to invite Vanessa out. I sometimes wonder if the child is lonely up there. Scotland always seems such an empty sort of country.'

'That's its attraction. Anyway, Gerard told you that there were lots of young men who were being attentive, and I can't imagine a stunning-looking female like Vanessa being short of companions.

'You're probably right,' agreed Amy. 'And anyway, I imagine Gerard is to the forefront of the attentive ones. I hope he can persuade Vanessa to become a little more literate when they are married.'

'Amy!' I cried, 'you are incorrigible! Let's go and change.'

'And then,' said Amy, 'we must do Vanessa's shopping. I have a feeling I shall never be paid for it.'

We had a splendid dinner, as usual, with lamb cooked in a particularly succulent sauce made with magnificent Cretan tomatoes and a touch of garlic. Afterwards we pottered round the shop and Amy bought a black scarf for Vanessa and some silver pendants for presents.

My purchases were more modest and consisted of attractive tiles which I hoped would be acceptable to Mrs Pringle and other kind souls who had made the holiday possible. Amy was admiring one of the beautiful gold plaited belts, and resisting temptation with remarkable strength of will. They were certainly expensive, and I hoped that she would not weaken and buy one, as I fully intended to get her one myself as a little thank-offering for her generosity over the past few weeks.

She left the belts reluctantly, and we returned to our little house with our purchases. The moon was out, and the night was calm.

We went out and descended the steps through the sweet-smelling night air. The scent of the lilies hung heavily about us. We walked in amicable silence along the seashore. Little waves splashed and sucked at the sand, and a flickering silvery pathway lay across the sea to the moon. It was one of those moments I should remember for the rest of my life, I knew.

We were in bed early that night, and Amy was asleep long before I was. Somehow, sleep evaded me. I could not get the memory of Toplou from my mind. That deserted place, with the wind crying in its courtyards, haunted me. And the tired patient face of the monk, so gently smiling and polite, floated before me in the moonlight. He seemed to embody the spirit of his surroundings, the lost splendour and the forgotten ardour.

The experience had shaken me, for it had presented me with the stark surprising fact that single people can be lonely. My own solitary state had always been a source of some secret pride to me. I was independent. I could do as I liked.

Now I had seen the other side of the coin, and found it daunting.

All my old night-time fears came flocking back. Suppose my health gave way? Suppose I outlived all my friends? And why didn't I set about buying a little house *now*, instead of shelving the idea? Someone else, all too soon, would need the school house when they took over my post. I must start facing things, or the bleakness of the monk's life would be echoed in mine.

Perhaps Amy was right to be so engrossed in matchmaking. Crippled though she was, at the moment, by the blows to her own marriage, maybe she was being true to a proper urge, something natural and normal, when she took such a keen interest in Vanessa's future. Some inner wisdom, as old as mankind itself, stirred Amy's endeavours. Maybe, in my comfortable arrogance, I was missing more than I cared to admit.

I thought how smug I had been when married friends had told me of their problems. How perfunctorily, for instance, I had disposed of Mrs Clark's dilemma. The truth was, I told myself severely, that, as in all things, celibacy has its good and bad sides. Nine times out of ten I was happy with my lot, which was as it should be. If I have to live by myself, it is as well to be on good terms with myself.

On the other hand, this salutary jolt would do me no harm. Toplou had made me suddenly aware, not only of the sadness of the solitary, but the warmth of loving companionship, which Amy had spoken of so movingly, which marriage can bring.

The dawn was flushing the sky with rose, and the small birds were twittering among the trees, before I finally fell asleep.

12. *The Last Day*

The last day of our holiday arrived much too quickly. My feelings were divided. On one side, I hated the idea of leaving this lovely place, probably for ever, for I doubted if I should be able to come again. On the other hand, the thought of going home to the waiting house and garden, to wicked Tibby and to all my Fairacre friends was wonderfully elating. I remembered Amy's amusement at my excitement on returning home from Bent. But surely wasn't that as it should be? How dreadful life would be if home were not the best place in it.

We decided to potter about the town and hotel rather than make a long excursion. We were to start at the gruelling time of five-thirty the next morning, catching an aeroplane from Heraklion a little before eight. If all went well, we should be home about tea-time.

After breakfast, Amy drove the car back to the garage from which we had hired it, and I was left to my own devices. The first thing I did was to hurry to the shop and select the finest gold belt available, taking advantage of Amy's absence.

Having secreted it among my pile of packing. I took my camera and set out on a last-minute filming expedition. A small private boatyard adjoined the hotel, and here I had been watching a young couple painting their boat in white and blue, with here and there a touch of scarlet. It was most attractive, and with the blue sea, and sky beyond it, would make a perfect colour photograph.

Then there were close-ups of some of the exotic flowers to take. I might have fallen down badly on Mr Mawne's Cretan hawk, but I intended to have something noteworthy to show the Women's Institute at some future meeting in Fairacre's village hall.

I was hailed by a voice as I passed the Clarks' house. Mrs Clark was sunning herself on the verandah.

'Are you off today?'

I said we were, unfortunately.

'We're staying another week. Do come and sit down. John has walked down to the town to get the newspapers.'

I sank into a deckchair and closed my eyes against the dazzling sunshine.

'I wonder if I shall ever feel sun as hot as this again at ten-thirty in the morning.'

'Of course you will. I've no doubt you'll come again next year, or sometime before long.'

'And what about you?'

'More hopeful, my dear. We are staying on this extra week for the express purpose of looking for something to rent, probably for a few months next winter.'

'So you are still thinking of coming here to live?'

Mrs Clark's expression became a trifle grim.

'John is. He found the most appalling house in Malia. Far too big, needing three servants at least, and crumbling into the bargain. I can't make him realize that, if I do come, we simply must have something we can manage on our own. We shall be far from rich on an army pension, and John still seems to imagine we shall have batmen hovering round us. I've persuaded him to try a short period here before we do anything drastic. I must say, he's agreed very readily.'

'It seems sensible,' I said.

'Well, we have to adapt, otherwise marriage could be a very uncomfortable state.'

She shifted her chair so that her face was in the shade. Her legs, I noticed, were a far more beautiful shade of brown than my own.

'Have you read *Mansfield Park*?' she asked unexpectedly.

'Constantly.'

'Do you remember a passage near the beginning when the Crawfords discuss matrimony? Mary Crawford says something to the effect that we are all apt to expect too much,"but then if one scheme of happiness fails, human nature turns to another – we find comfort somewhere." I often think of that. It's very true, and no marriage will work unless there is a willingness to adapt a little. I've no doubt we'll end very comfortably, one way or the other. The danger is in making long-term decisions too quickly, and I'm glad that I've made John see that.'

She sighed and wriggled her bare toes in the sunshine.

'Why I should worry you with my affairs, I can't think. It's that sympathetic face of yours, you know.'

There was the sound of footsteps on the path, and John appeared with the newspapers.

'I must go,' I said, after we had exchanged greetings. 'I'm off to take photographs of all the things I meant to take days ago. I shall see you again before we go.'

I left them together, John in my vacated chair. They were smiling at each other.

Plenty of give-and-take there, I thought, going on my way. But I hoped she would win.

We had our last lunch at a favourite restaurant nearby. Here the shrimps seemed to be larger than ever, the salads even more delicious. Two cats attended us, and obligingly cleared up the shrimps' heads and tails. Would Tibby have been so helpful? Perhaps, after her Spartan fare at the kennels . . .

We sauntered back, replete, to the welcome shade of our little house, and lay on our beds to rest. Outside, the light and heat beat from the white walls. All was quiet, wrapped in the hush on the beach below us.

'Must remember to put out my air-sick pills, yawned Amy. 'That's the thing to take shares in, you know. Wholesale chemists. When you think of the handful of pills the GPs hand out these days, you can't go wrong.'

'I'll remember,' I said, 'when I don't know what to do with my spare cash.'

'My Aunt Minnie,' went on Amy languidly, 'left me some hundreds of shares in something call Nicaraguan Railways or Peruvian Copper. I can't quite recall the name, but something far-flung in the general direction of South America. They bring in a dividend of about thirty-five pence every half year. James says for pity's sake sell 'em, but I don't like to. She was a dear old thing, though addicted to musical evenings, and she left me a beautiful ring.'

'The one you're wearing?'

Amy has a square-cut emerald which is my idea of a perfect ring.

'No. This is part of the product of five hideous rings my dear mother left me. She was left four of them by her older sisters, and every one was the same setting – a row of five diamonds like a tiny sparkling set of false teeth. I sold them when she died, and bought this instead, and put the rest in the Caxley Building Society. Very useful that money has been too, for this and that.'

Silence fell. It was very hot, even in our stone-built house, but I gloried in it. How long before I saw sunshine like this again, I wondered? Amy's eyes were closed and I was beginning to plan my packing when she spoke again.

'Did you have musical evenings when you were young? Aunt Minnie's were real shockers, especially as she made me accompany the singers, who were no keener on my assistance than I was on their efforts. She had a baby grand, covered with a horrible eastern scarf thing, ornamented with bits of looking-glass, and *nothing* would persuade her to open the lid. Mind you, it would have been a day's work to clear off all the silver-framed photographs, not to mention the arrangement of dried grasses. We all just soldiered on, while Aunt Minnie nodded her head and tapped her foot in approximate time to the music.'

'We got stuck with oratorios mainly,' I remembered. "Penitence, Pardon and Peace", "Olivet to Calvary", "The Crucifixion". My father could sing very well. Unfortunately, I couldn't play very well. Tempers used to get rather frayed, until we fell back on something simpler, like "The Lost Chord" or "Merry Goes The Time When The Heart Is Young".'

'I sometimes think,' said Amy, 'that people of our generation who are constantly mourning "the good old days" must have forgotten such things as musical evenings and starched knickers, and washdays tackled with yellow soap and a washboard.'

'And button-hooks that pinched your flesh, and elastic driving you mad under your chin,' I added. 'Children have such lovely clothes these days. No wonder they learn to dress themselves so much earlier than we did.'

'A case of have to, I expect, with all the mums having to rush off to work.'

Amy grunted contentedly and turned her face into the pillow. Peace descended again, and I lay listening to the gentle splashing of the waves and the chirruping of a nearby cricket until I too drifted into sleep.

We slept for over an hour and woke much refreshed.

'Let's ring for tea here,' suggested Amy, 'and remind them about early breakfast. What hopes of bread rolls. I wonder?'

It had been a standing joke. Each morning our tray had arrived with one bread roll each, a sweetish confection rather like a Bath bun without sugar, and a slice of sultana cake. Accompanying these things was a small dish of unidentifiable jam.

The bread rolls were excellent. The other things too cloying for our taste first thing in the morning. Marmalade we had on one unforgettable occasion. Our telephone conversation with the kitchen staff ran on the same lines each morning.

'Hello. This is room twenty-eight.'

'Ullo. Good morning. Breakfast?'

'Please, for two. Coffee for two.'

'Coffee for two.'

'Bread rolls for two. NO BUNS OR CAKE, PLEASE.'

'Bread rolls. No ozzer zings?'

'No, thanks. Just bread rolls.'

'Just blead rolls.'

'And *marmalade*, please, not jam.'

'Just marmalade. No nice jam?'

'No, thanks.'

'Bleakfast coming.'

'Thank you.'

'Okay. You're welcome.'

And within a few minutes the waiter would arrive with a beaming smile, and a few words of English, and a laden tray with exactly the same food as before.

'We might just as well save our breath,' Amy had said. But

I disagreed. It was part of the fun to keep trying, and as I pointed out, we had been given marmalade *once*.

I must say it seemed odd that with oranges and lemons bowing the trees to the ground with the weight of their fruit, marmalade seemed to be looked upon as a luxury. As it was, we had been obliged to buy a jar in town, and very poor stuff it was, reminding me of the jam manufacturer who made a fortune from his product SPINRUT, the main ingredient of which can be readily recognized by those who can read backwards.

Our tea tray arrived, and we were told that, as we had to make such an early start, our breakfast would be delivered in the evening, with the coffee in a flask. We received the news stoically, as befitted Britishers.

'At least it will wash down the Kwells,' Amy pointed out. 'Let's go and get some air.'

It was still too hot for much exertion, but we strolled in the shade of the trees, and watched the more energetic holiday-makers swimming in the pool. A gardener was pushing a hand mower very carefully and slowly over two tiny lawns. The hose and sprinkler lay nearby. I wished my lawn at Fairacre received such love. It would be the showpiece of the village. It was sad to think that this time tomorrow I should not be here to see the sprinkler at work on those two thirsty patches.

Later, after dinner, we took a last walk through the streets of Aghios Nikolaos, and stopped for coffee at our favourite café.

The night was velvety dark, and we sat at a table near the water's edge. The sea slapped the bottom of the moored boats as they swayed at anchor. Out to sea, a lighted ferry boat chugged across to Piraeus, and I wished that one day I might visit Greece itself.

As though reading my thoughts, Amy said: 'We haven't seen nearly enough, of course. Next time we must stop in Athens, and then come on to Crete and see the western end. The thing to do would be to spend six months or a year in these parts.'

'I can't see our Education Committee giving me leave of absence for that time,' I observed.

'If things don't turn out well at home,' said Amy slowly, 'it's a comfort to think there's so much to do here. I shall hang on to the idea. It would be a life-line to sanity, wouldn't it? I mean, in the presence of civilizations as old as these, one's own troubles seem pretty insignificant, Or so I've found, anyway,' she added, 'during the past fortnight.'

'I'm more glad than I can say, to hear you say that,' I told her soberly.

'And I can't thank you enough for coming. You've been the perfect companion for an old misery like me.'

'*Thank me*?' I cried. 'Why, it's entirely —'

But Amy cut me short.

'One word of thanks from you, my dear, and I shall throw these sandals you've just kicked off, into the sea, and you'll have to walk back to the hotel barefoot!'

The threat sufficed. Amy had won, as usual. We took our time over the coffee, and lingered to look at the sea on our way home.

Sure enough, on the low table in our room the breakfast tray waited for us. It was covered with a snowy cloth.

When we came to investigate we found one bread roll, one bun, one slice of cake and a dish of dark brown (fig?) jam apiece. Two stout flasks flanked our empty cups.

'Well, there we are,' said Amy, replacing the cloth. 'How about that at five in the morning? I don't think I'll be able to face a thing.'

'I shall,' I said robustly. 'Just think how far it is to England! Why, we may not be able to eat on the plane.'

'I shan't want to,' replied Amy, putting her Kwells on the tray, with a sigh.

We undressed and climbed into our beds for the last time. I meant to lie awake for a little, savouring all the pleasures of scent and sound that came drifting from the garden at night, but I scarcely had time to arrange my pillow before sleep overcame me, and a few minutes after that, it seemed, the telephone was trilling, telling us to get up in readiness for our departure.

13. *Going Home*

It was still dark when we set off along the bumpy road to Heraklion, but by the time we were in the aeroplane, the sky was filled with rows of little pink clouds, made glorious by the sunrise.

We circled the island, and I wondered, with a pang, if I should ever set foot there again. The experience had opened my eyes to a larger, more beautiful world, to an ancient culture happier than our own, and had given me a glimpse of 'the glory that was Greece'.

I felt wonderfully refreshed, and my arm and ankle were so much better that I discarded my sling whenever possible. Prudence, however, made me wear it on the flight. One gets jostled quite badly enough during travel when hale and hearty. With a slowly-knitting bone, I intended to take all precautions.

We made an unscheduled stop at Athens. The workmen were still pushing screaming machines over the marble floor, and the dust was as thick as ever. However, we found a cup of good coffee, and a very nasty chocolate biscuit apiece, while we waited, and then we were herded aboard the new aeroplane.

Amy had taken her Kwells, with a swig of flask coffee and much shuddering, and dozed for most of the journey. I had insisted that she sat by the window this time, so that I was in the middle seat of the three. There were a good many empty seats, so that I was somewhat surprised when a lone female came to sit by me.

'Haven't I seen you in Aghios Nikolaos?' she began.

I said indeed she might have done.

'I saw your friend had dropped off, and thought you might be glad of some company,' she said.

'How kind of you.'

'Well, I'm a schoolteacher, and I should think you are too, so I thought we might have something in common.'

Now, I am not ashamed of being a schoolteacher, rather the reverse, when I consider that I am still strong and healthy after so many years of classroom battling, but there is something depressing in being told that one wears one's profession like a brand upon one's forehead – the mark of a beast, in fact.

I said civilly that yes, I was a schoolteacher.

'There's a look, isn't there?' she prattled.

'Downtrodden? Hungry? Mad?'

'Not quite that. Shabby perhaps, and not much given to dressing well and making-up properly.'

This was really hard. I had visited the hairdresser at the hotel the night before, and she had given her all. Never had I looked so *bouffant*, so glossy, and so truly feminine. The sunshine had produced high-lights which I had never before seen in my normal mouse and I was looking forward to dazzling Fairacre with my new glamour, and my suntan.

I was also wearing an expensive – for me – pale pink linen dress and jacket, and Aunt Clara's seed pearls, not to mention new white sandals. And here was this stranger, bursting in upon my previous solitude, and generally undermining my self-confidence.

I was catty enough to notice her own crumpled floral print frock and dirty white cardigan, and also her undistinguished coiffure, but was humane enough to forbear to comment. Really, civility puts almost too great a strain on mankind at times.

Primitive woman, I reflected, under provocation, would have torn the greasy hair from this person's head in handfuls, and felt very much better for the exercise.

Instead, I asked her where she had stayed in Aghios Nikolaos and she mentioned a hotel near our own, which we had visited for lunch once.

'If I'd the money,' she said, 'I should have stayed where you were, but you can't do that on a teacher's salary.'

She sounded suspicious, and I wondered if she thought I had some secret source of income – heroin, perhaps, smuggled in the heels of my new shoes. Obviously, in her eyes, my age and dowdy appearance would exonerate me from any other immoral activity.

I did not rise to the bait, but asked if she had far to go when we reached Heathrow, and she told me that she lived at Chatham near the docks, and would be met by her fiancé and his twin brother. They were *exactly* alike, and went everywhere together.

I asked when she hoped to get married, and wondered, but didn't ask, if both twins would be together on the honeymoon.

'Next Easter,' she said, and went on to ask where I lived. I told her.

'It's so pretty round there,' she said enthusiastically. I agreed.

'You wouldn't like to exchange houses, I suppose? It sounds a lovely place for a honeymoon, and Chatham would make a nice change for you.'

'Frankly, no. I seldom leave home,' I said shortly.

I put one of my magazines firmly upon her knee, and opened my own.

She looked aggrieved, but opened it obediently, and silence fell.

I glanced at comatose Amy. One eye opened and shut again in a conspiratorial wink. Amy doesn't miss much.

A few minutes later she roused herself and sat up with a yawn.

'What a lovely nap! What's the time?'

The stranger told her, returned my magazine and stood up.

'I'll go back to my seat now,' she said, showing more tact than I imagined she had. On the other hand, it was said so primly, that maybe she had taken offence at my disobliging refusal to exchange houses. Whatever the reason, it was a great relief to see her depart, after such an unnerving encounter in mid-air.

We were late arriving at Heathrow and we seemed to wait for hours around the revolving contraption that disgorges one's luggage. Why is it, I wondered, that other people's luggage always seems superior in size, quality and polish to one's own? I was somewhat cheered by watching a red-faced man, very much like our local farmer Mr Roberts, collecting his pieces of battered luggage, each securely lashed with orange binder twine.

'I've lost two good leather straps up here in my time,' he said, catching my eye. 'They won't bother with binder twine, and if they do there's plenty more where that came from.'

Amy rang the garage whilst I collected our bags, and hours later, it seemed, we settled ourselves into her car.

The air was chilly, the clouds like a grey tent, low over us. Rain lashed the tarmac, umbrellas glistened all around, and goose-pimples stood on our arms. One could almost feel the tan fading.

We were in England again.

'What an extraordinary woman that was,' commented Amy, as we drove from the airport. 'I noticed her once or twice when we were walking about the town. She seemed to be holidaying alone.'

'I'm not surprised.'

'A typical case of someone who lives alone,' continued Amy, hooting at the motorist in front of us who had signalled that he was going left for the last half-mile, then right, and eventually went straight on.

'How do you mean?'

'Well there's a tendency for solitary people – *some* of them, I should say – to tag on to complete strangers and engage them in conversation. Lonely, of course, that's all, but a trifle disconcerting for those button-holed. And then these loners never stop talking. Most exhausting. I must say, you choked off that poor dear in a brutally efficient way.'

I began to feel qualms on two counts.

'I hope I wasn't brutal,' I said.

'Let's say *decisive*,' said Amy, 'and I really don't blame you after such cheek on her part.'

'And I hope I don't waylay people and talk too much,' I added, expressing my second fear.

Amy laughed indulgently.

'You silly old dear! You've always talked too much!'

I digested this unpalatable truth as we drove towards Bent. We had arranged to go straight to Amy's house from Heathrow, when we planned the holiday. It was nearer than Fairacre, and we both felt that a good night's sleep after our flight would enable us to face the home chores before us.

As always, Amy's house presented a calm and beautiful aspect. There were flowers in every room, no signs of dust, everything immaculate and welcoming. There was even a tray laid ready for two complete with biscuit tin, and Amy lost no time in putting on the kettle.

A pile of letters stood on the hall table, and Amy looked at it anxiously as we brought in her luggage from the car.

'I'll tackle that later,' she said.

I was in my old bedroom overlooking the corn fields. In the driving rain nothing was moving. No doubt the farmers were cursing all around, I thought, for some of the fields I could see were only half-cut.

But despite the rain, my spirits were high. We were home again, back among the wet fields, the dripping trees, the little runnels of brown rainwater chattering along the roadside. I thought of those two parched lawns at the hotel, as I gazed at Amy's lush slopes before me. A thrush, head cocked on one side, was listening for a worm, and three sparrows searched among the plants in the border, with raindrops splashing on their little tabby backs. Somewhere, far away, a sheep bleated, and another answered it. The fragrance of wet earth and leaves was everywhere, and I thanked heaven for the sights and scents of home.

Later that evening, Amy read her correspondence, sorting it into piles very tidily, while I read a gardening magazine and learnt about all the things I should have done last spring in order to have a flourishing flower border next season.

'Too late,' I said aloud.

'What is?'

'Taking pipings and cuttings, and sowing seeds ready for planting out this autumn, and a hundred other things. It's an extraordinary thing, but whenever I rush to the nurseryman in autumn, fired to have some particular plant, then the right time to put it in was last spring. And, of course, when I rush

there in the spring, the particular plants I'm mad for should have gone in last autumn.'

'I must remember to give you a basic gardening book for Christmas,' said Amy severely. 'You sound the most haphazard gardener. It's a wonder yours looks as well as it does. Mr Willet, I suppose.'

She patted her piles of correspondence into neat stacks.

'Friends who won't mind waiting. Friends who will mind waiting. Business and bills,' she said surveying them.

'Well, bills could go on the won't-mind-waiting stack, I should think.'

Amy shook her head.

'I was brought up as you were, my dear, to pay as I went along. I've a perfect horror of owing money, born of a frugal upbringing. As for hire purchase, my blood runs cold at the thought. Suppose I suddenly had no money –'

She stopped, and looked out at the grey evening. When she spoke again, her voice had altered.

'A letter from James among this lot.' It was in the friends who-will-mind-waiting pile, I noticed. 'He's still pressing for a divorce. What a hopeless situation this is! I wonder what the outcome will be? I felt so strong and sensible while we were away, but now I'm back I feel as wobbly as a jellyfish.'

'Put it out of your mind,' I advised. 'You've had a long

day travelling. Things will seem saner after a night's sleep. And if I were you,' I added, 'I should transfer his letter to the friends-who-*won't*-mind-waiting pile.'

Amy laughed, and did so. It seemed to give her some comfort.

Next morning the sky was blue, and our breakfast table was bathed in sunshine. I presented Amy with the plaited gold belt, with which she was agreeably delighted. Beside my plate was a large square parcel which turned out to contain a splendid book of photographs of Crete with short accounts of the different places. It was a perfect memento of a perfect holiday.

We drove back to Fairacre by way of the kennels, where Tibby sat on top of her sleeping house, looking aloof. I stroked her head, and muttered endearments to which she responded with a yawn.

Only when she was safely in the car, secured in the cat basket, did she deign to give tongue, and then only to keep up the nerve-racking caterwauling by which she registers strong disapproval of car travel.

'I hope you've got a supply of the tenderer portions of the most expensive rabbit,' shouted Amy, above the din.

'It's "Pussi-luv" or nothing,' I shouted back. 'If she can eat it in the kennels, she can eat it at home.'

We turned into the school lane. My hedge seemed to have grown six inches in the past fortnight, and the lawn needed cutting. But the border was full of colour, despite my abortive forays to the nurseryman.

I felt under the third stone on the right of the porch, and withdrew the key. The door was difficult to open, because there was a pile of letters still on the mat. One was stuck in the letter box.

It was a note in Mrs Partridge's handwriting, and I put it aside to read later. Probably, a change of date for the WI, I thought.

We picked up the letters and put them on the hall table. Tibby was released, and bounded into the garden, giving us time to look around us.

Something was wrong. The house smelt musty. Everything was tidy, but a fine layer of dust was everywhere. Unlike Amy's house, there were no flowers. Usually, Mrs. Pringle does me proud with a handful of marigolds stuffed in a mug, but today there was nothing.

'Come and sit down,' I said to Amy. 'This is all very strange. Something must have happened to Mrs P. There may be a note in the kitchen.'

But there was no note. The paint had been washed, the windows cleaned, the sink whitened with bleach, the dish-cloth draped along its edge, stiff and dry, but here too, dust lay.

I filled the kettle for coffee, remembered Mrs Partridge's note and read it while the kettle boiled.

So sorry to tell you that Mrs. Pringle is in hospital – probably appendicitis, nothing very serious, but she was worried because she could not get in the last-minute provisions.

If you are not too tired, do have dinner with us tonight. Very simple. About 7.30. Longing to hear about Crete. Cordelia Partridge

I handed it to Amy, and set about putting out the cups, I was sincerely sorry for my old sparring partner in hospital, and remembered how kind she had been to me at the beginning of the holiday when I had had my accident.

'Poor old girl,' I said, spooning instant coffee into the cups. 'I must ring the hospital later on. I suppose she'll be at Caxley.'

'I expect all this "bottoming" brought it on,' said Amy, gazing at my dazzling paintwork.

'Don't rub salt in my wounds,' I begged her. 'I'm already suffering from remorse for all the things I've said to her in my time.'

'She can take it,' said Amy robustly. 'And anyway, she gives as good as she gets, from all I hear.'

She finished her coffee, and stood up.

'Must be off. Dozen of things to do at Bent, and you have just as many here, I can see.'

I waved good-bye to her, watching until the car turned the bend in the lane, and went back to the garden.

My new rose bush had a dozen or more coppery buds on it, and the lavender hedge was in full flower. A few bumble bees buzzed lazily among the blossoms, and Tibby approached and weaved herself round my legs affectionately.

I picked up the exasperating animal and gave her a hug. 'Tibby,' I told her. 'We're really home!'

PART THREE

Return to Fairacre

14. Mrs Pringle Falls Ill

There is no doubt about it, going away does one so much good because, for one thing, it makes one's home seem doubly desirable.

I pondered on this truth as I walked round to the vicarage under my umbrella. The hotel could not be faulted, but how much cosier the small rooms of the school house seemed, and what a blessing it was to drink cold water straight from the tap, instead of having tepid mineral water, tasting faintly of soda, from a bottle!

And how green everything was! I looked with approval at the glistening hedges, the flowers drenched with rain, and the great green flanks of the downs where the sheep were grazing. I even felt kindly towards a worm which was struggling on Mrs Partridge's doorstep, and transferred it to a luscious wet garden bed. There had been no worms in Crete.

'Come in! Come in!' cried the vicar, and to my surprise he clasped me close to his Donegal tweed jacket, and kissed me on both cheeks. I felt as though I had returned from some long exile in the salt-mines.

'My dear, she's come!' he announced, ushering me into the drawing room where Mrs Partridge sat knitting.

'Bootees,' she said, after we had exchanged greetings and I had been supplied with a glass of sherry. 'For the sale, dear, but I've made a most unfortunate mistake. Can you see?'

Certainly, there was something strangely awry with the garment.

'I think you've knitted a row or two with a piece of wool that was hanging down, and not the main line, if you follow me.'

'Oh dear, it's these glasses! I've mislaid my others. They're bound to turn up, they always do. Last time they were in the laundry book. So I'm driven to wearing these.'

'Shall I undo it for you?'

Mrs Partridge looked anguished.

'*Must you?* Shall we put it aside for a bit, and just enjoy our drinks?'

We did so, and I answered a volley of questions about the holiday, until I could ask about Mrs Pringle.

'I did try to ring the hospital,' I said. 'Three times, but the exchange didn't answer.'

'I know. What has happened to all those nice girls who used to be so obliging years ago. I simply don't know. I can remember, many a time, asking for a number and the girl would say: "If it's Mrs Henry you want, I'm afraid she's out shopping. I saw her go into Boots not five minutes ago." So friendly, and always had time to let you know about their families. Gerald used to find them such a help when people needed visiting.'

'Those times have gone,' I agreed. 'I suppose it would be all the same if one were lying with two broken legs and a fire in the house, though no doubt 999 might answer.'

Mrs Partridge nodded thoughtfully.

'Except that you would not be able to get to the phone with two broken legs and the fire might be your side of it.'

'Tell me about Mrs Pringle,' I said. One can't afford to be too literal.

It appeared that she was taken ill in Caxley on market day.

'In Woolworth's, and I must say the manager sounds a thoroughly sensible fellow and deserves promotion, for he fetched a doctor, and she was taken straight to Caxley hospital.'

The vicar intervened.

'Don't tell her what they found, my dear,' he advised his wife. 'We are eating soon.'

I was grateful to him. He knows of my squeamishness.

Mrs Partridge looked disappointed, but loyally kept to generalities.

'Top and bottom of it was that they operated within an hour or two, and she'll be there for another week at least. But nothing serious. In fact, the hospital sister said she was comfortable when I inquired. It seemed a funny way to describe it when I know for a fact she was slit – '

'*Cordelia!*' said the vicar warningly.

'Sorry, sorry! Well, anyway, poor Mr Pringle had to go in, of course, taking nighties and things, and brought back the shopping, and was too upset to unpack it until next day. So the fish, my dear, from that jolly fellow in the market, was absolutely uneatable, and the cat was furious, Mrs Willet told me. You see, it *knows* it has fish on Thursdays.'

'Do you think our dinner is ready?' inquired the vicar.

'Of course it is. Come along,' said Mrs Partridge rising from the web of knitting wool criss-crossing the armchair.

'Cold chicken and salad,' she said, leading the way. 'I did warn you it would be simple, but I wish now I'd put some soup to heat. It's such a miserable evening for a cold meal. Shall I do that?'

We dissuaded her, protesting that cold chicken and salad would be splendid, and entered the dining room.

The meal was delicious, and afterwards, back in the drawing room, with the bootee growing even more grotesque, I caught up with the Fairacre news. Measles, it seemed, was now rife, and Mr Roberts' cowman had gone down with it and was in a very bad way.

'Of course, it will have its brighter side for you,' said Mrs Partridge. 'There won't be so many children next term, which will be a help with Mrs Pringle laid up.'

'I suppose I'd better look for someone else to stand in.'

'Well, Minnie Pringle won't be able to come. There's a new baby due, any minute now.'

'That's a relief. I shan't feel obliged to ask her. After ten minutes of Minnie's company, I'm nearly as demented as she is.'

'If the worst comes to the worst,' said the vicar, 'the older children must just turn to and help with the cleaning. Do it yourself, you know,' he added, beaming with pride at being so up-to-the-minute.

Mr and Mrs Mawne, it appeared, were in Scotland for a holiday, and I felt somewhat relieved. It would give me a breathing space before having to confess that I had no photographs of the Cretan hawk. The new people at Tyler's Row were repainting their house. Miss Waters' bad leg was responding to Dr Martin's liniment, and her sister had offered to embroider a new altar cloth.

At this stage, an enormous yawn engulfed me, which I did my best to hide, without success.

'It's time you were in bed,' said Mrs Partridge, looking over the top of the blameworthy glasses. 'You've had two busy days.'

It was true that I was almost asleep, but I did my best to look vivacious as I thanked her for a truly lovely evening, and departed into the rain.

Some poor baby, I thought, as I tottered home, was going to have a very odd bootee. Ah well, we all have to come to terms with life's imperfections, and one may as well begin young.

As might be expected, the minute I climbed into bed sleep eluded me, and I lay awake thinking about possible substitutes for Mrs Pringle, without success. I was going to visit her the next day, and hoped that she might have someone in mind. Otherwise, it looked as though the vicar's suggestion might have to be put into action.

After two hours or so of fruitless worrying, I heard St Patrick's clock chime, and then one solitary stroke. Very soon after this I must have fallen asleep, for I had a vivid dream in which the vicar was officiating at a marriage ceremony, clad in an improbable pale blue surplice. The bride was my importunate friend on the flight from Crete, and the groom was the monk from Toplou. Neither appeared to be interested in the ceremony, but were engrossed in a chess set which was lodged on the font.

I wonder what a psychiatrist would make of this?

The next morning I rang the hospital to inquire after my school cleaner. Mrs Pringle, I was not surprised to learn, was comfortable, and would be ready to receive visitors between two and four in the afternoon.

This was my first attempt at driving since the accident, and I was mightily relieved to find that I could do all that was necessary with my arm and foot.

Mrs Pringle, regal among her pillows, greeted me with

unaccustomed warmth, and admired the roses I had cut for her.

'A good thing I was handy for the hospital when it happened,' she told me. 'If I'd been slaving away at your place with nobody to call upon, I doubt if I'd be alive to tell the tale.'

I expressed my concern, and took the opportunity of thanking her for all the hard work she had put in at the school house, but I don't think she heard. Her mind was too full of more recent events.

'Ready to burst!' she told me with relish. 'Ready to burst! A mercy I didn't have to be jolted all the way to the County. I'd never have lasted out.'

She looked around her. Patients in neighbouring beds had fallen silent and were presumably listening to her saga. Mrs Pringle lowered her voice to a conspiratorial whisper.

'I'll tell you all about it when I'm back home,' she promised. 'There's some things you don't like to mention in mixed company.'

'Quite, quite,' I said briskly, thanking my stars for the

postponement. It seemed a good opportunity to ask when she might be back at Fairacre.

'They don't tell you nothing here,' she grumbled. 'But I heard one of the nurses say something about next week, if all goes well. It don't look as though I'll be fit for school work for a bit. I've been thinking about it, and you know our Minnie's expecting again?'

I said I had heard.

'How she does it, I don't know,' sighed Mrs Pringle. I assumed that this was a rhetorical question, and forbore to respond.

'To tell you the truth, Miss Read, I've lost count now, what with his first family, and hers out of wedlock, and then these others. Then of course his eldest two are married and having families of their own. When I visit there – which isn't often I'm glad to say – there are babies all over the place, and I'm hard put to it to say whose are whose. Sometimes I wonder if Minnie knows herself.'

'No other ideas, I suppose?'

'There's Pringle's young brother, if you're really driven to it. He's quite handy at housework, but of course he'd have to come out from Caxley on the bus, and he's a bit simple. Nothing violent, I don't mean, but you'd have to watch your handbag and the dinner money.'

'It would be better to get someone in the village,' I said hastily, 'if we can find one.'

'There's no one,' said Mrs Pringle flatly, 'and we both knows it. How many wants housework these days? And specially school cleaning! Thankless job that is, everlasting cleaning up after dozens of muddy boots. I sometimes think I must be soft in the head to keep the job on.'

Mrs Pringle's face was assuming its usual look of disgruntled self-pity, and I felt it was time to go.

'You're a marvel,' I told her, 'and keep the school beautifully. You deserve a good rest. We'll find someone, you'll see, and if the worst comes to the worst we shall have to do as the vicar suggested.'

'What's that?' asked Mrs Pringle suspiciously, on guard at once.

'Do it yourselves.'

'God help us!' cried Mrs Pringle, rolling her eyes heavenwards.

I made my farewells rapidly, before she had a total relapse.

Mr Willet turned up in the evening to cut the grass.

'I meant to have it all ship-shape for you when you got back,' he apologised, 'but what with the rain, and choir practice, and giving the Hales a hand with their outside painting when the rain let up – well, I never got round to it.'

I assured him that all was forgiven.

'That chap Hale,' he went on, 'got degrees and that, and a real nice bloke for a schoolmaster, but to see him with a paint brush is enough to make your hair curl! Paint all down the handle, paint all down his arm, drippin' off of his elbow – I tell you, he gets more on hisself than the woodwork! You could do out the Village Hall with what he wastes.'

He paused for breath. 'And how's the old girl?' he inquired, when he had recovered it. 'Still laughing fit to split?'

I said she seemed pretty bobbish, and told him about the dearth of supplementary school cleaners.

Mr Willet grew thoughtful.

'One thing, she did the place all through before she was took bad. I reckon we can keep it up together till she's fit again. After all, we shouldn't need to light them ruddy stoves she sets such store by. They're the main trouble. Won't hurt some of the bigger kids to lend a hand.'

'That's what the vicar said.'

'Ah!' nodded Mr Willet, setting off to fetch the lawn mower, 'and he said right too! Our Mr Partridge ain't such a fool as he looks.'

A minute later he wheeled out the mower. Above the clatter I heard him in full voice. He was singing:

> God moves in a mysterious way,
> His wonders to perform.

15. *Term Begins*

As always, the last week of the school holidays flew by with disconcerting speed. I had time to put the garden to rights, and to do a little shopping, but a great many other things, mainly school affairs, were shelved.

Nevertheless, I found time to call on Mrs Pringle, now at home and convalescent, and discovered, as we had all thought, that it would be two or three weeks before the doctor would allow her to resume work.

There was simply no one to be found who could take on her job, even temporarily. A fine look-out, I told myself, for the future, when Mrs Pringle finally retired. She obviously greeted my do-it-yourself plans with mixed feelings.

'It's a relief not to have our Minnie messing about with things,' she announced. 'Or anyone else, for that matter. I likes to know where to lay my hands on a piece of soap or a new dish-cloth, and where to hide the matches out of Bob Willet's way. I don't say he thieves. I'm not one to speak ill of anybody, but he sort of *borrers* them to light that filthy pipe of his, and pockets 'em absent-minded. It's better there's no stranger trying to run the place.'

'I'm glad you like the idea,' I said. I was soon put straight.

'I *don't* like the idea!' boomed Mrs Pringle fortissimo. She spoke with such vehemence that I trembled for the safety of her operation scar.

'But what can I do?' she continued. 'Helpless, that's what I am, and I must just stand aside and watch them stoves rust, and the floor turn black, and the windows fur over with dust, while you and Bob Willet and the children turns a blind eye to it all.'

I said, humbly, that we would do our best, and that Mrs Willet had offered to oversee the washing-up at midday.

Mrs Pringle looked slightly mollified.

'Yes, well, that's something, I suppose. A drop in the ocean

322

really, but at least Alice Willet knows what's what, and rinses out the tea cloths proper. Tell her I always hangs 'em on that little line by the elder bush to give 'em a bit of a blow, and then they finishes off draped over the copper.'

I promised to do so, and made a hasty departure.

'And tell Bob Willet not to lay a finger on them stoves,' she called after me. 'There's no need to light them for weeks yet.'

I let her have the last word.

Certainly, there was no need for the stoves on the first day of term. As so often happens, it dawned soft and warm, the morning sky as pearly as a pigeon's wing, and the children appeared in their summer clothes.

They all seemed to be in excellent spirits as I passed through the throng from my house to the school, and as far as I could see, attendance would not be appreciably lower, despite the measles epidemic.

A few were disporting themselves on the pile of coke, as usual, and came down reluctantly when so ordered. Unseasonably, a number of the girls were skipping together in the remains of someone's clothes line.

They were chanting: '*Salt, mustard, vinegar.*'

And then, with an excited squeal: '*Pepper!*'

At which, the line twirled frenziedly, and some of the skippers were vanquished.

Three mothers waited with new children by the door, and I ushered them all in to enter the children for school.

Two I knew well, for both had sisters at the school, but the third was a stranger, a well-dressed dark-eyed boy of about nine.

'We're living at the cottage opposite Miss Waters,' his mother told me. 'My husband is at the atomic energy station.'

I remembered Mrs Johnson, who had lived there before, and prayed that the present tenant would not be such a confounded nuisance. She certainly seemed a pleasant person, and it looked as though Derek would be an intelligent addition to my class.

'Show Derek where to put his things, and look after him,' I said to Ernest, who was hovering near the door, anxious not to miss anything.

His mother made her farewells to the child briskly, smiled at us all and departed – truly an exemplary mother, I thought, and the boy went willingly enough with Ernest.

The other two would be entering the infants' class, and their mothers were rather more explicit in their farewells.

'Now, don't forget to eat up all your dinner, and ask the teacher if you wants the lavatory, and play with Susie at play time, and keep off of that coke, and use your hanky for lord's sake, child, and I'll see you at home time.'

Thus adjured, the children were taken into the infants' room, and I went out to call in the rest of my flock.

By age-old custom, the children are allowed to choose the hymn on the first morning of term. Weaning Patrick from 'Now the day is over', at nine in the morning, and Linda Moffat from 'We plough the fields and scatter', as being a trifle premature, we settled for 'Eternal Father, strong to save', for although we are about as far inland at Fairacre as one can get in this island, we have a keen admiration for all sea-farers, and in any case, this majestic hymn is one of our favourites.

The new child, Derek, was standing near the piano and sang well, having a pure treble which might perhaps earn him a place at a choir school one day, I thought.

After prayers, we settled to the business of the day. Only five children were absent from my class, three with measles, one with ear-ache, and Eileen Burton for a variety of reasons supplied by her vociferous class-mates.

'Gone up her gran's,' said Patrick.

'No, she never then,' protested John. 'She's gone to Caxley with her mum about something on her foot.'

'A shoe perhaps,' commented some wag, reducing the class to giggles and much explaining of the joke to those who had been too busy chattering themselves to hear.

When order was restored, a more seemly set of reasons was offered for her absence. Someone said she was shopping, John stuck to the foot story with growing vehemence, someone else was equally positive that her mum was bad, while Joseph Coggs' contribution was that she was all right last night because she'd gone scrumping apples with him up Mr Roberts' orchard.

At this innocent disclosure, silence fell. I took advantage of it to point out, yet again, the evils of stealing, and, finally, requested Ernest and Patrick to give out the school books in preparation for a term of solid work.

Temporarily chastened, they settled down to some arithmetic in their rough books, with only minor interruptions such as:

'I've busted the nib off my pencil.'

'Patrick never give me no book,' and other ungrammatical complaints which I, and thousands of other teachers, deal with automatically, with no disturbance to the main train of thought.

Before half an hour had gone by, however, the infants' teacher appeared at the partition door, holding one of the newcomers by the hand.

The little girl's face was pink with weeping. Tears coursed downward, and it was quite clear that the hanky, thoughtfully pinned by her mother to her frock, had not been used recently.

'Don't worry,' I said. 'Let her stay here with Margaret.' Margaret, motherly in her solicitude, did some much-needed mopping, some kissing and scolding, and took her to sit beside her in the desk. The tears stopped as if by magic.

'Perhaps she would like a sweet,' I said, nodding towards the cupboard where a large tin of boiled sweets is kept for just such emergencies.

Margaret went to get it. There was an expectant hush in the classroom as the children watched the little one select a pear drop. Would I? Wouldn't I?

'You'd better take the tin round,' I said.

One needs something to help the first day along.

The golden day crawled by, and at the end of afternoon school I sauntered through the village to the Post Office to buy National Savings' stamps before Mr Lamb put up his shutters.

This was one of the jobs I should have done during the past week, but somehow the lovely holiday with Amy had unsettled me, and getting back to the usual routine had been extremely difficult.

I found my mind roving back to that delectable island, thinking of the white goats tossing their heads up and down as they nibbled carob branches, of the bearded priests, dignified in their black Greek Orthodox robes, of the smiling peasant we had met up in the hills, carrying a curly white lamb under each arm and the old woman sitting on her doorstep to catch the last of the light, intent upon her handspinning.

That dazzling light, which encompassed all out there, was unforgettable. It served, too, to make me more aware of the subtleties of gentler colour now that I was at home.

As I walked to the Post Office I saw anew how the terra cotta of the old earthenware flower pot in a cottage garden matched the colour of the robin's breast nearby. The faded green paint of Margaret Waters' door was echoed in the soft green of her cabbages. The sweet chestnut tree near the Post Office was thick with fruit, as softly-bristled as young hedgehogs, and matching the lime-green tobacco flowers which are Mr Lamb's great pride.

Mrs Coggs was busy filling in a form, assisted by the postmaster. She wrote painfully and slowly, far too engrossed in the job to notice me, and I waited while Mr Lamb did his instructing.

'Now just your name, Mrs Coggs. Here, on this line.'

The pen squeaked, and I thought how patient he was, bending so kindly over his pupil. He moved, and a shaft of sunlight fell across Mrs Coggs' arms. I was disturbed to see that they were badly bruised, and so was the hand that held the pen so shakily.

'And here?' she asked, looking up.

'No, no need for you to fill that in. I can do that for you. That's all now, Mrs Coggs. I'll see to it.'

She gave a sigh of relief, and turned. I saw that one eye was black.

'Lovely day, miss. Had a nice holiday?'

'Yes, thank you. Are you all well?'

'Baby's teething, but the rest of us is doin' nicely.'

She nodded and smiled, and went out to the baby who was gnawing its fists in the pram.

'Doing nicely,' echoed Mr Lamb, when she had pushed the pram out of earshot. He put Mrs Coggs' form tidily, with others, in a folder.

'Beats me why she stays with that brute,' he went on. 'Did you see her arms? And that black eye?'

I nodded.

'I bet she copped that lot last Saturday. Arthur had had a skinful down at "The Beetle and Wedge", I heard. That chap drinks three parts of his wage packet – when he earns any, that is – and she's hard put to it to get the rent out of him.'

'I thought things seemed better now they were in a council house.'

Mr Lamb snorted, and began to open the folder holding savings' stamps without even asking my needs.

'Better? You'll never alter Arthur Coggs even if you was to put him in Buckingham Palace! Usual, I suppose?' he said, looking up.

'Yes, please.'

'Pity she never left him before all those children came. Now she's shackled, and he knows it. Gets her in the family way every two years or so, and there she is tied with another baby and another mouth to feed, poor devil.'

'I wonder how we can help,' I said, thinking aloud. 'It might be an idea to have a word with the district nurse.'

'If you're thinking she can help with the pill and that,' said Mr Lamb, 'you'll have to think again. If Arthur got wind of anything like that, he'd knock the living daylights out of the poor woman.'

He folded the stamps and I put them in my bag. To my surprise, he looked rather embarrassed as he scrabbled in the drawer for my change.

'Shouldn't be talking of such things to a single lady like you, I suppose.'

I said that I had been conversant with the facts of life for some time now.

'Yes, well, no doubt. But you can take it from me, miss, you've a lot to be thankful for, being single. When I see poor souls like Mrs Coggs coming in here, I wonder women get married at all.'

'Mrs Lamb seems happy enough,' I observed. 'Not all husbands are like Arthur Coggs, you know.'

'That's true,' conceded Mr Lamb. 'But nevertheless, you count your blessings!'

I pondered on Mr Lamb's advice as I walked back to the school house through the sunshine. It reminded me again of Amy's plight, of Mrs Clark's at the hotel, and of all the complications which, it seemed, married life could bring. Somehow, in the last few months, the advantages and disadvantages of the single and married states had been thrust before me with disconcerting sharpness.

After tea, still musing, I took a walk through the little copse at the foot of the downs. Honeysuckle was in flower in the hedges, and the wood itself was heavy with the rich smells of summer. Yes, I supposed that I should count my blessings, as Mr Lamb had said. I was free to come and go as I pleased. Free to wander in a summer wood, when scores of other villagers were standing over stoves cooking their husbands' meals, or were struggling with children unwilling to go to bed whilst the sun still shone.

And yet, and yet . . . Was I missing something as vital as Amy insisted? I remembered the sad monk at Toplou, the garrulous schoolteacher, the victim of loneliness, on the flight home, and a dozen more single people who perhaps were slightly odd when one came to think about them. But any odder than married ones?

I began to climb the path up the downs beside a wire fence. A poor dead rook had been hung there, as a warning, I supposed, to others. I looked at the glossy corpse with pity as it hang upside down, its beautiful wings askew, like some wind-crippled umbrella. How quickly life passed, and how easily it was extinguished!

I looked up at the downs and decided I should turn back. Moods of melancholy are rare with me, and this one had quite worn me out. What, I wondered, besides the encounter with Mrs Coggs, had brought it on? Could I, at my advanced age, be love-lorn, regretting my lost youth, pining for a state I had never known? A bit late in the day for that sort of thinking, I told myself briskly, and not the true case of my wistfulness anyway.

It appeared much more likely to be caused by the first day of term combined with an unusually nasty school dinner.

I returned home at a rattling pace, ate two poached eggs on toast, and was myself again.

16. Gerard and Vanessa

One afternoon, a week later, I stood at my window and watched large hailstones bouncing on the lawn like mothballs. With any luck, the children should have got home before this sudden summer storm had broken, and any loiterers had only themselves to blame.

I was carrying out my tea tray to the kitchen when the telephone rang. It was Amy.

'Are you free this evening?'

'Yes. Anything I can do?'

'Yes, please. Come over to dinner. Gerard and Vanessa are here, just arrived. He's on his way to town, and has a lunch appointment tomorrow. I've persuaded him to stay the night. Do say you'll come.'

I said I should love to and would be with them at seven-thirty if that suited her.

'Knowing you,' said Amy, 'you will be on the doorstep at seven-ten, asking what's on the menu. I warn you, mighty little! It's the company you're coming for!'

She rang off, and I was left to wonder how many times Amy has upbraided me for punctuality. Personally, I cannot bear to wait about for visitors who have been asked for seven or seven-thirty, and who elect to come at eight-fifteen while the potatoes turn from brown to black, and I stand enduring a fit of the fantods.

It was good to be going out, and I put on a silk frock which Amy had not yet seen, and hoped it would please her eye. I had seen nothing of her since our return, although we had spoken briefly on the telephone once or twice. How things were going with naughty James, I had no idea.

The hailstorm was over by the time I set out – carefully not too early – but it was cold and blustery. I took the back way to Bent, enjoying the distant view of the downs with the grey clouds scudding along their tops.

Vanessa opened the door to me. She was looking very pretty in a long blue frock, and her favourite piece of jewellery without which I have never seen her. It consists of a hefty brown stone, quite unremarkable, threaded on a long silver chain which reaches to her waist. I have nicer looking pebbles in the gravel of my garden path, but obviously Vanessa sets great store by this ornament, and one can only suppose that she has sentimental reasons for wearing it.

'Lovely to see you again,' she said, kissing my cheek, much to my surprise. 'Come and see Gerard. He brought me down, as I've some leave due to me, and Aunt Amy said I could come here for a few days.'

Gerard was as pink and cheerful as ever.

'Doesn't he look well?' commented Amy. 'I'm so glad he's staying the night. He's meeting his publisher tomorrow. It sounds important, doesn't it?'

'It is to me,' said Gerard. 'They're suggesting that I attempt another book. We're meeting to see how the land lies.'

'But what about the Scottish poets?' I asked.

'Ticking over nicely. I should get them done within a month or so.'

We talked of this and that over our drinks, and I had to give him the latest news of Fairacre, with particular reference to Mr Willet and our local poet, Aloysius Stone, now long-dead, but not forgotten, in the parish.

Over dinner Amy told him about Crete with many inter-ruptions from me. The black silk scarf had been received by Vanessa with expressions of joy and, what's more, with an offer to pay for it which had taken Amy completely off-guard.

'Of course, I couldn't possibly allow it,' she said to me privately afterwards. 'But I was very much touched by the offer. I must say Eileen's brought her up very well.'

As always, Amy's scratch meal turned out to be far more sophisticated and enjoyable than one had been led to expect.

After avocado pears stuffed with shrimps, we had a beef casserole and then fruit salad. I sat enjoying the fruit and thinking idly how typical it was of Amy to be able to produce avocado pears, not to mention everything else, at an hour or so's notice.

'This sliced banana,' said Vanessa dreamily, 'lying on my plate, is wizened to the likeness of a cat's anus.'

'*Really!*' exclaimed Amy, putting down her spoon with a clatter.

'Oh, it's only a quotation,' explained Vanessa, becoming conscious of our startled gaze upon her. 'One of our waiters is a poet and he wrote it.'

'Well, I don't think he should be quoted at table, if that's typical of his work,' said Amy severely.

'He's really terribly gifted. He's had a book of poems published. I meant to tell you, Gerard dear. You may be able to help him. He paid three hundred pounds, he told me, to have them printed.'

'More fool him,' said Gerard.

'But couldn't you put in a word for him tomorrow when you meet your publisher?'

'I have more respect for my publisher than to lumber him with that sort of twaddle. I should say your waiter wants definite discouragement.'

'He's a very good waiter.'

'Then let him stick to his last,' advised Gerard. 'A good waiter's more use in the world than a poor poet.'

Vanessa sighed.

'I asked Angus if he could help. His father runs a Scottish evening paper, but they don't print poetry, he said.'

'Angus has tact.'

'And Ian Murray too, but he was no help. In fact, he used a terrible Scotch word about my poor little poet. I didn't quite understand it, and he refused to explain.'

'Ian Murray has been properly brought up.'

'And as for Andrew Elphinstone-Kerr, he simply roared his head off!'

'Do all your friends have such very Scotch names?' inquired Amy.

Vanessa's blue eyes opened very wide.

'Well they do *live* in Scotland, Aunt Amy, and were born and bred there, so it's hardly surprising, is it? Apart from being so horrid to my waiter,' she added, 'I love them all.'

'I'm glad to hear you've made so many friends,' said Amy.

'We were interested to hear you had met Hattie May. How is she?'

'Quite spry, really, considering she's so old.'

'So old?' we echoed in unison.

'What nonsense!' said Amy, 'she's only a year or two older than I am.'

'I'm sorry,' began Vanessa, 'I forgot that you used to see her.'

'We never missed one of her shows,' I said.

'They're reviving one,' said Gerard. 'In fact, Miss May is in town at the moment for the first night. There's to be a party afterwards.'

'And Gerard's been invited,' said Vanessa.

'Only because she heard that I would be in town,' explained Gerard. 'I knew her husband, years ago, and then we met in Scotland at Vanessa's hotel.'

'You'll have a super time,' Vanessa enthused. 'I hope your evening clothes are up to the occasion.'

'I shall do my best to appear respectable,' Gerard assured her.

'Come and have coffee,' said Amy, leading the way to the drawing-room. 'Would you like a tot of rum with it, Gerard?'

'Nothing I'd like more,' he replied.

Amy began clashing bottles in the cupboard.

'I'm so sorry, there doesn't appear to be any, and I was so looking forward to some myself. James usually keeps his eye on the drinks. Have whiskey instead?'

'Let me run to the local,' said Gerard, 'and get you some rum. It would do me a world of good to get five minutes' exercise.'

After polite expostulations on Amy's side, he had his way, and set off accompanied by Vanessa.

The coffee percolator belched and burped companionably on the side table, as we waited.

'I wonder,' said Amy, sounding usually wistful, 'whether anything will ever come of this affair. She seems so fond of Gerard.'

'She's also fond of half the eligible males in Scotland, as far as we can gather.'

'That's the pity of it. I really think that Gerard should realize that she won't hang about for ever. If he is really serious, I'm sure he should tell her so. Perhaps I could have a word with him. Tactfully, of course.'

'Amy,' I begged her. '*Say nothing!* They are both old enough to know what they are doing, and you will only cause everyone – including yourself – a great deal of embarrassment.'

'Perhaps you're right,' said Amy doubtfully. 'He's such a dear man, and it's time he was married. He'll start getting cranky if he waits much longer.'

'Gerard,' I said stiffly, 'is younger than I am.'

'That's what I mean,' replied Amy.

I was saved the necessity of answering by the arrival of Gerard, Vanessa and a large bottle of rum. And I was relieved to find that the rest of the evening passed without any reference to matrimony.

When the time came for me to go, Amy accompanied me to the car. A half-moon, low on the horizon and lying on its back, glowed as tawny as a ripe apricot.

'I haven't had a chance to tell you about James,' began Amy. She shivered. The night air was chilly.

'Get in the car,' I advised. 'We'll be more comfortable.'

'He came down last week-end, and we tried to have a straight talk. But oh, it's so sad! After all our years together we're becoming like strangers. I don't think I can bear it any longer. He's beginning to loathe me. I can see it in his face. Something will have to happen.'

'In what way?'

'I felt sure that I was right to give this matter time to fizzle out. Somehow I still think it will – but perhaps that's simply wishful thinking. I just don't know. All I can be sure of now, since we've been back from our holiday, is that he's getting more and more desperately unhappy.'

She fumbled for a handkerchief and blew her nose. After a moment or two, she went on.

'Now I ask myself, am I right in making three lives miserable? Has the time come to put my pride in my pocket and give in? Or am I right in thinking that one day he will give her up, and then need me? You can see how I torture myself. The position's getting more painful daily. What can I do?'

The question hung between us. A pinkish light from the rising moon warmed the front of Amy's pretty house. From the woods behind us, an owl cried.

'Amy,' I said slowly, 'I honestly don't know. I just can't think what sort of advice one could give in such a situation. I'm no help to you, and how desperately I wish I could be!'

Amy dabbled at her eyes.

'I wouldn't want my worst enemy to go through the misery I've had during these last few months. I feel torn this way and that. Whichever path I choose may be the wrong one.'

She sighed, put her damp cheek against mine, and then opened the door.

'I must go back. Thank you for coming, and for being such a prop in a tottering world. I'll give you a ring later on.'

I started the car and drove slowly down the drive. For the first time, the lonely figure I left standing in the door way looked old and defeated, and I drove home struggling with tears of my own.

Soon after this evening with Amy, I had to keep an appointment at Caxley Hospital. This was to check that the broken arm was in good trim, and as I could do practically everything with it I had no doubt that I should be paying my last visit there.

The time of the appointment was three-thirty on a Wednesday afternoon, which meant that I should have to leave school at three, no doubt arriving at the hospital room to find a score of other unfortunates called imperiously for exactly the same time.

I explained to my class that they must work on their own for the last half-hour or so, that Miss Edwards would leave the partition door ajar between the two rooms, and would keep an eye on them.

They knew, of course, that I was off to hospital, and were suitably impressed, not to say ghoulish about it.

'Will they have to break it again? They did my dad's – to reset it.'

'I sincerely hope not.'

'Will you be put to bed?'

'Good heavens, no.'

'Will you come to school tomorrow?'

'Of course. Now stop fussing and get on with your work.'

Reluctantly, they took up their pens again.

After play, the new child, Derek, distributed boxes of crayons and enormous sheets of paper.

'You can draw a picture,' I told them, 'about any episode in history that you like.' This, I felt, should provide plenty of scope for the boys, who would settle, no doubt, for scenes of warfare involving a great many human figures in various attitudes both upright and prone, and for the girls who would probably decide to illustrate such events as Queen Victoria hearing of her accession, or Henry the Eighth meeting one of his wives, and needing a good deal of detailed work on the costumes. Such subjects should keep them busily scribbling until the end of school.

But for good measure, I wrote my old friend CONSTANTI-NOPLE on the blackboard, and supplied an extra piece of paper, to be folded long-wise into four, for lists of words made from that trusted standby.

'And you are to work quietly,' I said, 'and be a good example to the infants.'

They assumed unnatural expressions of virtue and trustworthiness. I bade farewell to the infants' teacher, and set off.

I arrived at the hospital in good time, and followed a fellow-patient to the waiting room. She was on two sticks, and attended by an anxious daughter. The path led by a devious route to the back portions of the building and was composed of so much broken asphalt, pot-holes, manhole covers and the like, that it was a wonder that anyone arrived at the waiting room without injury, I reflected, as I picked my way cautiously between the laurel bushes.

There were quite a few of us hurt and maimed distributed on the benches. Legs in plaster casts, arms supported at shoulder level, people with slings, people with bandages – it might well have been the aftermath of just such a battle scene as those being created at Fairacre School.

I sat in the middle of an empty bench, but was joined within two minutes by a mountainous woman with a band-aged leg who told me, in hideous detail, what was concealed beneath her wrappings. I learnt more about the vascular system of the human frame, in that unfortunate ten-minute encounter, than I wished to know, and it was a relief to hear my name called and to be ushered into the doctor's presence.

He seemed a morose young man, and he had my sympathy.

'And how is it going, Mrs Potter?' he asked. I said I was Miss Read, and he put down the photographs he was studying rather hastily, and fished out another envelope.

'Of course, Mrs Read.'

'I'm single,' I said. He appeared not to hear, and I remained Mrs Read throughout the interview.

He felt my elbow, and then directed me to put my arm into various positions. The results seemed to depress him.

'Yes. Well, you shouldn't be able to do that with your injury. It pains you, I expect, Mrs Read?'

'Not at all.'

He looked disbelieving, and took a firm grip on the upper arm with one hand and the lower with the other hand, and tried a wrenching movement.

I yelped. An expression of satisfaction spread over his dour countenance.

'Still some need for improvement,' he said smugly. 'Keep on with the exercises. No need to come again, Mrs Read.'

He shook my hand warmly. No doubt about it, I had made his day.

The mountainous woman was on her way in as I came out.

'Coming again?' she asked.

'No!' I cried triumphantly, and made my escape into the sunshine.

17. A Visit from Miss Clare

One blue and white October day, I went to Beech Green to fetch Miss Clare who was going to pay a visit to Fairacre School where she had taught the infants for so many years.

Miss Clare, now a very old lady, lived alone in a thatched cottage which had been her home since early childhood. She was always invited to school functions, and was greeted with much affection by many of the Fairacre parents who owed their own early education to her efforts.

But today's visit was somewhat different. I had long been aware of the avid interest, shown by the older children, in the accounts of life in their village as remembered by their grandparents and other folk of that generation. Mr Willet's memories frequently enliven our schoolroom, and naturally, these first-hand accounts of local history have far more impact on the children than something read in a book.

Miss Clare, who had been a pupil as well as a teacher at our school, was willing to come and talk to the children, and as soon as school dinner was cleared away, I drove to Beech Green to collect her.

As always, she looked immaculate. She wore a navy-blue suit, and a very pale blue jumper under it. I admired the colour, which matched her eyes.

'Dear Emily knitted it a few months before she died,' she said calmly, speaking of her life-long friend who had shared her cottage for the last few years of her life. 'I keep it for best. I should like it to last.'

She was carrying a basket, covered with a white cloth, which she insisted on holding herself. She nursed it carefully throughout the journey and I wondered what it contained.

She was as long-sighted as ever, and on our drive back she pointed out a hovering sparrowhawk, which I confess I should have missed completely, and a weasel which emerged from the grass verge for an instant before turning tail and scurrying back to cover. Her mind was as keen as her eyesight, and she regaled me with snippets of Beech Green gossip, and with future plans for her garden, and a description of some new curtains she was sewing for her bedroom, until I began to feel lazier and more inefficient than ever.

She was greeted with enthusiasm by my class when we entered. Genuine affection, I knew, inspired nine-tenths of their exuberance, but I was aware that the fact that they would not need to exert themselves in work of their own that afternoon, partly contributed to their jubilation.

We set the most comfortable chair close to the front row, and the children at the back of the classroom came forward to squeeze companionably three in a desk, so that every word of Miss Clare's should be heard.

I sat at my desk and watched their intent faces. Certainly, Miss Clare had lost none of her old magic in holding children's interest.

The contents of the basket emerged one by one. The first object to be help up was a small china mug with a picture of Queen Victoria on the side.

'We all had one of these given to us,' she told the children, 'when the good Queen had reigned for sixty years. It was called her Diamond Jubilee, and you can see it written here.'

'Were you in this school then?' asked Linda Moffat.

'No, my dear, I was at Beech Green School then.' She went on to describe the junketings of that far-distant day when she was a young child, joining with her sister Ada, in the sports arranged in a nearby field.

She told them how she came to Fairacre School a year or two later, carefully omitting the reason, which I knew, for the move. A weak headmaster, with views too advanced for his time, had caused so much concern among the parents that several of them had transferred their children to other local schools, despite the long walks, in every kind of weather, which this involved.

Miss Clare described those daily walks. It was almost three miles from her cottage to the school, and she told the wondering class where she found a robin's nest one spring, and where a tiny river once overflowed one February, and she and

Emily Davis, her friend, took off their boots and stockings to paddle through the flood to get to school.

She showed them more treasures from her basket. A starched white pinafore, 'kept for Sundays', intrigued the girls who admired the insertion down the front as it was passed round the class for them to examine.

Her first copybook from Beech Green School with rows and rows of pot-hooks and hangers on the first few pages, and maxims of a strong moral flavour on the rest, was a source of wonder. The object, though, which gave them the most excitement was the photograph of the whole of Fairacre School taken outside in our playground with Mr Wardle, the then headmaster, his wife, the infants' teacher Miss Taylor, and Dolly herself and Emily Davis as pupil teachers, standing meekly at one side of the rows of children. The clothes of the latter caused hilarity and a certain amount of sympathy.

'What's he doin' with that great ol' thing round his neck?' asked Patrick, gazing with bewilderment at one sporting an Eton collar. And the fact that nearly all the children wore lace-up boots, despite the brilliant sunshine which had caused most of them to screw up their eyes against the dazzle, puzzled my class considerably.

She described the village as she remembered it so long ago, telling of houses and barns now vanished, of splendid trees, which had towered over the roofs, felled years before, of a disused chapel, now turned into a house, and a host of other changes in their environment. The questions came thick and fast, and she answered all with care and composure.

The last thing to be brought from the basket, for the children's delectation, was a fine Bible.

'I was lucky enough to win the Bishop's Bible,' she told them. 'I just sat there, where Ernest is sitting, and it rained so hard that we could hardly hear the question, I remember.'

The Bishop's Bible is still presented annually to the child who seems best grounded in religious knowledge, so that many a child in the class had just such a Bible at home, presented to a parent or relative years before. It seemed to bring home to them the continuity of tradition in this old school, and the bond between the Victorian child and those of the present day was forged even more firmly in Miss Clare's last few minutes with the class.

Patrick, primed and rehearsed beforehand, thanked her beautifully, and the children were sent to play.

I feared that she might be tired by her efforts, but she seemed stimulated, and insisted on calling on the infants after play where she spent the rest of the school afternoon.

'D'you reckon,' said Ernest, 'that you'll live as long as Miss Clare?'

I said I doubted it.

'Why not?' chorused the class.

'Children nowadays,' I told them, with as much solemnity as I could muster, 'are not as well-behaved as those Miss Clare taught. Teachers today get worn out before their time.'

They smiled indulgently at me, and at one another.

I would have my little joke!

Miss Clare came over to the school house for tea when school was over. One last object, not shown to the children, was produced. It was a pot of her own plum jam which made a most welcome addition to my larder.

The fire cracked merrily for I had slipped across during playtime to put a match to it. Outside, the shadows were already beginning to lengthen, and the chill of autumn became apparent as evening fell.

'It's a time of year I love,' said Miss Clare, stirring her tea. 'I love to see the barns full of straw bales, and to know the grain is safely stored, and to watch them ploughing Hundred Acre Field ready for another crop. I always feel when the harvest's home, that that's the true end of one year and the beginning of the next.'

'I must admit,' I agreed, 'that there's something very satisfying in pulling up all the tatty annuals and having a gorgeous bonfire in the garden. I like to think it's simply an appreciation of good husbandry, but I know that it's partly the thought of being relieved of gardening for a few months. And it's a positive pleasure to see the lawn mower go for its annual overhaul at the end of the summer. The older I get the less I enjoy pushing a mower. Mr Willet does it quite often, but he has so much to do in the village I don't rely on him.'

Miss Clare sighed.

'A man is *useful*! I suppose, if we're honest, we miss having husbands.'

'Like most things, there are points for and against husbands.' I told her about Mrs Coggs.

'I hope she's an exception, poor woman. It isn't only as a husband that Arthur Coggs fails. He's a complete failure at everything else. He won't work, he drinks, he lies and he sponges on the rest of us. But, after all, he's not typical of most men, and personally I very much regret that I did not marry.'

'You surprise me. I've always thought of you as one of the happiest, most serene people I know, with a perfectly full and satisfying life.'

Miss Clare smiled.

'I *am* happy. And, of course, one fills one's life whether single or married. I don't say that I sit and mope about being a spinster. I'm much too aware of my good fortune in having a home of my own, in a place I love, among a host of friends. But it's natural, I think, to wish to have someone of the next generation to carry on one's traditions and work. No, I think if I had been able to marry Arnold, I should truthfully have been happier still.'

She fingered the gold locket, which she always wears, containing the photograph of her fiancé so tragically killed in the First World War.

'After Arnold, there was nobody whom I could care for enough to marry. In any case, there was a dearth of young men after those terrible four years of war, and here in Fairacre and Beech Green, of course, men were few and far between anyway, and we hardly went further afield than Caxley to meet others.'

This was true. When one came to think of it, those couples of Miss Clare's generation were probably born and brought up within a very few miles of each other. More probably still, they were related, which accounted for the few names in those old registers shared by a large number of children.

'No cars, no holidays abroad,' I said, thinking aloud. 'It certainly restricted one's choice.'

'Not only that. There were so few openings for girls and boys. I could either go into domestic service, or a shop, or nursing or teaching. Really there was nothing else open to a girl from a poor home. Nowadays, the young things go all over the world, or get a grant for further education somewhere miles from their own area, where they meet scores of other young people from all walks of life. No wonder they seem so sophisticated compared with ourselves at that age!'

'But are they happier?'

'When it comes to marriage, I have my doubts. In our day, we took our marriage vows pretty seriously and divorce was difficult and expensive. You knew you must make a go of the affair. Maybe there was a lot of unhappiness which was kept hidden, but on the whole I think the young people did better when they waited for each other and got to know themselves more thoroughly.'

Tibby arrived on the window sill, mouthing her complaints. I hurried to let her in. Her fur was fresh and cold, smelling of dry grass, bruised leaves and all outdoors.

'You would make a very good wife yourself,' said Miss Clare, watching me pour some milk into a saucer for my domestic tyrant.

'The chance would be a fine thing,' I replied. 'No, I haven't the pluck to risk it, even if I did have the chance. The single state suits me very well.'

'Tell me more about Crete,' said Miss Clare, and in that moment I knew that Amy's troubles were known to her and, no doubt, to most other people in the neighbourhood. Nothing had been said, and certainly not by me, but here it was again – that extraordinary awareness by country people of what is going on about them.

I launched enthusiastically into an account of all the wonders I had seen, and out came the photographs and maps and guide books.

It was past seven o'clock when I finally drove her home, and never once was Amy's name spoken between us.

Nevertheless, I knew Amy's affairs were now common knowledge, and I was not surprised.

★

343

Mrs Pringle's return to her duties I greeted with mingled relief and apprehension. We had done our best, in the last few weeks, to keep things clean and tidy, but I doubted if our standards would please Mrs Pringle.

I did not doubt for long.

''Ere,' said the lady, issuing from the back lobby where the washing up is done. 'What's become of my mop? Alice Willet thrown it out?'

I said I did not know.

'Hardly worn, that mop. A favourite of mine. Hope nothing's become of it.'

I thought of the character in *Cold Comfort Farm* who had the same affection for his little twig mop.

'Perhaps it's been put somewhere different,' I suggested weakly.

'*Everything*, as far as I can see,' boomed Mrs Pringle, 'has been put somewhere different. And the bar soap's almost gone, and them matches is standing for all to see and help themselves to.'

This was a side-swipe at Mr Willet, luckily not present, or battle would have been joined without hesitation.

'And where's the little slatted mat I stands on at the sink?' demanded the lady.

'I think it got broken.'

'Then the office should send out another. If I have to stand on damp concrete, in my state of health, I'll be back in Caxley Hospital before you can say "knife".'

I said that I would indent for another mat without delay.

Mrs Pringle prowled around my classroom, sniffing suspiciously.

'Funny smell this place has got. You been letting mice in?'

'Is it likely?' I responded coldly. 'Do you imagine I spread a mouse banquet of cheese crumbs and bacon rinds and then open the door and invite them in?'

'There's no saying,' was Mrs Pringle's rejoinder. She ran a fat finger along the top of a door and surveyed the resulting grime.

'And not much dustin' done neither,' she commented.

'The children can't reach the tops of the doors.'

'There's others who can,' she answered.

As usual, I could see that I should lose this battle. Luckily, at this juncture, the new boy Derek appeared on the scene with a cut finger, and I was obliged to break off our exchanges and attend to him.

As I wrapped up his finger, I noticed his eyes were fixed on Mrs Pringle who still roamed the room, sniffing and making small noises of disapproval as she examined cupboard tops, window sills, and even the inside of the piano.

'Off you go,' I said, when I had completed my first aid. 'Try and keep it clean.'

Mrs Pringle made her way into the infants' room. No doubt she would find plenty there to gloat over, I thought.

Through the open window I became conscious of two voices. One belonged to Derek.

'Who's that lady in there?'

'Ma Pringle.'

'What does she do? Is she a teacher?'

'Nah! Old Ma Pringle? She's the one what keeps the school clean.'

'But I thought we did that?'

'You thought wrong then, mate. We done a bit while she was ill, but I bet Ma Pringle don't reckon we've kept it clean!'

Too true, I thought, too true!

18. *Autumn Pleasures*

Saturday mornings are busy times for schoolteachers. It is then that they usually tackle the week's washing, any outstanding household jobs and, of course, the week-end shopping.

The latter can usually be done in Fairacre, but this Saturday in question I found that I needed such haberdashery items as elastic and pearl buttons. As there were one or two garments to be collected from the cleaners as well, I faced the fact that I must get out the car and make a sortie into Caxley.

While I was choosing a piece of rock salmon for Tibby and two fillets of plaice for myself, Amy smote me on the back.

As usual, she was looking as if she had come out of a bandbox, elegant in dark green with shoes to match. I became conscious of my shabby camel car coat, heavily marked down the right sleeve with black oil from the lock on the car door, and my scuffed car shoes.

'Nearly finished?' she asked.

'Just about. A pound of sprouts, and I'm done.'

'Let's have a spot of lunch together at "The Bull",' suggested Amy. 'They do some very good toasted sandwiches in the bar, and I'm famished.'

'So am I. An hour's shopping in Caxley finishes me. Partly, I think, it's the smug pleasure with which half the assistants tell you they haven't got what you want.'

'And that it's no good ordering it,' added Amy. 'I know. I've been suffering that way myself this morning.'

I bought my sprouts, and we entered 'The Bull'. A bright fire was welcoming and we sank gratefully into the leather armchairs to drink our sherry. We were the only people in the bar at that moment, for we were early. Within a short time, the place would be crowded.

'Vanessa's back at work,' said Amy.

'Did Gerard take her to Scotland?'

'Oh no, he's back in London in his little flat, putting the

final touches to the book, I gather. A very personable young man picked her up. I never did catch his name. Could it have been Torquil?'

'Sounds likely. I take it he was a Scot?'

'They're *all* Scots at the moment, which makes me anxious about Gerard. He really should be a little more alert if he wants to capture Vanessa.'

'Perhaps he doesn't.'

Amy's mouth took on a demented line.

'I'm quite sure *she* is fond of him. She talks of him such a lot, and is always asking his advice. You know, she really *respects* Gerard. Such a good basis for a marriage where there is a difference in age.'

'Well, there is nothing you can do about it,' I pointed out. 'Have another sherry?'

I went to get our glasses refilled. Amy was looking thoughtful as I replaced them on the table by the sandwiches.

'James was down during the week,' she said. 'He looks worried to death. I don't know whether the girl is wavering and he is having to increase his efforts, or whether he senses that *I'm* wavering, but something's going to give before long. And I've a horrible feeling it's going to be me. It's an impossible situation for us all. What's more, I keep getting tactful expressions of sympathy from people in the village, and I'm not sure that that isn't harder to bear than James's indiscretions.'

I remembered Miss Clare.

'You can't keep any secrets in a village,' I said. 'You know that anyway. Don't let that add to your worries.'

'But how do people find out? I've not said a word to a soul. Even Mrs Bennet, our daily, knows nothing.'

'You'd be surprised! A lot of it's guesswork, plus putting two and two together and making five. Bush telegraph is one of the strongest factors in village life, and works for good as well as ill. Look how people rallied when I broke my arm!'

'Which reminds me,' said Amy, looking at her watch, 'I must get back to pack up the laundry. Mrs Bennet hasn't been for the last two days. She's down with this wretched measles. Caught it from her grandchild.'

'There's a lot about. Three more cases last week in the infants' room.'

'There's talk of closing Bent School,' Amy told me. 'Actually, they rang up last week to see if I could do some supply work there, but I felt I just couldn't with James coming down, and so much hanging over me. They're two staff short, and no end of children away.'

'Have you had it?'

'What, measles? Yes, luckily, at the age of six or seven, and all I can remember is a bowl of oranges permanently by the bedside, and the counterpane covered with copies of *Rainbow* and *Tiger Tim's Annual*.'

We collected our shopping and made for the door, much fortified by 'The Bull's' hospitality.

'I wonder if I've got the stamina to go looking for a new winter coat,' I mused aloud.

Amy eyed my dirty sleeve.

'You certainly look as though you need one,' she commented.

'The thing is, should it be navy blue or brown? In a weak moment last year I bought a navy blue skirt and shoes, and I ought to make up my mind if I'm to continue with navy blue, which means a new handbag as well, or play safe with something brown which will go with everything else.'

Amy shook her head sadly.

'Well, I can't spare the time to come with you, I'm afraid. What problems you set yourself! And you know why?'

I shook my head in turn.

'*No method!*' said Amy severely, waving good-bye.

She's right, I thought, watching her trim figure vanishing down the street.

I decided that I could not face such a problem at the moment, collected my car and drove thankfully along the road to Fairacre.

The conker season was now in full swing. Rows of shiny beauties, carefully threaded on strings, lined the ancient desk at the side of the room, and as soon as playtime came, they were snatched up and their owners rushed outside to do battle.

There were one or two casualties understandably. Small boys, swinging heavy strings of conkers, and especially when faced with defeat, are apt to fly at an opponent. One or two bruises needed treatment, usually to the accompaniment of heated comment.

'He done it a-purpose, miss.'

'No, I never then.'

'I saw him, miss. Oppin' mad, he was, miss.'

'Never! I saw him too, miss. They was jus' playin' quiet-like. It were an accident.'

'Cor! Look who's talking! What about yesterday, eh? You was takin' swipes at all us lot, with your mingy conkers.'

'Whose mingy conkers? They beat the daylights out of yourn anyway!'

Luckily, the conker season is a relatively short one, and the blood cools as the weather does.

Out in the fields the tractors were ploughing and drilling. We could hear the rooks, dozens of them, cawing as they followed the plough, flapping down to grab the insects turned up in the rich chocolate-brown furrows.

The hedges were thinning fast, and a carpet of rustling leaves covered the school lane. Scarlet rose hips and crimson hawthorn berries splashed the hedgerows with bright colour, and garlands of bryony, studded with berries of coral, jade and gold, wreathed the hedges like jewelled necklaces.

The children brought hazel nuts and walnuts to school, cracking them with their teeth, and as bright-eyed and intent as squirrels as they examined their treasures. Their fingers were stained brown with the green husks from the walnuts, and purple with the juice from late blackberries. Plums and apples from cottage gardens joined the biscuits on the side table ready for playtime refreshment. Autumn is the time of plenty, of stocking up for the lean days ahead, and Fairacre children take full advantage of nature's bounty.

So do the adults. We were all busy making plum jam and apple jelly, and keeping a sharp eye on the wild crab apples which would not be ready until later. There are several of these trees among the copses and hedges of Fairacre, and most years there is plenty of fruit for everyone. One year, however, soon after I arrived in Fairacre, there was a particularly poor crop of these lovely little apples. A newcomer to the village, one of the 'atomic wives', living in the cottage now inhabited by young Derek and his parents, was rash enough to pick the lot, much to the fury of the other good wives of Fairacre. I remember, in my innocence, attempting to be placatory, suggesting that ignorance, rather than greed, had prompted her wholesale appropriation.

'We'll learn her!' had been the vengeful cry. And they did. Perhaps it was as well that her husband was posted elsewhere after this unfortunate incident. I can't think that she really enjoyed her crab apple jelly.

There is a very neighbourly feeling about picking these wild fruits, and very few would strip a hedge of nuts or blackberries. Leaving some for the next comer is usual. It is as though the generosity of nature communicates itself to those blessed by it, and many a time I have heard the children, and their parents, recommending this hedge or that tree as the best place to try harvesting.

One of the group of elms at the corner of the playground was considered unsafe and had to come down. The children were allowed to watch the operation at a respectful distance. The two men had the small branches off, the trunk sawn through and the giant toppled, all within the hour.

It fell with a dreadful cracking sound, and thumped into Mr Roberts' field beyond. The children raised a great shout of triumph, but one of the infants grew tearful and said:

'I don't like it falling down.'

'Neither do I,' I said. We seemed to be the only two who felt saddened at the sight. Everyone else rejoiced, but I cannot see a tree felled, particularly a majestic one such as this was, without a shock of horror at the swift killing of something which has taken a hundred years or more to grow, and has given shelter and beauty to the other lives about it.

However, I was not too shattered to be grateful for some of its logs which Mr Willet procured for me. I helped him to stand them in my wood shed one afternoon after school.

The sky was that particularly intense blue which occasionally occurs in October. Across the fields, in the clear air, the trees glowed in their russet colours. It was invigorating handling the rough-barked wood, knowing that the winter's fires would be made splendid with its burning.

But it was cold too. Mr Willet, stacking the final few, blew out his moustache.

'Have a frost tonight, you'll see. Got your dahlias up?'

I had not. Mr Willet evinced no surprise.

'Shall I do 'em for you now?' he offered.

'No need. I've kept you long enough. It's time you were home.'

'That's all right. Alice has gone gadding into Caxley to a temperance meeting.'

Gadding seemed hardly the word to use under the circumstances, I felt.

'Come and have a cup of tea with me then,' I said. We stood back to admire the stack of logs before making for the kitchen.

'That baby of Mrs Coggs has got the measles, they say,' said Mr Willet, stirring his tea. 'Them others away from school?'

'Not today. I'd better look into it. Two more infants are down with it, but we're not as badly off as Bent.'

I told him what Amy had said about the possibility of the school there having to close.

'And how is your friend?' inquired Mr Willet. 'I did hear,' he added delicately, 'that she was in a bit of trouble.'

Here we were again, I thought. I had no desire to snub dear old Mr Willet, but equally I had no wish to betray Amy's confidences.

'Aren't we all in a bit of trouble, one way or the other?' I parried.

'That's true,' agreed Mr Willet. 'But you single ones don't have the same trouble as us married folk. Only got yourself to consider, you see. Any mistakes you make don't rebound on the other like. Take them dahlias.'

'What about them?'

I was relieved that we seemed to have skated away from the thin ice of Amy's affairs.

'Well, if my Alice'd forgot them dahlias, I should have cut

up a bit rough, seeing what they cost. But you, not having no husband, gets off scot free.'

'Not entirely. I shall have to pay for any new ones.'

'Yes, but that's your affair. There ain't no *upsets*, if you see what I mean. No bad feelings. You can afford to be slap-dash and casual-like. Who's to worry?'

I laughed.

'You sound like Mrs Pringle! Am I really slap-dash and casual, Mr Willet?'

'Lor, bless you,' said Mr Willet, rising to go, 'you're the most happy-go-lucky flibbertigibbet I've ever met in all me born days! Many thanks for the tea, Miss Read. See you bright and early!'

And off he went, chuckling behind his stained moustache, leaving me dumb-founded – and with all the washing-up.

I had time to savour Mr Willet's opinion of me as I sat knitting by the fire that evening. I was amused by his matter-of-fact acceptance of my shortcomings. His remarks about the drawbacks of matrimony I also knew to be true. Any unsettled feelings I had suffered during the holidays had quite vanished, and I realized that I was back in my usual mood of thinking myself lucky to be single.

For some unknown reason I had a sudden craving for a pancake for my supper. I had not cooked one for years, and thoroughly enjoyed beating the batter, and cutting a lemon ready for my feast. I even tossed the pancake successfully, which added to my pleasure.

If I were having to provide for a husband, I thought, tucking into my creation, a pancake would hardly be the fare to offer as a complete meal. No doubt there would be 'upsets', as Mr Willet put it. Yes, there was certainly something to be said for the simple single life. I was well content.

The fire burnt brightly. Tibby purred on the rug. At ten o'clock I stepped outside the front door before locking up. There was a touch of frost in the air, as Mr Willet had forecast, and the stars glittered above the elm trees. Somewhere in the village a dog yelped, and near at hand there was a rustling among the dry leaves as some small nocturnal animal set out upon its foraging.

With my lungs full of clear cold air I went indoors and made all fast. I was in my petticoat when the telephone rang.

It was Amy. She sounded incoherent, and quite unlike her usual composed self.

'James has had an accident. I'm not sure where. In the car, I mean, and the girl, Jane, with him. I'm just off.'

'Where is he?'

'Somewhere near Salisbury, in a hospital. I've got the address scribbled down.'

'Shall I come with you?'

'No, no, my dear. I only rang because I felt someone should know where I was. Mrs Bennet's not on the phone, and anyway, as you know, she's ill. I must go.'

'Tell me,' I said, wondering how best to put it, 'is he much damaged?'

'I don't know. They told me nothing really. The hospital people found his address on him and simply rang me to say he was there. He's unconscious – they did say that.'

I felt suddenly very cold. Was this the dreadful way that Amy's affairs were to be settled?

'Amy,' I urged, 'do let me come with you, please.'

I could hear crying at the other end. It was unendurable.

'No. You're sweet, but I must go alone. I'll be careful, I promise. And I'll ring you first thing tomorrow morning when I know more.'

'I understand,' I said. 'Good luck, my love, and call on me if there's anything I can do to help.'

We hung up. Mechanically, I got ready for the night and climbed into bed, but there was no hope of sleeping.

I think I heard every hour strike from the church tower, as I lay there imagining Amy on her long sad journey westward, pressing on through the darkness with a chill at her heart more cruel than the frosts around her.

What awaited Amy at the end of the dark road?

19. *James Comes Home*

After my disturbed night I was late in waking. Fortunately, it was Saturday, and my time was my own.

I went shakily about the household chores, alert for the telephone bell and a message from Amy.

Outside, a wind had sprung up, rattling the rose against the window and ruffling the feathers of the robin on the bird table. Frost still whitened the grass, but great grey clouds, scudding from the west, promised rain before long with milder weather on the way.

The hands of the clock crept from nine to ten, from ten to eleven, and still nothing happened. My imagination ran riot. Was James dying? Or dead, perhaps, and Amy too distraught to think of such things as telephone calls? And what about the girl? Was she equally seriously injured? And what result would this accident have upon all three people involved?

I made my mid-morning coffee and drank more than half before realizing that the milk was still waiting in the saucepan. A shopping list progressed by fits and starts, as I made one entry and then gazed unseeingly through the window.

Suddenly, the bell rang, and I was about to lift the receiver when I realized that it was the back door bell.

Mrs Pringle stood on the doorstep holding a fine cabbage.

'Thought you could do with it,' she said. 'I was taking the school tea towels over to the kitchen so thought I'd kill two birds with one stone.'

I thanked her and asked if she would like some coffee.

'Well now,' she said graciously, 'I don't mind if I do.'

I very nearly retorted, as an ex-landlady of mine used to do when encountering this phrase:

'And I don't mind if you *don't*!' but I bit it back.

Mrs Pringle seated herself at the kitchen table, loosening her coat and rolling her hand-knitted gloves into a tidy ball.

I switched on the stove to heat the milk again. As one

354

might expect, it was at this inconvenient moment that the telephone bell rang.

'Make the coffee when it's hot,' I cried to Mrs Pringle, and rushed into the hall.

It was Amy.

She sounded less distraught than the night before, but dog-tired.

'Sorry to be so late in ringing, but I thought I'd wait until the doctor had seen James, so that I had more news to tell you.'

'And what is it?'

'He's round this morning, but still in a good deal of pain. The collar bone is broken and a couple of ribs cracked, and he's complaining of internal pains. Still, he's all right, the doctor says, and can be patched up.'

'What about his head? Did he have concussion?'

I was suddenly conscious of Mrs Pringle's presence and, without doubt, her avid interest in the side of the conversation she could hear. Too pointed to close the kitchen door, I decided, and anyway too late.

'Yes. He was knocked out, and has a splitting head this morning, but, thank God, he'll survive.

'Now, my dear, would you do something for me?'

'Of course. Say the word.'

'Could you pop over to Bent and take some steak out of the slow oven? Like an ass, I forgot it in the hurry last night. It's been stewing there for about fourteen hours now, so will probably be burnt to a frazzle.'

'What shall I do with it?'

'Let Tibby have it, if it's any use. Otherwise, chuck it out. And would you sort out the perishables in the fridge? And cancel the milk and bread? I'm sorry to bother you with all this, but I've decided to stay nearby. There's a comfortable hotel and James won't be able to be moved for a bit. Mrs Bennet isn't on the phone, and I don't like to worry her anyway while she's ill.'

I said I would go over immediately, scribbled down her forwarding address, and was about to put down the receiver when, luckily, Amy remembered to tell me where the spare key was.

'I've moved it from under the watering-can,' explained Amy, 'and now you'll find it inside one of those old-fashioned earthenware honey pots, labelled CARPET TACKS, on the top shelf at the left-hand side of the garden shed.'

I sent my love and sympathy to James.

'I'll ring again tomorrow,' promised Amy, and then the line went dead.

Mrs Pringle looked up expectantly as I returned, but I was not to be drawn.

'Have a biscuit, Mrs Pringle,' I said proffering the tin.

She selected a Nice biscuit with care. It was obviously a poor substitute for a morsel of hot news, but it had to do.

Half an hour later, I was on my way to Amy's, and it was only then that I remembered that nothing had been said about James's companion – Jane, wasn't it? What, I wondered, had happened to her?

The wind buffeted the car as I drove southward. The sheep were huddled together against the hedges, finding what shelter they could. Pedestrians were bent double against the onslaught, clutching hats and head-scarves, coat-tails flapping. Cyclists tacked dangerously to and fro across the road, dogs, exhilarated by the wind, bounded from verges, and children, screaming with excitement, tore after them.

The leaves of autumn, torn from the trees, fluttered down like showers of new pennies, sticking to the windscreen, the bonnet, and plastering the road with their copper brightness. Amy's drive was littered with twigs and tiny cones from the fir tree which must have caught the full brunt of some particularly violent gust.

I found the key in the honey pot, and went indoors. A rich aroma of stewed beef greeted me, and my first duty was to rescue the casserole. Amazingly, it still had some liquor in it, and the meat had fallen into deliciously tender chunks. I decided that I should share this largesse with Tibby that evening.

Amy's refrigerator was far better stocked than mine, and much more tidy. There was little to remove – some milk, a portion of apricot pie, four sardines on a saucer, just the usual flotsam and jetsam of daily catering.

There were a few letters which I re-addressed, and then I wrote notes to the baker and milkman, before going round the house to make sure that the windows were shut and that any radiators were left at a low heat.

All seemed to be in order. I checked switches, locked doors, and took a final walk around Amy's garden, before replacing the key. It was while I was on my tour of inspection, that I saw a man battling his way from the gate.

He looked surprised to see me.

'Oh good morning! My name's John Bennet. My wife works here and asked me to come and see everything's all right.'

I asked after her.

'Getting on, but it's knocked all the stuffing out of her. These children's complaints are no joke when you're getting on.'

'So I believe. Don't worry about the house. Mrs Garfield asked me to look in. She's been called away.'

'Yes, we knew she must have been. That's why I came up. My sister, who lives just down the road from us, saw her setting off last night – very late it was – and looking very worried. My sister was taking out the dog, and guessed something must be up.'

I had imagined that Mrs Bennet had been concerned for any possible gale damage, but now revised my views.

'Mr Garfield,' I explained, 'has had a car accident, but is getting on quite well, I gather, and should be home before long. Tell Mrs Bennet not to worry. I'll keep an eye on the place while she's laid up, and if she wants to get in touch tell her to phone me.'

We took a final turn round the windy garden together before parting. All seemed well.

I got back into the car and set off for home, marvelling, yet again, at the extraordinary efficiency of bush telegraph in rural areas.

The gales continued for the rest of the week, and the children were as mad as hatters in consequence.

Wind is worse than any other element, I find, for causing chaos in a classroom. Snow, of course, is dramatic, and needs to be inspected through the windows at two-minute intervals to see if it is 'laying'. But this is something which occurs relatively seldom in school hours.

Sunshine and rain are accepted equably, but a good blustery wind which bangs doors, rattles windows, blows papers to the floor, and the breath from young bodies, is a fine excuse for boisterous behaviour.

Up here, on the downs, the wind is a force to be reckoned with. Not long ago, an elm tree crashed across the roof of St Patrick's church, and caused so much damaged that the village was hard put to it to raise the money for its repair. Friends from near and far rallied to Fairacre's support, and the challenge was met, but we all (and Mr Willet, in particular, who strongly suspects any elm tree of irresponsible falling-about through sheer cussedness), watch our trees with some apprehension when the gales come in force.

The only casualty this time, as far as I knew, was a venerable damson tree in Ernest's garden. He brought the remaining fruit to school in a paper bag, and the small purple plums were shared out among his school fellows.

I watched this generous act with some trepidation. Damsons, even when plentifully sugared, are as tart a fruit as one could wish to meet. To see the children scrunching them raw made me shudder, but apart from one or two who complained that 'they gave them cat-strings' or 'turned their teeth all funny', Ernest's largesse was much enjoyed.

My own share arrived in the form of a little pot of damson cheese, made by Ernest's mother, and for this I was truly thankful.

Apart from fierce cross-draughts, and a continuous whistling one from the skylight above my desk, we were further bedevilled by smoke from the tortoise stove. Even Mrs Pringle, who can control our two monsters at a touch, confessed herself beaten, so that we worked with eyes sore with smoke and much coughing – most of it affected – and plenty of smuts floating in the air.

Amy rang twice during the few days after the accident. The car, she said, on the first occasion, was beyond repair and James had been lucky to escape so lightly.

'And Jane?' I dared to ask.

'Simply treated here for superficial cuts on her face and a sprained wrist. She'd gone home by the time I arrived, fetched by mother. At least she'd had the sense to be wearing her seat belt. It saved her from hitting her head on the windscreen which is what happened to James.'

'And how is he?'

'Still running a temperature, which the doctor thinks is rather peculiar, I gather. He's very restless, and in pain, poor thing. He was terribly worried about Jane, but they've put his mind at rest about that.'

'Any chance of bringing him home?'

'They don't seem in any hurry to get rid of him. He's been strapped up and the collar bone set, and so on. And I'm afraid his beauty has been spoiled, at least for a time, as a little slice was cut off the end of his nose by the glass of the windscreen.'

'Oh, poor James!'

'He doesn't care about the look of it, but curses most horribly whenever he needs to blow it.'

I sent my sympathy, assured Amy that all was well at Bent, and we rang off.

I had not mentioned it to my old friend, but this was the evening when I had undertaken to give a talk to Fairacre Women's Institute about our holiday in Crete.

Accordingly, soon after her telephone call, I dressed in my best and warmest garments and got ready for my ordeal. The Mawnes had promised to bring a projector and I had looked out my slides into some semblance of order. Amy had offered her own collection, but under the circumstances, I had to make do with my inferior efforts. Luckily, the brilliant Cretan light had guaranteed success with almost all the exposures.

The village hall was gratifyingly full and a beautiful flower arrangement graced the W.I. tablecloth. Listening to the minutes, from the front row, I studied its form. This was obviously the handiwork of one of 'the floral ladies', expert in arrangement of colour and form with no 'Oasis' visible at all, as is usual with us lesser mortals. The whole thing had been fixed, with artistic cunning, to a mossy piece of wood, and I was so busy trying to work out how it was done, that it came as a severe shock to hear my name called and to be obliged to take the floor.

I began by a brief description of our journey out, and of the attractions of the hotel. The projector, operated by Mr Mawne, worked splendidly for he had brought the correct plug for the village hall socket, a rare occurrence on these occasions, and we were all duly impressed at such efficiency and foresight.

The vivid colours of the Cretan landscape were even more impressive on a grey October evening. The animals evoked cries of admiration, although someone commented that the R.S.P.C.A would never have let a poor little donkey *that* small, hump a great load like that! I had to explain that, despite appearances, those four wispy legs beneath the piles of brushwood were really not suffering from hardship and that the load was light in weight.

Knossos, of course, brought forth the most enthusiastic response. The great red pillars and the beautiful flights of stairs made spectacular viewing, and the frescoes of dolphins and bulls were much admired. Even the topless ladies were accepted, except for one gasp of shock from Mrs Pringle in the front row.

I ended in good time, for I had seen Mrs Willet go quietly into the kitchen to attend to the boiling water in the urn, and knew that coffee break was scheduled.

My final word was of thanks to Mr Mawne, who had so nobly coped with the projector, and to whom I felt I owed an apology as I had been unable to photograph the Cretan hawk for him.

At this, Mr Mawne came forward and began a description of the elusive bird. I must say, his grasp of the subject was profound, and by the time he had described its appearance in detail, its mode of flight and its diet, a good many ladies were consulting their wrist watches while Mrs Willet hovered by the kitchen door, coffee pot in hand.

Meanwhile, I had sat down in the front row beside Mrs Pringle, the better to enjoy Mr Mawne's impromptu discourse. It is such off-the-cuff situations which give village meetings their particular flavour. Who wants to stick to such a dreary thing as an agenda? As everyone knows, the *real* business takes place on the way home, or an hour after the meeting finished, in the local pub.

Henry Mawne was just about to begin on the breeding habits and nesting sites of the hawk, and had broken off to suggest that he would just slip down to his house to fetch a reference book on the subject, if the ladies were agreeable, when Mrs Partridge, as President, bravely rose and checked the flow with her usual charm and aplomb. What was more, she invited her old friend to speak at one of the monthly meetings next year about any of his favourite birds.

'I am sure that they will soon be our favourites as well,' she finished, with a disarming smile, and Henry resumed his seat, flushed with pleasure, while Mrs Willet hastened to bring in the coffee amidst general relief.

I was presented with the magnificent flower arrangement, so that, all in all, the evening was a resounding success.

Amy's second call came soon after I returned from school the next day.

'There's a bit of a panic here,' said Amy calmly. 'Don't laugh, but poor James has the *measles*!'

'Oh, no! As though he hasn't enough to put up with.'

'Exactly. I suppose he picked it up when he was at home recently. Mrs Bennet was about in the house then. It might have been contact with her. But there, it could have been *anyone*! The point is, the hospital people seem dead anxious to get rid of him before he gives it to the rest of the ward, so they tell me he is fit enough to go home tomorrow.'

'I bet he's pleased.'

'He is. So am I. It's funny they didn't spot this rash earlier, but I think they put it down to a fairly common reaction to antibiotics, and in any case, he hasn't got a great many spots.'

'Can I do anything this end?'

'Yes, please. Could you turn up the heating, and get some milk and bread for us? I'll shop the next day when he's settled in.'

I said I could do whatever was needed.

'He's still at the soup and egg-and-milk stage. A front tooth was knocked out, which gives him a piratical look, and his mouth hurts him quite a bit.'

'He sounds as though he's taken quite a pasting.'

'Well, evidently he was turning right, and a van was coming behind him pretty swiftly, and James caught the full force of the impact. Luckily, nothing too serious seems to have resulted apart from the collar bone and ribs. It's just that he looks rather odd with his sliced nose and gappy smile. And, of course, it is rather ignominious to have the measles in your fifties! In fact, rather a humiliating end altogether to what was going to be a glamorous few days in Devonshire.'

'Does he feel that?' I asked hesitantly.

'Yes, he certainly does,' said Amy. 'Wasn't it Molière who said: "One may have no objection to being wicked but one hates to be ridiculous"? Well, that sums up James's feelings at the moment.'

The pips went for the second time, and I felt we should terminate our conversation.

'What time do you expect to be home?'

'During the late afternoon, I imagine. We'll have to see the doctor here, and I shall drive slowly. The poor old thing is pretty battered and bruised. He'll go straight to bed, of course.'

I said that I would put hot bottles in the beds, and we rang off.

An hour or so later, I drove over to Bent to do my little duties.

I took with me a few late roses to cheer the invalid's room, and half a dozen of Mrs Pringle's new-laid eggs.

On the way, I left a message at the dairy and collected a brown loaf. The house struck pleasantly warm when I entered, but I duly turned up the heating and set a fire ready in the sitting room for Amy to light on her return.

There was little else to do except to fill the hot-water bottles and to transfer the few letters from the floor to the hall table. I was home again by eight o'clock to join Tibby by my own fire.

Leg upraised, she washed herself industriously, spitting out little balls of goosegrass on to the hearthrug. As cat-slave, I transferred them meekly from the rug to the fire, my thoughts with Amy and James.

They were much in my mind throughout lessons the next day. Soon after five, Amy rang to thank me for my ministrations.

'What sort of journey?'

'Better than I thought. He stood it very well, and feels easier now that he's in his own bed. His temperature is almost back to normal. I shall get our own doctor to call in tomorrow, but I think he'll mend fast now.'

There was relief and happiness in Amy's voice which I had not heard for many months.

And I knew, as Amy certainly must know, that, in every sense of the expression, James had come home.

20. The Final Scene

The autumn gales gave way to a spell of quiet grey weather, and we were all mightily relieved. The stoves behaved properly, the children almost as well, and their parents finished tidying their gardens and generally set about preparations for the winter ahead.

Mist veiled the downs from sight. It hung, swirling sluggishly, in the lanes, and everything outdoors was damp to touch. Flagged paths and steps glistened, little droplets hung on the hedges, and nothing stirred.

All sound was muffled. Mr Roberts' sheep, in the field across the playground, sounded as though they bleated from as far away as Beech Green. The dinner van purred to a halt as mellifluously as a Rolls. Even the children's voices, as they played up and down the coke pile, were pleasantly muffled.

The measles epidemic seemed to be on the wane. Children returned, a little peaky perhaps, and certainly with tiresome coughs which persisted long after they were pronounced cured, but seemingly ready for work and secretly glad, I suspected, to have something to occupy them.

James's measles, and his general injuries, kept him resting for some time after his return home. Amy rang me one evening when I was busy with the local paper.

'Getting on quite well,' she replied in answer to my inquiries. 'But I really rang about something quite different. Have you seen the paper today?'

'I'm holding it.'

'Good. Look at page fourteen.'

'Hang on while I turn it over.'

I spread the paper on the hall floor and turned the pages.

'What about it?' I asked.

'Well, look at the photograph!'

Amy sounded impatient. I looked obligingly at some

twenty photographs of local houses. At least six pages of the *Caxley Chronicle* are devoted to housing advertisements.

'Which one?'

'What do you mean, which one? There is only one.'

'On page fourteen? It's one of the advertisement pages. There are about two dozen photographs.'

There was an ominous silence. When Amy spoke next it was in the quiet controlled voice of a teacher driven to desperation by some particularly obtuse pupil.

'Which paper are you looking at?'

'The *Caxley Chronicle*. You said "The Paper". On Thursday, naturally, "The Paper" is the local one.

'I didn't mean that thing!' Amy shouted, with exasperation. 'How parochially minded can you get? Look at the *Daily Telegraph*.'

'I shall have to fetch it,' I said huffily. 'I haven't had time to look at it yet.'

I found page fourteen in the right periodical, and called excitedly down the telephone.

'Yes! Good heavens! Gerard!'

'As you say, "Good heavens, Gerard!" What do you think of that?'

The photograph showed a pretty woman in a fur coat holding hands with Gerard, who was looking remarkably smug and had a wisp of hair standing up in the wind like a peewit's crest.

Underneath it said:

'Miss Hattie May, the well-known musical comedy actress, after her marriage to Mr Gerard Baker at Caxton Hall.'

'It's staggering, isn't it?' I said. 'And they've even got the names right!'

'It's not the reporters I'm concerned with,' said Amy severely, 'it's poor Vanessa. What will she be feeling?'

'I don't imagine she'll be too upset,' I said. 'I never did think she was in love with him.'

This was plain speaking, but I was still smarting from Amy's high-handedness about parochial minds.

'I don't expect a single woman like you to be particularly sensitive to a young girl's reaction to an attractive and mature man like Gerard,' said Amy, with *hauteur*. She was obviously going to return blow for blow, no doubt to the enjoyment of the telephone operator. I determined not to be drawn. In any case, I had some gingerbread in the oven and it was beginning to smell 'most sentimental', as Kipling said. This was no time for a brawl.

'Look, Amy,' I said swiftly. 'I honestly think Vanessa is completely heart-whole — at least, as far as Gerard is concerned, so don't upset yourself on her behalf.

Amy accepted the olive branch and spoke graciously.

'I hope you're right. You often are,' she added generously. 'I wondered if I should ring her at the hotel, but perhaps I'll wait.'

'Good idea,' I said, trying to keep the relief from my voice. Amy, in meddlesome mood, is dangerous. 'No doubt, she would prefer to get in touch with you.'

'Yes, yes, that's so!' agreed Amy. She sounded thoughtful.

I rang off before she could start the discussion again, and made swiftly for the oven. The gingerbread could not have stood another two minutes.

I discovered, with some surprise, that half-term occurred the next weekend. So much had happened already this term, that I had not really collected my wits sufficiently to look ahead. What with Amy's affairs, the last trivial discomforts of my own injuries, Mrs Pringle's tribulations, the measles and the ordinary run of day-to-day school events, time had whirled by.

Miss Edwards, my infants' teacher, a pleasant girl who had been with me for two years since the departure of Mrs Bonny, brought to my notice the fact that, if we were proposing to have a Christmas concert, as usual, then we should start preparing for it.

She was right, of course, but the thought depressed me.

'What about a carol service with the nine lessons?' I countered weakly. 'We shall have the usual Christmas party in the school.'

She looked disappointed.

'Let me think about it over half-term,' I said, and we shelved the subject.

'And another thing,' she said. 'I'm getting married next Easter, so of course I shall give in my notice, and go at the end of next term. It's early to tell you, but I thought you'd like to know in good time.'

There was nothing to do but to congratulate her, but my heart was leaden. I broke the news to the vicar when I saw him.

His face lit up with joy.

'What good news! She will make an excellent wife and mother.'

'There are too many girls running out of teaching to become excellent wives and mothers,' I said sourly. 'Especially infant teachers. Heaven knows when we'll get a replacement. After all, the colleges don't let the girls out until June or July. We shall have a whole term to fill in.'

This is a situation which has faced us often enough, but every time it brings pain and perplexity.

Mr Partridge trotted out his usual optimistic hopes.

'There's dear Miss Clare – ' he began.

'Much too old, and not fair to her or the children.'

'Well, Mrs Arnett, perhaps?'

'She's two children of her own and a husband, and an old blind aunt coming for the summer.'

'Really? What a kind person she is! Lives for others, and an example to us all.'

I agreed. A heavy silence fell as we wrestled with the problem.

'Now, what about that good friend of yours who is so competent? The lady from Bent? She helped us once or twice, I believe.'

I said that Amy might manage the odd day or two, but was far too busy a person to commit herself to a whole term's teaching.

'Besides,' I said, 'Amy's methods are the same vintage as mine, and I think she'd find our infant room far too chaotic under today's conditions.'

'But I thought that was as it should be these days?' protested Mr Partridge, looking bewildered. 'That last inspector who called – the one with no collar, you remember, and long hair

– he said that young children needed to make a noise to develop properly. I recall his words quite clearly: "Meaningful activity creates noise".'

'So do other things,' I remarked tartly. 'The point is that to get a competent teacher for the infant room is going to be a headache.'

'I shall see that the post is advertised in good time,' said the vicar. 'After all, one never knows. Providence has been good to us before, and Fairacre is doubly attractive in the summer. I will have a word with the Office at once.'

'That might be a help,' I agreed.

'I must go and see Miss Edwards,' he said, 'to congratulate her. Are you sure you can't persuade your friend to come over from Bent for that term? It's not too bad a journey.'

'I will ask her, but I don't think there's much hope there. Her husband is recovering rather slowly from a car accident, complicated by catching measles.'

'Poor fellow,' said Mr Partridge sincerely. 'I heard he had been injured. He's lucky to have such a good wife to nurse him back to health.'

If he had added: 'And to his responsibilities as a married man,' I should not have been surprised. Clearly, the vicar knew exactly what had been happening at Bent.

One morning, during half-term, I was surprised and pleased to have a visit from Amy.

'Mrs Bennet's back,' she explained. 'Still a trifle wobbly, but it means I can get out now and again. James is in bed most of the day, so he's not in the way of Mrs Bennet's Hoover.'

She presented me with a splendid bunch of late chrysanthemums.

'By the way, you were right about Vanessa. She rang the very same night that we saw the photograph of Gerard and Hattie. I don't know if she was putting on a stout act, or whether she was genuinely pleased, but I must say she sounded so.'

I could afford to be magnanimous in the face of this.

'Well, naturally, as an aunt, you would be more anxious

about Vanessa's feelings than I needed to be. But I always thought that Gerard's manner was more *avuncular* than *amatory*.'

'At Gerard's age,' commented Amy, 'it might well be both. He is practically the same age as James.'

We seemed to be treading close to dangerous ground.

'What did Vanessa say?' I asked hastily.

'Well, it seems that Gerard had confided to Vanessa his hopes of wooing Hattie some time ago. You remember she bought that house near the hotel? Evidently he was a constant visitor. Of course, all this is Vanessa's story, you understand. She may well be putting a good front on a somewhat humiliating episode.'

'I don't think so for a minute,' I said stoutly.

'He knew Hattie years ago. In fact, it was his friend who cut him out, so Vanessa says, which is why he's never married. It's rather romantic, isn't it, to think of him being faithful for all those years?'

'Maybe he didn't meet anyone he liked.'

'Trust you to throw cold water on any small fire of passion,' observed Amy, but she was smiling.

'I'm very glad it's ended this way,' I told her. 'Hattie May was always a darling, and the more I see of Gerard the better I like him. I look forward to meeting them both.'

'And so you shall,' declared Amy, 'for I'm inviting them down for a weekend as soon as James has properly recovered.'

She looked at me speculatively, as if weighing up something in her mind. I wondered what was worrying her.

'Have some coffee?' I suggested.

Amy shook her head.

'Not at the moment, thanks. I just wanted to let you know how things have worked out for James and me. You were such a help, when I was in the depths. It's only right that you should know the end of the story.'

'Amy,' I protested, 'there's absolutely no need!'

'Don't get alarmed! I shan't tell you any details that might bring a blush to your maiden cheek, I assure you.'

'Thank God for that! You know I hear far too many confidences for my peace of mind as a spinster.'

Amy looked suddenly contrite.

'I hope I didn't burden you too desperately,' she said, in a low voice. 'Perhaps I imposed on you as thoughtlessly as so many others do. I'm sorry.'

'Your troubles are quite different,' I said. 'And if two old friends like us can't help each other in a fix, it's a pity. You rallied to my support when I needed it. I hope I helped a little when things were tough with you. So, rattle away, and tell me what happened. Of course I want to know. It's just that I don't want you to feel obliged to *Tell All*.'

Amy laughed.

'Well, poor James has had long enough to think about things. I was careful not to press him too much. It was plain that he was desperately unhappy, and one evening after we were back at home he volunteered the information that Jane's affections had been cooling for some time. In fact, it was for this reason that he had insisted on taking her away for the week-end to see if they couldn't make things up. I think he was feeling pretty silly too, as he had asked me for a divorce, and now the girl was about to ditch him.'

'But surely, it would have been more sensible to have broken with Jane then, rather than pursue her further?'

'Being sensible is not the usual state of mind when a man's in love. Especially a middle-aged man. And you know James! Love him as I do, I face the fact that he is a terrible show-off, and always has been. The handmade shoes, the vastly expensive suits, the fast cars – they're all the dreary old status symbols that James loves to play with. They've never impressed me particularly, as he well knows, and perhaps that's where I have been wrong – in letting him see that I have simply indulged his weakness for his toys instead of letting him think I'm dazzled by them. Well, we live and learn, and we've both learnt the hard way these last few months.'

'It's over now,' I said consolingly.

'Yes, I think it is, as far as our natures will allow it to be. If only we'd had children, I think we should have escaped some of this damage.'

'There would have been other risks. They might have

turned out unsatisfactorily in one way or another, and I think that's harder to bear than any result of one's own actions.'

Amy nodded and sighed.

'I suppose the old saying that man is born to trouble as the sparks fly upward, is pretty true. However, our particular trouble has a funny side.'

'Tell me.'

'Well, on the day of the accident, evidently, Jane was being remarkably offhand and James was doing his best to impress her as they drove – much too fast, I gather – down to Devon. According to him, she picked a quarrel about the best route to take, and was actually tugging at his arm when he was turning right, shouting that it was the wrong road.

'I think there may be some truth in this. James isn't a liar about matters of this sort, and it's unlike him to have missed seeing the van coming up behind him. He drives much too fast, I always think, but he prides himself on being a good driver, and really he is.'

'So she may have caused the accident?'

'Who's to say? Anyway, she was furious with him. I heard a bit about her behaviour from the hospital staff. And she wouldn't answer the telephone when James tried to ring her. After some time, he began to accept the position, and it was then that he told me all about it.'

'Was he very miserable?'

'I think he'd begun to get over that. Let's say he was beginning to be more clear-headed, and to face the fact that he'd behaved badly. Also, that he was well out of a situation which would have been distinctly uncomfortable. Jane's mother, I gather, is a holy terror.

'Anyway, recovery was complete last week when a letter came from Jane. I've brought it for you to read.'

'Oh no!' I demurred. 'I'm sure James would be horrified if he knew you'd shown it to me!'

'Not he! Here, take it.'

She handed over the sheet of bright blue paper. In a large schoolgirl scrawl was Jane's final communication, presumably, to James.

It said:

Dear James,

This is to give in my notice. I don't want to set foot in that office again, or to see you.

My mother says I should sue you for damages, but I've told her I don't want anything more to do with you. I must have been mad to waste my time with someone so old and dotty he can't even drive.

Jane

P.S. Yesterday I got engaged to Teddy Thimblemere in Accounts and we are getting married at Christmas.

'And how did James take that?' I asked, handing it back.

'He lay back on the pillow with his eyes closed, and then he began to shake. I was quite worried, until I realized it was with laughter. He laughed until the tears ran down his cheeks, and of course that set me laughing too! You should have heard the hullabaloo, and poor James gasping for breath, and saying: "Oh God, my poor ribs hurt so!" And me, wiping my eyes and saying: "Try *not* to laugh, darling, you'll burst something!" And, after a bit, he would quieten down, and then remember some particular phrase like "so old and dotty he can't even drive", and double up all over again. It did us both a world of good!'

'Not enough laughter about these days,' I agreed.

'It's as good a healer as time,' said Amy, putting the letter into her bag. 'That little bout certainly restored us to happier days.'

'And so, all's well again?'

'As well as one can expect in an imperfect world,' said Amy. 'I daresay James will recover enough to turn to look at a pretty girl again, when he's had his nose patched up and a false tooth put in the gap. And no doubt I shall be as bossy and bitchy as I am at times. But somehow, I feel sure, nothing quite so serious will ever happen again.'

'I'm glad you told me,' I said. 'I like a happy ending.'

'Then let's have that coffee,' said Amy.

A week or so later, I was talking to Mr Willet in the playground after school, when a long low sports car of inordinate length drew up outside the school house.

It was a dashing vehicle, bright yellow in colour, with

enormous headlamps and one of those back windows on top
of the car like a skylight. The bonnet seemed about six feet in
length, and the whole thing was dazzlingly polished.

'My word,' said Mr Willet, with awe, 'that must've cost a
pretty penny! One of your millionaire friends droppin' in?'

'Strangers to me,' I was saying, when the door by the
passenger's seat opened, and Vanessa emerged.

'Hello!' I welcomed her. 'How lovely to see you!'

'We're on our way to see Aunt Amy,' said Vanessa, kissing
me, and enveloping me in fair hair and expensive scent. 'And
this is Tarquin.'

An enormous young man disengaged himself from the interior of the car, and shook my hand so warmly that I
wondered if I should ever be able to part my fingers again.
He was so good-looking, however, that I readily forgave
him, and they came with me into the sitting room.

I thought I had never seen Vanessa quite so lively. It was
quite apparent that Gerard's affairs were not worrying her.

On the contrary, she spoke of his marriage with the greatest joy.

'Wasn't it fun? That's really why he was off to town last time we called. He really deserves someone as nice as Hattie. He's so *kind*! I can't tell you how good he's been to me. I've *always* asked his advice about *everything*, and he's never failed me. And see what else he did?'

She gazed fondly upon Tarquin, who gazed back in an equally besotted fashion.

'He introduced me to Tarquin. And here, you see, we are! Just engaged!'

I hastened to congratulate them.

'We're not sure if we're on our heads or our heels,' said the young man. 'We rang Vanessa's father and mother last night, and we're going to stay there over the week-end.'

'And I said,' broke in Vanessa, 'we simply *must* call in on you on the way, and Aunt Amy, because we wanted you to know before it was in the paper.'

'Well I call it uncommonly nice of you,' I said, 'and I very much appreciate it. When will the wedding be?'

'Tomorrow,' said Tarquin, 'if I had my way.'

'Dear thing!' said Vanessa indulgently. 'Probably early in the New Year.'

'As long as that?' exclaimed the young man.

I asked them to have a drink in celebration, but they looked at the clock, and each other, and said that they must go.

They fitted themselves skilfully into the gorgeous car. I kissed Vanessa, and kept my hands out of the way as I wished Torquil good-bye.

The car roared away. Mr Willet, who was carrying a bucket of coke to make up the stoves for the night, set it down, and pushed his cap to the back of his head with a black hand.

'You was cut out, I see,' he observed. 'That young lady saw him first.'

Sadly, I had to agree.

Three days later, Amy rang me.

'Have you seen the paper? And I *don't* mean the *Caxley Chronicle*!'

'Why? Is Vanessa's engagement in it?'

'Yes. Have you read it?'

'I had an accident with the paper today.'

'How do you mean?'

'I muddled it up with yesterday's, and gave it to the children to tear up for papier mâché bowls.'

'Really! The things you do! Sometimes I despair of you!'

'I despair of myself.'

'Well, listen! I'll read it to you.'

' "The engagement is announced between Tarquin Ian Angus, only son of Wing Commander and Mrs Bruce Cameron of Blairlochinnie Castle, Ayrshire, and Vanessa Clare, only daughter of Mr and Mrs Charles Hunt of Hampstead, London." '

'And will she live at Blair Tiddlywinks Castle?'

'Not for a long time. Tarquin's father is in splendid health, I gather, and I don't think the banks and braes are altogether to Torquil's taste just yet. You know what he does?'

'No.'

'He's a band leader. And fairly rolling in money. No, I think London will be the place for those two.'

'Have they fixed the wedding date?'

'Yes. It's to be the first week in January. You're going to be invited, so you'd better start looking for that winter coat.'

'I will,' I said meekly.

'We shall be back for the wedding, of course,' said Amy.

'Back?' I echoed.

'From our holiday. James wants to go as soon as he's fit again, and that won't be long now.'

'And where are you going?'

Amy laughted. 'Can't you guess? To Crete.'

'Perfect!' I cried.

In a flash, I saw again the golden island, and breathed the heady scent of flowers and sun-baked earth. One day, I knew suddenly, I should go there once more.

'Give it all my love,' I said.

Village Affairs

To Anthea and Mac
with love

CONTENTS

PART ONE

The Rumours Fly

1. Forebodings

It is an undisputed fact that people who choose to live in the country must expect to be caught up, willy-nilly, in the cycle of the seasons.

Spring-cleaning is done to the accompaniment of the rattle of tractors as they drill up and down the bare fields outside. Lambs bleat, cuckoos cry, blackbirds scold inquisitive cats, while upstairs the sufferers from spring influenza call hoarsely for cold drinks.

Summer brings its own background of sights and sounds and the pace of village life quickens as fêtes follow cricket matches, and outings, tennis parties and picnics crowd the calendar.

There is not quite so much junketing in the autumn, for harvest takes pride of place, and both men and women are busy storing and preserving, filling the barns and the pantry shelves.

It is almost a relief to get to winter, to put away the lawn mower, to burn the garden rubbish, and to watch the ploughs at work turning the bright corn stubble into dark chocolate ribs ready for winter planting, while the rooks and peewits flutter behind, sometimes joined by sea-gulls when the weather is cruel elsewhere.

For each of us in the country our own particular pattern of life forms but a small part against the general background of the seasons. If you are a schoolmistress, as I am, then the three terms echo in miniature the rural world outside. The Christmas term brings the arrival of new children to the school, harvest festival and, of course, the excitement of Christmas itself.

The spring term is usually the coldest and the most germ-ridden, but catkins and primroses bring hope of better times, and summer itself is the crown of the year.

It is good to have this recurring rhythm, this familiar shape of the year. We know – to some extent – what to expect, what to welcome, what to avoid.

But there is another aspect of country life which is not so steady. There are certain topics which crop up again and again.

Not, to be sure, as rhythmically as primroses and harvest, but often enough over the years to give us a little jolt of recognition. There is the matter of the village hall, for instance. Is it needed or not needed? And then there is the parlous state of the church organ and its eternal fund. And Mrs So-and-so is expecting again for the twelfth – or is it the thirteenth? – time, and something must be done about her house, or her husband, or both.

It is rather like watching a roundabout at a Fair. The galloping horses whirl by, nostrils flaring, tails streaming, and then suddenly there is an ostrich, strange and exotic in its plumage among the everyday beasts. The merry-go-round twirls onward and we begin to sink back again into our pleasant lethargy when, yet again, the ostrich appears and our interest is quickened once more. So it is with these topics which disappear for a time whilst we are engrossed with everyday living, and then reappear to become the chief matters of importance, our talking points, things which have startled us from our normal apathy and quickened our senses.

Just such a recurring topic is the possible closure of Fairacre School. I have been headmistress here for a number of years, and talk of closing it has cropped up time and time again, diverting attention from the Church Organ Fund and the Village Hall as surely as the ostrich does from the horses. Naturally, after a week or two, the excitement dies down, and we continue as before with feelings of relief, until the next crisis arrives.

The cause varies. The true difficulty is that our numbers at the school scarcely warrant two teachers. One-teacher schools are considered undesirable, rightly, I think, and have been closing steadily in this area. Every now and again, the word goes round that Fairacre School really only needs one and a half teachers, and this half-teacher problem cannot be overcome, although one has the pleasing fancy that a great deal of ruler-gnawing in county offices goes on while the matter is being given consideration.

Usually, Providence steps in. A new family of six children appears, and is joyously added to the register. Cross parents refuse to send their young children by bus to the next village, or some other benign agency gets to work, and the matter of Fairacre School's closure is shelved once more.

I had become so used to the ostrich appearing, that I confess I could scarcely distinguish him from the galloping horses.

Until one evening, when Mr Annett, the headmaster of neighbouring Beech Green School, startled me with his disclosures.

As well as being a headmaster, George Annett is choirmaster and organist of St Patrick's, Fairacre. On Friday evenings he drives over from Beech Green, a distance of some three miles, to officiate at choir practice.

For a small village we have quite a flourishing choir. Two of the stalwarts are Mr Willet, part-time caretaker of the school, sexton, grave-digger and general handyman to the whole village, and Mrs Pringle, our lugubrious school cleaner, whose booming contralto has been heard for long – far too long, according to the ribald young choristers – resounding among the rafters of St Patrick's roof.

On this particular Friday, George Annett called at the school house where I was busy putting away the week's groceries and trying to recover from the stunning amount I appeared to owe for about ten everyday items.

'Have a drink,' I said. 'I reckon I need a brandy when I see the price of butter this week.'

'A spot of sherry would be fine,' said George. 'Not too much. Can't arrive at church smelling of alcohol, or Mrs P. will have something to say.'

'Mrs Pringle,' I told him, with feeling, 'always has something to say. And usually something unpleasant. That woman positively invites assault and battery.'

'Heard the latest? Rumour has it that my school is being enlarged.'

'I've heard that before. And Fairacre's closing, I suppose?'

George studied his sherry, ignoring my flippancy. His grave face sobered me.

'It rather looks like it. The chap from the office is coming out next week to see me. Don't know why yet, but this rumour has reached me from several sources, and I believe something's in the wind. How many children do you have at the moment?'

'We're down to twenty-eight. Pat Smith has fifteen infants. I have the rest. Incidentally, she's going at the end of term, so we're in the throes of getting a new appointment.'

'No easy task.'

'No. I expect we'll have to make do with a number of supply teachers, until next term when the girls are appointed from college.'

George Annett put down his glass and rose to his feet.

'Well, I'll let you know more when I've seen Davis next week. I can't say I want a bigger school. We'll have the upheaval of new building going on, and a lot of disgruntled parents who don't want their children moved away.'

'Not to mention disgruntled out-of-work teachers.'

'You won't be out-of-work for long,' he smiled. 'Perhaps you'll be drafted to Beech Green?'

'And where should I live? No doubt the school and the school house would be sold together pretty quickly, and I certainly can't afford to buy either. I'm going to need a sub from the needlework tin, as it is, to pay for this week's groceries!'

George laughed, and departed.

I might have ignored this rumour, as I had so many others, if it had not been for Mrs Pringle.

She arrived at the school house on Saturday morning with a nice plump chicken, of her own rearing, in the black oilcloth bag which accompanies her everywhere.

'Have a cup of coffee with me,' I invited.

'I don't mind if I do,' replied Mrs Pringle graciously.

I recalled a forthright friend who used to reply to this lack-lustre acceptance by saying:

'And I don't mind if you don't!' But, naturally, I was too cowardly to copy her.

I took the tray into the garden, Mrs Pringle followed with the biscuit tin. Spring at Fairacre is pure bliss and I gazed fondly at the almond blossom, the daffodils and the pink haze of a copper beech in tiny leaf.

'I see you've got plenty of bindweed in your border,' said Mrs

Pringle, bringing me back to earth with a jolt. 'And twitch. No need to have twitch if you weeds regular.'

It sounded like some nervous complaint brought on by self-indulgence – a by-product of alcoholism, perhaps, or drug addiction. However, the sun was warm, the coffee fragrant, and I did not intend to let Mrs Pringle deflect me from their enjoyment.

'Have a biscuit,' I suggested, pushing the tin towards her. She selected a chocolate bourbon and surveyed it with disapproval.

'I used to be very partial to these until they doubled in price pretty nearly. Now I buy Osborne. Just as nourishing, and don't fatten you so much. At least, so Dr Martin said when he gave me my diet sheet.'

'A diet sheet?'

'Yes. I'm to lose three stone. No starch, no sugar, no fat, and no alcohol – though the last's no hardship, considering I signed the pledge as a child.'

'Then should you be eating that biscuit, and drinking coffee with cream in it?'

'I'm starting tomorrow,' said Mrs Pringle, taking a swift bite at the biscuit.

'I see.'

'You've heard about our school shutting, I suppose?' said the lady, her diction somewhat blurred with biscuit crumbs.

'Frequently.'

'No, the latest. My cousin at Beech Green says they're going to build on to Mr Annett's school, and send our lot over there in a bus. Won't suit some of 'em.'

A vague feeling of disquiet ran through me. Mrs Pringle was so often right. I remembered other dark warnings, airily dismissed by me, which had been proved correct, as time went by.

Mrs Pringle dusted some crumbs from her massive chest.

'Some seems to think the infants will stay here,' she went on, 'but I said to Florrie – that's my cousin at Beech Green, and a flighty one she used to be as a girl, but has steadied down wonderful now she's got eight children – I said to her, as straight as I'm saying to you now, Miss Read, what call would the Office have to keep open all that great school for a handful of fives to sevens? "Don't make sense," I said, and I repeat it now: "It just don't make sense."'

'No indeed,' I agreed weakly.

'Take the heating,' continued Mrs Pringle, now in full spate. She held out a large hand, as though offering me the two tortoise stoves in the palm. 'Sacks of good coke them stoves need during the winter, not to mention blacklead and brushes and a cinder pail. They all takes us taxpayers' money. Then there's brooms and dusters, and bar soap and floor cloths, which costs a small fortune – '

'And all the books, of course,' I broke in.

'Well, yes,' said Mrs Pringle doubtfully, 'I suppose they needs *books*.' She spoke as though such aids to learning were wholly irrelevant in a school – very small beer compared with such things as scrubbing brushes and the other tools of her trade.

'But stands to reason,' she continued, 'that it's cheaper for all the whole boiling to go on the bus to Beech Green, though what the petrol costs these days to trundle them back and forth, I shudders to think.'

'Well, it may not happen yet,' I said, as lightly as I could. 'We've had these scaremongering tales before.'

'Maybe,' said Mrs Pringle, rising majestically, and adjusting the black oilcloth bag over her arm. 'But this time I've heard it from a good many folk, and when have our numbers at Fairacre School ever been so low? I don't like it, Miss Read. I feels in my bones a preposition. My mother, God rest her, had second sight, and I sometimes thinks I take after her.'

I devoutly hoped that Mrs Pringle's premonition meant nothing, but could not help feeling uneasy as I accompanied her to the gate.

'You wants to get rid of that bindweed,' was her parting shot, 'before it Takes Over.'

That woman, I thought savagely as I collected our cups, always has the last word!

By Monday morning my qualms had receded into the background, as they had so often before. In any case, everyday problems of the classroom successfully ousted any future threats.

Patrick had been entrusted with a pound note for his dinner money and had lost it on the way. He was tearful, fearing awful retribution from his mother.

'It was in my pocket,' he sniffed, mopping his tears with the back of his hand. 'All scrunched up, it was, with these 'ere.'

He produced four marbles, a stub of pencil, a grey lump of bubblegum and a jagged piece of red glass.

'You'll cut yourself on that,' I said. 'Put it in the wastepaper basket.'

He looked at me in alarm. A fat tear coursed unnoticed down his cheek.

'But it's off my brother's rear lamp,' he protested.

'Well, put it in this piece of paper to take home,' I said, giving in. 'And put all that rubbish on the side table. Now *think*, Patrick. Did you take the pound note out of your pocket on the way?'

'Yes, he did, miss,' chorused the class.

'He showed it to me,' said Linda Moffat. 'He said he betted I didn't have as much money.'

'That's right,' agreed Ernest. 'And it was windy. Blowing about like a flag it was. I bet it's blown over the hedge.'

'And some old cow's eaten it.'

'Or some old tramp's picked it up.'

'Or some old bird's got it in its nest.'

At these helpful surmises, Patrick's tears flowed afresh.

'You must go back over your tracks, Patrick, and search,' I told him. 'And someone had better go with him. Two pairs of eyes are better than one.'

Silence descended upon the class. Arms were folded, chests stuck out, and expressions of intense capability transformed the countenance of all present. What could be better than escaping from the classroom into the windy lane outside?

'Ernest,' I said, at last.

There was a gust of expelled air from those waiting lungs, and a general slumping of disappointed forms.

Ernest and Patrick hastened from the room joyfully, almost knocking over Joseph Coggs who was entering with a bunch of bedraggled narcissi. He looked bemused.

'I bin and brought you some flowers,' he said, holding them up.

'My auntie brought them on Saturday, but my mum says they'll only get knocked over, so you can have them.'

'Well, thank you. Fetch a vase.'

When he returned, I added:

'You're late, you know, Joseph.'

His lower lip began to droop and I feared that we should have yet another pupil in tears.

'A policeman come,' he said.

Everyone looked up. Here was real drama!

'From Caxley,' faltered Joseph. Bright glances were exchanged. This was better still!

'He wanted to see my dad, but he was in bed. My mum give me these flowers and said to clear off while she got dad up. The policeman's waiting in our kitchen.'

'Well, there's no point in worrying about that,' I said reassuringly. 'Your mother and father will see to it.'

The class looked disappointed at the dismissal of such an enthralling subject. What spoilsports teachers are, to be sure!

By the time prayers had been said, a hymn sung and the rest of the pupils' dinner money safely gathered into my Oxo tin, the hands of the great wall clock stood at a quarter to ten. Patrick and Ernest were still at large in the village, and no doubt enjoying every minute of it.

'We're having a mental arithmetic test this morning,' I announced, amidst a few stifled groans, 'and I shall want someone to give out the paper.'

At that moment, there was a cry from the back of the room, and Eileen Burton stumbled down the aisle with a bloodied handkerchief clapped to her streaming nose.

This is a frequent occurrence and we all know what to do.

'Lay down, girl!' shouted one. I should like to have given – not for the first time – a short lecture on the use of the verbs 'to lie' and 'to lay', but circumstances were against me. As it was, I fetched the box of paper handkerchiefs and assisted the child to a prone position by the stove.

'Shall I get the cold water?'

'Do she need a cushion, miss?'

'She wants a bit of metal down her neck, miss.'

I fetched the cutting-out scissors, a hefty chunk of cold steel, and put them at the back of her neck, substituting, at the same time, a wad of paper tissues for the deplorable handkerchief. Eileen remained calm throughout, accustomed to the routine.

We left her there, and set about the test.

'Number down to twenty,' I told them. Would we never get started?

There was a clanging noise as feet trampled over the iron scraper in the lobby. Ernest and Patrick entered, wind-blown and triumphant, Patrick holding aloft a very dirty pound note.

'We found it, miss!' they cried. 'Guess where?'

'In the hedge?'

'No.'

'In the duck pond?' shouted someone, putting down his pen.

'No.'

'In your pocket after all?'

'No.'

By now, pens were abandoned, and it was plain that the mental arithmetic test would be indefinitely postponed unless I took a firm hand.

'That's enough. Tell us where.'

'In a cow pat. So stuck up it was, it couldn't blow away. Weren't it *lucky*?'

They thrust the noisome object under my nose.

'Wipe it,' I said faintly, 'with a damp cloth in the lobby, then *bring it back*. Don't let go of it for one second. Understand?'

By now it was a quarter past ten and no work done.

'First question,' I said briskly. Pens were picked up, amidst sighing.

'If a man has twelve chickens,' I began, when the door opened.

'And about time too,' I said wrathfully, expecting Ernest and Patrick to appear. 'Get into your desks, and let's get some work done!'

The mild face of the Vicar appeared, and we all rose in some confusion.

2. News of Minnie Pringle

The Reverend Gerald Partridge has been Vicar of this parish for many years. I have yet to hear anyone, even the most censorious chapel-goer, speak ill of him. He goes about his parish duties conscientiously, vague in his manner, but wonderfully alert to those who have need of his sympathy and wisdom.

In winter, he is a striking figure, tramping the lanes in an ancient cape of dramatic cut, and sporting a pair of leopard skin gloves, so old, that he is accompanied by little clouds of moulting fur whenever he uses his hands. It is commonly believed that they must have been a gift from some loving, and possibly beloved churchgoer, in the living before he came to Fairacre. Why otherwise would he cling to such dilapidated articles?

Fairacre School is a Church of England School, standing close to St Patrick's and the vicarage. The Vicar is a frequent visitor, and although I have heard the ruder boys mimicking him behind his back, the children are extremely fond of him, and I have witnessed them attacking a stranger who once dared to criticize him.

'I'm sorry to interrupt,' he said, 'but I was just passing and thought I would have a word with you.'

'Of course.'

I turned to the class.

'Turn over your test papers and write out the twelve times table,' I directed. Long-suffering glances were exchanged. Trust her to want the twelve times! One of the nastiest that was! Their looks spoke volumes.

'What on earth is the matter with that child?' asked the Vicar, in a shocked tone, his horrified gaze upon the prone and bloodied figure of Eileen Burton.

'Just a nose-bleed,' I said soothingly. 'She often has them.'

'But you should have a key,' cried Mr Partridge, much agitated, 'a *large* key, to put at the nape of the neck –'

'She's got the cutting-out scissors –' I began, but he was now too worried to heed such interruptions.

'My mother always kept a large key hanging in the kitchen for this sort of thing. We had a parlour maid once, just so afflicted. What about the key of the school door? Or shall I run back to the vicarage for the vestry key? It must weigh quite two pounds, and would be ideal for the purpose.'

His face was puckered with concern, his voice sharp with anxiety.

At that moment, Eileen stood up, dropped the paper handkerchief in the wastepaper basket, and smiled broadly.

'Over,' she announced, and put the scissors on my desk.

'Take care, dear child, take care!' cried the Vicar, but he sounded greatly relieved at this recovery.

He picked up the cutting-out scissors.

'A worthy substitute,' he conceded, 'but it would be as well to get Willet to screw a hook into the side of one of the cupboards for a key. I can provide you with one quite as massive as this, I can assure you, and I really should feel happier if you had one on the premises.'

I thanked him, and asked what it was he wanted to tell me.

'Simply a rumour about the school closing. I wanted you to know that I have had no official message about such a possibility. I pray that I may *never* have one, but should it be so, please rest assured that I should let you know at once.'

'Thank you. I know you would.'

'You have heard nothing?'

'Only rumours. They fly around so often, I don't let them bother me unduly.'

'Quite, quite. Well, I must be off. Mrs Partridge asked me to pick up something at the Post Office, but for the life of me I can't remember what it is. I wonder if I should go back and ask?'

'No doubt Mr Lamb will know and have it waiting for you,' I suggested.

Mr Partridge smiled with relief.

'I'm sure you're right. I will call there first. No point in worrying my wife unnecessarily.'

He waved to the children, and made for the door.

'I won't forget to look out a suitable key,' he promised. 'My mother would have approved of having one handy at all times. First aid, you know.'

The door closed behind him.

'First question,' I said. 'If a man had twelve chickens – '

Although I had told the Vicar that I was not unduly bothered by the rumours, it was not strictly true. Somehow, this time, as the merry-go-round twirled, the ostrich had a menacing expression as it appeared among the galloping horses. Perhaps, I told myself, everything seemed worse because I had heard the news from several sources in a very short space of time.

After school, I pottered about in the kitchen preparing a salad, which Amy, my old college friend, was going to share that evening. She had promised to deliver a pile of garments for a future jumble sale, and as James, her husband, was away from home, we were free to enjoy each other's company.

Apart from a deplorable desire to reform my slack ways, Amy is the perfect friend. True, she also attempts to marry me off, now and again, to some poor unsuspecting male, but this uphill job has proved in vain, so far, and I think she knows, in her heart, that she will never be successful.

It was while I was washing lettuce, that Mr Willet arrived with some broad bean plants.

'I saw you'd got some terrible gaps in your row, miss. Bit late perhaps to put 'em in, but we'll risk it, shall us?'

I agreed whole-heartedly.

He departed along the garden path, and I returned to the sink.

'*No rose in all the world,*' warbled Mr Willet, '*until you came.*'

Mr Willet has a large repertoire of songs which were popular at the beginning of the century. They take me back, in a flash, to the musical evenings beloved of my parents. Mercifully, I can only remember snippets of these sentimental ballads, most of which had a lot of 'ah-ah-ah'-ing between verses, although a line or two, here and there, still stick in my memory.

'*Dearest, the night is over*' (or was it 'lonely'?)

'*Waneth the trembling moon*' and another about living in a land of roses but dreaming of a land of snow. Or maybe the other way round? It was the sort of question to put to Mr Willet, I decided, when Amy arrived, and Mr Willet and the ballads were temporarily forgotten.

★

'Lovely to be here,' sighed Amy, after we had eaten our meal.

She leant back in the armchair and sipped her coffee.

'You really do make excellent coffee,' she said approvingly. 'Despite the haphazard way you measure the beans.'

'Thank you,' I said humbly. I rarely get praise from Amy, so that it is all the more flattering when I do.

She surveyed one elegant hand with a frown.

'My nails grow at such a rate. I always remember a horrifying tale I read when I was about ten. A body was exhumed, and the poor woman's coffin was full of her own hair and immensely long finger nails.'

'Horrible! But it's common knowledge that they go on growing after death.'

'A solemn thought, to imagine all those dark partings on Judgement Day,' commented Amy, patting her own neat waves. 'Well, what's the Fairacre news?'

I told her about the school, and its possible closure.

'That's old hat. I shouldn't worry unduly about that, though I did hear someone saying they'd heard that Beech Green was to be enlarged.'

'The grape vine spreads far and wide,' I agreed.

'But what about Mrs Fowler?'

'Mrs Fowler?' I repeated with bewilderment. 'You mean that wicked old harridan who used to live in Tyler's Row? Why, she left for Caxley years ago!'

'I know she did. That's why I hear about her from my window cleaner who lives next door to her, poor fellow. Well, she's being courted.'

'Never! I don't believe it!'

Amy looked pleasantly gratified at my reactions. 'And what's more, the man is the one that Minnie Pringle married.'

This was staggering news, and I was suitably impressed. Minnie Pringle is the niece of my redoubtable Mrs Pringle. We Fairacre folk have lost count of the children she has had out of wedlock, and were all dumb-founded when we heard that she was marrying a middle-aged man with children of his own. As far as I knew, they had settled down fairly well together at Springbourne. But if Amy's tale were to be believed, then the marriage must be decidedly shaky.

'Mrs Pringle hasn't said anything,' I said.

'She may not know anything about it.'

'Besides,' I went on, 'can you imagine anyone falling for Mrs Fowler? She's absolutely without charms of any sort.'

'That's nothing to do with it,' replied Amy. 'There's such a thing as incomprehensible attraction. Look at some of the truly dreadful girls at Cambridge who managed to snaffle some of the most attractive men!'

'But Mrs Fowler – ' I protested.

Amy swept on.

'One of the nastiest men I ever met,' she told me, 'had four wives.'

'What? All at once? A Moslem or something?'

'No, no,' said Amy testily. 'Don't be so headlong!'

'You mean headstrong.'

'I know what I mean, thank you. You rush *headlong* to conclusions, is what I mean.'

'I'm sorry. Well, what was wrong with this nasty man you knew?'

'For one thing, he cleaned out his ears with a match stick.'

'Not the striking end, I hope. It's terribly poisonous.'

'*Whichever* end he used, the operation was revolting.'

'Oh, I agree. Absolutely. What else?'

'Several things. He was mean with money. Kicked the cat. Had Wagner – of all people – too loud on the gramophone. And yet, you see, he had this charm, this charisma – '

'Now there's a word I never say! Like "Charivari". "Punch or the London" one, you know.'

Amy tut-tutted with exasperation.

'The point I have been trying to make for the last ten minutes,' shouted Amy rudely, '*against fearful odds*, is that Minnie Pringle's husband must see something attractive in Mrs Fowler.'

'I thought we'd agreed on that,' I said. 'More coffee?'

'Thank you,' said Amy faintly. 'I feel I need it.'

The fascinating subject of Mrs Fowler and her admirer did not crop up again until the last day of the spring term.

Excitement, as always, was at fever-pitch among the children. One would think that they were endlessly beaten and bullied at school when one sees the joy with which they welcome the holidays.

Pat Smith, who had been my infants' teacher for the past two years, was leaving to get married at Easter, and we presented her with a tray, and a large greetings card signed by all the children.

The Vicar called to wish her well, and to exhort the children to help their mothers during the holidays, and to enjoy themselves.

When he had gone, I contented myself with impressing upon them the date of their return, and let them loose. Within minutes, the stampede had vanished round the bend of the lane, and I was alone in the schoolroom.

I always love that first moment of solitude, when the sound of the birds is suddenly noticed, and the scent of the flowers reminds one of the quiet country pleasures ahead. Now, freed from the bondage of the clock and the school timetable, there would be time 'to stand and stare', to listen to the twittering of nestlings, the hum of the early foraging bees, and the first sound of the cuckoo from the coppice across the fields.

Spring is the loveliest time of the year at Fairacre, when

everything is young, and green, and alive with hope. Soon the house martins would be back, and the swifts, screaming round and round the village as they selected nesting places. Then the swallows would arrive, seeking out their old familiar haunts – Mr Roberts' barn rafters, the Post Office porch, the loft above the Vicar's stables – in which to build their nests.

Someone had brought me a bunch of primroses as an end of term present. Holding the fragrant nosegay carefully, I made my way through the school lobby towards my home across the playground, full of anticipation at the happiness ahead.

The door scraper clanged. The door opened, and Mrs Pringle, her mouth set grimly, confronted me.

'Sorry I'm a few minutes late,' she began, 'but I'm In Trouble.'

In Fairacre, this expression is commonly used to describe pregnancy, but in view of Mrs Pringle's age, I rightly assumed that she used the term more generally.

'What's wrong?'

'It's our Minnie,' said Mrs Pringle. 'Up my place. In a fair taking, she is. Can't do nothing with her. I've left her crying her eyes out.'

'Oh, dear,' I said weakly, my heart sinking. Could Amy have heard aright?

I smelt my sweet primroses to give me comfort.

'Come to the house and sit down,' I said.

Mrs Pringle raised a hand, and shook her head.

'No. I've come to work, and work I will!'

'Well, at least sit on the bench while you tell me.'

A rough plank bench in the playground, made by Mr Willet, acts as seat, vaulting horse, balancing frame and various other things, and on this we now rested, Mrs Pringle with her black oilcloth bag on her lap, and the primroses on mine. In the hedge dividing the playground from the lane, a blackbird scolded as Tibby, my cat, emerged from the school house to see why I was taking so long to get into the kitchen to provide her meal.

'That man,' said Mrs Pringle, 'has up and left our Minnie. What's more, he's left his kids, and hers, and that one of theirs, to look after, while he gallivants with that woman who's no better than she should be.'

'Perhaps he'll come back,' I suggested.

'Not him! He's gone for good. And d'you know who he's with?'

'No,' I said, expecting to be struck by lightning for downright lying.

'You'll never guess. That Mrs Fowler from Tyler's Row.'

I gave a creditable gasp of surprise.

'The scheming hussy,' said Mrs Pringle wrathfully. A wave of scarlet colour swept up her neck and into her cheeks, which were awobble with indignation.

'It's my belief she knew he had an insurance policy coming out this month. After his money, you see. Well, it wouldn't have been his looks, would it?'

I was obliged to agree, but remembered Amy's remark about the plain girls and the young Adonises at Cambridge. Who could tell?

'But, top and bottom of it all is – how's Minnie to live? Oh, I expect she'll get the Social Security and Family Allowance, and all that, but she'll need a bit of work as well, I reckons, if she's to keep that house on at Springbourne.'

'Won't he provide some money?'

'That'll be the day,' said Mrs Pringle sardonically. 'Unless Min takes him to court, and who's got the time and money to bother with all that?'

Mrs Pringle's view of British justice was much the same as her views of my housekeeping, it seemed, leaving much to be desired.

'If she really needs work,' I said reluctantly, 'I could give her half a day here cleaning silver, and windows, and things.'

Mrs Pringle's countenance betrayed many conflicting emotions. Weren't her own ministrations on my behalf enough then? And what sort of a hash would Minnie make of any job offered her? And finally, it was a noble gesture to offer her work anyway.

Luckily, the last emotion held sway.

'That's a very kind thought, Miss Read. Very kind indeed.'

She struggled to her feet, and we stood facing each other.

Tibby began to weave between our legs, reminding us of her hunger.

'But let's hope it won't come to that,' she said. I hoped so too, already regretting my offer.

Mrs Pringle turned towards the lobby door.

'I'll let you know what happens,' she said, 'but I'll get on with a bit of scrubbing now. Takes your mind off things, a bit of scrubbing does.'

She stumped off, black bag swinging, whilst Tibby and I made our way home.

3. Could it be Arthur Coggs?

The policeman from Caxley, who had called upon the Coggs household, was making inquiries, we learnt, about the theft of lead in the neighbourhood.

Scarcely a week went by but the *Caxley Chronicle* reported the stripping of lead from local roofs around the Caxley area. Many a beautiful lead figure too, which had graced a Caxley garden for generations, was spirited away under cover of darkness, lead water tanks and cisterns, lead guttering, lead piping, all fell victim to a cunning band of thieves who knew just where to collect this valuable metal.

It so happened that the Mawnes had an ancient summer house, with a lead roof, in their garden.

Their house had been built in the reign of Queen Anne, and the octagonal summer house, according to Mr Willet, who considered it unsafe and unnecessarily ornate, was erected not long afterwards, although it was, more likely, the conceit of some Victorian architect. It was hidden from the house by a shrubbery, and nothing could have been easier for thieves than to slip through the hedge from the fields adjoining the garden to do their work in privacy.

The lead was not missed until a thundery shower sent cascades of water through the now unprotected roof into the little room below. A wicker chair and its cushion were drenched, a water colour scene, executed by Mrs Mawne in her youth, became more water than colour overnight, and a rug, which Mr Mawne had brought back from Egypt on one of his bird-watching trips, and which he much prized, was ruined. Added to all this was the truly dreadful smell composed of wet timber and the decaying bodies of innumerable insects, mice, shrews and so on, washed from their resting places by the onrush of rain.

Fairacre was shocked at the news. It was one thing to read about lead being stolen from villages a comfortable distance from their own, in the pages of the respected *Caxley Chronicle*.

It was quite another to find that someone had actually been at work in Fairacre itself. What would happen next?

Mr Willet voiced the fears of his neighbours as he returned from choir practice one Friday night.

'What's to stop them blighters pinching the new lead off the church roof? Cost a mint of money to put on. It'd make a fine haul for some of these robbers.'

A violent storm, some years earlier, had damaged St Patrick's sorely. Only by dint of outstanding efforts on the part of the villagers, and never-to-be-forgotten generosity from American friends of Fairacre, had the necessary repairs been made possible. The sheets of lead, then fixed upon much of the roof, had formed one of the costliest items in the bill. No wonder Fairacre folk feared for its safety, now that marauders had visited their village.

'They wouldn't dare to take the Lord's property,' announced Mrs Pringle.

'I don't think they care much whose property it is,' observed Mr Lamb from the Post Office. 'It's just how easy they can turn it into hard cash.'

'My sister in Caxley,' replied Mrs Pringle, still seeking the lime-light, 'told me the most shocking thing happened all up the road next to hers.'

'What?' asked Mr Willet. The party had reached the Post Office by now and stopped to continue the conversation before Mr Lamb left them.

Twilight was beginning to fall. The air was still and scented with the flowers in cottage gardens.

Mrs Pringle looked up and down the road before replying. Her voice was low and conspiratorial. Mr Willet and Mr Lamb bent their heads to hear the disclosure.

'Well, these lead thieves came one night and went along all the outside lavatories, and cut out every bit of piping from the cistern to the pan.'

'No!'

'They did. As true as I'm standing here!'

'What! Every house?'

Mrs Pringle shifted her chins uncomfortably upon the neck of her cardigan.

403

'Not quite all. Mr Jarvis, him what was once usher at the Court, happened to be in his when they reached it, so they cleared off pretty smartly.'

'Did they catch 'em?'

'Not one of 'em!' pronounced Mrs Pringle. 'Still at large, they are. Quite likely the very same as took Mr Mawne's lead off the summer house.'

'Could be,' agreed Mr Lamb, making towards his house now that the story was done. 'Thought I heard as Arthur Coggs might be mixed up with this little lot.'

'Now, now!' said Mr Willet, holding up a hand in a magisterial gesture. 'No hearsay! It's not right to go accusing people. Us doesn't know nothing about Arthur being connected with lead stealing.'

'He's connected with plenty that's downright dishonest,' rejoined Mr Lamb, with spirit. 'Dam' it all, man, he's done time, he's a poacher, he's been had up, time and time again, for stealing. And he ought to be had up for a lot of other things, to my mind. Wife-beating for one. And dodging the column for another. Why, that chap hasn't done a day's work for weeks, and all us old fools keeps him by giving him the dole and the family allowances. Makes my blood boil!'

'We knows all that,' agreed Mr Willet, taking a swipe at a passing bat with a rolled-up copy of Handel's *Messiah*. 'But you just can't pin everything that's crooked on Arthur Coggs.'

'Why not?' asked Mrs Pringle belligerently. 'More times than not you'd be right!'

And on this note the friends parted.

Human nature being what it is, there were far more people in Fairacre who shared Mrs Pringle's view than Mr Willet's.

Arthur Coggs was the black sheep of the village, and his wife greatly pitied. He was supposed to be a labourer, although his neighbours stated roundly that labour was the last thing Arthur looked for.

He occasionally found a job on a building site, carrying a hod, or wheeling a barrow slowly from one place to the next. But he rarely stayed long. Either he became tired of the work, or more often, his employer grew tired of paying him to do nothing.

The greater part of his money went on beer, and he was a regular customer at 'The Beetle and Wedge' in Fairacre. He and his family had once occupied a tumbledown cottage, one of four in Tyler's Row, now made into one long attractive house occupied by a retired schoolmaster from Caxley and his wife.

The Coggs family had been rehoused in a council house which was fast becoming as dilapidated as their last abode. Mrs Coggs, with a large family to cope with, and very little money with which to do it, struggled to tidy the house and garden, but never succeeded. Over the years she had grown thinner and greyer. Her highest hopes were that Arthur would stay sober and that he would provide more housekeeping money. So far, her hopes had not been realized.

Now and again, Arthur would appear to have money in his pocket and this she felt certain was the result of some dishonest dealings. Arthur had appeared in the Court at Caxley on many occasions, and his list of previous convictions, handed up for the Bench to study, included such offences as theft, receiving goods knowing them to have been stolen, shoplifting, burglary and house-breaking.

Mrs Coggs knew better than to question Arthur about any unusual affluence. A black eye, or painful bruises elsewhere would have been the outcome. But experience had given her some cunning and she had sometimes been able to abstract a pound note or some change from his pocket, when he was fuddled with drink.

Pity for Arthur's wife had prompted several people in Fairacre to employ her dissolute husband over the years. Mr Roberts, the local farmer, had taken him on as a farm hand, only to find that eggs vanished, one or two hens disappeared, as well as sacks of potatoes and corn. The other men complained that they were doing Arthur's work as well as their own and they were right. Mr Roberts dispensed with Arthur's services.

Mr Lamb had tried to employ him as a jobbing gardener, but again found that vegetables were being taken and the jobs set him were sketchily done, and the local builder's patience snapped when he caught Arthur red-handed, walking home with a pocketful of his tools.

The plumber at Springbourne, whose soft heart had been

touched by the sight of Mrs Coggs and her four children all in tears one morning as he passed through Fairacre, was moved to take on Arthur for a week's trial. By Wednesday he discovered that a considerable amount of copper piping had vanished, and Arthur was sacked once again.

Virtually, he was unemployable, and soon realized that he was far better off collecting his social security allowance and other moneys disbursed by a benevolent government, and indulging his chronic laziness at the same time.

He was known to be in tow with some equally feckless and dishonest men in Caxley, and, in fact, Arthur frequently acted as look-out man when the more daring of the gang were breaking-in. His wages for this kind of work were in proportion to the loot obtained, but always far less than the share each burglar received.

'You didn't take much risk, chum,' they told him. 'Piece of cake being look-out. You can reckon yourself lucky to get this bit.'

And Arthur agreed. As long as it helped to keep him in beer, there was no point in arguing.

For a while, immediately after the discovery of the loss of Mr Mawne's roofing lead, Fairacre folk were extra careful about making their homes secure. People actually shut their front doors on sunny days, instead of leaving them hospitably open for neighbours to enter. They began to hunt for door keys, long disused, and some very funny places they were found in after the passage of time. Mr Willet, after exhaustive searching, admitted that he found his front door key at the bottom of a biscuit tin full of nuts, bolts, screws, hinges, padlocks, latches, tacks, brass rings, and other useful impedimenta vital to a handyman.

His neighbour found his on top of the cistern in the outside lavatory. The two Misses Waters, Margaret and Mary, who had a horror of burglars but so far relied on a stout bolt on both back and front doors, now scoured their small cottage in vain for the keys they had once owned. It was Margaret who remembered eventually, at three o'clock one morning, that they had hidden them under the fourth stone which bordered their brick path, when they were going away for a brief holiday some years earlier. At first light, she crept out, and unearthed them, red with rust. She remained in a heady state of triumph all day.

Mr Lamb, it seemed, was the only householder in Fairacre who locked up and bolted and barred his premises methodically every night. But then, as people pointed out, as custodian of the Queen's mail he'd have to see things were done properly or he'd soon get the boot. No one gave him credit for his pains, and to be honest, Mr Lamb was sensible enough not to expect any. But at least he was spared the searching for keys, for his own hung, each on its hook and carefully labelled, ready for its nightly work.

For a time, even the children caught the fever and became aware that it was necessary to be alert to dishonesty.

One Caxley market day, Linda Moffat and Eileen Burton arrived each with a door key on a string round their necks.

'My mum's gone on the bus to buy some material for summer frocks,' said Linda, 'and she may not be back when I get home.'

'And mine's gone to buy some plants,' announced Eileen. 'Ours never come to nothing.'

'If they never come to nothing,' I said severely, 'then they must have come to something. Say what you mean.'

The child looked bewildered.

'I did, miss. Our seeds never come – '

'*Your seeds did not come up*,' I said, with emphasis.

'That's what I said.'

'You did not say that,' I began, and was about to embark, for the thousandth time, on an elementary grammar lesson, when Mr Willet intervened. He had been listening to the exchange.

'Your mum's seeds never come up,' he said forcefully, 'because she used that plaguey compost muck out of a bag. She wants to mix her own, tell her, with a nice bit of soft earth and dung and a sprinkle of sharp sand. Tell her they'll never come to nothing in that boughten stuff.'

I gave up, and turned to the marking of the register.

It came as no surprise to the good people of Fairacre when they heard that a week or two after the visit of the police to the Coggs' house Arthur Coggs was to appear in Court charged, together with others, with stealing a quantity of lead roofing, the property of H. A. Mawne, Esq.

At the time of the theft, the *Caxley Chronicle* had given some prominence to the affair, enlarging upon Mr Mawne's distinction as an ornithologist, and reminding its readers that the gentleman had frequently contributed nature notes to the paper's columns. News must have been thin that week for not only was Mr Mawne given an excessive amount of type, but a photograph was also included, taken by one of the younger staff against the background of the depleted summer house.

Even the kindest readers were at a loss to find something nice to say about the likeness, and the subject himself said it looked to him like an explosion in a pickle factory, adding tolerantly that maybe he really looked like that and had never realized.

'There's three other chaps,' Mr Willet told me. 'Two of 'em is Bryants – that gipsy lot – and the third's a real bad 'un from Bent. I bet he was the ringleader, and that poor fool of an Arthur Coggs told him about the roof here. I still reckons we ought to keep watch on the church, but the Vicar says we must trust our brothers.'

'He's a good man,' I commented.

'A sight too good, if you ask me. "There's brothers and brothers," I told him. I wouldn't want any of them four for brothers, and I wouldn't trust them no further than that coke-pile, idle thieving lot.'

'We don't know that they're guilty yet,' I pointed out.

'I do,' said Mr Willet, picking up his screwdriver.

I overheard a conversation in the playground as I strolled round holding my mug of tea. It was a glorious May morning. The rooks cawed from the elm trees as they went back and forth feeding their hungry nestlings, and the children were sitting on the playground bench, or had propped themselves against the school wall, legs outstretched, as they enjoyed the sunshine.

Joseph Coggs sat between Ernest and Patrick, all three oblivious of the condition of their trouser seats in the dust.

'Saw your dad in the paper,' said Ernest.

'Ah,' grunted Joseph.

'Bin pinchin', ain't he?' said Patrick.

'Dunno.'

'That's what the paper said.'

Joseph scratched a bite on his leg and said nothing.

'That's what the copper come about,' said Ernest to Patrick.

'Is he in prison?' asked Patrick conversationally of Joseph.

'No,' shouted Joseph, scrambling to his feet. His face was red, and he looked tearful. He rushed away towards the boys' lavatories, obviously craving privacy, and I approached his questioners.

They gazed up at me innocently.

'You should stand up when ladies speak to you,' I told them, not for the first time. They rose languidly.

'And don't let me hear you upsetting Joseph with questions about his father. It's none of your business and it's unkind anyway.'

'Yes, miss,' they replied, trying to look suitably chastened.

One or two of the other children hovered nearby, listening to my brief homily, and I was conscious of meaning glances being exchanged. It was difficult to be critical. After all, the Arthur Coggs affair was the main subject of spicy conjecture in their homes at the moment, and it was hardly surprising that they shared their parents' interest.

That afternoon when the sun was high in the heaven, and the

downs were veiled in a blue haze of heat, I decided that a nature walk was far more beneficial to my pupils than a handwork lesson.

As the sun was so hot, we kept to the lanes, in and around the village, which are shaded by fine old trees. The hawthorn hedges were sprouting young scarlet shoots, and in the cottage gardens the columbines were out. The children call them 'granny's bonnets', and they are exactly like the beautifully goffered and crimped sun bonnets that one sees in old photographs.

Some of the lilac flowers were beginning to turn rusty, and the old-fashioned crimson peonies were beginning to droop their petals in the heat, but the scent was heavy, redolent of summer and a whiff of the long days ahead.

The children straggled along in a happy and untidy crocodile, chattering like starlings and waving greetings to friends and relations as they passed.

Fairacre, I told myself, was the perfect place to live and work, and early summer found it at its most beautiful. I stopped to smell a rose nodding over a cottage gate, and became conscious of voices in the garden. Two neighbours were chatting over their boundary hedge.

'And if it isn't Arthur Coggs, then who is it?' asked one.

I sighed, and let the rose free from my restraining hand.

Every Eden seemed to have its serpent, Fairacre included.

4. *Mrs Pringle has Problems*

With the departure of the infants' teacher, Pat Smith, we were back in the familiar circumstances of looking for a second member of staff.

As it happened, only two children arrived for the summer term, both five-year-olds, making the infants' class seventeen in all. Altogether we had now thirty children on roll, and although this might sound a laughably small number to teach compared with some of the gigantic classes in overcrowded urban primary schools, yet there were considerable difficulties.

I struggled alone for two weeks before a supply teacher could be found.

It meant a proliferation of groups working in the one class-room, and an impossible situation when one tried to play games, or choose a story or a song, which could be enjoyed by five-year-olds and eleven-year-olds at the same time. I always feared that some accident might happen, when the sole responsibility rested on me to get help and to look after the rest of the school at the same time. It was a worrying time and I was mightily relieved when Mrs Ansell arrived to share the burden.

She was a cheerful young woman in her thirties whom I had met once or twice at teachers' meetings in Caxley. She had a young son of two, and had not taught since his birth, but her mother lived nearby in Caxley, and was willing to mind the child if Mrs Ansell wanted to do occasional supply teaching.

All went well for a fortnight, and the children were settling down nicely under their new regime, when the blow fell. She rang me one evening to say that her mother had fallen down in the garden and damaged her hip. She was in Caxley hospital, and of course quite unable to look after Richard.

I expressed my sympathy, told her we could manage, and hung up.

Now what, I wondered? Supply teachers are as rare and as precious as rubies. Most of those local few who were in existence

lived in Caxley and preferred to attend the town schools. I had
been lucky enough to get Mrs Ansell because she particularly
wanted to teach infants, liked country schools, and had her own
car.

'I shall have to ring that office again in the morning,' I told
Tibby gloomily. 'And what hope there?'

Tibby mewed loudly, but not with sympathy. Plain hunger
was the cause, and I obediently dug out some Pussi-luv and put
it on the kitchen floor. I then supplied my own supper plate
with bread and cheese.

It was while I was eating this spare repast that I thought of
Amy. She has helped us out on occasions, and there is no one I
would sooner have as my companion at Fairacre School.

'Are you in the middle of your dinner?' was Amy's first
remark.

'It's only the last crumb of bread and cheese,' I assured her.

'Is that all you have had?'

'Yes. Why?'

'I really do think you should be a little less slapdash with your
meals,' said Amy severely. 'And on your lap, I suppose. It's
ruination to the digestion, you know, these scrambled snacks.'

'Well, never mind that,' I said impatiently, and went on to
tell her our troubles.

'Could you?' I finished.

'I could come on Monday,' said Amy, 'not before, I'm afraid,
as I'm helping Lady Williams with the bazaar for the Save The
Children Fund on Friday.'

'Come and save my children instead.'

'And it can't be for long,' went on Amy, 'as I have Vanessa
coming some time next month.'

'But you could come for a week or two?'

'Probably three weeks. James is off to Persia on some trade
mission or other, and then to Australia, I believe, unless it was
New Zealand. They're so close, one gets confused.'

'I believe they are thousands of miles apart, and they get
pretty stroppy about being muddled up. It's like the Scandina-
vian countries, isn't it? Do you know which is top and bottom
of that craggy looking piece of coastline?'

'No, I don't. But I remember it was always a great help to

trace the outline on the way home in the train. The movement was invaluable round the fiords.'

'You are a darling to come,' I said, reverting to the main topic. 'I'll ring the office in the morning and get things straight, and let you know the result. It really is murder trying to cope alone. One grazed knee or a pair of wet knickers is enough to stop us all in our tracks.'

'Never fear,' cried Amy, 'help is on its way!'

'The relief of Mafeking,' I told her, 'will be nothing to it.'

Jubilantly, I hung up.

The office gave its blessing to my arrangements, and we all awaited Amy's coming with varying degrees of pleasure.

My own feeling was of unadulterated relief. The Vicar, who has a soft spot for Amy, said it would be delightful to see her again, and how very generous she was with her time when one considered that she had a husband and a house to look after.

Mr Willet was equally enthusiastic.

'I can ask her about those pinks cuttings I give her,' he said. 'Always a bit tricky pinks are, if the soil's not to their liking. I'd dearly love to go over to Bent to keep an eye on 'em, but I don't want to push meself forward.'

I said I felt sure that Amy would welcome his advice, and he retired to the playground humming cheerfully.

Mrs Pringle greeted the news with modified rapture. Amy is too well-dressed, drives too large a car, and altogether has an aura of elegant affluence which Mrs Pringle disapproves of in a teacher. I think she feels that anyone as comfortably placed as Amy should do a little voluntary work for some deserving charity, but to take on a teaching job smacks too much of depriving some poor wretch of her rightful dues.

Since taking to her slimming diet, Mrs Pringle seems to be even more martyr-like than usual. She received the news of Amy's arrival on Monday with a resigned sigh.

'Best get both gates wide open,' she said, 'for that great car of hers. I take it you'll tell the children to keep off of it? It's a big responsibility havin' an expensive motor like that on the premises, and I haven't got eyes in the back of my head.'

I reassured her on that point.

'And last time she come, she didn't eat no potatoes I noticed. Now that's a bad example to the children. We tells 'em to eat up all they've got, and then they sees their teachers pickin' and choosin'. Just drop a word, Miss Read. She's your friend after all.'

'How's the dieting?' I asked, hoping to change the subject.

Mrs Pringle's gloom deepened.

'That Dr Martin's getting past it. Fairly snapped my head off when I went to get weighed, just because I've only lost two pounds in a month! I told him straight: "Well, at least I've *lost* it. There's no call to get so white and spiteful. Anyone'd think I'd *put on* two pounds!" He calmed down a bit then, and made me write down all I'd eaten since Sunday.'

'Could you remember?'

'Most of it. And when I gave him the list, he shouted out so loud that Mrs Pratt's baby started hollering in the waiting room.'

'Why, what was wrong?'

'You may well ask. He shouted: "I said no cakes, no bread, no potatoes, and no sugar!" And I said to him: "How's a body to drink tea without sugar? And what's tea time without a slice of cake? And what's a dinner plate look like without a nice little pile of potatoes?" He never answered. Just went a bit pink, and hustled me out, telling me to do what he'd said. No sense to him these days. Too old for the job, if you ask me.'

'But he's right, you know. You won't lose weight unless you cut out all those lovely fattening things.'

'I don't call them *fattening*,' said Mrs Pringle, with immense dignity. 'They're *sustaining*! A woman what works as hard as I do needs nourishment. The days I've given up me bread and that, I've felt proper leer. Me knees have been all of a tremble. With this job to do, let alone my own home, I needs the food.'

There seemed little to add. Mrs Pringle shuffled off, limping slightly, a sure sign that her bad leg was giving trouble, as it always does in times of stress.

As she went, I noticed she did up a button on her cardigan which had burst from its buttonhole under excessive strain. The two pounds had not been lost from that portion of her anatomy obviously.

Come to think of it, I pondered, watching her massive rear vanish into the lobby, it would be difficult to say just where she had lost those pounds.

The hot weather continued, showing May in all her glory. In my garden the pinks began to break, shaking their shaggy locks from the tight grey cap which held them.

On the front of the school house, the ancient Gloire de Dijon rose, planted by one of my predecessors, turned its fragrant flat-faced flowers to the sunshine in all its cream and pink splendour.

The hay crop looked as though it would be heavy this year, and the bees were working hard. A field of yellow rape made a blaze of colour across one of Mr Roberts' stretches of land, and it was this, I suspect, that attracted so many bees to the area.

The copper beech was now in full leaf, and the box edging to the garden beds gave off its peculiar aromatic smell as the noonday sun drew out all the delicious scents of summer.

The school room door was propped open with a large knobbly flint, turned up by the plough in the neighbouring field. The sounds and scents wafted in, distracting the children from their work, so that I often took them all into the grass under the trees, and let them listen − or not − to a story. The daddy-long-legs floated round us in the warm air, small birds chattered and squeaked in the branches above, and only the sound of Mr Roberts' tractor in the distance gave any hint of the village life which was going on around us. They were lovely sessions, refreshing to body and mind, and we always returned to the classroom in a tranquil state of mind.

Amy arrived on Monday morning, wearing a beautiful pale pink linen suit, but with her usual foresight had brought with her a deep rose-pink overall to ward off such infant room hazards as sticky fingers, spilt milk, and chalk dust.

Some of the children knew her already, and it was not long before her calm efficiency had made friends of them all. I closed the infants' room door with a sigh of relief, and set out to catch up with many neglected lessons with my older children.

Things went swimmingly all the week until Friday morning.

'Guess who I saw at the bus stop in Caxley,' said Amy, trying to adjust her hair by the reflection from 'The Light of the World' behind my chair.

'Haven't a clue,' I replied.

'Why don't you have a mirror somewhere? I see there isn't one in the lobby either. Where do you do your hair?'

'At home.'

'But surely, when you've been in the playground on a windy day, you – and the children, for that matter – need to tidy up.'

'We manage.'

'By just leaving things, I suppose,' said Amy. 'It's too bad of you, you know. The children should be set an example of neatness. And did you know that the hem is coming down on that frock?'

'I had a suspicion. There was an ominous tearing sound when I caught my heel in it this morning, but no time to investigate.'

'Dreadful!' murmured Amy, more in sorrow than anger. She does try so hard to improve me, with practically no success.

'You were telling me,' I said, 'about someone at the bus stop. Miss Clare?'

'At eight-thirty in the morning? Don't be silly.'

'Who then?'

'Mrs Fowler and Minnie Pringle's husand, whatever he's called.'

'What? Waiting for the bus to Springbourne?'

'It looked remarkably like it.'

I pondered upon this snippet of news.

'Do you think they might be going to collect his children from Minnie's?'

'It would be a jolly good thing if they did,' said Amy forthrightly, 'but I doubt it. They've managed quite happily without them, as far as one can see, so why suddenly want a family reunion now?'

'It certainly seems odd,' I agreed. 'Perhaps Mrs Pringle will be able to throw light on the matter.'

Sure enough, when Mrs Pringle arrived for her after-school duties, it was quite apparent, from the important wobbling of her chins, that she had great news to impart.

'Well, I've got that Minnie of mine back again. I've left her

416

grizzling in the kitchen and the children are in the garden. I've
dared them to put a foot on the flower beds, unless they want to
be skinned alive. I can't say fairer than that to them.'

'What's the matter this time?' I asked. Amy who had picked
up her handbag ready to depart, put it down again and perched
on the front desk to observe the scene.

Mrs Pringle looked at her with some dislike, but aquiver as
she was with her momentous news, she decided to ignore her
presence and tell all.

'That man had the cheek to come out to Minnie's this
morning, with that woman who's no better than she should be,
and I'll not soil my lips by repeating her name, and ask for his
furniture back.'

'But can he? Isn't it the marital home, or whatever they call it
in Court?'

'Whether he can or he can't,' boomed Mrs Pringle, 'he's done
it. And that Mrs Fowler – '

'With whose name you wouldn't soil your lips,' I remembered
silently.

'Well, she was at the bottom of it. It was that cat as put him
up to it. And her nephew had his van waiting by Minnie's gate
to put the stuff in. All planned and plotted you see. And off

they drove, leaving our Minnie without a frying pan in the house.'

'Nothing at all?' I said horrified.

Mrs Pringle tutted with impatience.

'No, no, they never took *the lot*, I'll give 'em that, but they took two armchairs, and the kitchen table, and no end of china, and the upstairs curtains, and some cooking pots and the frying pan, so of course Minnie and the kids have had no dinner.'

I could not quite see why the frying pan was the only utensil needed to cook the family's food, but this was no time to go into all that, and I was beginning to feel very sorry for poor luckless Minnie, and for Mrs Pringle too, when her next remark cooled my sympathy.

'So it looks to me, Miss Read, as Minnie will be very glad to take up your offer of some work. She's got all that stuff to buy anew, and money's very tight anyway. I told her to come up and see you to arrange things some time.'

'Thank you,' I said faintly. It was an appalling prospect, and I cursed myself for ever making such an idiotic suggestion. I avoided meeting Amy's gaze. She appeared to be struggling to hide her very ill-timed amusement. Like Queen Victoria, my amusement was nil.

'Well, I'd better get on with my tidying up and then hurry back to see what damage them little varmints of Minnie's have done. When shall I tell her to come?'

'She'd better come one evening,' I said. 'There's no hurry, tell her, and if she gets a post elsewhere I shall quite understand.'

Amy suffered a sudden fit of coughing which necessitated a great deal of play with her handkerchief. At times, she can be very tiresome.

'Right!' said Mrs Pringle, shaking out a clean duster from her black oilcloth bag. 'I'll let her know. But I wouldn't trust her with glass, if I were you, or any china. She's a bit clumsy that way.'

She went into the infants' room and vanished from our sight.

'Come and have tea with me,' I said to Amy.

'No, I really must get back, but I couldn't possibly leave before knowing the outcome of this morning's activities.'

We walked out into the sunlit playground. Overhead the

swifts screamed and whirled, and the air was deliciously fresh after the classroom.

'Looks as though I'm saddled with that ghastly Minnie,' I remarked.

'You should have been firm from the outset,' replied Amy.

'I didn't get much chance,' I protested. 'She practically told me she was coming. What on earth could I do?'

'You could have said that you had offered the job to someone else, and it had been accepted.'

'What? In Fairacre? Be your age, Amy! Everyone knows I haven't a job to offer! It's as much as I can cope with having Ma Pringle bullying me about the house. I don't want more.'

'You should have thought about that earlier,' said Amy primly. 'I'm always telling you how you rush headlong into things.'

'Well, don't keep rubbing it in,' I retorted crossly. 'It's quite bad enough having to face the possibility of Minnie wrecking my home weekly, without enduring your moralizing.'

Amy laughed, and patted my shoulder.

'What you need is a nice husband to protect you from yourself.'

She slid into the driving seat.

'That I don't,' I told her, through the car window. 'I've quite enough troubles already, without a husband to add to them.'

Amy shot off with an impressive turn of speed, and I waved until my maddening old friend had disappeared round the bend in the lane.

5. *Hazards Ahead*

One Friday evening, George Annett called in on his way to St Patrick's. I could see at once that he was the bearer of bad tidings.

'There's definitely something in the wind,' he said, in answer to my queries. 'I've had several chaps from the office measuring the school and offering me a temporary classroom to be erected across the playground, complete with washbasins and lavatories.'

'When?'

'No one can say definitely. Obviously, they're just making sure I can cope with the extra numbers. It may never happen. You know how these things hang on.'

'I remember Dolly Clare telling me that poor Emily Davis, who was head at Springbourne, had this closure business hanging over her for nearly ten years.'

'There you are then! Don't get steamed up yet. But I thought I'd let you know the latest. Had any luck with applicants for the teaching post?'

'Not yet. Amy is coping for a little longer, then it will be another supply until the end of term, if I'm lucky.'

George laughed, and rose to go across to his duties.

'You will be.'

He patted my shoulder encouragingly.

'Cheer up! I'd take a bet on Fairacre School remaining as it is for another thirty years.'

'I wonder. Anyway, there's a managers' meeting soon, and perhaps we'll learn something then.'

'Ask Mrs Pringle what's going on,' shouted George, as he went down the path. 'She'd be able to tell you.'

At that moment the lady was approaching, also on her way to choir practice, and had obviously heard the remark.

I was amused to notice George's discomfiture, as he wished her 'Good evening' in a sheepish fashion.

★

The night was hot, and I could not sleep – a rare occurrence for me.

There was a full moon, and the room was so light that it was impossible to lie still, and equally impossible to draw the curtains on such a torrid night.

The longer I stayed awake, the more I worried. What would become of me if the school closed? I had no doubt that I should be treated honourably by the education authority. Whatever teaching post I was offered would provide me with my present salary, but that was the least of my worries.

Not for the first time, I blessed my single state. I had only myself to fend for, and I thought of other teachers who were widowed with young children, or those who supported aged parents, or invalid relatives, and whose salary had to be stretched much farther than my own. Amy often told me that I led a very selfish life and perhaps it was true, but when one was faced with a situation such as that which I now contemplated, there were compensations. No one depended on me. No one offered me disturbing advice. No one would blame me for any decision I took, however disastrous it turned out to be.

I left my hot and rumpled bed, and hung out of the window. The shining rose leaves glittered in the bright moonlight. The sky was clear, and the evening star hung low over the village, as brilliant as a jewel.

Here was the heart of my grief. To leave this – my well-loved school house, and its garden, shady with trees planted by other teachers, long dead, but remembered by me daily for their works which still endured.

I could truthfully say that I relished every day that I spent in Fairacre. It was not only a beautiful place, backed by the downs, open, airy, and dominated by St Patrick's spire thrusting high above the thatched and tiled roofs around it. It was also a friendly place, as I soon found when I had arrived as a newcomer some years earlier.

The thought of leaving Mr Willet, Mr and Mrs Partridge, the Mawnes – even Mrs Pringle – was unbearable. My life was so closely bound with theirs, in fact, so closely woven with all those living in the village, that I should feel as weak and withered as an uprooted plant, if circumstances forced me to go.

As for the children, to part with them would be the hardest blow. I loved them all, not in a sentimental fashion but because I admired and respected their sound country qualities.

I loved their patience, their docility, their efforts to please. Certainly, at times, these very virtues exasperated me. Then I would find them unduly slow, complacent and acquiescent, but when I took stock I had to admit that it was often impatience on my part which roused my wrath. How could I ever leave them?

I returned to my bed, and now it was practical matters which bedevilled me. Why on earth hadn't I bought a house for myself, instead of living in a fool's paradise in the school one? The times I had thought about it – and the times Amy had admonished me on the same subject – were beyond counting.

But somehow, I had let matters drift. I had never seriously thought of leaving Fairacre, apart from the odd urge to make a change which sometimes hit me in the Spring. Even then, just reading the advertisements in *The Times Educational Supplement* had usually been enough to quench my brief ardours. To slide gently from middle age to retirement in Fairacre seemed such a serene and mellow way to face the future. Of course, I realized that one day, when I had left, someone else would live in my dear house and teach in the school, but it all seemed so far away, that I was lulled into a dream-like state of bliss.

Now had come the rude awakening. It was E. M. Delafield, I believe, who said she wanted seven words on her tombstone:

'*I expected this, but not so soon.*'

They echoed my own thought absolutely.

All the cocks in Fairacre were crowing before I fell into an uneasy sleep.

It was the following evening, when I was making plans for an early night, that I saw, with horror, the untidy figure of Minnie Pringle coming up the path.

I think it is uncommonly sensible and prudent of Minnie to buy her clothes at local jumble sales, and I have often recognized old garments of mine among her wardrobe. But what irks me is the way she wears them without the slightest attempt to adapt them to her skinny figure.

She is particularly fond of a dilapidated fur coat which was once Mrs Mawne's. It is a square garment, made from square pieces of moulting fur. A great many squares are parting from their neighbours, and as the whole thing swamps Minnie, it would have seemed reasonable to remove one row of squares to make it fit, or at least to mend the slits and tie a belt round it. As it is, Minnie's hands are hidden about six inches up the sleeves, the hem, which is coming undone, reaches her calves, and the rest of the tent-like object swings about Minnie's frame like a scarecrow's coat on a broomstick.

On this occasion, as the evening was warm, I was spared Mrs Mawne's ex-coat, for Minnie was wearing a shiny mauve blouse over a wrap-around skirt whose pattern seemed vaguely familiar to me. On her bare feet were black patent evening sandals with high heels ornamented with diamanté studs.

I braced myself for the interview and invited her in.

'Auntie says as you could do with some help,' began Minnie, once settled in an armchair.

'Would two hours a week suit you?'

I had given some thought to this problem of my own making, and had decided that, with some contriving, I could find her work within her limited ability which would not conflict too obviously with Mrs Pringle's duties. It was going to be a delicate matter trying to keep her off her aunt's preserves, such as cleaning my few pieces of silver and washing the kitchen floor with as much care as one would sponge a baby's face, and I guesseed that my efforts were probably doomed to failure at the outset. But surely, in two hours even Minnie could not do much harm.

Also, two hours of work were really all I could afford to pay on top of Mrs Pringle's weekly dues. I awaited Minnie's reaction with mixed feelings.

Minnie scratched her tousled red locks with a silver-varnished nail of inordinate length.

'Same pay as auntie?' she inquired at length.

'Yes.'

'OK. What wants doin'?'

'I'll show you in a minute,' I said, feeling that we were going along rather fast. 'When can you come? I gather you have some work already.'

'You can say that again,' said Minnie, lying back and putting

423

her sandals on the coffee table. 'I goes to Mrs Partridge Mondays – the Vicar fixed that.'

My heart bled for poor Mrs Partridge, at the mercy of her husband's Christian charity. The havoc Minnie could cause in that fragile collection of old glass, Hepplewhite chairs and china cabinets made one shudder to contemplate.

'Then I goes to Mrs Mawne on Wednesday morning, but that's all scrubbin'. Mr Mawne don't want no one to touch his butterfly drawers and stuffed birds and that, though I offered to give 'em a good dusting. He's a funny chap, ain't he?'

I forbore to comment, but my opinion of both Mr and Mrs Mawne's good sense rose considerably.

'And Thursday evenings I does out the hall, 'cos Auntie says she's getting a bit past it, and the committee gentlemen said it was all right for me to do it, though I don't know as I shall stick it long.'

'Why not?'

'Mucky. Bits of sausage roll and jam tart squashed between the floor boards, and the sink gets stopped up with tea leaves.'

'Don't they use tea bags?'

Minnie's mouth dropped open. She looked as though she had been coshed. I began to feel alarmed, but at last she spoke.

'Cor!' she whispered. 'You're a marvel! I'll tell 'em that! It's the cricket tea ladies as does it, I reckons, though them Scouts and Cubs isn't above mucking things up in spite of them oaths they take. Tea bags is the answer. Of course it is.'

I said I was glad to have been of help, and wondered how soon I should be ostracized by all those who managed the village hall kitchen.

'Is that all the work you do?'

'I has to keep my own place tidy at Springbourne,' said Minnie, looking suddenly truculent.

I hastened to apologize.

'Of course, of course! I meant any more work in Fairacre.'

Minnie sat up, removed her sandals from the table top, and surveyed her grubby toe nails.

'I likes to keep Saturday free.'

'Naturally. I shouldn't want you to give up your weekends. What about Friday afternoons?'

'I shops on Fridays.'

'Wednesday then?'

'Auntie comes up here Wednesdays.'

'Oh, of course. Tuesday any good?'

'I goes to Springbourne Tuesdays, 'cos it's double Green Shield Stamp day at the shop.'

'What's wrong with Monday?'

'The Vicar.'

I was beginning to get desperate. Did Minnie want work or did she not? Heaven alone knew I would be happy to dispense with her services, but having got so far I felt I must soldier on. I changed my tactics.

'Well, Minnie, when *could* you come?'

'Friday afternoon.'

I took a deep breath.

'But I thought you said you went shopping on Friday.'

'Not till six o'clock. It's late night Caxley.'

I controlled a sudden desire to scream the place down.

'Very well then, let's say from two until four on Friday afternoon. Or one-thirty to three-thirty, if that suits you better.'

'Is that harpast one?'

'Yes,' I said weakly. Whoever had had the teaching of Minnie Pringle deserved deep sympathy, but not congratulation.

There was silence as Minnie scratched her head again, and thought it out.

'Well, that's fine and dandy. I'll come up harpast one and do two hours, and go at – what time did you say?'

'Harpast – *half past* three,' I said faintly. 'I shall be back from school soon after that.'

'What about me money then?' She sounded alarmed.

'I shall leave it on the mantelpiece,' I assured her, 'just as I do for Mrs Pringle. Now, come and look at the work.'

I proposed that she took over window-cleaning and the upstairs brasswork, and bath and basins. This meant that she would be out of Mrs Pringle's way, and could not do too much damage.

I showed her where the dusters and cleaning things were kept, and she looked doubtfully at the window-cleaning liquid.

'Ain't you got no meth. and newspaper? It does 'em a treat. Keeps the flies off too.'

I said shortly that this was what I used, and that I disliked the smell of methylated spirits.

'My uncle drinks it,' she said cheerfully. 'Gets real high on it. They picks 'im up regular in Caxley, and it's only on meths!' She sounded proud of her uncle's achievements.

I led the way downstairs.

'You want the grandfather clock done? I could polish up that brass wigger-wagger a treat. And the glass top.'

There was a gleam in her mad blue eyes which chilled me.

'Never touch that clock!' I rapped out, in my best schoolmarm voice.

'O.K.,' said Minnie, opening the door. 'See you Friday then, if not before.'

I watched her totter on the high heels down the path, still trying to remember where I had seen that skirt before.

'Heaven help us all, Tibby,' I said to the cat, who had wisely absented herself during Minnie's visit. 'Talk about sowing the something-or-other and reaping the whirlwind! I've done just that.'

I felt the need for early bedtime more keenly than ever. Just before I fell asleep, I remembered where I had seen Minnie's skirt before.

It had once been my landing curtain. I must say, it looked better on Minnie than many of her purchases.

Notice of the managers' meeting arrived a few days after Minnie's visit. It was to be held after school as usual, on a Wednesday. There was nothing on the agenda, I observed, about possible closure of the school. Could it be village rumours once again?

The Vicar called at the school on the afternoon following the receipt of our notices. He was in a state of some agitation.

'It's about the managers' meeting. I'm in rather a quandary. My dear wife has inadvertently invited all the sewing ladies that afternoon, so the dining-room will be in use. The table, you know, so convenient for cutting out.'

'Don't worry,' I said. 'We could meet here, if it's easier.'

We usually sit in comfort at the Vicar's mahogany dining-table, under the baleful eye of an ancestor who glares from a massive gilt frame behind the chairman's seat. Sometimes we have met in the drawing-room among the antique glass and the china cabinets.

'And the drawing-room,' went on Mr Partridge, looking anguished, 'is being decorated, and everything is under shrouds – no, not *shrouds* – furniture covers – no, *loose* covers – no, I don't think that is the correct term either – '

'Dust sheets,' I said.

His face lit up with relief.

'What a *grasp* you have of everything, dear Miss Read: no wonder the children do so well! Yes, well, you see my difficulty. And my study is so small, and very untidy, I fear. I suppose we could manage something in the hall, but it is rather draughty, and the painters are in and out, you know, about their work, and like to have their little radios going with music, so that I really think it would be *better*, if you are sure it isn't inconveniencing – '

'Better still,' I broke in, 'have it in my dining-room. There's room for us all.'

'That would be quite perfect,' cried the Vicar, calming down immediately. 'I shall make a note in my diary at once.'

He sighed happily, and made for the door.

'By the way, no more news about the possible closing. Have you heard anything?'

'Not a word.'

'Ah well, no news is good news, they say. We'll hear more perhaps on Wednesday week. I gather that nice Mr Canterbury, who is in charge of Caxley Office, is coming out himself.'

I thought that sounded ominous but made no comment.

'No,' said the Vicar, clapping a hand to his forehead. 'I don't mean *Canterbury*, do I? Now, what is that fellow's name? I know it's a cathedral city. Winchester? Rochester? Dear, oh dear, I shall forget my own soon.'

'Salisbury,' I said.

'Thank you. I shall put it in my diary against Wednesday week. I shouldn't like to upset such an important fellow.'

He vanished into the lobby.

'It's more likely,' I thought, 'that the important fellow will upset us.'

6. The Managers' Meeting

Amy's last week at Fairacre School arrived all too soon, and I was desolate. She was such good company, as well as being an efficient teacher, that I knew I should miss her horribly.

'Well, I'd stay if I could,' she assured me, 'but Vanessa arrives next week, and I hope she'll stay at least a fortnight. She's rather under the weather. There's a baby on the way. Or *babies*, perhaps!'

'Good heavens! Do they think it will be twins?'

'The foolish girl has been taking some idiotic nonsense called fertility tablets, so it's quite likely she'll give birth to half-a-dozen.'

'But surely, the doctors know what they're doing?'

'Be your age,' said Amy inelegantly. She studied the lipstick with which she had been adorning her mouth. 'I must have had this for years. It's called "Tutankhamen Tint".'

'It can't date from that time.'

Amy sighed.

'The Tutankhamen Exhibition, dear, which dazzled us all some years ago. Everything was Egyptian that year, if you remember. James even bought me a gold necklace shaped like Cleopatra's asp. Devilish cold it is too, coiled on one's nice warm bosom.'

'I'm glad about Vanessa's baby,' I said. 'I'll look foward to knitting a matinée jacket. I've got a pattern for backward beginners that always turns out well. Is she pleased?'

'After eleven in the morning. Before that, poor darling, she is being sick. Tarquin is terribly thrilled, and already planning a mammoth bonfire for the tenants on the local ben, or whatever North British term they use for a mountain in Scotland.'

'He'll have to build six bonfires if your fears prove correct.'

'He'd be delighted to, I have no doubt. He's a great family man, and I must say he's very, very sweet to Vanessa. They seem extremely happy.'

She snapped shut her powder compact, stood back and surveyed her trim figure reflected murkily in 'The Light of the World'.

'I think I might present Fairacre School with a pier-glass,' she said thoughtfully.

'It would never get used,' I told her, 'except when you came.'

We went to let in the noisy crowd from the playground.

Mrs Pringle's slimming efforts seemed to be having little result, except to render her even more morose than usual.

I did my best to spare her, exhorting the children to tidy up carefully at the end of afternoon school, and putting away my own things in the cupboards instead of leaving them on window sills and the piano top, as I often do.

Luckily, in the summer term, the stoves do not need attention, but even so, it was obvious that she was finding her work even more martyr-making than before. I was not surprised when she did not appear one morning, soon after Amy's departure, and a note arrived borne by Joseph Coggs.

He pulled it from his trouser pocket in a fine state of stickiness. I accepted it gingerly.

'How did it get like this, Joe?'

'I gotter toffee in me pocket.'

'What else?'

'I gotter gooseberry.'

'Anything else?'

'I gotter bitter lickrish.'

'You'd better turn out that pocket!'

'I ain't gotter –'

'And if you say: "I gotter" once more, Joseph Coggs, you'll lose your play.'

'Yes, miss. I was only going to say: "I ain't gotter thing more."'

He retired to his desk, after putting his belongings on the side table, and I read the missive.

Dear Miss Read,

Have stummuck upset and am obliged to stay home. Have had terrible night, but have taken nutmeg on milk which should do the trick as it has afore.

Clean clorths are in the draw and the head is off of the broom.
Mrs Pringle

I called to see my old sparring partner that evening. She certainly looked unusually pale and listless.

'I'm rough. Very rough,' was her reply to my inquiries. 'And there's no hope of me coming back to that back-breaking job of mine this week.'

'Of course not. We'll manage.'

Mrs Pringle snorted.

'But what I mind more, is not doing out that dining-room of yours for the managers tomorrow.'

'I'll do it. It's not too bad.'

She gave me a dark look.

'I've seen your sort of housework. Dust left on the skirting boards and the top of the doors.'

'I don't suppose any of the managers will be running their fingers along them,' I said mildly. 'Has the doctor been?'

'I'm not calling him in. It's him as started this business.'

'How do you mean?'

'This 'ere diet. Drinking lemon juice first thing in the morning. That's what made my stummuck flare up.'

'Then leave it off!' I cried. 'Dr Martin wouldn't expect you to drink it if it upset you!'

'Oh, wouldn't he? And the price of lemons what it is too! I bought a bottle of lemon juice instead. And that's just as bad.'

She waved a hand towards a half empty bottle on the sideboard, and I went to inspect it. It certainly smelled odd.

'Is it fresh?'

Mrs Pringle looked uneasy.

'I bought it half-price in Caxley. The man said they'd had it in some time.'

'Chuck it away,' I said. 'It's off.'

The lady bridled.

'At fifteen pence a bottle? Not likely!'

'Use oranges instead,' I urged. 'This is doing you no good, and anyway oranges are easier to digest.'

She looked at me doubtfully.

'You wouldn't tell Dr Martin?'

'Of course I wouldn't. Let me empty this down the sink.'

Mrs Pringle sighed.

'Anything you say. I haven't got the strength to argue.'

She watched me as I approached the sink and unscrewed the bottle. The smell was certainly powerful. The liquid fizzed as it ran down the waste pipe.

'One thing,' she said, brightening, 'it'll clean out the drain lovely.'

It was certainly a pity that Mrs Pringle had not given the dining-room the attention it deserved, but I thought it looked quite grand enough to accommodate the managers.

There are six of them. The Vicar is Chairman and has been for many years, and the next in length of service is the local farmer Mr Roberts.

When I first was appointed I was interviewed by Colonel Wesley and Miss Parr, both then nearing eighty, and now at rest in the neighbouring churchyard. Their places were taken by Mrs Lamb, the wife of the postmaster, and Peter Hale, a retired schoolmaster from Caxley, who is very highly regarded by the inhabitants of Fairacre and brings plenty of common sense and practical experience of schooling to the job.

The other two managers are Mrs Mawne and Mrs Moffat, the latter the sensible mother of Linda Moffat, the best dressed child in the school. She is particularly valuable, as she can put forward the point of view of parents generally, and is not too shy to speak her mind.

On Wednesday we had a full house, which is unusual. It is often Mr Roberts who is unable to be present and who sends a message – or sometimes puts an apologetic face round the door – to say a ewe or cow is giving birth, or the harvest is at a crucial stage, and quite rightly we realize the necessity for putting first things first, and the meeting proceeds without him.

As well as the six managers Mr Salisbury arrived complete with pad for taking notes. I had a seat by him, with my usual brief report on such school matters as attendance, social activities and the like. Also in evidence were the log book of the school and the punishment book – the latter with its pages virtually unsullied since my advent.

The Vicar made a polite little speech about the pleasure of using my house for the meeting. The minutes were read and signed and I gave my report.

There were the usual requests to the office for more up-to-date lavatories and wash-basins. The skylight, which had defied generations of Fairacre's handy men to render it rainproof, was mentioned once more, and Mr Salisbury solemnly made notes on the pad. We fixed a date for our next term's meeting, and then settled back for Any Other Business.

'Is there any message, in particular,' asked Gerald Partridge, 'from the office? We have heard some disquieting rumours.'

'Oh?' said Mr Salisbury. 'What about?'

'Might close the school,' said Mr Roberts, who does not mince words.

'*Really?*' cried Mrs Moffat. 'I hadn't heard a thing! Now that I get my groceries delivered I hardly ever go to the shop, and it's amazing how little one hears.'

'I've taken to going into Caxley for my provisions,' said Mrs Mawne conversationally. 'I can't say I enjoy these super-markets, but when soap powder is ten pence cheaper it makes you think.'

'And bleaching liquid,' agreed Mrs Moffat, 'and things like tomato ketchup.'

'I make my own,' broke in Mrs Lamb. 'We grow more tomatoes than we can cope with, and it's no good trying to freeze them, and bottled tomatoes are not the same as fresh ones, are they? If you are interested, I've a very good recipe for ketchup I can let you have.'

The ladies accepted the offer enthusiastically. The Vicar wore his resigned look. Most of our village meetings get out of hand like this, and he is quite used to waiting for these little asides to resolve themselves.

Mr Salisbury, tapping his expensive pen against his expensive false teeth, looked rather less patient, and cast meaning glances at the chairman.

Mrs Moffat had just embarked on a long and somewhat

confused account about pickling walnuts when the Vicar rapped gently on the table and said kindly: 'Order please, dear ladies, I think Mr Exeter has something to tell us.'

Mr Salisbury, taking his new name in his stride, put down the pad and assumed an expression of disarming candour.

'Well, I don't quite know just *what* you have been hearing at Fairacre, and I can assure you that the office would always consult with the managers of any school as soon as the possibility of closure cropped up.'

'And has it?' asked Mr Roberts.

'There is always some chance of really small schools becoming uneconomic,' began Mr Salisbury cautiously.

He's been through this hoop many times before, I thought to myself. How far would he commit himself today?

'Fairacre's not really small,' said Mrs Mawne.

'I like a small school anyway,' pronounced Mrs Moffat.

'Much more friendly,' agreed Mrs Lamb.

'There are certain disadvantages,' said Mr Salisbury. 'Lack of team games, for instance. No specialist teachers on the staff for certain subjects. Older children get deprived.'

'*Deprived?*' squeaked Mrs Lamb. 'Our children aren't *deprived* are they, Miss Read?'

'I hope not,' I said.

'But what about Fairacre?' persisted Mr Roberts. 'Are you sharpening the knife for us?'

'Nothing will be done without your knowledge and cooperation,' repeated Mr Salisbury.

'But it's on the cards?' asked Peter Hale quietly. 'Is that it?'

'Numbers are going down steadily,' replied Mr Salisbury. 'We have to assess each case on its merits. Certainly, Fairacre is costing us a lot of money to maintain and the children might well be better off at a larger school.'

'Such as Beech Green?'

'Such as Beech Green,' agreed Mr Salisbury.

'When?' said Mr Roberts.

Mr Salisbury put down his pen and tilted back in his chair. I hoped that the rear legs of my elderly dining-room chair would stand the strain.

434

'It might be years. It all depends on numbers, on getting staff – a problem you are facing at the moment – and the feelings of managers and parents of the school.'

The Vicar was looking unhappy.

'But what about Miss Read? It is unthinkable that she should have her school taken from her.'

There was a rumble of agreement round the table.

Mr Salisbury smiled at me. I felt like Red Riding Hood facing the wolf.

'Miss Read's welfare is our concern, of course. There would always be a post for her in the area. That I can promise you.'

'But we want her *here*!' wailed Mrs Lamb. 'And we *don't* want our school to close!'

'Absolutely right!' said Mrs Mawne. 'People in Fairacre simply won't stand for their children being uprooted, and carted away in buses like so many – er, so many – '

'Animals?' prompted Mr Roberts helpfully.

'No, no, not *animals*,' said Mrs Mawne testily. 'Animals don't go in buses! What I mean is, we won't have it. We'll never let Fairacre School close.'

She looked round the table. Her face was red, her eyes bright.

'Agreed?'

'I do for one,' said Mr Roberts. 'I never heard such a shocking thing in my life. The idea of some of our little tots being hauled off to Beech Green fair gives me the shudders. This school's served the village for over a hundred years, and I don't see why it shouldn't go on doing so for another hundred.'

'Hear! Hear!' said Mrs Lamb.

Mr Salisbury scribbled something on his pad, then looked up. 'Well, Mr Chairman, I have noted the objections of the managers, though I must point out that no decision of any kind has been taken by the committee about Fairacre School.'

'I hope nothing will ever happen to disturb the *status quo*,' said the Vicar. 'We are all extremely happy with our little school. We should be deeply distressed if anything were done to close it, and we rely upon you to keep us informed of any developments.'

Mr Salisbury nodded agreement, and began to put his things together. The Vicar glanced at the clock.

'If that is all our business then nothing remains for me to do but to thank Mr Wells for coming here today and to remind you of the date of the next meeting.'

Mr Salisbury smiled at us all, shook my hand warmly and departed.

'He'd better not try any funny business with our village school,' said Mr Roberts, watching the car drive away. 'And don't you bother your head about all that nonsense, Miss Read. We're all behind you in this.'

'Indeed we are,' said the Vicar.

'They closed Springbourne though,' said Mrs Moffat thoughtfully.

'Took 'em ten years,' observed Mr Roberts. 'A lot can happen before they think of Fairacre again. In any case, we can all have a dam' good fight over it, and I bet we'd win. The parents would be with us, that I do know.'

One by one, the managers left, until only Mr Partridge remained with me.

'We don't seem to have gone very far with this business,' he remarked, 'but at least it has been mentioned, and I think that is a good thing. He seems a good fellow, that Mr Wells – Winchester, I mean – '

'Salisbury,' I interjected.

'*Salisbury*, yes, *Salisbury*. I feel he would act honourably and not do anything without letting us know first.'

'So I should hope.'

'Don't upset yourself about it, dear Miss Read. I cannot believe that it would ever happen here.'

'Let's hope not,' I said. I really felt that I could not discuss the wretched business any more, and I think the Vicar sensed this, for he patted my shoulder encouragingly, and made his departure.

I felt more shaken by the meeting than I would have admitted to anyone. My mouth was dry, my knees wobbly. I tottered into the garden and sat on the seat.

Everything around me burst with healthy life. Sparrows flashed from plum tree to cherry tree. A peacock butterfly flapped its bejewelled wings from a daisy top. The pinks gave out their heady scent. The rose buds opened gently in the warm air. Even Tibby displayed every sign of well-being, with her stomach exposed to the sun, and her eyes blissfully closed.

Only I, it seemed, was at odds with my surroundings. Their very beauty emphasized my own malaise. Should I ever come to terms with this horrible nagging uncertainty? Would it be better to take the bull by the horns, and apply for another post now? If I kept putting it off I should be too old to be considered by other managers. Perhaps I was too old already? How old was Emily Davis, I wondered, when she first heard that Springbourne was going to close? How long did Mr Roberts say that was hanging over her? Ten years? The suspense could not be borne.

At least, I told myself, no one need know yet about the shadow coming nearer. Enough to let the rumours die down, as they were doing quite comfortably, before stirring them up again like a swarm of angry bees.

I went indoors, at length, and tried to busy myself with bottling gooseberries, but the operation did not get my whole attention. I was glad when Mr Willet knocked at the back door and asked if he could borrow my edging shears.

It was a comfort to exchange a few general remarks with him on the state of our gardens, and the surprising need for rain at this time of year.

I accompanied him to the gate.

'All right if I bring these 'ere cutters back in the morning?' he asked.

'Fine,' I told him. 'I shan't be doing any gardening tonight.'

'I'd have an early night if I was you,' he advised me. 'You looks a bit peaky. I hears they brought up that school closing business again at your meeting. Bit of a shock, no doubt, but you put it out of your head.'

I was too stunned to reply.

He smiled kindly upon me.

'Us'll rout anyone who tries to shut up our school! You can bet your last farthing on that!'

He strode down the lane, my edging-shears across his shoulder like a gun.

'There goes a militant Christian,' I said to Tibby, 'but how on earth did he know?'

7. *Troubles Never Come Singly*

Now that Amy had gone to attend to her other commitments, I was left to cope alone once again.

Luckily, it would be only for one week – or so the office told me. After that, help was at hand in the form of Mrs Rose who had been Headmistress of a small school near by. That school had been closed for some two years, and Mrs Rose was now euphoniously termed 'a peripatetic teacher'.

This meant that she moved from school to school, sometimes helping children who found reading difficult, and sometimes acting as a supply teacher when staff was short.

I viewed her advent with mixed feelings. She was over sixty, and was in this present job because she was in the last stages of her forty years' service. Her health was not good, and she was a martyr to laryngitis.

On the other hand, she was of a gentle disposition, anxious to fit in, open to suggestions, and generally amenable. And, in any case, the mere presence of another human being – even one as frail as Mrs Rose – on the other side of the glass partition, was a great comfort and support.

In the meantime, I soldiered on and was relieved, in a way, to have the school to myself in order to try to come to terms with the dreadful possibility of becoming, like Mrs Rose, a teacher without a school of my own.

Despite my airy dismissal of rumours on so many earlier occasions, this time I had an uncomfortable feeling that change was in the wind. Something in Mr Salisbury's manner at the managers' meeting made me fear the worst, and I was surprised to find how upset I was.

Normally, I slept for nine hours, drugged with work and good downland air. Now I took an hour or more before drifting off, as I tossed and turned trying to decide what to do. Even my appetite suffered, a most unusual symptom, and I found myself nibbling a biscuit and cheese rather than facing a square meal in the evening. What Amy would have said if she could have witnessed my more than usually casual eating habits, I shuddered to think.

Now and again, I found myself trembling too. Good heavens, was I becoming senile into the bargain? Fat chance I should have of landing another teaching post if I appeared before strange managers with my head shaking and possibly a drop on the end of my nose!

It was all extremely unnerving, and I was grateful for the children's company in my alarming condition.

There were other disquieting factors. The weather had turned cold and blustery, despite the fact that June had arrived. We could have done with some heating from the tortoise stoves, but that, of course, was out of the question.

Then Minnie Pringle's presence about the house on Friday afternoons was distinctly unsettling. On the first visit, she had managed to drop a jar of bath salts into the hand basin, smashing the former and badly cracking the latter.

Also, in a fit of zeal, she had attacked my frying pan with disinfectant powder kept for the dustbin, and some steel wool, thus effectively removing the non-stick surface.

'I thought as it was Vim,' she explained, in answer to my questioning.

'But it says DISINFECTANT POWDER on the tin!'

'Can't read them long words,' said Minnie truculently.

'But you can read "Vim", can't you? And this tin didn't have "Vim" written on it.'

'Looked the same to me,' replied Minnie, and flounced off, tripping over a rug on the way, and bringing the fire-irons into the hearth with a fearful crash.

I fled into the garden, unable to face any more destruction. So must victims of earthquakes feel, I thought, as they await the next shattering blow.

It was during this unsettled period that the case of Arthur Coggs and his companions was heard at Caxley.

As they appeared in Court on market day, several people from Fairacre were interested spectators, among them Mr Willet. He had travelled in by bus to pick up some plants from the market, and having two hours to spare before the bus returned, decided to witness the fate of the four accused.

Mr Lovejoy, the most respected solicitor in Caxley, was defending all four, as he had done on many previous occasions.

'And an uphill job he'll have this time,' commented Mr Willet to me. 'They had the sauce to plead Not Guilty, too.'

'Perhaps it's true,' I said.

Mr Willet snorted, puffing out his stained moustache.

'Want to bet on it? Anyway, old Colonel Austin was in the chair, and he read out a bit, before they got started, about committing 'em to Crown Court if they was found guilty. Something about their characters and antecedents, whatever that means. But it made it plain that they could get clobbered for more than six months, if need be, and I'd stake my oath that's where they'll end up. All four's got a list as long as my arm, as everyone knows.'

'A man is innocent,' I said primly, 'until he is proved guilty.'

'Them four,' replied Mr Willet, 'are as innocent as Old Nick hisself. My heart bleeds for that chap Lovejoy trying to whitewash them villains. It'd turn my stomach to do a job like that. I'd sooner dig Hundred Acre Field with a hand fork, that I would!'

On Monday morning, Mrs Rose arrived in good time, in a little car, shabby and battered enough to win approval from Mrs Pringle, in whose eyes it appeared a very suitable form of transport for teachers. Amy's large high-powered beauty had always offended Mrs Pringle's sense of fitness. She opened the gates for Mrs Rose's vehicle with never a trace of a limp, or a word of complaint. Clearly, Mrs Rose was accepted, and that was a great relief to me.

She looked frailer than ever, and also decidedly chilly in a sleeveless cotton frock.

'I'd no idea it would be so cold,' she said, clutching her goose-fleshed arms. 'It is *June*, after all!'

'It's always colder up here on the downs,' I told her, 'and these old buildings are pretty damp. We grow quite a good crop of toadstools in the map cupboard when the weather's right.'

She was not amused. I hastily changed my tactics.

'Come over to the house,' I urged, 'and we'll find you a

cardigan. It will be too big, I fear, but at least you will be warm.'

Tibby greeted us effusively, no doubt imagining that the morning session had gone by with unprecedented speed, and it was now time for a mid-day snack.

Mrs Rose paused to take in my accommodation and furnishings before coming upstairs with me.

'I used to have a nice little house like this,' she mourned.

I felt very sorry for her, and slightly guilty too. I certainly was lucky, that I knew. All the old fears of losing my home came fluttering back as we mounted the stairs. I did my best to fight them off.

I set out a selection of woollen garments, and she chose a thick shetland wool cardigan which would have kept out an arctic wind. It would certainly mitigate the chill of Fairacre School in June.

Her eyes wandered over the bedroom as she did up the buttons.

'You have made it so pretty and snug,' she said enviously. 'I had much the same curtains when I was in the school house at Bedworth.'

'I always admired the garden when I passed that way,' I said hastily, trying to wean her from her nostalgia. 'The roses always seemed so fine in that part of the country. Clay soil, I suppose. What sort of garden do you have now in Caxley?'

I could not have done worse.

'I've no garden at all! Just a window box in my upstairs flat. I can't tell you how much I miss everything.'

The sound of infants screaming in the playground saved me from commenting.

'I think we'd better go back,' I said, leading the way downstairs, 'or we may find spilt blood.'

But all was comparatively calm, and I led Mrs Rose inside to show her the infants' room, and to introduce her to Mrs Pringle.

That lady was leaning against the doorway, upturned broom in hand, looking rather like Britannia with her trident, but a good deal less comely. She bowed her head graciously to Mrs Rose.

'We met at Mrs Denham's auction sale,' she reminded the new teacher. 'I remember it well because you bid against me for a chest of drawers.'

Mrs Rose looked nervous.

'Not that you missed much,' continued Mrs Pringle. 'Even though it was knocked down to me at four pounds. The bottom drawer jams something cruel, and them handles pulls off in your hand. We've had to glue 'em in time and time again.'

I thought, once again, on hearing this snippet of past history, that life in a small community is considerably brightened by such memories as this one of a shared occasion. Some of these joltings of memory are caused by pure happiness – others, as in this present case, owe their sharpness to a certain tartness in the situation. Obviously, Mrs Pringle's bad bargain had caused some rankling since the day of the ladies' battle for the chest of drawers.

'Miss!' shouted Ernest, appearing on the scene. 'Can I ring the bell, miss? Can I? Can I ring the bell?'

'Yes, yes,' I replied. 'And there's no need to rush in here as though a bull were after you.'

I ushered Mrs Rose into the infants' room as the bell clanged

443

out its message to my tardy school children still in the fields and lanes of Fairacre.

The *Caxley Chronicle* carried a full report of Arthur Coggs' case that week, and eagerly devoured it was by all his neighbours in Fairacre. There is nothing so comforting as reading about others' tribulations. It reminds one of one's own good fortune.

The prosecution's most weighty piece of evidence, in more senses than one, was the entire piece of lead roofing which was carried into Court by six sweating policemen.

A plan was handed up to the Bench, and the magistrates were invited to compare the shape of the roof displayed on the paper before them, with that of the lead, now being unrolled and stamped into place beneath large feet, on the floor below.

After old Miss Dewbury's plan had been put the right way up for her by a kindly fellow-justice, the magistrates gave their attention to the matter with more than usual liveliness.

Amazing how they come to life, thought Mr Lovejoy, when a few pictures or objects to play with are handed up! Glazing eyes sparkled, sagging shoulders were braced. Could it be that addresses given by prosecution and defence sometimes bored the Bench? Not, thought Mr Lovejoy seriously, when he addressed them. He had a turn of phrase, he fancied, which commanded respect as well as attention to his cause, but possibly some of his learned colleagues were less fortunate in their powers. (Mr Lovejoy, it will be noted, was without humour.)

Certainly, there was a surprising likeness between the plan and the cumbersome evidence on the floor. The lead undoubtedly came from a small building with an octagonal roof like Mr Mawne's. It had been found, the magistrates were told, hidden under a pile of sacks in the Bryant brothers' outhouse. They looked suitably impressed.

Mr Lovejoy, on the other hand, looked calm and faintly disdainful. His eye fixed on the pitch-pine ceiling of the Victorian court house, he was clearly rehearsing his speech which would show that a person or persons unknown had humped the lead, from a source equally unknown, and dumped it upon the Bryants' premises with the intention of getting them into their present unfortunate position.

The case ground on for the rest of the morning, and continued after the lunch break. Witnesses were called, by the indefatigable Mr Lovejoy, who testified to the fact that the accused had been in their company, regularly each evening, whilst imbibing, in a modest fashion, as befitted their unemployed state, at local hostelries.

At four o'clock Miss Dewbury was nudged into wakefulness, the accused men were told that the charge against them had been proved, and the prosecutor handed up long lists of previous convictions for the Bench to study.

The Chairman, Colonel Austin, after a brief word with his colleagues, then committed them in custody to the Crown Court for sentence, just as Mr Willet had prophesied, and they left the Court escorted by two policemen.

Mr Lovejoy shuffled his papers together, bowed politely, and hurried after his clients.

'That is the business of the Court,' announced the clerk, 'and the business of the day is over.'

'And only just in time,' observed old Miss Dewbury as she departed. 'I put a beef casserole in the oven at lunch time, and it must be nearly dry by now.'

'Never like sending chaps to prison,' grunted Colonel Austin to his male colleague, as they reached for their hats. 'But what can you do with four like that? How many times have we seen 'em, John?'

'Too many,' replied his friend, 'and we'll see them again the minute they're out!'

In Fairacre, reaction to the Court's decision was mixed. Most agreed that Arthur Coggs was only getting his just deserts, and speculated upon how long the Judge would give all four when the time came. But more were concerned about the effect of Arthur's absence on his wife and family.

'She'll be a dam' sight better off without him around,' said Mr Willet. 'What good's he to her, poor soul? She'll get the social security money to herself now, instead of watching Arthur swilling it down his throat at 'The Beetle'. Besides, she won't get knocked about. Make a nice change for her, I'd say, to have a peaceful house for a time.'

445

To my surprise, Mrs Pringle took another view.

'She'll miss him, I'll be bound, bad lot though he is. A woman needs a man's company about the house.'

'I can't say I've missed it,' I observed. 'And I could well do without Arthur Coggs' company, at any time.'

'Yes, well,' admitted Mrs Pringle, 'there's some as lead an *unnatural* life, so their opinions don't altogether matter.'

'Thank you,' I said. My sarcasm was ignored, as Mrs Pringle followed her train of thought.

'I knows he keeps her short of money. I know he raises his hand to her – '

'And his boot,' put in Mr Willet.

'And I knows his language is plain 'orrible when he's in liquor, but then she's used to it, and used to having him around the place. She'll be terrible lonely with him gone.'

Several other people echoed Mrs Pringle's comments, but the general feeling was that Mrs Coggs must be relieved she was safe from physical assault, at least for a year or more. A number of inhabitants went even further in their concern, among them Gerald Partridge the Vicar, who spoke about the family to me.

'I am right in thinking that the Coggs children get free dinners?'

I reassured him on this point.

'And their clothing? Shoes and so on. Are they adequately provided for? I should be only too happy to give something, you know, if it could be done without causing distress to poor Mrs Coggs. She has enough to bear as it is.'

I said that I tried to keep an eye on that side of things, and had been lucky enough to get Mrs Moffat and other generous parents to hand down garments that were little worn directly to Mrs Coggs, instead of sending them, in the usual way, to our local jumble sales.

'She won't be too badly off,' I promised him. I could not bear to see his gentle face puckered with anxiety. 'And now Arthur is out of the way, I believe she will take on more work.'

'Yes, indeed. Mrs Mawne is having her there for a morning. I gather that Minnie Pringle insisted on dusting some very precious glass cases housing some of Mr Mawne's rarer birds,

446

and two were broken, most unfortunately. Mr Mawne was a little put out about it, and fired the girl on the spot.'

Later I was to hear from Minnie's own lips, the exact words used by her irate employer – short, brutal, words of Anglo-Saxon origin – which, I felt, had been put to their proper use under the circumstances.

'Well, I'm glad to know Mrs Coggs has got the job,' I said. 'It will give her an added interest as well as more money. But don't worry too much about her. The social security office will see she is looked after, and really she's so much better off without that ghastly husband.'

The Vicar looked shocked.

'Strong words, Miss Read, strong words! He is one of my flock, remember, even if he has strayed, and I can only hope that his present afflictions will make him change his ways.'

'That'll be the day,' I said.

But I said it when the Vicar had departed.

PART TWO

Fairacre Hears the News

8. A Welcome Diversion

One summer afternoon, soon after the Vicar's visit, I had a
surprise call from Amy and Vanessa.

The children had just run home, glad to be out in the sunshine,
and I was just about to make tea.

Vanessa, a niece of James, Amy's husband, was always
attractive, but now, in pregnancy, had that added lustre of skin
and hair which so often goes with the condition. I said,
truthfully, how radiant she looked.

'But *enormous!*' protested Vanessa, holding out her arms
sideways, the better to display her bulging form. 'I'd no idea
one could stretch to this size. All those women's magazines chat
away about letting out skirts a few inches, as time goes by! My
dear, *look* at me! This is a shirt which was too big for Tarquin,
who stands six feet four as you know, and even this is getting
tight. I'm thinking of hiring a bell tent.'

'A dirndl skirt's the answer,' said Amy, 'with a huge smock
over it. Or a kaftan, perhaps.' She gazed at Vanessa with a
thoughtful smile. 'There's no denying that one really does need
a *waist* for most clothes.'

'Well, I hope to have one again in a few weeks' time,' replied
Vanessa, settling her bulk on the sofa.

'Put your feet up,' I urged.

'Too much effort, darling. I really don't recommend this baby
business. Don't attempt it.'

'I should get the sack if I did,' I told her.

'Which reminds me,' said Amy, 'what news of Fairacre School
closing?'

I felt Amy could have been a little more tactful, but forbore
to comment upon it.

'Not much, but something's in the wind. George Annett has
been asked to send in lists of equipment he would need if another
class were added to his school – or possibly two classes.'

'It does sound ominous.'

'It does indeed. But there's mighty little one can do until I hear something more definite. It seems silly to try for another post when I'm so settled here, and in any case, all this may come to nothing.'

Amy fixed a steady gaze upon me.

'Poor old dear,' she said, so sympathetically that I was glad to turn away from her and busy myself with pouring tea.

'Vanessa is staying for a whole week,' she went on, 'and I wondered if you would come over for dinner one evening?'

'You know I'd love to,' I said, carrying a cup to the recumbent figure on the sofa. Vanessa struggled to a more upright position.

'I'll just lodge it on this bulge,' she said with a dazzling smile. 'It really comes in quite useful, this extra shelf. I shall miss it. Sometimes I think I shall give birth to at least *three* babies.'

'Don't the doctors know?'

'My own, who is a sweetie, says twins. The other chap, a top-flight gynaecologist, won't commit himself, but then he's terribly cautious. Always worrying about his hypocrites' oath, I think.'

'*Hippocrates*, Vanessa!' exclaimed Amy. 'Really, when I think of the money spent on your education and see the result, I shudder!'

'I have a cosy little argument with him sometimes,' continued Vanessa unabashed, 'just to stretch his mind, you know. "If I had a tumour on the brain, which meant I was a living vegetable, don't you think you should put me gently to sleep?" I ask him. Of course, he gets in a terrible fluster, and talks about this old hypocrites' oath he took when he was a beardless boy, and we both thoroughly enjoy a little abstract thinking after all the dreadfully coarse back-and-forth about bowels and heartburn.'

Vanessa sighed, and the teacup wobbled dangerously.

'I must say it will be quite a relief to know how many. Luckily, I've been given enough baby clothes for a dozen. Tarquin's mother is a great knitter, and does everything in half-dozens. Even *binders*! I don't think babies have them now, but I haven't the heart to tell her. She's also presented me with a dozen long flannel things, all exquisitely feather-stitched, which have to be pinned over the baby's feet to keep it warm. I can't see the monthly nurse using those.'

'You're having it at home then?' I said.

'Good heavens, yes! All the family's babies have to be born in the castle, and the piper waits outside – for days sometimes – ready to play the bagpipes to welcome the child.'

'I'd have a relapse,' I said. 'To my Sassenach ear "The Flowers of the Forest" sounds exactly like "The Keel Row".'

'Well, don't let Tarquin know,' advised Vanessa. 'The sound of the bagpipes brings tears to his eyes.'

'He's not the only one,' I told her, rescuing her empty cup.

On the Saturday following Amy's visit, I was invited to attend a lecture by Henry Mawne. It was to be held in the Corn Exchange in Caxley, and the subject was 'European Birds of Prey', illustrated by slides taken by the speaker.

I was a little surprised by the invitation. The Mawnes are always very kind to me, but we do not meet a great deal, except by chance, in the village. The Vicar and Mrs Partridge were also going, and several other people from Fairacre.

All had been invited to lunch with the Mawnes at the Buttery, a restaurant in Caxley, conveniently placed near the hall, and offering a varied menu at modest prices. The Buttery is always busy, and many a local reputation has been shredded beneath its oak beams.

If I had been rather more alert when Mrs Mawne invited me I might have excused myself, for Saturday afternoons are usually taken up with household chores, cooking, mending, or entertaining, which get left undone during the week. But as usual, I was not prepared, and found myself at twelve o'clock on the Saturday in question, trying to decide between a long-sleeved silk frock (too dressy?) or a pink linen suit, rather too tight in the skirt, which Amy had kindly told me made me look like mutton dressed as lamb.

I decided on the latter.

There were four cars going from Fairacre, and I went with Diana and Peter Hale.

'Wonder how long this affair will last?' mused Peter Hale. 'I want to drop in at school to see some of the cricket. Diana will drive you home. I'm getting a lift with the new classics man. He passes the house.'

'I think, you know,' said Diana gently, 'that Henry Mawne is afraid that the Corn Exchange is going to be far too big for this afternoon's lecture. I hear that he suggested that a party from Beech Green might help to swell the ranks.'

Light began to dawn.

'He'll need several hundreds to make a good sprinkling in that barn of a place,' I said. 'Why not find something smaller?'

'Everything was booked up,' said Peter, jamming on his brakes as a pheasant strolled haughtily across the road. 'Half the jumble sales and bazaars seem to take place on Saturdays. I can't think why.'

'Most people have been paid on Friday,' I told him. 'It's as simple as that.'

We had the usual trundling round Caxley to find a place to leave the car, and were lucky enough to snap up the last place in a car park fairly near the restaurant. Secretly, I was glad. It was not the pink skirt alone that was tight. My new shoes were killing me. Could I be growing a corn on my little toe? And if so, would I need to go to a chiropodist? What a terrible thought! Hopelessly ticklish, I should be hysterical if my feet were handled, and what if she – or he, perhaps? – wanted to file my toe-nails? That could not be borne.

A prey to these fears, I hobbled in the wake of the Hales and entered the bustle and heat of the Buttery.

The Mawnes greeted us cheerfully, and we were seated at the Buttery's largest table. It was clear that we should be about a dozen in all, and the manager had done us proud with six pink carnations in a hideous glass vase with coloured knobs on it.

Margaret and Mary Waters, two spinster sisters who share a cottage in Fairacre, arrived, with the Vicar and Mrs Partridge, and four more friends of the Mawnes made up the party.

Menus were handed round, and we studied them seriously. For most of us it was a pleasure to have a choice of dishes. After all, I was usually grateful, at this time of day, for a plain school dinner. To be offered such attractions as melon, prawn cocktail, pâté or soup – for first course alone – was wholly delightful, and I began to enjoy myself enormously.

Our host did not appear to be so happy. I remembered that

his wife had once told me that he dreaded any sort of public speaking, and was a prey to nerves before these events.

'What is this blanket of veal?' he was asking her crossly.

'You won't like it. It's veal in white sauce.'

'How disgusting! *Blanket*'s just about the right word for it.'

He turned to the Vicar.

'Don't you hate white gravy, padre? It's like cold soup – dead against nature.'

'I must admit,' replied Gerald Partridge, 'that I rather like things in white sauce. So bland, you know. Take tripe, for instance – '

'No, *you* take tripe,' exclaimed Henry, shuddering, 'I never could face that awfully rubbery flannel look, let alone put it in my mouth.'

'Done with onions,' said Margaret Waters earnestly, 'it can be quite delicious. And so nourishing. My poor father practically lived on it for the last few weeks of his life.'

Peter Hale caught my eye across the table, and I had to concentrate on the carnations to preserve my sobriety.

'I should have the lamb chops, Henry,' said Mrs Mawne decisively. 'I see there are new potatoes and peas, and you know you always enjoy them.'

Henry brightened a little.

'But what about our guests? Come now, Miss Read, what are you having?'

I said I should like melon, and then, bravely, the *blanquette de veau*.

The waiter, who had been leaning against a nearby dresser looking bored to distraction, now deigned to approach and started to take down orders.

As always, the meal was good. Caxley people are fond of their food, and are quite ready to complain if it is not to their liking. The Buttery knows its customers, and does its best to give satisfaction.

By the time the cheese board was going the rounds we were all in fine spirits, except for poor Henry Mawne who was becoming more agitated as the dreadful hour drew near.

'I've forgotten my reading glasses,' he exclaimed fretfully, slapping each pocket in turn. '*Now*, what do I do?'

Mrs Mawne remained calm.

'You use your bifocals, as you always do, Henry. Really, *the fuss!*'

'You know I never feel right with bifocals at a lecture,' wailed Henry, for all the world like one of my eight-year-olds. Gerald Partridge leant forward anxiously.

'Shall I get the car, and go back for them?' he offered. 'I could be back here in half an hour.'

Mrs Mawne took charge.

'Certainly not, Gerald. I won't hear of it! You are the soul of kindness, but there is absolutely *no need* for Henry to have his reading glasses. And well he knows it!'

She looked severely at her husband, who seeing himself beaten, turned his attention to a splendid Stilton cheese clothed in a snowy napkin, and began to look less fractious.

His guests became more relaxed, and the conversation turned to Arthur Coggs and his future.

'A friend of mine,' said Mary Waters, 'was in court when they carried in that massive piece of lead. Poor Albert Phipps nearly had a rapture!'

'A careless one?' inquired Peter Hale.

'You mean a *rupture*, dear,' said her sister reprovingly. 'You always get that word wrong. A *rapture*, as Mr Hale has reminded us, is what dear Ivor Novello wrote about.'

'I'm sorry,' said Peter, 'I was being flippant.'

'My English teacher once said: "Flippancy gets you nowhere,"' remarked his wife. 'I'd been trying to show off, I remember, about "trembling ears" in Milton. I said that the phrase smacked of the asinine, and was ticked off, quite rightly. Schoolgirls must be very trying to teach.'

'No worse than schoolboys,' commented Henry.

'I agree with that wholeheartedly,' said Peter Hale, schoolmaster.

Someone then looked at the clock and murmured that perhaps we should be moving. Henry Mawne's agitation returned.

'The bill, waiter! Quickly, my dear fellow. We mustn't be late.'

The waiter ambled off at a leisurely pace, while we collected bags and gloves and various other impedimenta, and Henry

Mawne started his pocket-slapping again in the frenzy of finding his cheque book.

'Henry,' said his wife, with a look which could have stopped a rogue elephant in its tracks. 'Calm down! You know perfectly well that I have the cheque book in my handbag. Now, if you will make sure that you have your notes and your bifocals, I will take charge of the account and meet you outside.'

We gave our sincere thanks to the Mawnes for the delicious lunch as we made our way to the Corn Exchange. The Caxley market square was gay with stalls, and I should dearly have loved to buy some eggs and cheese from my favourite stall-holder, but this was not the time, I realized, to clutch a piece of ripe gorgonzola for an hour and a half.

The hall was half full, which was a creditable number to assemble on a Saturday afternoon. As we were the speaker's party, we were shown to the front row. On the way to our august places, I was delighted to catch sight of a contingent from Beech Green. Among the party I saw George and Isabel Annett and dear Miss Clare, who taught for many years at Fairacre School, sitting with them.

I was seated by Mrs Mawne, who remained completely unmoved by the pathetic sight of her husband trying to arrange his papers with shaking hands.

The chairman was the president of Caxley's Nature Conservancy Trust and was doing his best to put Henry at his ease before starting the meeting. He might just as well have saved his breath, for Henry took not the slightest notice, and brought matters to a climax by dropping all his papers on the floor.

With startled cries, the two men bent to retrieve them, cracking their skulls together, thus occasioning further cries from the audience. The papers were collected, Henry shuffled them together with a look of utter despair, and the chairman rose to introduce him.

Once Henry was on his feet, and the clapping had died away, he became wonderfully calm and happy. He smiled at us all, as though he were truly glad to tell us about the birds which gave such zest and joy to his life. It was difficult to believe that less than half an hour ago, he had been as nervous as a fretful baby.

It was an enthralling talk, and the slides were superb. When

he ended, the audience applauded enthusiastically. Clearly, here was a man who was master of his subject and able to transmit his own excitement to others.

As we drove home again, Diana Hale summed up the feelings of us all.

'He's a man who can make you forget your own world, and carry you into his.'

With a start, I realized how true this was.

For the first time for weeks, I had forgotten the shadow which hung menacingly over my future, and gratitude mingled with admiration for our old friend Henry Mawne.

9. Mrs Pringle Goes to War

Minnie Pringle continued to wreak havoc in my house every Friday afternoon. I did my best to forestall trouble, but was far from successful.

Now that I realized that she could not read, I tried to put out the bottles and tins she would need for any specific job. Sometimes it worked. Sometimes such bottles as that containing window-cleaning liquid would be put in the bathroom cabinet beside witch hazel or gargle. It was all a little unnerving.

My vacuum cleaner was maltreated weekly by having its cord twisted tightly into figures of eight round the handle, and the plug became so cracked with being dropped on the tiled floor of the kitchen, that I was obliged to renew it. Maddening though she was, I did not want to find Minnie electrocuted on my premises.

She also had a peculiar way with dusters. Somewhere along the extensive line of previous employers, she had picked up the wholly admirable habit of washing dusters before leaving work.

Unfortunately, how to dry them seemed to be beyond her. I had indicated a small line conveniently near to the back door, but this was ignored. Sometimes she hung a wet duster on the newel post at the foot of the stairs, so that anyone mounting clapped her hand upon the clammy object. When remonstrated with, Minnie changed her tactics and draped them along the newly polished dining-room table, or over the padded back of an armchair.

Irritation gave way to incredulity, and I used to return to my home on Friday afternoons wondering what Minnie had got up to this time. There was always something untoward to greet me. If there were not some new places for the dusters to dry, then it might be a few broken shards of a favourite cup, carefully arranged on a half-sheet of newspaper, on the draining board. At least, she did not try to cover up her little mishaps with my property. I supposed it was something to be thankful for, but I longed for the day when Minnie's future took her far, far away.

Her own domestic affairs seemed to be shrouded in mystery. I had heard rumours about Mrs Fowler and her new paramour, and some said that she was asserting her authority to such an extent that it was likely that Minnie's husband might return to his wife and children. Others said that Minnie too was finding consolation elsewhere, and that the under-gardener at Springbourne Manor had been seen leaving Minnie's premises at some very odd times.

I rarely saw Minnie, only the results of her labours, and that was quite enough for me. Mrs Pringle, who usually volunteered any village news, was unusually taciturn these days, and I put it down to the debilitating effects of the diet. Not that she seemed any thinner, but she was certainly paler, and her limp seemed to be permanent these days.

I ventured to ask how the dieting was progressing one day.

'You wants to ask Dr Martin,' she said sourly. 'It's him what does the worrying. I told him straight: "Them scales of yourn are wrong," but he never batted an eyelid. He reckons I've only lost another two pound, after all this time. Not my fault, you know, I sticks to what's writ down.'

It did seem odd.

'Of course, I eats what's put afore me if I'm invited out. Stands to reason you can't offend people when they've slaved over a hot stove getting a nice bit of roast pork and potatoes ready, and a good suet pudden to follow.'

'But do you go out often?'

'Twice a week to my sister's. And of course I have her back, and have to do much the same for her.'

'That can't help,' I felt obliged to point out.

Mrs Pringle bridled.

'I've halved my chocolate! I'm used to what we knew as a tuppeny bar in the old days, after my tea. Well, I makes that do for two days now, and I only takes one spoonful of sugar instead of two in my tea. No call for Dr Martin to be so sharp with me, I tell him. After all, I'm still *losing* weight, aren't I?'

I began to feel sorry for Dr Martin.

460

'Couldn't you use those sweeteners instead of sugar, and perhaps have half an apple instead of the chocolate?'

Mrs Pringle looked at me as if I were an earwig discovered in the bedclothes.

'And start my heart-burn up again? It's plain to see, Miss Read, as you and Dr Martin is hand in glove. If you wants me to go on working here, day in and day out, giving of my best and my heart's blood to this 'ere thankless job, then I must have a bit of nourishing food.'

She made her way towards the door, limping heavily.

I said no more. I know when I am beaten.

The second half of the summer term brought some of the hottest weather of the century. Day after day dawned clear and cloudless, and by half past ten in the morning, it was beginning to get too hot for comfort outside.

Our ancient schoolroom was one of the coolest places in the village. With its lofty ceiling and high windows, it was remarkably airy, and the gnarled elder trees which tapped against the west-facing windows, cast a green shade which was more than welcome.

The door was propped open permanently to let in any stray breeze. It also let in Tibby, much to the rapture of the children, and an assortment of wild life ranging from wasps – which threw the children into violent demonstrations of assumed fear – to butterflies, and once, a fieldmouse.

The latter threw *me* into a transport of fear, which was certainly not assumed, but which I tried to hide from the children. My efforts were not completely successful.

'Shall I whack it on the 'ead?' inquired Ernest, advancing with his geography reader in hand.

'No, no,' I said hastily. After all my exhortations on kindness to animals, it was disappointing to see Ernest's bloodthirsty reaction to the intruder. 'It will find its way out in a minute.'

Nose twitching, it scampered along by the map cupboard, watched by the class. I observed its movements with inward horror. Suppose it turned in my direction?

As luck would have it, Patrick gave an enormous sneeze,

461

which sent it bolting from the room, and out once again to the field from which it had emerged.

I breathed again.

The afternoons were so hot that it was impossible to expect much in the way of work from the children. The older ones went by school bus to Caxley once a week for a swimming lesson, and were the envy of all those left behind to swelter in the heat of Fairacre.

I did my best to make their lot easier by taking them outside. We have one particularly fine beech tree near the edge of the field which borders the playground, and here the shade was deep and refreshing on those baking afternoons.

I read them folk tales, and let them lie as they pleased, flat on their backs, or lodged on an elbow, their hair lifting in the light wind that stirred the leaves above them. What did it matter if they heard little of the story? On those golden afternoons they absorbed more than any printed page could give them – happy summer memories which would remain with them for a lifetime.

Whether it was the heat, or Mrs Pringle's growing touchiness, or a combination of both, which triggered off the great row between that lady and inoffensive Mrs Rose, it is impossible to say.

It began one hot after-dinner session, and the battleground was the lobby at the back of the school where Mrs Pringle does the washing-up.

It is usually a peaceful period, preceding the afternoon session, and occasionally running into the first lesson. I am quite used to giving out handwork material to the background of clashing cutlery and Mrs Pringle's contralto rendering of the more lugubrious numbers from *Hymns Ancient and Modern*.

The first I heard was the sound of infants on the move next door. They were obviously surging towards the door leading into the lobby. Adult voices were raised, one shrill, one booming. The latter was only too familiar to me, but I could not think who the other shrill-voiced contestant could be.

Daring my children to bat an eyelid, I strode forth to investigate.

'Into your seats this minute!' I bellowed at Mrs Rose's excited children, who were milling round the door. Reluctantly they obeyed, and I posted the largest infant at the front to tell me on my return who had been the quietest. The battle was gaining in volume and speed of action behind me.

It was now plain that Mrs Rose was engaged in combat with Mrs Pringle, and I quaked at the thought of what I might see by – or even under – the lobby sink.

There was something Wagnerian about the sight which met my eyes. Steam from the washing-up bowl wreathed the forms of the two martial bodies. Mrs Pringle held a saucepan aloft as though about to cleave Mrs Rose's skull, some inches below her own. Mrs Rose, her normally pale face suffused with blotchy red patches, clung to Mrs Pringle's flowered overall and screamed her head off.

'*Ladies!*' I shouted. It seemed a singularly inappropriate title to bestow upon the two viragos before me, but was the best I could manage. At least it had the desired effect, and the combatants parted and faced me, bosoms heaving and eyes flashing. They were too winded with warfare to speak.

'What on *earth*,' I said sternly, 'are you two doing? You are frightening the life out of the children.'

This was not strictly true. Even now, some bold bad infants had crept to the doorway and were surveying the scene with every appearance of joy. This little contretemps would soon be common knowledge in Fairacre, I surmised.

'Stand back,' I hissed. 'Into your seats this instant! The very idea!'

This last phrase, idiotic though it may be, has an uncanny power over the young, if expressed forcibly. It worked yet again, and the faces vanished.

Mrs Rose tidied her hair, and without a word, followed her pupils, leaving Mrs Pringle muttering malevolently to herself.

'I don't know what all that was about, and I don't *want* to know,' I said loftily, 'but if it happens again we shall have to look for another cleaner.'

'And lucky you'll be to get one with that old cat on the premises,' boomed Mrs Pringle, as I departed with as much dignity as I could muster.

Mrs Rose was tying a shoelace with trembling fingers, as I passed through the infants' room on the way to my own.

'Sorry about that,' she whispered. 'I'll tell you all at playtime.'

A rare silence had fallen upon her class. They gazed upon her round-eyed. I left her to face the infants alone.

My own children were equally silent, but their eyes were bright with expectation.

'See if you can stay as quiet as that for the next ten minutes,' I said frostily, propping myself on the edge of the table, and trying to regain composure.

Long-suffering looks were exchanged. Obviously not a word of explanation was going to be given them. Was there no justice?

I saw Mrs Pringle departing soon afterwards, her black bag swinging on her arm, her stout back registering martyrdom, and her limp much in evidence.

Mrs Rose, calmer now, told me about the cause of the fuss, as we sipped our tea in the playground.

The real culprits were some new babies who had emptied their dinner scraps into the wrong bucket. It was as simple as that.

From time immemorial, Mrs Pringle has taken home a dank

parcel of plate-scrapings for her chickens. This is one of the many uses to which her black oilcloth bag is pressed. One bucket stands beneath the sink for such revolting left-overs as fat-trimmings, tough morsels of cabbage stalk and so on, combined with gobbets of custard, jelly or pastry from the second course.

Sometimes, turning from this receptacle with nausea, I am reminded of the tubs which are reputed to have been left outside the gates of Blenheim Palace, years ago, for the poor of Woodstock. It took an American Duchess to suggest that at least the savoury matter could be put in a separate container from the sweet. Mrs Pringle's chickens are not so fortunate, but appear to thrive on what they get.

The second bucket contains the true rubbish destined for the dustbin, along with the contents of the waste paper baskets. What had happened was that four or five innocents had scraped their plates into the latter, and such delicacies as half chewed gristle, dear to the hearts of Mrs Pringle's hens, were in danger of being thrown out.

Nagged by pain from her empty stomach, Mrs Pringle reacted furiously to this scandalous filching from her hungry hens, and began berating the poor babies who soon began to weep.

Mrs Rose, as zealous for her children as Mrs Pringle was for her chickens, rushed to their defence, and the ugly scene then ensued.

'She had no business to shout at the children like that,' asserted Mrs Rose, pink at the memory. 'Nor at me. I've never in my life been subjected to such impertinence.'

'I think you could have been a little more tolerant,' I said mildly. 'You know what Mrs Pringle is – and since this confounded dieting she's been twice as touchy.'

'She's not going to yell at my babies and get away with it! I shall expect an apology!'

'You won't get it.'

And of course she didn't. Mrs Pringle wrapped herself in majestic silence, and so did Mrs Rose, so that the atmosphere fairly quivered with taut nerves whenever the two ladies were in the same room.

It was a trying time for us all, and the fact that nothing more had been said, one way or the other, about Fairacre School's possible closure, I found particularly unnerving. More measuring had been going on at Beech Green School, according to Mr Annett, but otherwise he too was in the dark.

'I think it will all blow over,' he told me one sunny Friday evening. He had called before choir practice to lend me an American treatise on educating young children which he thought I might enjoy.

I had not the heart to tell him that any book more than three inches thick, with footnotes and five appendices, killed any desire to read it, from the start. A quick look inside had confirmed my suspicions that this one had been written in the brain-numbing sort of jargon I cannot abide. There was no doubt about it. It was one of those books one keeps safely for a decent interval, dusts, and returns, praying that the lender refrains from asking questions on it.

'After all,' he continued, 'it always has before. Why should they close Fairacre at this particular moment?'

'I don't know, but the numbers are dwindling. We're down to twenty-six this term, and somehow there was a look in Mr Salisbury's eye which I didn't like.'

'He's always got that,' said George cheerfully. 'Comes of working in an office all day.'

He put down his glass and sprang nimbly to his feet.

I sighed and rose too.

'You sound uncommonly sad,' he said. 'Old age?'

'Probably. How long notice would I get, do you think, if they do decide to close?'

'Years.'

'Honestly? Really *years*?'

'I believe so. Why, you'd probably be about to retire anyway by the time they get round to it.'

We walked together towards the church. The lime trees buzzed with scores of bees, and the scent from the creamy flowers was delicious – the essence of Summer. Fairacre seemed very dear and sweet.

'You've got a good spot here,' said George, as if reading my thoughts.

'None better,' I told him, as bravely as I could.

10. Who Shall it be?

One afternoon, towards the end of term, four candidates for the post of infants' teacher arrived for interview.

It was a sweltering day. The distant downs shimmered in a haze of heat, and the flowers drooped in the border. Tibby had found a cool spot among some thick grass under the hedge, and lay comatose. Even the sparrows were too exhausted to twitter from the school gutters.

Mrs Rose was taking charge of the school for an hour while I attended the interviewing session in my own dining-room, grudgingly polished by Mrs Pringle.

I had hoped that Mrs Rose might feel like applying for the post. She was not ideal, I know, but better the rogue one knew than the devil one didn't. However, since the row with Mrs Pringle, I was relieved to know that she would be leaving at the end of term, as had first been arranged. The frosty silences and cutting looks, which occurred when they met, may have given them some warped satisfaction, but I found the whole business extremely distasteful and childish.

The Vicar, as chairman of the managers, was being supported by Peter Hale. As a retired man, he seemed freer than the other managers, and anyway his experience and wisdom, as a schoolmaster, should prove a help on this occasion.

I had had the job of making a short list from the surprisingly large number of applicants for this modest post. It was a sign of the times, of course, as so many teachers were out of work. Normally, we are lucky, at Fairacre, to get two or three applicants. This time there were over fifty, and it had been difficult to choose four for interview.

They were all young. For too long we have had elderly ladies in charge of our youngest children, and though their motherly qualities were endearing, I felt that we were falling behind in up-to-date methods of teaching. It was time to have a change.

From my own point of view too, I wanted someone who

could be trained towards my aims with the children. It is doubly important to have a united team when the staff is small, and I was getting heartily sick of trying to keep the boat up straight with people like Mrs Rose who were set in their ways before they even came to Fairacre, and who had no intention of changing them.

Two of the applicants had been teaching for two or three years. The others had just finished their training and would be in their probationary year if they were appointed. We saw them first.

'Charming girls,' said the Vicar enthusiastically, as the second one closed the door behind her.

'They are indeed,' agreed Peter Hale. Both girls were remarkably pretty, and I began to wonder if I were going to get an unbiased assessment of their teaching powers from two males who, although elderly, were clearly still susceptible to female good looks.

The first, a fresh-faced blonde, had answered our questions with intelligence, but was not very forthcoming about methods she would use in teaching reading and number, which I found slightly daunting. She was engaged to be married, but intended to go on teaching for a few years before thinking of starting a family.

The second, Hilary Norman, was a red-head, with the creamy pallor of complexion which so often accompanies auburn hair. Her paper qualifications were very good, and she was thoughtful in her answering. Her judgement, in my opinion, was in advance of her years, and she seemed to have a delightful sense of humour. I warmed to her at once, and said so to my fellow-interviewers.

'She'll have to get digs near by,' observed Peter Hale, studying her address. 'Home is somewhere in Herefordshire. Too far to travel. Know anyone in Caxley who might put her up?'

'Not a soul,' I said.

'And really there's no one now in the village,' lamented the Vicar. 'And the bus service gets worse and worse.'

'I think we ought to see the others before going any further,' said Peter Hale. 'Let's have Mrs Cornwall, shall we?'

We turned our papers over, and the Vicar ushered in the lady.

To my eyes, she seemed just as attractive as the other two, and I could see that I should easily be out-classed in looks next

term – not that that would take much doing, I am the first to admit.

She was very calm and composed, and I could well imagine that the infants would behave angelically in her care. But, as the questioning went on, I began to wonder if she would be able to stimulate them enough. Country children are often inarticulate – not dumb by any means, they often chatter quite as volubly as their town cousins – but they are not as facile in expressing themselves and are basically more reserved.

She had wonderful references, drove her own car, and I felt she would be a loyal aide. But would she stay in Fairacre long enough to be of use?

'If my husband is posted abroad, of course I shall go too, but it might not be for another two years.'

It clinched matters for me, I fear.

The last applicant was Amazonian in build, and if anything even better-looking than those who had gone before. She would be jolly useful, I thought, in forcing open the high windows which so often stuck fast at Fairacre School, and her appearance alone would cause respect among her pupils. One sharp slap from that outsize hand would be enough to settle the most belligerent infant.

Again, her qualifications were outstanding, and she excelled in all kinds of sport. This worked both ways, of course, in our tiny school. Would she miss team games? Would there be enough scope for her with small children, and a small class of them at that? I had the feeling that she would be happier in the livelier atmosphere of a large school, and would find Fairacre too confining before long.

It was certainly a problem that faced us, when at last she had returned to await her fate in my sitting-room.

'Fine-looking set of girls,' said Peter Hale. 'Must be something to do with all that National Dried Milk they were brought up on.'

'I thought that finished years ago,' I said.

'I've never even heard of it,' admitted the Vicar. 'Is it the same as pasteurized?'

This is the way decisions get made in village life, and only a fool would get impatient with the meandering paths that lead to our end, but Peter Hale brought us back to the point.

'Perhaps it would be sensible to use the eliminating method here. We've four excellent candidates. Has Miss Read any doubts about any of them?'

'After all,' put in the Vicar, 'you have to work with the lady, and at close quarters. You must find her compatible.'

'Well, I feel that the married lady won't stay long. She was quite frank about it, and it seems as though she fully expects her husband to be sent overseas within two or three years. I'd sooner have someone willing to stay longer.'

'Agreed,' said my two colleagues, putting aside one set of papers.

'And in a way, that goes for the engaged girl too, although I'm sure she would be able to give a reasonable length of service.'

'I liked that little red-haired girl,' confessed the Vicar. 'She is so lively. I'm sure the children would respond to her.'

'But we haven't gone steadily through our eliminating yet,' protested Peter Hale. 'Let's be methodical.'

'My dear fellow, I do apologize,' said the Vicar, flustered. 'How far had we got? Not the married one, wasn't it?'

'Provisionally,' I agreed guardedly.

'Nor the engaged one? Really, it looks as though you disapproved of matrimony, Miss Read! A holy state, we're told, a holy state!'

'My mind is open, I hope. I just think she is less quick than Miss Norman. She was pretty vague about methods she would use, and I suspect the children might find her too easy-going and get out of hand.'

'Right!' said Peter Hale, putting aside another set of papers. The Vicar sighed.

'She had a remarkably sweet expression, I thought. Reminded me of the early Italian Madonnas.'

'What about the large lady?' asked Peter, ignoring the Vicar's gentle lamentations.

'Useful type,' I said. 'Could do all the jobs Mr Willet can't manage. Why, she could lift Mrs Pringle up with one hand!'

'If that should ever be called for,' agreed Peter gravely. 'But what about working with her? Her qualifications are excellent, and she looks in spanking health.'

'I have a feeling that she would find Fairacre a little constricting. She's obviously cut out for a much more demanding post, a bigger staff, older children and so on. There's not enough scope for her here. I wouldn't mind betting that she'll be a head teacher in a big school within ten years. It's like putting a lion in a rabbit hutch.'

'But why did she apply then?' asked the Vicar.

'Not enough jobs going.'

'I'm sure that's it,' I said. 'And we shall find that it's a side-step for this girl, that she'll regret it herself before long.'

'Then that leaves Miss Norman whom you liked from the first. Still feel the same?'

I closed my eyes and thought again. It really is a staggering decision to make, this choosing someone to share one's life so closely in a remote school. Things can so easily go wrong.

I remembered Miss Jackson who had been with me some years earlier. It had been a disastrous appointment, and yet just as much care had gone into considering her.

The fact is that it is virtually impossible to sum up a person until you have lived and worked with them through good times and bad. Paper qualifications, references, examination successes, can only play a small part, and one interview, with the applicant highly nervous and on her best behaviour, can tell little more. Much must be taken on trust.

'Well?' said the Vicar and Peter together.

I opened my eyes.

'Yes,' I said. 'I'd like Hilary Norman, if you feel the same.'

'I think it's the best choice,' said Peter.

'Without doubt,' said the Vicar. 'And so pretty.'

He turned to Peter.

'Would you like to ask her in again, and apprise the unsuccessful candidates of the result?'

Peter took it like a man.

'I'll go and break it gently,' he said, and vanished to carry the good – and bad – news to the waiting four.

Amy came over that evening, bearing a beautiful bouquet of roses from her garden, and the news that Vanessa had produced a son and heir, weighing eleven pounds.

'Good grief!' I exclaimed. 'Poor girl! How is she?'

'Absolutely fine amidst all the rejoicing. It all sounds delightfully feudal, I must say. Tarquin rang last night amidst sounds of revelry in the background, and a bonfire to beat all bonfires blazing on the hill, or ben. It is "*ben*"?'

'Either that or "butt",' I told her. 'I'm not conversant with the lingo. But tell me more.'

'She had what is euphemistically termed "a good time", I gather.'

'Meaning what?'

'Oh, sheer unadulterated misery for twenty-four hours instead of forty-eight or more. But she's remarkably resilient, you know. Takes after Eileen who thought nothing of a twelve-mile walk as a girl. Uphill at that.'

'And what is he going to be called?'

'Donald Andrew Fraser Tarquin. One thing, people will know the land of his birth.'

'But the initials spell DAFT,' I pointed out. 'He'll have hell at school.'

Amy looked shocked.

'How right you are! What a blessing you noticed it! I shall let Vanessa know at once.'

She put her head on one side, and considered me carefully. I waited for her usual derogatory comments on some facet of my appearance.

'You know, you are remarkably astute in some ways.'

I began to preen myself. I so seldom receive a compliment from Amy.

'It's a pity you're so pig-headed with it,' she added.

I rose with dignity.

'Come and help me put these roses in water,' I said. 'I intend to ignore that quite unnecessary last remark.'

'Hoity-toity,' said Amy, following me into the kitchen, and watching me start my flower arranging.

'Are you going to see Vanessa?'

'Yes, quite soon. James has to go to Glasgow on business, and we thought we'd have the weekend with them. There's one thing about being a Scottish laird. It seems that there are hosts of old loyal retainers to help with the cooking and housework. Why, Vanessa even has an under-nurse to help the monthly one! Can you imagine such luxury?'

'Would you take the matinée jacket I've just finished? It's pink, of course, but that's like life.'

'No bother at all,' said Amy. 'By the way, do you really want that red rose just there?'

'Why not?'

'It breaks the line.'

'What line?'

'Aren't you taking the eye down from that dark bud at the top to the base of the receptacle and below?'

'Not as far as I know. I was simply making sure that they were all in the water.'

Amy sighed.

'I do wish I could persuade you to come to the floral classes with me. It seems so dreadful to see you so ignorant of the basic skills of arrangement. You could really benefit with some pedestal work. Those roses call out for a pedestal.'

'At the price pedestals are, according to Mrs Mawne, these

roses can go on calling out,' I said flatly. 'What's wrong with this nice white vase?'

'You're quite incorrigible,' said Amy, averting her eyes. 'By the way, how's Minnie Pringle?'

'In smashing form, as the music hall joke has it.'

I told her about some of Minnie's choicer efforts, particularly the extraordinary methods used for the drying of dusters.

'You won't believe this,' I told her, 'but last Friday she had upturned the vegetable colander on the draining board, and had draped a wet duster over that. Honestly, I give up!'

'Perhaps you won't have her much longer. I hear that Mrs Fowler has ejected Minnie's husband. My window cleaner says the rows could be heard at the other side of Caxley.'

My spirits rose, then fell again.

'But it doesn't mean that he'll come back to Springbourne necessarily, and in any case, Minnie will probably still need a job. I don't dare hope that she'll leave me.'

'He'll have to sleep somewhere,' Amy pointed out, 'and obviously his old home is the place.'

'Minnie might demand more money, though, and let him stay on sufferance,' I said, clinging to this straw like a drowning beetle, 'then she wouldn't need to come to me on Fridays.'

'I think you are going too fast,' said Amy, lighting a cigarette and inserting it into a splendid amber holder. 'It's a case of wishful thinking, as far as you are concerned. I imagine that he'll return to Minnie, make sure she's bringing in as much money as possible, and will sit back and pretend he's looking for work. Minnie really isn't strong enough to protest, is she?'

Sadly, I agreed. It looked as though I could look forward to hundreds of home-wrecking Friday afternoons.

'Mrs Coggs,' I said wistfully, 'is doing more charring now that Arthur's inside. I gather she's a treasure.'

'You shouldn't have been so precipitate in offering Minnie a job,' reproved Amy. 'Incidentally, Arthur's case comes up at Crown Court this week. It was in the local paper.'

'I missed that. Actually this week's issue was handed by that idiotic Minnie to Mrs Pringle to wrap up the chickens' scraps, before I'd read it.'

'Typical!' commented Amy, blowing a perfect smoke ring,

an accomplishment she acquired at college along with many other distinctions, academic and otherwise.

'Well, if you've quite finished ramming those roses into that quite unsuitable vase,' said Amy, 'can I beg a glass of water?'

'I'll do better than that,' I told her, bearing my beautiful bouquet into the sitting-room. 'There's a bottle of sherry somewhere, if Minnie hasn't used it for cleaning the windows.'

11. Problems

As always, everything seemed to happen within the last two weeks of term.

At the beginning of every school year, I make all sorts of good resolutions about being methodical, in time with returning forms and making out lists, arranging programmes well in advance and so on. I have a wonderful vision of myself, calm and collected, sailing through the school year's work with a serene smile, and accepting graciously the compliments of the school managers and the officials at the local education department, on my efficiency.

This blissful vision remains a mirage. I flounder my way through the multitudinous jobs that surround me, and can always still be far behind, particularly with the objectionable clerical work, when the end of the year looms up.

So it was this July. The village fête in aid of Church Funds, as usual, had to have a contribution from the school, and as Mrs Rose became less and less capable as the end of her time drew nigh, and more and more morose since the tiff with Mrs Pringle, I was obliged to work out something single-handed.

It is difficult to plan a programme which involves children from five to eleven taking part, but with all the parents present at the fête, and keen to see their own offspring in the limelight, it was necessary to evolve something.

After contemplating dancing, a play, a gymnastic display and various other hoary old chestnuts, I decided that each of these activities needed more time and rehearsing than I could possibly manage. In the end I weakly fell back on folk songs, most of which the children knew already.

Mrs Rose gave half-hearted support to this proposal, and the air echoed each afternoon as we practised. Meanwhile, there were the usual end of term chores to do, and the heat continued, welcome to me, but inducing increasing languor in the children.

It was during this period that Arthur Coggs and his partners in crime appeared at Crown Court.

As Mr Willet had forecast, all the accused were given prison sentences. The brothers Bryant were sent down for three years and Arthur Coggs for two.

'Not that he'll be there all that time,' said Mr Willet. 'More's the pity. They takes off the time he's been in custody already, see, and if he behaves himself he'll get another few months cut off his spell inside. I reckons he's been lucky this time. We'll have him back in Fairacre before we've got time to turn round, darn it all!'

Mrs Coggs, it was reported, had gone all to pieces on hearing the sentence. Mrs Pringle told me the details with much relish.

'As a good neighbour,' she added, 'I lent that poor soul the *Caxley Chronicle* to read the result for herself, and I've never seen a body look so white and whey-faced as what she did! Nearly fell off of her chair with the shock,' said Mrs Pringle with evident satisfaction.

'Wouldn't it have been kinder to have told her yourself, if she'd asked?'

'I didn't trust myself not to break down,' responded the old humbug smugly. 'A woman's heart's a funny thing, you know, and she loves that man of hers despite his little failings.'

'I should think, *little failings* hardly covers Arthur's criminal activities,' I said, but Mrs Pringle was in one of her maudlin moods and oblivious to my astringency.

'I was glad to see the tears come,' went on that lady. 'I says to her: "That's right! A good cry will ease that breaking heart!"'

'Mrs Pringle,' I cried, 'for pity's sake spare me all this sentimental mush! Mrs Coggs knew quite well that Arthur would go to prison, and she knew he deserved it. If I'd been in her shoes, I'd have breathed a sigh of relief.'

Mrs Pringle, cut short in the midst of her dramatic tale, looked at me with loathing.

'There's some,' she said, 'as has no feeling heart for the misfortunes of others. It's plain to see it would be useless to come to you in trouble, and I'm glad poor Mrs Coggs had my shoulder to weep on in her time of affliction. One of these fine days, you may be in the same boat,' she added darkly, and limped from the room.

Heaven help me, I thought, if that day should ever come.

As it happened, trouble did come, but I managed to cope, without weeping on Mrs Pringle's ample bosom.

I received a letter from the office, couched in guarded terms, about the authority's long-term policy of closing small schools which were no longer economic to run. It pointed out that Fairacre's numbers had dwindled steadily over the years, that the matter had been touched on at the last managers' meeting, and that local comment would be sought. It emphasized the fact that nothing would be done without thorough consultation with all concerned, and that this was simply a preparatory exploration of local feeling. Closure, of course, might never take place should numbers increase, or other circumstances make the school vital to the surroundings. But should it be deemed necessary to close, then the children would probably attend Beech Green School, their nearest neighbour.

A copy of the letter, it added, had been sent to all the managers.

I felt as though I had been pole-axed, and poured out my second cup of coffee in a daze.

The rooks were wheeling over the high trees, calling harshly as they banked and turned against the powder-blue morning sky. The sun glinted on their polished feathers, as they enjoyed the Fairacre air. How long should I continue to enjoy it I wondered?

By the time I had sipped the coffee to the dregs, I was feeling calmer. In a way, it is always better to know the worst, than to await tidings in a state of dithering suspense. Well, now something had happened. The rumours were made tangible. The ostrich on the merry-go-round had come to a stop in full view of all of us. Now we must do something about it.

I washed up the breakfast things, put down Tibby's mid-morning snack, washed my hands, and made my way across to the school.

*

Now what should I choose for our morning hymn? 'Oft in danger, oft in woe' might fit the case, or 'Fight the good fight' perhaps?

No, let's have something bold and brave that we could roar out together!

I opened the book at:

'Ye holy angels bright
Who wait at God's right hand'
and looked with approval at the lines.

'Take what He gives, and praise Him still.'
Through good or ill, whoever lives.'

That was the spirit, I told myself, as the children burst in, breathless and vociferous, to start another day beneath the ancient roof which had looked down upon their parents and their grandparents at their schooling years before.

I guessed that the Vicar would pay me a visit, and before playtime he entered, holding his letter, and looking forlorn. The children clattered to their feet, glad, as always, of a diversion.

'Sit down, dear children,' said the Vicar, 'I mustn't disturb your work.'

That, I thought, is just what they want disturbed, and watched them settle down again reluctantly to their ploys.

'I take it you have had this letter too?'

'Yes, indeed.'

'It really is most upsetting. I know it stresses the point of there being no hurry in any of these decisions, nevertheless I feel we must call an extra-ordinary meeting of the managers, to which you, naturally, are invited, and after that I suppose we may need to have a public meeting in the village. What do you think?'

'See what the managers decide, but I'm sure that's what they will think the right and proper thing to do. After all, it's not only the parents, though they are the most acutely involved, but everyone in Fairacre.'

'My feelings exactly.'

He sighed heavily, and the letter which he had put on my desk, sailed to the floor. Six children fell upon it, like starving dogs upon a crust, and it was a wonder it was not torn to shreds before the Vicar regained his property.

After this invigorating skirmish, they returned to their desks much refreshed. The clock said almost a quarter to eleven, and I decided that early playtime was permissible under the circumstances.

They clattered into the lobby and the clanging of milk bottles, taken from the metal crate there, made a background to our conversation.

'You see there was some foundation for those rumours,' commented Mr Partridge. 'No smoke without fire, as they say.'

'It began to look ominous when the measuring started at Beech Green,' I responded. 'And Mr Salisbury was decidedly cagey, I thought. Oh dear, I hope to goodness nothing happens! In a way, the very fact that it's going to be a long drawn-out affair makes it worse. I keep wondering if I should apply for a post elsewhere, before I'm too old to be considered.'

The Vicar looked shocked.

'My dear girl, you mustn't think of it! The very idea! *Of course*, you must stay here, and we shall all see that you do. That's why I propose to go back to the vicarage and fix a date for the managers' meeting as soon as possible.'

'I do appreciate your support,' I said sincerely, 'it's just this ghastly hanging about. You know,

"The mills of God grind slowly
But they grind exceeding small."'

The Vicar's kind old face took on a look of reproof.

'It isn't God's mill that's doing the grinding,' he pointed out. 'It's the education office's machinery. And that,' he added vigorously, 'we must put a spoke in.'

If he had been a Luddite he could not have sounded more militant. I watched him cross the playground, with affection and hope renewed.

They say that troubles never come singly, and while I was still reeling under the blow of that confounded letter, I had an unnerving encounter with Minnie Pringle.

Usually, she had departed when I returned to my home after school on Fridays. I then removed the wet dusters from whatever crack-brained place Minnie had left them in, put any broken

480

shards in the dustbin, and set about brewing a much-needed cup of tea, thanking my stars that my so-called help had gone home.

But on this particular Friday she was still there when I entered the house. A high-pitched wailing greeted me, and going to investigate I found Minnie sitting on the bottom stair with a broken disinfectant bottle at her feet.

She was rocking herself back and forth, occasionally throwing her skirt over her mop-head of red hair, and displaying deplorable underwear including a pair of tights more ladders than fabric.

I was reminded suddenly of those Irish plays where the stage is almost too murky to see what is happening, the only light being focused dimly on a coffin with four candles, one at each corner, and a gaggle of keening women, while a harp is being plucked, in lugubrious harmony, by some unseen hand.

'What on earth's the matter, Minnie? Don't cry about a broken bottle. We can clear that up.'

'It ain't the *bottle*!' wailed Minnie, pitching herself forward with renewed energy.

'What is it then?'

She flung herself backward, hitting her head on the fourth stair up. I hoped it might knock some sense into her.

'Ah-ah-ah-ah!' yelled Minnie, and flung her skirt over her head once more.

I took hold of her skinny shoulders and shook her. The screaming stopped abruptly, and the skirt was thrown back over the dreadful tights.

'Now stop all this hanky-panky,' I said severely, 'and tell me what's wrong.'

Snivelling, Minnie took up the hem of her skirt once more, but this time applied it to her weeping eyes and wet nose. I averted my gaze hastily.

'Come on, Minnie,' I said, more gently. 'Come and have a cup of tea with me. You'll feel better.'

She sniffed, and shook her head.

'Gotter clear up this bottle as broke,' she said dimly.

'Well, let's find the dustpan and you do that while I make the tea.'

She accompanied me to the kitchen, still weeping, but in a less hysterical fashion. I found the dustpan – for some reason, best known to Minnie, among the saucepans – and handed it over with a generous length of paper towel to mop up her streaming face. I then propelled her into the hall, and returned to prepare the tea tray.

'At this rate,' I muttered to myself, 'I shall need brandy rather than tea.'

Five minutes later, sitting at the kitchen table, the tale unfolded in spasmodic fashion.

'It's Ern,' said Minnie. 'He's comin' back.'

Ern, I knew, was the husband who had so recently deserted her.

'And you don't want him?'

'Would you?'

'No!' I said, without hesitation. 'But can't you tell him so?'

'What, Ern? He'll hit me if I says that.'

'Well, get the police.'

'He'll hit me worse if I tells them.'

I changed my tactics.

'Are you sure he's going to come back?'

'He wrote to Auntie – she can read, you see – and said his place was at my side.'

'What a nerve!' I exclaimed. 'It hasn't been for the last few months, has it?'

'Well, it's different now. That Mrs Fowler don't want 'im. She's turned 'im out.'

So Amy was right after all, I thought.

'And when's he supposed to be coming?'

Minnie let out another ear-splitting yell, and I feared that we were in for another period of hysteria.

'Tonight, 'e says. And I'm too afeared to go home. And what will Bert say?'

'Bert?' I echoed, in perplexity.

'My boy friend what works up Springbourne Manor.' Minnie looked coy.

I remembered the rumour about the under-gardener who had been consoling Minnie in her loneliness.

'What about Bert?'

'He'll hit him too,' said Minnie.

'Your husband will?'

'Yes. Bound to. And Bert'll 'it 'im back, and there'll be a proper set-to.'

Minnie's fears seemed to be mingled with a certain pleasurable anticipation at the prospect, it seemed to me.

'Well, you'd better let Bert know what's happening,' I said, 'and he can keep away. That is, if Ern comes at all. Perhaps he's only making threats.'

Minnie's eyes began to fill again.

'He'll come all right. He ain't got nowhere to sleep, see. And I dursn't face him. He'll knock me about terrible, and the kids. What am I to do?'

'You say Mrs Pringle had the letter?'

'Yes. She read it out to me.'

'She'll be over at the school now,' I said, putting down my cup. 'I'll go and see her while you have some more tea.'

I left her, still sniffing, and sought out her aunt, who was balanced on a desk top dusting the partition between the two classrooms.

'My, what a start you gave me!' she gasped, one hand on her heart.

483

'Can you come down for a minute?' I said, holding out my hand for support. 'It's about Minnie.'

Mrs Pringle, twisting my hand painfully, descended in a crab-wise fashion, and sat herself on the front desk. I faced her, propped on my table.

'She's in tears about that husband of hers, and seems afraid to go home.'

'I knows that. She's been no better than she should be while he's been away. He's promised her a thundering good 'iding.'

'But he's threatening her just because he wants somewhere to sleep. It all seems most unfair to me. After all, he left her.'

'Maybe. But his place is in his own home, with Minnie.'

'But, he's intimidating her!'

'Natural, ain't it? How else did she get her last baby?'

I felt unequal to explaining the intricacies of the English language to Mrs Pringle, and let it pass.

'The point is, Mrs Pringle, that it really wouldn't be safe to let her go home if he intends to come and knock her about. Should we tell the police?'

Mrs Pringle bridled.

'What, and let the neighbours have a free show? Not likely.'

'But the children –'

Mrs Pringle's face became crimson with wrath. She thrust her head forward until our noses were almost touching.

'Are you trying to tell me what to do with Minnie's children? I'll tell you straight, I'm not having that tribe settling on me with all I've got to do. I'm sick and tired of Minnie and her lot, and the sooner she pushes off and faces up to the trouble she's made the better.'

'So you won't help?'

'I've done nothing but help that silly girl, and I'm wore out with it.'

'I can understand that, and I think you've been remarkably patient. But now what's to be done? I really think the police should be warned that there might be trouble.'

Mrs Pringle's breathing became heavy and menacing.

'You just try it! You dare! I've been thinking about the best way to tackle this ever since I got that Ern's letter. He can talk –

going off with that old trollop who's old enough to be his mother!'

I began to feel dizzy. Whose side was Mrs Pringle on?

'What I'm going to do,' said my cleaner, 'is to go back with Minnie and the kids tonight, and to sleep the night at her place, with the rolling pin on one side of me and the poker on the other. I'll soon settle that Ern's hash if he dares put a foot inside the place. We don't need no police, Miss Read, that I can tell you!'

'Splendid!' I cried. 'Can I go and tell Minnie?'

'Yes. And I'll be ready to set off in half an hour sharp, tell her, just as soon as I've got the cobwebs off this partition.'

She heaved herself up on to the desk again, duster in hand, and I returned home, thinking what a wonderfully militant band we were in Fairacre, from the Vicar to Mrs Pringle.

12. Militant Managers

The extra-ordinary managers' meeting was called during the last week of term, and great difficulty the Vicar had encountered before gathering them all together.

The long hot spell had advanced harvest, and Mr Roberts was already in that annual fever which afflicts farmers at this time of year, when the Vicar rang. However, he nobly put aside his panic and agreed to spend an hour away from his combine harvester, as the matter seemed urgent.

Mrs Lamb was supposed to be at a flower arranging meeting at Caxley where someone, of whom Mrs Lamb spoke with awe in her voice, was going to show her respectful audience how to make Large Displays for Public Places from no more than five bought flowers and the bounty culled from the hedgerows. Mrs Lamb, whose purse was limited but who enjoyed constructing enormous decorations of bullrushes, reeds, branches, honesty and even beetroot and rhubarb leaves, was looking forward to learning more, but gave up the pleasure to do her duty.

Mrs Mawne had a bridge party arranged at her house, but was obliged to do a great deal of telephoning to get it transferred to another player's. As all the ladies vied with each other in preparing exotic snippets of food to have with their tea, this meant even further domestic complications. However, it was done.

Mrs Moffat was busy putting the final touches to a magnificent ball dress which was destined to go to a Masonic Ladies' Night, but set aside her needle to be present, while Peter Hale, recently retired from the local grammar – now comprehensive – school, cursed roundly at ever being fool enough to agree to being a manager when the grass wanted cutting so urgently.

Resigned to their lot, therefore, they assembled in the Vicar's dining-room one blazing afternoon and accepted a cup of tea from Mrs Partridge before she departed to her deck-chair under the cedar tree, there to read, or rather to skip through, the final chapters of a very nasty book, strongly recommended by the book critics of the Sunday papers, and dealing with the incestuous relations of a sadistic father and his equally repulsive teenage daughter. The fact, much advertised by the publishers, that it had already sold thirty thousand copies and was now reprinting, gave Mrs Partridge more cause for regret than rejoicing, but she was determined to turn over the pages until the end, so that she could give her trenchant comments on the work, and truthfully say she 'had been through it', in more ways than one.

No one appeared from the office on this occasion, but I was invited, and enjoyed my cup of tea, and the comments of the managers.

'We've got to be firm about this,' said Mr Roberts. 'Say "No" from the outset. I mean, what's village life coming to?'

'How do you mean?' asked Mrs Moffat.

'Well, we used to have a village bobby. Remember Trumper, padre?'

The Vicar said he did, and what a splendid fellow he was.

'Exactly. Used to hear old Trumper puffing round the village every night about two o'clock making sure everything was in order.'

'So sensible,' agreed Mrs Mawne. 'We need more police. That's half the trouble these days.'

'And what's more,' went on Mr Roberts, 'he gave any young scallywag a good clip round the ear-'ole, on the spot, and stopped a peck of wrong-doing. What happens now? Some ruddy Juvenile Court six months later when the kid's forgotten all about it.'

The Vicar coughed politely.

'Quite. We take your point, but it is the school closure we are considering.'

'It's the same principle,' said Peter Hale, coming to Mr Roberts' support. 'You need direct contact – that's the unique quality of village life. If we lose the village bobby it's a link broken. Far worse to lose our village school.'

'Too little spread too thin,' said Mrs Lamb. 'Same as having to share you, Mr Partridge, with Beech Green and Springbourne. Why, I remember the time, before your day, of course, when the Vicar was just for Fairacre, and you could reckon to see him any time you wanted, if you were in trouble. He'd be in his study or the garden, or in the church or visiting in the parish. Now he can be anywhere.'

The Vicar nodded and looked unhappy.

'Not that it can be altered,' added Mrs Lamb hastily, 'and a marvellous job you do, but nevertheless, it's not the same.'

'I suppose there's no hope of this school staying open for infants only?' asked Mrs Mawne. 'The biggest objection is hauling the babies to Beech Green, I think.'

'It's too small as it is,' I said. 'Even if the Beech Green infants were brought here, both schools would still be too small according to the authority.'

The arguments went on. I was touched to see how concerned they all were, not only for the children's sake and mine, but for the destruction of a tradition which went back for over a hundred years.

'If we give in,' said Mr Roberts, 'we're betraying the village, as I see it. Our Fairacre children get a jolly sound grounding. You've only got to look at the percentage we used to get through the eleven-plus exam to go on to the grammar school, before it turned into this blighted whatever it's called. I propose we send a reply to the office saying we're firmly against the idea of closure.'

This proposal was carried unanimously, and the Vicar promised to write the letter that evening.

The clock stood at four-thirty. Mr Roberts rushed back to his combine, Mrs Moffat to her ball gown, Mrs Lamb to the telephone to hear all about the flower-arranging from a friend, Mrs Mawne to studying the bridge column in last Sunday's paper in lieu of her game, and Peter Hale to his lawn mower.

I stood in the vicarage garden and looked across at our modest weatherbeaten school across the way.

'Never fear,' said the Vicar, clapping me on the shoulder. 'It will be there for another hundred years, believe me.'

'I hope so,' I said soberly.

Amy called unexpectedly that evening while my head was still humming with the memory of the managers' meeting.

I told her a little about it. To my surprise, she seemed to think that Fairacre School was doomed to close, and that it would be a good thing.

'Well, I'm blowed!' I exclaimed. 'A fine friend you are! I suppose you want to see me queuing up for my dole before long?'

'Well, no,' replied Amy, with what I thought quite unnecessary hesitation. 'Not exactly, but I do think this place is an anachronism.'

'How can it be if it serves a useful purpose in the village?'

'I sometimes wonder if it does. Oh, I know all about fathers and grandfathers doing their pot-hooks and hangers under these very windows, but it's time things changed.'

'My children don't do pot-hooks and hangers.'

'Don't snap, dear. What I'm trying to point out is that things have altered considerably. For one thing, those grandfathers came to Fairacre School when it boasted a hundred children or more, as the log books show. It was a real *school-sized* school then, and enough boys present to play a decent game of football or cricket among themselves if they wanted to.'

'Team games aren't everything.'

'And then this building,' continued Amy, waving a hand. 'It's really had its time, you know. The very fabric is crumbling, as Mrs Pringle points out daily. And those antiquated stoves! And that ghastly sky-light forever letting in rain and a wicked draught! It's really not good enough. I wonder the parents haven't complained before now.'

I was speechless before this onslaught. Perhaps Amy was right. She often was, as I knew to my cost.

I changed the subject.

'You were right about Mrs Fowler by the way. She's pushed out Minnie's husband, and Minnie's afraid he'll come back to her.'

'With that row of children to look after, I should think she might welcome him.'

I told her about Minnie's fears of aggression, and how Mrs Pringle had gone into attack. Amy listened avidly.

'And did he come?'

'No, thank heaven, but they expect him daily and barricade

the door with the kitchen table whenever they go out. The children think it is terrific fun.'

'Children are odd,' agreed Amy. 'I remember how Kenneth used to insist on having the more lugubrious parts of *Black Beauty* read to him, while the tears rolled down his cheeks. He was about six then.'

Kenneth was a brother of Amy's who was killed in the last war. I met him occasionally, and could never take to him, finding him boastful, selfish, and frequently untruthful. He was a confounded nuisance to his parents in his teens, as so many boys are, and they were wonderfully realistic and cheerful about it.

However, no sooner had he died than their attitude to the young man was completely transformed. To hear them talk of Kenneth, after his death, one would have imagined him to be a paragon of all the virtues, kind, noble, a loving son and devoted friend to many. So does death transfigure us. Perhaps it is as well, but personally I think one should cling to the truth – in charitable silence, of course – and not try to deceive oneself, or others, about the rights of the matter.

Even now, so long after, Amy's voice took on a reverent note when Kenneth's name was mentioned. I was glad that she remembered him with love, but wondered if such an outstandingly honest and downright person as dear Amy really conned herself into believing Kenneth the complete hero.

'He was the handsomest of us all,' went on Amy, gazing across the fields outside the window. 'Our Aunt Rose always gave him a better birthday present than the rest of us. We used to resent it dreadfully.'

'Quite natural, I should think.'

'And it's about Aunt Rose I've come tonight,' said Amy, becoming her usual brisk self. 'She died a fortnight ago and I'm clearing out the house for her. When you break up, could you spare a couple of afternoons to help?'

I said I would be glad to.

'It's no joke, I can tell you,' warned Amy. 'She seems to have kept every letter and photograph and Christmas card since about 1910.'

'They'd probably make a fortune at Sotheby's,' I said.

'Make a hefty bonfire,' commented Amy, picking up her handbag. 'Anyway many thanks for offering. I'll pick you up one afternoon next week, and we'll get down to it. I should bring a large overall and tie up your hair.'

'How's Vanessa?' I said, as Amy slammed the car door.

'Besotted with motherhood,' said Amy. 'I think she's going to be one of those mammas who keep a diary of daily progress. You know the sort of thing:

Thursday: Baby dribbled.
Friday: Baby squinted.
Saturday: Baby burped.

'It's because it's the first,' I said indulgently.

'Well, her only hope is to have about half a dozen. Surely she would be more reasonable then.'

She drove off, and I returned to prepare a snack for the ever-voracious Tibby.

The last day of term passed off jubilantly, its glory only partly clouded by my secret fears that this might be perhaps the last day of a school year spent under Fairacre School's dilapidated roof.

However, I put such dismal thoughts aside, and fell to tidying cupboards, dismantling the nature table, removing the children's art-work from the walls and ruining my thumb nail as a result, as I do regularly. A broken thumb nail and arthritis in the right shoulder, caused by writing on the blackboard, are just two of a teacher's occupational hazards, I have discovered. Increasing impatience, over the years, seems to be another, certainly in my case.

But today in the golden haze of breaking up, all was well. The children were noisy but busy. The sun blazed down as though it would continue to do so until Christmas. Mr Roberts' combine provided a pleasant humming from some distant field, and a drowsy bumble bee droned up and down one of the school windows.

The afternoon flew by. We stood for grace in the unusually tidy and bare classroom, our voices echoing hollowly, and

praised God for mercies received and blessings to come, before the tumultuous rush for home.

Joseph Coggs was the last to leave.

'You want any gardening done this 'oliday?' he asked in his husky voice.

'Why, yes,' I said untruthfully.

It was plain that he needed occupation as well as a little pocket money.

'Can your mother spare you?' I asked. 'Or should you be helping with the baby?'

'The baby goes with 'er,' said Joseph, running a grubby finger along the table edge. 'Anyway the twins does that all right.'

'Well, if you're sure,' I said, making up my mind to have a word with Mrs Coggs before he came, 'then perhaps one morning next week, if it stays fine.'

'Cor!' was all he said, but he raised his dark eyes to mine, and unalloyed delight shone from them.

I patted his shoulder. I have a very soft spot for young Joseph, and life has never treated him well. Despite that, he has a sweetness of disposition which one rarely meets. Things must be pretty grim at home, and pretty tight too. I should be glad to have him to help, if only to enjoy his obvious pleasure at being of use.

'Off you go then,' I said. 'I'll call at your house soon to fix things up.'

He skipped off, and I followed him.

The sun had beaten down upon the faded paint of the school door all the afternoon, and it was almost too hot to touch. In the distance, the downs trembled through veils of heat haze, and my spirits rose at the thought of weeks of summer holiday stretching before me.

I skipped, almost as blithely as young Joseph, across the playground towards my home.

13. Other People's Homes

As promised, I went to see Mrs Coggs one evening during the first week of the holidays.

I knew better, as a country dweller, than to knock at the front door. In most cases, the knocker is securely fastened by layers of paint and the grime of years, except in the case of those once termed gentry, who still have polished knockers on their front doors, and use them.

The concrete path leading to Mrs Coggs' back door was so narrow and flush with the wall that it was quite a balancing feat to remain on it. The surface was badly cracked, and here and there an iron manhole cover added to the hazards. Fairacre 'went on the mains' a few years ago and we seem to have sprouted more covers than taps in the village.

At the back door three scraggy chickens pecked idly at the concrete, scattering with a squawk when they saw me, and fleeing to cover among some gooseberry bushes almost hidden in long grass. It was apparent that no gardener's hand had been at work here for many a long year, and I wondered if the Council had issued any reprimand about the state of its property.

Mrs Coggs appeared at the door looking like a startled hare. Her eyes bulged and her nose was atwitch.

'I didn't mean to frighten you,' I began.

She wiped her wet hands on the sacking apron which girt her skinny form, and pushed wisps of dank hair from her face.

'You best come in,' she said resignedly, and stepped over the threshold into the kitchen. I followed her.

I nearly stepped straight back again, stunned by the appalling smell. Mrs Coggs was busy wiping the seat of a wooden chair with the useful sacking apron and had her back to me, so that I hoped she had not seen my dismay.

The twins, runny-nosed despite the hot day, now came to the door which led into the remaining room where most of the

494

living was done. They looked as startled as their mother, and put grimy thumbs into their mouths for comfort.

'Clear off!' said Mrs Coggs. 'Miss Read don't want you lot 'anging around, and no more don't I!'

While I was engaged mentally in correcting the grammar of this last phrase, the two little girls sidled past me nervously, and bolted into the garden. The toddler, who had been hiding behind the back of the sacking apron, now set up a terrible hullabaloo. Mrs Coggs sat down at the kitchen table and hoisted him on to it among towers of dirty saucepans, plates, old newspapers, and a broken colander which seemed to contain a multitude of fish heads. It was this last, I guessed, which contributed the largest and most potent part of the general stench.

'It's gone your bed-time, ain't it, lovey,' she crooned, her face as suffused with tenderness, as she surveyed her youngest, as it had been with exasperation at the sight of the twins only a minute before. I was reminded of mother cats who adore their tiny babies, and cuff them unmercifully as soon as they think they should be off their hands.

'It was about Joe that I've come,' I said. 'I wondered if he could help me in the garden now and again during the holidays.'

She continued to stroke the baby's hair and did not answer. I began to wonder if she were becoming deaf, or if she were still too bemused by her change of fortune to take in anything she was asked. She certainly looked white and pinched, and I wondered if she were getting enough to eat.

'Perhaps one morning a week?' I said. 'He could stop and have his midday dinner with me, if that fits in with your plans.'

The mention of food seemed to rouse her.

'He'd like that. Always likes 'is school dinners, that one. More'n the twins does. They eats next to nothing.'

'What do they like?' I inquired.

'Bread and sauce,' she replied. 'They has that most days. Saves cooking.'

I pointed to the nauseating collection of fish heads.

'Are you going to cook those?' I inquired tentatively.

She surveyed them with some surprise, as though she had only just noticed their presence, although heaven above knew, they made themselves felt quite enough.

'Fishmonger give 'em to me yesterday, and said to boil 'em for soup or summat. But we'd never eat that stuff. I likes tomato out of a tin.'

I could not probe too deeply into Mrs Coggs' culinary arrangements though I was dying to know how she fed the family. Surely they didn't live on bread and sauce exclusively? I returned to Joe's arrangements.

'What about Tuesday mornings?' I suggested.

'Yeh, that's fine. I goes out all day Tuesday charring. I takes the baby, and the twins can come too in the holidays, but I usually leaves 'em 'ere, out of the way.'

'That's settled then,' I said, making my way to the door, and anxious to get a breath of fresh air after the foetid atmosphere inside. Spread over the hedge, I saw some shrunken and torn garments, fit only for polishing rags. Their washing had been sketchy, and they were still stained in many places. The over-powering smell of poverty and neglect saddened me.

'Mrs Coggs,' I said, able to bear it no longer, 'are you being looked after by the Social Security people? I mean, you are getting money regularly?'

Her face lit up.

'I gets over a pound for each kid now and Joe gets a pound too. And there's me own supplementary. I've never 'ad so much in me life. We gotter telly now.'

'But what about food?'

She looked bewildered.

'They has what they likes best. I told you, bread and sauce, and now I buys a few cakes and sweets. We ain't hard up, Miss, if that's what's worrying you. And I've got me work.'

I turned away, sighing. It was quite apparent that Mrs Coggs' home conditions were the result of lack of management rather than lack of money. I guessed that she was brought up in a home as feckless as her own, and marriage to Arthur could not have helped her, but how sad it all seemed! Sad and wasteful!

'Then I'll look forward to seeing Joe next Tuesday,' I said retracing my steps over the manhole covers. 'About ten, shall we say? And I'll send him home about one, after he's had lunch with me.'

She nodded vaguely, and lifted the child from her hip to the ground, where he sat in the dust. His bottom, I noticed, was completely bare. His hand was already reaching for a dollop of dried chicken's mess.

I escaped into the lane, and picked the first sprig of honeysuckle I could find. It mitigated the reek of fish only a little, but it helped.

Amy came to lunch before we both drove over to her late aunt's house, some miles beyond Springbourne, to sort out the old lady's things.

Still worried about the Coggs family, I poured out an account of my visit. Amy remained unperturbed.

'I can't think why you worry yourself so much about other people's affairs,' she said. 'I imagine Mrs Coggs muddles along quite satisfactorily. After all, she's still alive and kicking, and the children too, despite her appalling housekeeping.'

'But it's all so *unnecessary*,' I began.

'It's purely relative,' said Amy, accepting a second helping of gooseberry pie. 'I mean, look at the way I could worry myself stiff about you – but what good would it do?'

'How d'you mean?' I said, bridling.

'Well, the slapdash way you go about things. This pastry for instance. I imagine it's frozen, or something like that?'

'Of course it is. I make ghastly pastry, and the kitchen floor wants a good scrub after I've done it. Why, does it taste horrible? You've had two helpings, so it can't be too bad.'

'I was always brought up,' said Amy, touching her lips delicately with her napkin, 'in the belief that it was excessively rude to comment on the amount eaten by one's guests.'

'Oh, come off it,' I said. 'What I want to know is why you compare me with Mrs Coggs?'

'Simply this. *You* worry about Mrs Coggs because she is so inefficient. I *could* worry about *you* because you, in your way, are just as feckless. Fancy spending all that money on frozen pastry when it would cost you about half to make your own!'

'Don't nag,' I said. 'All right. I take your point, and I'll try

497

not to get too worked up about the bread and sauce menu at the Coggs'. But I shall see Joe gets a decent meal on the days he comes here.'

We washed up amicably, drank a cup of coffee (instant) apiece and drove over the hill towards Aunt Rose's establishment.

There had been a thunderstorm in the night, and the air was fresh and moist. The road ran between thick woods which gave off a delicious scent of wet leaves and moss. A slight mist hung over the little tributary of the Cax at Springbourne, and a flotilla of ducks splashed happily by the hump-back bridge.

A magpie flew chattering across the road, just in front of the car.

'*One for sorrow*,' quoted Amy. 'Did you spit?'

'Spit?'

'How ignorant you are! You should always spit if you see a magpie alone. It takes the venom out of the spell.'

'I had no idea you were superstitious.'

'I'm not. But I do spit at one magpie, and I make a cross in spilt salt, of course, and I wouldn't dream of cutting my nails on a Friday, but I wouldn't consider myself superstitious.'

'What about walking under ladders?'

'Common sense not to. Someone might drop a pot of paint over you.'

I pondered on the fact that no matter how long one knows people there still remain depths unplumbed in their make up.

Aunt Rose's house lay some two miles along a narrow and twisted lane. A charm of goldfinches fluttered from the high hedges, bound, I felt sure, for some thistle seeds which were growing near by. A crow was busy pecking at the corpse of a poor squashed hedgehog, victim, no doubt, of a car during its night time foraging. It was being watched by a pony whose shaggy head hung over a five barred gate. Animals, it seemed, enjoyed each other's company, and were as curious about each other's activities, as any of us village folk at Fairacre.

The house had a forlorn look as we approached it. The curtains were half-drawn and every window tightly shut. It was deathly quiet and still when we went inside, and smelt of dust and old clothes.

'Leave the front door wide open,' directed Amy, 'and let's open a few windows, before we go upstairs.'

It had been built in the thirties, when Aunt Rose's father had died, leaving her comfortably off. It was quite a period piece and a very pleasant one too, with its cream walls and paintwork, its fawn tiled hearth, the standard lamp crowned with its beige bell-shaped shade, and the oatmeal-coloured great Knole settee tied at the corners with silk cord.

On the wide window sills stood the sort of flower vases one rarely sees these days – pottery posy rings, a glass bowl containing a heavy glass holder with bored holes, and several fine lustre jugs. On a little table near by lay a half-finished piece of knitting in pale blue wool. It looked like part of a jumper sleeve, and a spider had spun a long gossamer strand across its dusty surface. It brought home to me, with dreadful poignancy, the swift transition from life to death, when our toys are set aside and we have to leave our playing.

We made our way upstairs where a smell of lavender greeted us. A bowl of dried flowers stood on the table on the landing and scented the whole top floor. Amy wanted to go through her aunt's clothes before tackling anything else, and we set to with a will.

Out of the wardrobe came the sort of clothes which a repertory theatre would welcome. There were coats trimmed with silver fox fur, black evening gowns, ablaze with sequins at the neck, and a musquash coat from which flew several moths as we dumped it on the bed.

On the rack at the bottom of the wardrobe we removed beautiful cream kid shoes with Louis heels, and some later ones with stiletto heels and sharply pointed toes. Everything was in apple pie order.

'Now, what I propose to do,' said Amy, 'is to make three piles. One for myself, one for friends and relatives, and one for local jumble sales. Let's make a start.'

It all seemed very well thought out, until we began. Amy's pile was extremely modest. She put aside two almost new tweed skirts and a pretty little fur stole. It was the division of the rest between relatives and jumble which gave us a headache. Amy proved surprisingly dithery over the allotment.

'I think we ought to let the two nieces have a look at these woollies. After all, they're practically new and came from Harrods. Perhaps they're too good for the jumble pile.'

And so they would be transferred, changing places – but only temporarily – with four pairs of elbow-length gloves with rows of pearl buttons.

My head was beginning to buzz by the time Amy called a halt and we went downstairs for a change of occupation.

Aunt Rose, methodical to the last, had left a list of objects which she wanted close friends to have. Our job was to tie on labels bearing the new owner's name.

It was not quite so exhausting as the upstairs sorting, and we duly affixed labels to pieces of beautiful Wedgwood, Venetian glass, a nest of tables, two bronze clocks and a few choice pieces of furniture.

I found the job rather sad. It seemed such a pity that all these lovely things, which had lived together cheek-by-jowl for so many years, should now be parted. But I comforted myself with the thought that no doubt they were going to homes where they would be cherished as dearly as they had been by Aunt Rose.

The sky was overcast as we locked up and drove away.

'More rain tonight,' forecast Amy, dodging a rabbit that

sprinted across the narrow lane. 'Bang goes any idea of mowing the lawn tomorrow. Can you come again tomorrow afternoon to finish off upstairs?'

'I've got Joseph Coggs to lunch,' I said, 'but I could be ready by two.'

'You and your gentlemen friends,' commented Amy. 'I only wish this one were more your age and you took him seriously.'

She drew up at the school house, and shook her head when I asked her in.

'No, I must get back. But a thousand thanks for helping. I'll see you tomorrow.'

She let in the clutch, and then shouted over her shoulder as the car moved forward.

'Give Joe a good lunch!'

14. *The Summer Holiday*

The clock of St Patrick's was striking ten when Joseph Coggs arrived. The sun was beginning to break through the clouds which had brought more rain at dawn, and gilded the wet paths and sparked tiny rainbows from the droplets on the hedge. My temporary gardener looked remarkably happy.

'Wodjer want doin', miss?' he inquired after our greetings. He surveyed the garden appreciatively.

'What about weeding the border?'

'I likes weedin'!' said Joe, accepting a bucket and small fork, 'but if I don't know which is which I'll 'ave to 'oller to you.'

I agreed that that would be wise, and watched him tackle the job. He was quick and neat in his movements, and the groundsel and twitch were soon mounting in the bucket. There is one thing about neglecting a border. By the time you get down to it the results are really spectacular.

Joe began to hum happily to himself and I returned to the kitchen.

I had prepared a chicken casserole, and as the oven was in use I decided to make a treacle tart, for where would you find a small boy who doesn't like treacle tart? With Amy's rebuke still ringing in my head, I resolved to make my own pastry.

I must admit, I found the task quite rewarding, despite the shower of crumbs which managed to leap from the bowl on to the floor. I found myself becoming quite dreamy as I rolled the pastry. It was such a soporific exercise that I was quite startled when Joe appeared at the open window before me. His eyes were bright as he watched me at work.

'Us havin' poy then?'

'Treacle tart.'

'Cor!' breathed Joe. He rested his elbows on the outside window sill and settled down to watch. It was not long before his gaze became as bemused as I guessed my own was. Perhaps it was the rhythmic movement of the rolling pin, I thought.

'I loves pastry,' growled Joe. 'Bein' made, I mean, as well as when I eats it.'

I nodded in reply, and lifted the floppy material on to a shallow dish.

'Like sittin' by the fire, or sleepin' with your back against your mum,' went on Joe, suddenly loquacious. 'You want that bit what's cut off?'

'No,' I said, handing over a strip. 'But should you eat it raw?'

'Gives you worms, my mum says,' said Joe contentedly, retreating rapidly with his booty, 'but I still likes it.'

He returned to the border leaving me to ponder on the primitive needs which still make themselves felt, and which had given Joe such unusual powers of expression.

The chicken stew was relished as keenly as the treacle tart, and while we were demolishing my handiwork we chatted of this and that, his next gardening spell with me, why rabbits have so many babies, what happens to your inside if you eat soap, why Mrs Partridge has summer curtains as well as winter ones, and other interesting topics.

'Is our school truly going to shut?' he said suddenly, spoon arrested halfway to his mouth. A thread of treacle drooped dangerously tableward, and I steered his hand over his plate.

'I don't know. I hope not.'

'Mrs Pringle told me mum it was going to.'

I should like to have said: 'Don't believe anything Mrs Pringle tells you,' but civility and the enforced camaraderie of those in authority forbade.

'No one knows yet.'

Joe's dark eyes looked troubled.

'Well, I don't want to go off in a bus to that ol' Beech Green.'

'Why not?'

Joe twirled his spoon slowly, winding up the treacle.

'I'm afeared of that Mr Annett. 'E walloped my cousin Fred 'orrible.'

'He probably misbehaved,' I said primly. 'Mr Annett doesn't punish children unless they've been really bad.'

'Well, I'm not going anyways,' said Joe, looking mutinous. 'I 'ates going on buses away from Fairacre.'

'Why? Do you feel ill?'

'No. But I bin to Caxley sometimes, and to Barrisford on the outings, and I don't like it. I don't like being so far away.'

I remembered his look when he described the comfort of sleeping with his back against his mother.

'I likes to be home,' he sighed. 'It's right to be home. It's safe there.'

The vision of that appalling kitchen rose before me, the stinking fish heads in the colander, the dirty rags on the draining board, the grease on the floor, the meals of bread and sauce consumed at that filthy table. But to Joe it meant happiness.

Miss Clare, I remembered, had a sampler hanging on her cottage wall, by the fireplace.

'*Home is where the heart is*' it said in cross-stitch. It certainly seemed to apply in the case of Joseph Coggs.

I told Amy about Joe's disclosure as we continued to sort out Aunt Rose's effects that afternoon.

'It seems to me that everyone in Fairacre is taking it for granted that the school is going to close,' I said, holding up a pair of vicious-looking corsets with yards of pink lacings hanging from them.

Amy took them from me and deposited them on the jumble pile.

'Well, what do you expect? After all, it affects everybody and you know what village life is like, better than most. If there isn't a real drama going on then someone will invent one.'

'But nothing has been decided yet.'

'All the more fun. You can make your own ending, can't you? I suppose you realize that you are the central character?'

'How? I've said nothing.'

'A dispossessed person, you'll be. The evicted innocent cast out into the snow, frail, noble and uncomplaining. The village is dying to rally to your support.'

'That'll be the day!'

'Or maybe you'll be rescued, just in time to save you from complete penury, by some gallant hero who marries you in Fairacre Church while the children throw rose petals in your path.'

'Lumps of coke, more likely, knowing them.'

I held up a vest which looked remarkably short.

'What's this?'

'A *spencer*, dear. It's time they came back. You wear it under or over your petticoat in cold weather. A very sensible garment. Put it on my pile. It'll be just the thing for next winter.'

I did as I was bid.

'I hope you're wrong,' I went on, 'about village feelings. Lord knows there's enough to keep all the gossip-mongers busy at the moment, what with Minnie Pringle's affairs, and Mrs Pringle's spasmodic dieting, and talk of Dr Martin retiring at last, and Mr Lamb's brother and his family coming over from America very soon, and the mystery of two dead rats in the rainwater butt outside the vestry door.'

Amy broke into a peal of laughter, and sat down on the side of the bed clutching a black velvet evening cape to her ribs.

'Heavens, how you do go on in Fairacre,' she managed to gasp. 'No wonder you don't want to leave with all that happening around you! But, mark my words, there will still be time left to attend to you and your affairs, even if they do have to compete with two dead rats in the vestry's rainwater butt.'

She shook out the velvet cape and studied it with her head on one side.

'For bridge parties, should you think?'

'For the jumble pile,' I told her.

And, for once, she obeyed.

A few days later, I set off for a short holiday in East Anglia, staying with friends and revisiting on my way to Norfolk the little resort of Walton-on-the-Naze where I had stayed as a child with my grandparents. The air was still as bracing as I remembered it from my youth, and I felt no desire to plunge into the chilly waves of the North Sea, despite the sunshine.

I forgot my cares as I travelled. It was a relief to leave all the gossipers to get on with their tongue-wagging and wonderful not to have to guard my own conversation. I returned to Fairacre, after nine days of enjoyment, much refreshed.

It was Mrs Pringle's day for 'doing' me, and she was in the kitchen when I went in, doing something complicated with an old toothbrush at the sink.

'A dirt-trap, these 'ere taps,' was her greeting. 'I'd like to meet the fellow as designed 'em. No room to get behind 'em to scrub out the filth. And filth you can always reckon to find in .this kitchen, I can tell you!'

She did, quite often, but I forbore to say so.

'I'm having a cup of tea,' I said. 'Will you have one too?'

'I don't mind if I do,' she said graciously, attacking the crack behind the taps with renewed vigour.

'Well,' I said, when the tray was ready, 'what's the news?'

'Plenty,' she said. 'Our Minnie goes from bad to worse.'

'What now? Is she moving?' I asked, my heart taking a hopeful leap. Would Friday afternoons revert to their former tranquillity again?'

'Moving? I wish she was! No, *she's* not moving, but that dratted Bert of hers is. He's moving in.'

'But what about her husband? Ern, isn't it? I thought *he* was going to move in.'

'I settled him,' said Mrs Pringle grimly. I remembered her threat of sleeping with the rolling pin on one side and the poker on the other. Perhaps Ern had met his match.

'After all Ern's hullabaloo Bert said his place was at Minnie's side.'

'But that's just what Ern said!' I expostulated. If all the men who had received Minnie's favours over the years suddenly decided that their place was at her side, she would undoubtedly have to look for larger premises.

Mrs Pringle blew heavily upon her tea, creating a miniature storm in the cup.

'Well, Bert's not a bad chap, although no better than he should be, of course, when it comes to Minnie, and no doubt he could settle Ern's hash if he comes back in a fighting mood. So he's gone to live with our Min. In the spare room, of course,' she added austerely.

'A lodger.'

'A *paying guest*,' corrected Mrs Pringle. 'Five pounds a week. All found.'

I was musing upon the expression 'all found' when Mrs Pringle casually threw in her bombshell.

'So maybe she won't need to do as much cleaning work now. I'll find out if she wants to give you up, for one, shall I?'

'Yes, please,' I said fervently.

I poured Mrs Pringle a second cup. My feelings towards Bert, the philanderer, whose relationship with Minnie I had hitherto deplored, became suddenly much warmer. When it came down to brass tacks – Minnie's moral welfare versus my self-preservation – the latter won hands down.

As always, the holidays rushed by at twice the speed of term-time, reminding me of vague wisps of Einstein's theory of relativity which was once explained to me at Cambridge and involved something to do with Wordsworth's 'Ode on Intima-tions of Immortality from Recollections of Early Childhood'. I may have taken in one hundredth of the explanation at the time, but now I remember nothing clearly, except the fact that things are not what they seem. Certainly, this time business is purely relative, and I give Einstein points for that.

Hilary Norman was there in the infants' room, looking remarkably fresh and competent on her first morning, in a pale blue denim trouser suit.

The children, round-eyed, and in an unusually quiet mood, studied her with curiosity. I don't think they can ever have had quite such a young teacher before, and they were enchanted. Later I heard that one of them had told his mother that: 'We've got a little girl to teach us now.'

We pushed back the partition between the two classrooms, to the accompaniment of ear-splitting squealings from the steel runners, and embarked on a full assembly, starting with 'We plough the fields and scatter the good seed on the land' which seemed a little premature to me at the end of August, until I looked out of the window to see one of Mr Roberts' tractors busily turning the golden stubble into lovely long ribs of chocolate-coloured earth. Farmers, these days, certainly hurry along with their work, and the gulls were having a splendid time following close behind, mewing and squawking like a trodden cat, as they swooped upon the bounty below them.

As they sang lustily, and not very tunefully – music is not one

of our stronger accomplishments – I thought how small the school was just now. Despite the fact that two new infants had joined Hilary Norman's class, we were two down on last term's numbers, as one family had moved into Caxley, taking four children whom we could ill afford to lose at this critical stage.

What would happen to us? I was surprised that nothing further had been heard from the office, but supposed that the summer holidays had meant a postponement of any decision. No doubt we should hear in good time. It seemed that the general feeling was that closure was inevitable. Far better to know the worst than to hang on like this in horrible suspense.

The matter was further aggravated for me at playtime when, mugs of tea in hand, my assistant and I roamed the playground to keep an eye on would-be fighters and coke-pile climbers.

Things were remarkably tranquil, reflecting the golden summer day about us, and I was beginning to relax into my usual mood of vague well-being when Hilary spoke.

'I heard that the school may have to shut before long? Is there any truth in it?'

I came to earth with a jolt.

'Where did you hear of this?'

'Oh, at my digs. My landlady's old friend was visiting her yesterday evening, and she lives at Beech Green, and there seemed to be a pretty strong rumour that our children will be going there before long.'

So our affairs were already being discussed in Caxley! Not that I was surprised, having lived in a village and knowing how rapidly word is passed from one to another. Nevertheless, it was beginning to look as though something definite must be heard soon from official sources if so many people were assuming that the matter was settled.

'If it's true,' continued Hilary, 'I don't think I should have applied for this post. It's very unsettling to have a short time in one's first school and then have to find somewhere else.'

I could quite see her point of view. She was beginning to wonder if we had kept things from her, and I hastened to explain.

'Truthfully, these are only rumours, and we are no nearer a decision now than we were when you came for interview. If there had been anything known definitely, you would have been told. General policy is to close small schools, but it may be years before Fairacre's turn comes.'

I felt it right that she should know that the managers were resisting any such move, and that if need arose there might well be a village meeting to find out more about local opinion, and I told her so.

'This far from happy position lasted for over ten years at Springbourne,' I told her. 'It's always a long drawn out thing. I feel sure that your post wouldn't have been advertised at all, if there had been any thought of closing in the near future, so I think you can look forward to several years here, if you want to stay.'

The girl looked much relieved.

'I think I *shall* want to, you know. It's a lovely place to teach, and the children seem angelic.'

At that moment, two children fell upon each other with the ferocity of starving tigers upon their prey, and a ring of interested spectators assembled to cheer them on.

'You spoke too soon,' I said, striding into the centre of things.

August slipped into September, and the signs of early autumn were all around us. Already the scarlet berries of the wild roses and crimson hawthorn beaded the hedges, and old man's beard made puffs of smoke-like grey fluff here and there.

In the cottage gardens, the dahlias made a brave show, and the last of the summer annuals, love-in-a-mist, marigolds and verbena added colour in the borders. It was a time to enjoy the last of the summer, for already it was getting chilly in the evenings, and I had lit an occasional fire in my sitting-room, much to Mrs Pringle's disgust.

I had purposely refrained from asking about Minnie's affairs. The lady still flapped about my premises on Friday afternoons, like a demented hen, and wet dusters appeared in the unlikeliest places. By now I was resigned to my lot and had given up hope of ever being free of her attentions.

But one afternoon, Mrs Pringle accosted me when she appeared to wash up the crockery after school dinner. Her mouth was turned down ominously, and her limp seemed more pronounced to me.

'Got trouble at 'ome,' she said. 'I'll be off as soon as I've done the pots.'

'What is it? Not Minnie again?'

She nodded portentously, like a Chinese mandarin at his most impressive.

'Ah! Minnie it is! That girl and them kids of hers come up my place just now, because Ern's arrived.'

'Where? At Springbourne?'

'That's right. She left him cooking sausages and chips. I must say he'd had the decency to bring the sausages with 'im. Probably knew our Minnie wouldn't 'ave nothing worth eating in the house. Strikes me they lives on cornflakes.'

'Is she staying with you?'

'She'd better not. She knows my feelings on the matter. I've told her to clear off home, but she won't take a hint, that girl.'

Some hint, I thought, but Mrs Pringle was in full spate and I was obliged to listen to the unedifying tale.

'She seems scared stiff of that fellow, and I reckons when Bert turns up after work, there'll be a proper set-to atween 'em. Well, I told her straight: "The house is in your name now. You pays the rent to the Council, so your place is inside it." After all, that Ern – or Bert, for that matter – is no more than paying guests, only they don't pay, and if Minnie would only stand her ground, she could get rid of both of them.'

'But will she?' I managed to slip in, as Mrs Pringle drew breath.

'You may well ask,' said Mrs Pringle, unrolling a flowered overall and donning it ready for her session at the sink.

'Sometimes I wonders,' she went on, 'if our Minnie is quite right in the head, I really do.'

I could have told her, but common civility kept me silent.

PART THREE

Fate Lends a Hand

15. Two Ladies in Trouble

Autumn is one of the loveliest times at Fairacre. We are not as wooded as Beech Green, but small copses at the foot of the downs turn to bronze and gold as soon as the first frosts come, and the tall elm trees near the school send their lemon-yellow leaves fluttering down. A few sturdy oak trees rise from the neighbouring hedges, and these are the last to turn, but when they do, usually sometime in November, their colour is superb.

Now the children arrive with poisonous-looking toadstools for the nature table, and sprays of blackberries, mostly hard and red fruits remaining, as the juicy black ones have vanished down young throats on the way.

We do well for nuts too, in this area, and walnuts from cottage gardens, sweet chestnuts and beech nuts from the woods, and hazel nuts from the hedgerows also find their way to school. Horse chestnuts, of course, are put to more vigorous use, and the strings of conkers lie coiled on the long desk at the side of the classroom, awaiting their owners at playtime.

This year we were lucky enough to have a sunny October, with those peculiarly clear skies of Autumn which show up the glory of blazing leaves. We took a great many nature walks, watching the flocks of rooks stabbing the newly ploughed furrows for worms and leatherjackets, and noting the starlings, excited and chattering as they wheeled around the sky, the flock getting larger and larger until the great day came to set off together.

The swallows had already gone. For weeks past, they had perched upon telegraph wires in the village, preening themselves and twittering noisily, preparing for their flight of thousands of miles to warmer sunshine than Fairacre could provide.

In village gardens, the first bonfires of Winter were appearing, and wreaths of blue smoke scented the air with the true essence of Autumn. Mr Willet was already planning where to plant his broad beans: 'You can't beat Aqua-Dulce Long-pod for planting in November,' he assured me. 'A good sturdy grower, and it beats that blighted black fly if it gets a fair start.'

The holidaymakers were back from exotic climes, and comparing notes on the beauties of Spain and Italy, and the price of a cup of coffee in Paris and St Mark's Square, Venice. These people, of course, were the more leisured among us. Most of us had taken our breaks, if any, in July or August, ready for the new school year.

I was invited to a cheese and wine party at the Mawnes. Proceeds were to go to the Royal Society for the Protection of Birds, of which both Mawnes were strong supporters. As the house is a lovely Queen Anne specimen, and the furniture is a joy to behold, I walked along the village that evening with more than usual pleasure. The older I get the less I want to leave my own home in the evenings, particularly bleak winter ones, but it was pleasant to stroll through the gentle darkness, catching sight of the various village cats setting off on their hunting expeditions, and savouring the whiff of bonfires still hanging upon the quiet air.

The house was ablaze with lights, and more than a dozen cars were lined up in the drive. I was glad I had not brought mine to add to the congestion. Far too often I have been the poor wretch penned in behind some glossy monster whose owner always seems to be the last to leave.

The village seemed to have turned out in force, and I was soon going the rounds, glass in hand, meeting Mary and Margaret Waters, two elderly spinsters of whom I am very fond, the Lambs from the Post Office, with Mr Lamb's brother from America and his wife, the Hales from Tyler's Row, a comparative newcomer, Miss Quinn, with her landlady Joan Benson, and a host of other friends.

Mrs Mawne, resplendent in black and gold, introduced me to a middle-aged man called Cecil Richards.

'A fellow ornithologist of Henry's,' explained Mrs Mawne. 'Well more than that really. Sissle here has just had a book published. About fishing, isn't it?'

'Yes, indeed. *With Rod in Rutland* is the title.'

I said I must look out for it.

'And Sissle has had others published,' said Mrs Mawne proudly. 'Wasn't *Beagling in Bucks* the last one?'

'No. *Hunting in Hereford*,' replied Cecil reprovingly.

I felt tempted to ask when *Winkling in Wilts* was coming out, but restrained my flippancy. Obviously, this particular writer took his work seriously, unlike Basil Bradley, our local novelist, who turns out a well-written book a year with a Regency buck as hero and a score of gorgeous girls with ringlets and fans. He aims to entertain, and makes no secret of it.

'You must find writing very hard work,' I said politely.

'Not at all. I find it pleasantly relaxing.'

I remembered reading that: 'Anyone who claims to write easily must be either a terrible writer or a terrible liar,' but naturally did not quote this to Cecil Richards.

'Ah,' said Mrs Mawne, 'here comes Diana Hale. I know she wants to meet Sissle.'

I bowed away gratefully, only to find that I was in the midst of a three-cornered discussion on holidays.

'You really need a couple of years in Florence to see it properly,' Henry Mawne was saying to Mrs Partridge. 'Did you see Michelangelo's house?'

'We saw his "David",' replied Mrs Partridge.

'Well, naturally,' said Henry. 'But *everyone* sees his "David". The house brings it all to life. You went to Siena, of course?'

'Well, no. We didn't have time.'

'Siena is a *must*,' said Joan Benson. 'I think I really enjoyed Siena more than Florence itself. Those beautiful Duccios in the museum by the Duomo! You really should have gone to Siena.'

'I found the leather school at the Santa Croce one of the most interesting things,' continued Henry. 'I bought this wallet there.' He fished in a back pocket, juggling dangerously with his wine glass, and produced a wallet worn with age.

'Lovely,' agreed Mrs Partridge. 'I bought a handbag on the Ponte Vecchio.'

'On the Ponte Vecchio?' echoed Henry, with horror. 'My dear lady, you must have been mad to buy anything there! You can get the same thing much cheaper in those nice shops near the Bargello!'

I was beginning to feel very sorry for poor Mrs Partridge being batted between the two Florence-snobs.

Henry suddenly became conscious of my presence.

'And where did you go this year?' he asked.

'Clacton,' I said, and was rewarded with Mrs Partridge's smile.

Half-term came and went, and a long spell of dark weather, with pouring rain and high winds, set in.

School playtimes became an endurance test for all. Deprived of their usual exercise in the playground, the children became cross at their enforced incarceration. The tattered comics reappeared, the jigsaw puzzles, the second-best sets of crayons, and the balls of plasticine, multi-hued by careless hands which had rolled various colours together, were brought out of the cupboard to try to assuage their frustration.

It was uphill work to keep them happily occupied. The first colds of winter swept the classroom, and sneezes, sniffs and coughs rent the air. A large box of tissues seemed to be exhausted in two days, and my pleas for them to bring their own, or to bring a handkerchief, fell on deaf ears. The tortoise stoves took to smoking, as they do when the wind gets into a certain quarter, and the skylight, as always, dripped steadily, as the rain swept viciously across the playground.

It was during this bleak period that I received another missive from the office. It informed me that due note had been taken of the findings at the managers' meeting held some time earlier, and that my own comments were being considered. It was only right to point out, it went on to say, that reorganization of schools in the area was now advancing steadily, and that the possible closure of Fairacre School could not be ruled out.

'Back to square one,' I observed to Tibby, who was trifling with a portion of expensive cat food, much appreciated by the cat in the television advertisement, but not by my fastidious friend.

'Now what?' I wondered.

My problems were further complicated on the next Friday by Minnie Pringle's.

My heart sank when I opened the door and heard the crash of the hand-brush against the sitting-room skirting board. Since Minnie's advent all the skirting boards have been severely dented, and now resemble hammered pewter. I think she feels that the edge of the carpet has not been properly cleaned without a hefty swipe at the skirting board with each movement. My remonstrances have made not the slightest impression, and I doubt if Minnie realizes the damage she is doing. At one stage, I forbade her to touch the hand brush, but that too was ignored.

'You're working overtime, Minnie,' I said.

She looked up from her demolition work, with a mad grin.

'It don't matter. I ain't got nowhere to go.'

I took the brush from her hand and put it on the table.

'You'd better sit down and tell me,' I said resignedly. At least the skirting board was spared for a time, but I had no doubt that my nerves would take a similar pounding.

Minnie sat on the extreme edge of a Victorian buttoned armchair, which, I knew from experience, was liable to tip forward abruptly if so used.

'Sit back, Minnie,' I advised her.

She wriggled forward another two inches, and I gave up. With any luck, her light weight would not affect the chair's balance.

'What's the matter now?'

'It's Bert. Him and Ern has been fighting.'

'Can't you tell them to go? I gather it's your house now, or so your aunt says.'

Minnie's eyes grew round with horror.

'Tell 'em to go?' she echoed. 'They don't take no notice of what I says. Anyway, Ern's gone.'

'Then what's the trouble? I thought Bert was a lodger – paying guest, I mean – so surely you can give him notice, if you want to?'

'He don't pay.'

'All the more reason for pushing him out!'

Minnie twisted her dirty fingers together unhappily.

'It's not that. It's 'is 'itting me I don't like.'

'I thought you said it was Ern and Bert that were fighting.'

'Well, it was, first off. Then when Ern went back to Caxley to give old Mrs Fowler a piece of 'is mind, Bert turned sort of nasty and took a strap to me.'

I thought that 'turned sort of nasty' was the understatement of the year if it involved attacking the minute Minnie with a strap.

'Look here,' I said, 'I think you had better have a word with Bert's employers at Springbourne Manor. Let them speak to him.'

Minnie looked more horrified than ever.

'They'd give 'im the sack, most like, and then 'e'd take it out on me. He's 'orrible strong, is Bert. I'd almost sooner have Ern. 'E never used the strap.'

'Well, you seem in a pretty pickle, I must say,' I said severely. 'Why has Ern gone back to Caxley? I thought he had left Mrs Fowler.'

'She gave him the push, and now he's hollering for the furniture what he pinched from our house. 'E reckons Mrs Fowler's flogged it.'

Despair began to overtake me. Heaven knows, I do my best to simplify my own life, and even so I am beset by irksome complications. To confront someone like Minnie, whose relationships with others are a hopeless tangle, makes my rational mind boggle. Where can one begin to help?

'Well, Minnie, what do you propose to do? I take it Mrs Pringle can't put you up, and you certainly can't stay here. You really must try and get Bert to go away if he's becoming violent.'

Minnie looked vaguely surprised, and wriggled nearer the edge of the chair. As expected, it tipped forward and pitched her on to the carpet, where she remained seated, looking perfectly at ease.

'Oh, I don't want Bert to go. 'E's a good chap apart from the strap. I daresay 'e'll be all right if I gets 'im a good bit of steak for his tea.'

I began to feel somewhat dizzy. This frequently happens during a conversation with Minnie. She veers from one point to another like a storm-battered weathercock.

'Surely, that will cost a mint of money? I shouldn't feel inclined to cook an expensive steak for someone who hit me.'

'Only with a strap,' said Minnie earnestly. 'Could have been 'is belt. Buckle end.'

I gave up, and rose to end the interview.

'Your money's on the mantel shelf,' I said wearily.

She gave me a radiant smile.

'Do just right for Bert's steak,' she said, reaching for the hand brush.

But I got there first.

Not long after this encounter, the village was staggered to hear that Mrs Coggs had been caught shop-lifting in Caxley, and was due to appear in Court.

I could not believe it when Mrs Pringle informed me of the fact.

'But it seems so absurd,' I protested, 'when she's better off now than ever she was! She told me herself that she had never had so much money to manage on.'

'That's why she went to Caxley,' said Mrs Pringle, with a trace of smugness which riled me. 'When she didn't have no money to spend she stayed home. Come she got to the shops in Caxley she was Tempted and Fell.'

It all seemed very odd, and very sad, to me. What had she bought, I asked?

Mrs Pringle bridled.

'She never *bought*. That was the trouble. She *thieved*. As far as

I can gather, it was things like rashers and sausages and a great bag of them frozen chips.'

At least a change from bread and sauce, I thought, though no doubt the poor children were still having that ghastly fare.

'Perhaps she just forgot to pay,' I said. 'It happens.'

Mrs Pringle snorted.

'Likely, ain't it! Anyway, she said straight out she'd nicked 'em.'

Her dour countenance showed a rare streak of pleasure.

'D'you reckon she'll get put inside? Fancy them both being in prison, at the same time!'

'I shouldn't think so for a moment,' I said shortly. 'And isn't it about time the stoves were filled?'

If looks could have killed, I should have been a writhing corpse by the fireguard, but I was only vouchsafed the back view of my cleaner retreating from the fray with a heavy limp.

Most people, it transpired, felt as bewildered as I did at Mrs Coggs' behaviour, and the general feeling in the village was one of sympathy. The Vicar had promised to appear in Court to speak on her behalf, and one of Mr Lovejoy's juniors was to appear for her. Mrs Coggs herself, I heard, hardly seemed to realize what was happening. She made no attempt to excuse her actions, not in any mood of defiance, but simply in her usual mood of apathy. It was all very puzzling.

Our butcher's comments seemed to echo Mrs Pringle's way of thinking.

'She's a poor tool as we all know, Miss Read. Let's face it, she wasn't born over-bright, and any wits she had have been knocked out of her by Arthur. I reckon she got carried away when she saw all the things in Caxley.'

'But she is better off now than ever,' I repeated.

'Yes, but not all that much better off. I mean, she's had a taste of spending a bit extra, and it's gone to her head. When she lives as she usually does, it's hand-to-mouth. She comes in here for a chop for Arthur, never anything for herself and the children. To tell you the truth, I've often given her meat scraps and told her to make a stew or a pudding, but it's my belief she doesn't know how to cook at all. How they manage I can't think.'

Another customer arrived, and we were forced to terminate our conversation, but it gave me food for thought.

We all agreed that as this was a first offence, imprisonment surely was out of the question, although Mr Roberts with unusual severity, said it might be an example to other light-fingered neighbours. However, as we heard later, twenty or so sheep belonging to him had that night been stolen from the downs, within two miles of his home, and naturally his judgement was coloured by his loss.

'And if she's fined, then who is to pay it?' asked another. 'The Social Security people? Meaning us?'

'She might just get a ticking-off,' said one hopeful. 'That Colonel Austin's got a sharp tongue they tells me, specially with poachers.'

'She might get a conditional discharge,' said Mr Lamb, with such authority that his few customers awaiting their pensions or postage stamps began to wonder if he had first-hand knowledge of Courts and their procedure.

It was thus that we anticipated the Court's decision. Meanwhile, we had to wait and hope that, when the time came, Mrs Coggs' case would evoke mercy as well as justice from the Bench.

16. Snow

The end of the Christmas term came suddenly upon us, and we were caught up in a whirl of parties, concerts, and carol services. Added to these school and village activities were the personal ones of shopping for Christmas presents, trying to find out the correct time to post parcels to friends overseas, and stocking the larder for what looked like being the longest public holiday on record.

'You wouldn't think the country was dead broke,' commented Peter Hale acidly, when I met him in the village street, 'when you hear that the local factories are closing until January the fourth or roundabout.'

I found myself buying mounds of food against the siege, and having considerable difficulty in packing it away. Does everyone, I wondered, as I stacked away tins of this and that, imagine that starving families are going to arrive after all the shops have shut, and will be obliged to stay for days because of sudden blizzards? I always over-estimate my own – and my imaginary visitors' – needs, at these times, and never learn my lesson.

Because of this unwanted bustle, the question of the closure of Fairacre School seemed to be in a state of suspended animation, and I was relieved to have something else to worry over.

But, all too soon, the festivities were over, the Christmas decorations were taken down, I continued to eat left-overs and term started.

It was quite apparent that we were in for a bleak spell of weather. The wind had whipped round to the north-east, and every night brought us frost. The ground was sodden after the heavy rains of Autumn, and long puddles in the furrows froze into hard ice. At the sides of the lanes of Fairacre more ice lay in the gutters, and the children had a wonderful time making slides on their way to school.

'Cruel weather,' said Mr Willet. 'My greens look fair

shrammed. What with the weather, and the pigeons, and all them other birds, I sometimes wonder why I bothers to grow them. If I had my way I'd stick to root crops, but my old woman says we must have a bit of winter greens, so I doos my best. 'Tis a thankless task though, when the winter's like this.'

'As long as we don't get snow,' I said.

Mr Willet looked surprised.

'Snow?' he echoed. 'You'll get that aplenty, my dear, and afore the week's out too.'

As usual, he was right.

It began during the dinner hour, while the children were tearing about digesting, I hoped, steak and kidney pie and pink blancmange. Hilary was on playground duty, and I was cutting up painting paper for the afternoon session, when the classroom door burst open to reveal a knot of panting children, proudly displaying the spatters of snow on their clothes.

'Snowing, miss! Ennit lovely? It's snowing! And it's laying too.'

They were much too excited to have understood the different uses of the verbs 'to lie' and 'to lay', and anyway I have almost given up hope of any success in that direction.

I contented myself with telling them to let Miss Norman know that they must all come in to school.

They clanged over the door scraper with enough noise for a mechanized army, and I went to the window to see the worst.

The snowflakes were coming down in great flurries, whirling and turning until the eyes of the beholder were dazzled. The icy playground was white already, and the branches of the elm trees would soon carry an edging of snow several inches deep. Across the playground, sitting inside the window of my dining-room, I could see Tibby watching the twirling flakes as interestedly as I was doing.

The snow hissed against the glass, but that sibilant sound was soon drowned in the stamping of feet in the lobby and the excited voices of the children. I could see we were in for a boisterous afternoon. Wind is bad enough for raising children's spirits to manic level. Snow is even more potent a force.

I judged it best to give out the paints and paper as soon as the register had been called, for it was quite apparent that my voice could never compete with the drama that was going on outside the windows.

'You can paint a snow scene,' I said, working on the principle that if you can't beat your rival you join him.

'What like?' said Ernest.

Our Fairacre children are chary of anything involving the imagination. If I had told them to paint the tasteful arrangement of dried flowers and leaves, concocted by Amy and kept on my desk, they would have set to without a word. But to be asked to create a picture from nothing, as it were, filled them with dismay.

I used to be rather hard on them, refusing to suggest themes, and urging them to use their imaginations. But they are genuinely perturbed by these forays into the unknown, and advancing age has made me somewhat kinder.

'Well, now, you could make a picture of yourselves running about in a snowy playground. Or making a slide.'

'Or a snowman?' suggested Patrick, in a burst of inspiration.

'Quite. Or a picture of men clearing the snow away from the roads. Perhaps digging a car out of a snow drift.'

'Or a bus,' said Ernest. 'Only I ain't got much red for a bus. Might do a tractor.'

They seemed to be fairly launched now, and they began their attempts without too much hesitation. A fierce argument broke out, at one point, about the best way of depicting snow flakes which looked black as they came down, but which one knew were white really, and anyway *turned white* when they reached the ground. Linda Moffat said she was going to leave spots of paper showing through her sky, to look like snow. Joseph Coggs said they'd look like stars then, and anyway the sky wasn't blue like that, it was 'grey sort of'.

Altogether, it was a distracting art session, considerably enlivened by the constant uprising of children looking to see how deep the snow was in the playground. Certainly, by the time their afternoon break arrived, the snow was thick enough for Hilary to consult me about sending the infants home early.

'I think the whole school had better go early,' I replied. The sky was low and heavy with snow to come, and there was no respite from the blizzard around us.

The news was greeted with even greater excitement. One or two were apprehensive because their mothers were still at work.

'I knows where our key is,' said one. 'It's in the secret place in the coal hole. I can easy get in.'

'Old Bert can come in my house till his mum gets back,' offered another, and gradually we were able to account for all the children's safety from the storm.

Except, as it happened, for the Coggs children. No one seemed to offer to have them. Mrs Coggs was out at work and would not be home until after three-thirty. I was not very surprised that there were no invitations from the other children. For one thing, the Coggs had no near neighbours with children at the school. For another, the Coggs family has always been a little ostracized by the more respectable villagers, and I had a suspicion that since Mrs Coggs' shop-lifting escapade, the family was even less popular. So far, her case had not been heard, but as she herself admitted her guilt, there were quite a few who censored her, and the innocent children.

'You'd better come home with me,' I said to the three, 'and I'll run you home when your mother is back.'

They waited patiently by the tortoise stove, warming their grubby hands, while Hilary and I buttoned and tied the others into their outdoor clothes and threatened them with all manner of retribution if they forbore to go straight home.

They vanished with whoops of joy into the veils of snow which swept the outside world, and I ushered my three visitors across the playground to my warm sitting-room.

I had had the foresight to light the fire at dinner time, and by now it was a clear red glow, ideal for making toast, which no doubt would be welcomed before taking the children home.

Joseph was inclined to be unusually self-confident in front of his little sisters. After all, his attitude seemed to say, I know this place. You don't.

They watched me cut some substantial slices of bread. The toasting fork intrigued them, and I set them to make toast while I brewed a pot of tea which I really did not need, but it made an excuse to pass the time before Mrs Coggs returned.

Their faces were flushed with heat and excitement. They handled the toast reverently.

'Never cooked toast,' announced Joseph. 'Never knew a fire done cooking like this.'

I remembered that the Council houses had a closed stove for cooking and heating the water. But surely, there was an open fire in the living room?

'We never lights that,' said Joseph, slightly shocked. 'Us has the electric if it's cold.'

And pretty cheerless too, I thought. No wonder that the children enjoyed my fire, and their first attempts at toast-making.

They demolished several slices of their handiwork, plentifully spread with butter and honey. Outside, the snow drifted along the window ledges, and settled on the roofs and hedges. It was time we made a move before the snow became too deep to open the garage door.

Mrs Coggs had just arrived home when we reached their house. I saw them indoors with a sinking heart. It looked as sordid, and was certainly as smelly, as ever.

Driving back through the driving snow, I pondered on the differences between neighbours and their surroundings in such a tiny place as Fairacre. I was not comparing the fairly well-to-do such as the Mawnes and Hales, with those who had very little, but people like the Willets, for instance, or my sparring partner Mrs Pringle, who really had no more money coming into their homes than Mrs Coggs had at the moment. In most of the homes in Fairacre, one could be sure of finding a welcome. There would be a fire in winter, a cup of tea or coffee offered, biscuits or a slice of home-made cake, or a glass of home-made wine (deceptively innocuous incidentally) put into one's hand. The house would be as welcoming as the householder. There would be the smell of furniture polish, the gleam of burnished brass and copper, and a bunch of flowers from the garden standing on the window sill.

It was lucky that Mrs Coggs was in the minority in our little community, I thought, as I put away the car and shuffled through the snow to my own home.

But hard luck on those children!

It snowed, off and on, for over three weeks, and a very trying time was had by all. Mrs Pringle seemed to take the snow as a personal insult directed towards her by a malevolent weather-god, and loud were her daily lamentations about the state of the school floors, and the wicked way the children brought the snow inside on their boots.

It was useless to try and placate her, and useless too to bully the children into greater care. The snow was everywhere, and after a time, I decided that the only thing to do was to be philosophical about it.

'It can't last for ever,' I said, trying to comfort my surly cleaner. 'Look, the catkins are showing on the hedge!'

'Sure sign the spring-cleaning will want doing,' replied Mrs Pringle, enjoying her misery. Irritated though I was by her dogged determination to see the gloomy side of things, I was not blind to the fact that she was not looking at all well.

One day I ventured to comment on it. Was she still dieting?

She gave a grunt.

'I lost two pounds last month, and even that never pleased Dr Martin. He's a hard taskmaster that one. I wouldn't care to be

under the knife when he's holding the handle. "Got no feelings,"
I told him straight. I get the stummer-cake something awful
some nights, but he only laughs when I tell him.'

'Perhaps you are doing too much,' I said, in an unguarded
moment.

Mrs Pringle rose to the bait beautifully.

'Of course, I'm doing too much! It's me nature. "You're a
giver, not a taker, my girl," my old mother used to say, and I
fair gets wore out. What with this 'ere school to keep clean –
well, try to keep clean would be truer – and our Minnie driving
me mad and the worry over this place closing next year – '

'Closing next year?' I echoed in astonishment. 'Who told you
that?'

Mrs Pringle looked surprised in her turn.

'Why, it's general knowledge in the village! And at Beech
Green, and at Caxley, come to that. Why else are they havin'
new buildings at Mr Annett's? And what about that managers'
meeting? I tell you, Miss Read, you must be the last person to
know. It's the talk of the parish, and a fine old rumpus there's
going to be before long!'

I gazed at her, speechless with dismay. All my old worries,
suspended for some weeks, and ignored because of more pressing claims on my time, now flocked back to haunt me, like so
many evil birds.

'So it's no wonder I'm not meself,' continued Mrs Pringle,
with some satisfaction. 'I can feel meself growing old afore my
time. It's as much as I can do to get round my own housework
these days, let alone this lot. You'll see my place looking like
Mrs Coggs' before long, I shouldn't wonder.'

'Never!' I said, finding my voice.

'Which reminds me,' said my cleaner, picking a piece of
squashed clay from the front desk, 'that silly woman's been in
Court, and got to go again in three weeks.'

'Why?'

'Them magistrates want reports on her before passing sentence. At least that's what the *Caxley Chronicle* said.'

She snorted with disgust.

'Reports! I ask you! I could have given 'em a report on Mrs

Coggs, on the spot. It wouldn't have needed three weeks, if I'd been consulted!'

She straightened up and went, limping pathetically, to the lobby.

'Bring any more of that dratted snow in here,' I heard her shout threateningly, 'and I'll larrup the lot of you!'

'Can't help it,' Patrick shouted back impudently. 'And anyway, it's started again, so there'll be lots more, for days and days and days!'

He sounded exceedingly happy about it. Mrs Pringle's rumblings could be heard in answer, but I could not catch the exact words.

Above the turmoil Patrick's clear treble rang out triumphantly.

'And anyway, I likes it!'

17. Renewed Fears

The Court at Caxley meets twice a week, and Mrs Coggs duly appeared three weeks after her first attendance.

The Vicar had promised to escort her, and to make himself available to speak on her behalf, should the magistrates so allow, but on the very day of the hearing Mr Partridge was stricken with gastric influenza, and was obliged to keep to his bed.

Mrs Partridge, having left various drinks and some very unpleasant medicine on the bedside table, left the patient and collected Mrs Coggs herself. The Vicar, ill as he was, nevertheless struggled into an upright position for long enough to write a letter to the Court expressing his view on Mrs Coggs' hitherto blameless character, and his apologies for absence.

Armed with this, Mrs Partridge entered the annexe to the Court and prepared to wait indefinitely with her luckless companion.

When the case was called, Mrs Coggs faced the bench with apathetic bewilderment, and Mrs Partridge sat at the back, feeling over-awed by the general solemnity.

Reports were handed up to the magistrates by the probation officer, and silence reigned as they perused them. Every now and again old Miss Dewbury gave a snort of disgust. Her fellow-magistrates were quite used to this. It did not express shock at the facts presented by the probation officer, but simply impatience with such dreadful phrases as 'peer group', 'siblings' and 'meaningful relationship' with which such reports are invariably sprinkled, and which drove Miss Dewbury, as a lover of plain English, near to despair.

Mrs Partridge gave the Vicar's letter to the usher, who duly gave it to the clerk, who gave it to the magistrates, to add to their papers.

At length, Colonel Austin rose saying gruffly: 'The bench will retire to consider this case,' and the three magistrates, papers in hand, made their way to the fastness of the retiring room. The clerk to the justices, the usher, the solicitors and general public were just wondering if there would be time for a quick cup of hot liquid, from a machine in the lobby labelled TEA or COFFEE but bearing no resemblance to either, or better still a hasty smoke, when the magistrates returned and hope was deferred.

'We propose,' said Colonel Austin to the trembling Mrs Coggs, 'to make a probation order for a period of two years. Just listen carefully.'

He turned over a dozen or so pages of a booklet before him. His fellow-magistrates were used to this delay, and their chairman's growing impatience as he stumbled through 'Taking the Oath on the Koran', 'Conditional Discharge' and other irrelevant matters, and were relieved when their ever-ready clerk leapt to his feet and found the place for him, with the sort of fatherly smile fond papas give their offspring when they have tracked down the collect for the day at matins.

Colonel Austin read out the order in a military fashion, and on being asked if she would comply with the requirements, Mrs Coggs said:

'Yes, please, sir. Yes, sir, thank you.'

'You may stand down,' said Colonel Austin, and Mrs Coggs, still quaking, was led by the usher to Mrs Partridge who accompanied her from the Court, closely pursued by the probation officer.

'She got off lightly,' said Mrs Pringle later to me. 'Wouldn't have got probation in my mother's day. I wonder they didn't let her off altogether.'

'It means that someone will have access to the household,' I said mildly, 'and surely that's a good idea. Arthur will be out before her probation order ends, and I think it is a very good thing that she'll be having some guidance then.'

'But what about them things she took? Never paid for 'em!'

'They were returned at the time,' I said.

'Well, I wouldn't want to eat anything Mrs Coggs had been handling,' said Mrs Pringle, determined to have the last word and making sure by leaving me rapidly.

*

The rumours of closure still rumbled about the village, but I did my best to ignore them, despite inner qualms.

George Annett, however, brought all my fears to the fore again by calling in on choir practice night to acquaint me with a new problem.

'I heard today,' he said, 'that Mrs Allen is leaving at the end of this term. She's only got a couple of years to do, but her husband has had a stroke, and she's decided to give up now. What about it?'

I felt a little nettled. I like plenty of time to consider things. Too much, Amy tells me. Some things are better decided at once.

'What about what?' I said, to gain time.

'Putting in for the post, of course,' said George impatiently. 'It's one of the largest junior schools in Caxley, and very well thought of. Suit you well.'

'I don't think I really want it,' I said slowly, 'and anyway, after such a small school as this one, I doubt if I stand a chance.'

'Rubbish!' exclaimed George. 'You're dam' well qualified, and you know the county want to appoint from their own people at the moment, before advertising. You stand as good a chance, or better, than the rest. You think about it, my girl.'

He vanished churchwards, and left me in turmoil.

How I hate having to make a decision! I have the reputation, I heard once with amazement, of making up my mind very swiftly. The answer is that I find suspense so exhausting that I decide quickly in order to cut short the agony.

Now, here I was again, faced with 'Shall I?' or 'Shan't I?' and very unpleasant I found it. Mrs Allen's school was on one of the new estates on the edge of Caxley, and had earned a shining reputation for solid schooling with fun thrown in. It would be a post which would attract a great many applicants, and I spoke truly when I told Mr Annett that my chances would be slight.

On the whole, I felt that I should be wasting my time to apply. Then too, there was the problem of a house. No doubt, I should be allowed to stay on at Fairacre for a time, but if the school closed, then presumably the school house would be sold when the rest of the property came on the market.

I certainly had no money to buy a house in Caxley, and

anyway, would I want one? Oh dear, why did George have to unsettle me like this?

I pottered about distractedly in the kitchen, wet dishcloth in hand, wiping the top of the cooker. The stains seemed worse than usual and I squeezed a large dollop of liquid cleaner on to the top and rubbed bemusedly.

If only I could hear something definite from the office! It would be disastrous if I applied for that post and got it – some hope, I thought – and then found that Fairacre School was to stay as it was. What a problem!

The stains seemed to be a problem too, and on investigation, I found that I had squeezed a dollop of hand lotion instead of cleaner on to the surface. The stove was not improved.

I chucked the dishcloth into the sink and went to get a glass of sherry. At times, drink is a great solace.

The snow lingered on into February, lying under the hedges and along the sides of the lanes.

'Waiting for more to come,' Mr Willet told me, with morose satisfaction. 'I fair 'ates to see it laying this time of year! Still plenty of weeks to get another lot.'

'Cheer up,' I said. 'There are some snowdrops in bud at the end of the garden, and some lovely yellow aconites showing. And the children brought catkins for the nature table – a bit stubby yet, but cheering all the same.'

'Well, you was always one for looking on the bright side,' said Mr Willet. 'Heard any more about this 'ere school closing? Someone told me Mrs Allen's leaving. That'd suit you a treat, that school of hers. Should think about it, if I was you.'

As I had done exactly that for a considerable time, with no firm result, I found Mr Willet's remarks a little trying.

'No, I haven't heard any more,' I said, 'and I don't think I should get that job, even if I wanted it.'

'Well, there's plenty in the village thinks you would, when this place shuts up –'

'What do you mean? "When this place shuts up?" We don't know that it will!' I broke in crossly.

'No need to fly off the handle,' said Mr Willet. 'I'm only saying what's going the rounds in Fairacre. If you ask me, it's

time the village had a say in this business. It's fair upsetting for us all, and we don't want to see you go. You knows that.'

I began to feel ashamed of my rudeness, and apologized.

'Oh, don't you let that trouble you,' replied Mr Willet easily. 'It's a worrying time, especially for you, and at a funny age.'

And on this unsatisfactory note he left me.

The Vicar appeared at playtime, and I took him across the playground, dodging boisterous children in full flight, to have a cup of coffee while Hilary coped with playground duty.

The gastric influenza, which had prostrated him at the time of Mrs Coggs' court appearance, had left him looking remarkably pale and shaky, and he seemed glad to put his moulting leopard skin gloves on the table, and sip hot coffee. Tibby, unused to mid-morning visitors, graciously climbed on to his lap and purred a welcome.

'You really have the gift of making a proper home,' smiled Mr Partridge. 'And, of course, a cat is absolutely essential to that. I hope you'll be here for many, many years.'

'It rather depends on the county,' I told him. 'If only we knew!'

'It's about that that I've come,' said the Vicar. My heart sank. Had he, as chairman of the managers, heard at last?

'I've no further news from the office,' he said, and my heart started beating again. 'But there are so many rumours and conjectures going round the village, that I've had a word with the other managers, and we feel we should call a public meeting to air our views.'

'An excellent idea!'

'I'm glad you agree. I feel we should put everything possible before that fellow Rochester – '

'*Salisbury*,' I broke in. 'Rochester was in *Jane Eyre*.'

'Of course. Salisbury then – so that the authority has some idea of the strong reaction to this proposal of closing the school. You'll be there, naturally.'

'When?'

'Now you're asking! It will need to be in the village hall, and what with the Cubs and Brownies, and square dancing, and Women's Institute and the muscular dystrophy jumble sale and three wedding receptions, it's quite a problem to find a date. However, something will turn up, and meanwhile we must put up posters, and perhaps the children could write a note to take home?'

'Willingly, but we shall have to know the date.'

The Vicar picked up his gloves, deposited Tibby tenderly on another chair, from which the animal got down immediately with umbrage, and made for the door.

'So you will! What a wonderful grasp of affairs you have, Miss Read! I wish I were as practical. I think I'd better spend the rest of the morning working out a few dates with the managers, and then I'll call again with the result.'

He ploughed his way to the gate through the screaming mob, and smiled kindly upon one bullet-headed urchin who butted him heavily in the stomach as he fled from a pursuing playmate.

'A thoroughly good man!' I told Tibby, as I collected the coffee cups.

Amy called a few evenings later with an invitation to drinks at her house in Bent.

'And stay on to eat with us,' said Amy. 'The rest of them should have gone by eight, and we'll have a nice little cold collation ready, and a good natter.'

'Suppose they don't go?' I queried. 'I've been to lots of these dos – particularly before Sunday lunch, where the joint is getting more and more charred as the visitors all wait for other people to make a move, not realizing that the luckier ones are staying on.'

'That's why it will be cold,' said Amy. 'Please allow me to run my own parties as I wish. Sometimes you are a trifle bossy.'

'*Well!*' I said, flabbergasted. 'Talk about the pot calling the kettle black! You're the bossy one, as well you know!'

Amy laughed.

'I didn't come here to have a vulgar brawl, darling, but I should love a cigarette if you have such a thing in this non-smoking Paradise.'

'Of course, of course!' I said, reminded of my duties as a hostess. 'They're donkey's years old, as I only buy them when I go abroad and get them duty free, as you know. Still they should be a good vintage by now.'

Amy puffed elegantly, and seemed quite content.

'Are you trying for Mrs Allen's job when she goes?'

Not again, I thought despairingly.

'No, I don't think I am. I've been turning it over, and I really feel I can't be bothered until I know more definitely about the plans for this school.'

'I believe Lucy Colgate is trying for it,' said Amy, naming a contemporary of ours at college, whom I always detested.

'She's welcome,' I said shortly.

'She'll be at the party, incidentally,' said Amy, tapping ash from her cigarette with a rose-tipped finger.

'Well, it's your party, as you've already pointed out. I can be as civil as the next, I hope.'

'I can't think why you dislike her.'

'I don't actively dislike her. I just find her affected and a liar to boot.'

'She's very well connected. Her uncle's the Bishop of Somewhere.'

'So what! It doesn't alter Lucy Colgate for me. However, I promise to behave beautifully when we meet.'

'She would have loved this place, you know. She always

hoped you would apply for another job, so that she could come here.'

I began to feel decidedly more cheerful.

'Well, she won't have the opportunity now, will she? If Fairacre stays, then I do. If it closes, no headmistress will be necessary – not even horrible Lucy Colgate!'

Amy began to laugh, and I followed suit.

'Tell me the latest about Vanessa,' I said, changing the subject. 'How's that baby?'

'My dear, she's having another.'

'She can't be! She's only just had this one!'

'It can happen,' said Amy. 'It's not due for another seven months. She told me on the phone last night. I must say, that in my young days one waited until one was quite five months gone, as the vulgar expression is, before admitting coyly to one's hopes. But there. I gather from a doctor friend, that you have to book your nursing home bed quite twelve months in advance, so I suppose there's no encouragement to be over-modest about the proceedings.'

'I'd better look out my knitting patterns for baby clothes again,' I said. 'I suppose she wouldn't like a tea-cosy this time? I'm halfway through one.'

'Try her,' advised Amy, looking at the clock. 'I suppose there's no chance of a cup of coffee?'

'I do apologize,' I said, making for the kitchen. 'I seem to have forgotten my manners.'

'You must take a lesson from dear Lucy,' said Amy wickedly, following me. 'Her manners are quite perfect, and what's more, she makes delicious coffee.'

'So do I,' I told her, putting on the kettle. 'When I think of it.'

A few days later the Vicar appeared, waving a slip of paper in triumph.

'At last, my dear Miss Read! We have fixed a date, though at what cost of time and telephone calls I shudder to think. Here we are! It is for March the first, a Friday. That seems to be the only free day for most of the managers. Henry Mawne has a lecture on sea-birds to give in Caxley, but Mrs Mawne says she has heard it dozens of times and there will be no need for her to attend.'

I remembered how competently she looked after her dithering husband on these occasions, and asked if he would be able to manage without her support.

'Oh yes, indeed. George Annett is going and says he will see that Henry has his papers in order, and his spectacles and so on.'

As George Annett can be just as scatter-brained as Henry Mawne under pressure, I felt that it would be a case of the blind leading the blind, but forbore to comment.

'We'll copy this out today,' I assured the Vicar, securing the slip of paper under the massive brass inkstand which has adorned the head teacher's desk here since the time of Queen Victoria.

'Splendid, splendid!' said Mr Partridge making for the door. 'It will be a good thing to see how the wind blows in the village. Nothing but good can come of airing our feelings, I feel sure.'

'Help me up with the blackboard, Ernest,' I said, as the door closed behind the Vicar. 'We'll start straightaway on these notices.'

'Good,' said Ernest with approval. 'Save us doin' them 'orrible ol' fractions.'

'They'll come later,' I told him.

18. *A Battle in Caxley*

Spring came suddenly. We had grown so accustomed to the miserable dark days, and to the flecks of snow still dappling the higher ground, that to awake one morning to a blue sky and the chorus of birds seemed a miracle.

The wind had veered to the south-west at last, and moist warm air refreshed us all. The elms were beginning to show the rosy glow of early budding. The crocuses were piercing the wet ground, the birds were looking about for nesting sites and the world seemed decidedly more hopeful.

Even Mrs Pringle seemed a little less morose as she went about her duties and was heard singing 'Who Is Sylvia?' instead of 'Lead Kindly Light Amidst the Encircling Gloom'.

I complimented her, and was told that she 'learnt it up the Glee Club as a girl'.

It was good to have the schoolroom windows open, although I had to call upon Mr Willet to leave his usual coke-sweeping in the playground to give me a hand.

'They're stuck with the damp,' puffed Mr Willet, smiting the wooden frames with a horny hand. 'Needs to be planed really, but then, come the summer you'd get a proper draught. Bad as that there skylight.'

He looked at it gloomily.

'Useless to waste time and money on it. Been like that since I sat here as a boy, and will be the same when I'm dead and gone, I shouldn't wonder.'

'You're down in the dumps today,' I teased. 'Not like you.'

Mr Willet sighed.

'Had bad news. My brother's gone home.'

'I'm sorry,' I said, and was doubly so – for his unhappiness and for my own misplaced levity. The old country phrase for dying, 'gone home', has a melancholy charm about it, a finality, a rounding off.

'Well, he'd been bad some time, but you know how it is, you

don't ever think of anyone younger than you going home, do you?'

'It's a horrible shock,' I agreed.

'That's the third death this year,' mused Mr Willet, his eyes on the rooks wheeling against the sky. The fresh air blew through the window, stirring the scant hair on his head.

'Like a stab wound, every time,' he said. 'Leaves a hole, and a little of your life-blood drains away.'

I could say nothing. I was too moved by the spontaneous poetry. Mr Willet's utterances are usually of practical matters, a broken hinge, a tree needing pruning or a vegetable plot to be dug. To hear such rich imagery, worthy of an Elizabethan poet, fall from this old countryman's lips, was intensely touching.

Mrs Pringle's entry with a bucket of coke disturbed our reverie.

'Well,' said Mr Willet, shaking himself back to reality. 'This won't do. Life's got to go on, ain't it?'

And he stumped away to meet it.

Minnie Pringle was still about her ministrations when I returned home on Friday afternoon. She was flicking a feather brush dangerously close to some Limoges china dishes which I cherish.

'Lawks!' she cried, arrested in her toil, 'I never knew it was that late! I never heard the kids come out to play, and the oil man ain't been by yet.'

'Well, it's quarter to four by the clock,' I pointed out.

Minnie gazed blearily about the room.

'On the mantelpiece,' I said. 'And there's another in the kitchen.'

'Oh, the *clock*!' said Minnie wonderingly. 'I never looks at the *clock*. I don't read the time that well. It's them two hands muddles me.'

I never cease to be amazed at the unplumbed depths of Minnie's ignorance. How she has survived so long unscathed is astounding.

'How do you know what time to set out from Springbourne to get here?' I asked.

'The bus comes,' replied Minnie simply.

I should like to have asked what happened if there were a bus strike, but there is a limit to one's time.

'I'd best be going then,' announced Minnie, collecting an array of dusters from an armchair.

'Don't bother to wash them, Minnie,' I said hastily. 'I'll do them later on. I have to wash some tea towels and odds and ends.'

It would be a treat, I thought, to see the dusters hanging on a line for a change. Their last Friday's resting place had been over a once shining copper kettle which stands in the sitting-room.

Minnie shrugged herself into a fur fabric coat which pretended to be leopard skin, and would have deceived no one – certainly not a leopard.

'Had a bust-up down home,' said Minnie, her face radiant at the memory.

'Not Ern!'

'Ah! It was too. 'E turned up when I was abed. Gone twelve it was 'cos the telly'd finished.'

'Good heavens! I hope you didn't let him in.'

'No, I done what Auntie said, and put the kitchen table up agin the door, and I 'ollered down to him from the bedroom window.'

'And he went?'

Minnie sniffed, grinning with delight.

'Well, after a bit he went. He kep' all on about 'aving no place to sleep, and I said: "What about that ol' Mrs Fowler then?" and what he says back I wouldn't repeat to a lady like you.'

'I thought he'd left her long ago.'

'He went back for the furniture, and she wouldn't let 'im in, so he chucked a milk bottle at her, and there was a real set-to until the neighbours broke it up.'

'Who told you all this?'

'Jim next door. He took Ern into Caxley when 'e went in for the night shift. Said it was either that, or 'e'd tell the police 'e was molesting me.'

'He sounds a sensible sort of neighbour.'

'Oh, Jim's all right when he's not on the beer.'

'So what happened to Ern?'

'Jim dropped 'im at the end of the town. Ern's got a sorter cousin there would give 'im a doss down probably.'

'Well, I only hope he doesn't come again,' I said. 'You seem to have managed very well.'

543

'It's Auntie really,' said Minnie. 'She's told me what to do, and I done it. Auntie nearly always wins when she has an up-and-a-downer with anybody.'

I could endorse that, I thought, seeing Minnie to the door.

I heard more about Ern's belligerence from Mrs Pringle, and later from Amy, whose window cleaner had the misfortune to live next door to Mrs Fowler in Caxley.

Town dwellers who complain of loneliness and having no one to talk to, should perhaps be thankful that they do not live in a village. Here we go to the other extreme. I never cease to be astonished at the speed with which news gets about. In this instance I heard from three sources, Minnie, Mrs Pringle and Amy, of the Caxley and Springbourne rows, and all within three or four days. It is hopeless to try to keep anything secret in a small community, and long ago I gave up trying.

'Heard about that Ern?' asked Mrs Pringle.

I said I had.

'I must say our Minnie settled him nicely.'

'Thanks to you, I gather.'

Mrs Pringle permitted herself a gratified smirk.

'Well, you knows Min. She's no idea how to tackle anyone, and that Ern's been a sore trial to us all. She gets in a panic for nothing.'

'I don't call midnight yelling "for nothing",' I objected.

'Well, they're married, aren't they?' said Mrs Pringle, as though that explained matters.

'Mind you,' she went on, lodging a full dust-pan on one hip, 'we ain't heard the last of him. Now Mrs Fowler's done with him, I reckon he'll badger Min to take him back.'

'Where is he now?'

'Staying with that cousin of his, but she don't want him. He's got the sofa of nights, and the springs won't stand 'is weight. She told me herself when I saw her at the bus stop market day.'

'Is he working?'

Mrs Pringle snorted in reply.

'He don't know the meaning of the word! Gets the dole, I suppose. I told our Minnie: "Don't you have him back on no account, and certainly if he's out of a job! You'll be keeping 'im all 'is days, if you don't watch out." But there, I doubt if she really took it in. She's a funny girl.'

Amy's account, at second or third hand, covered the Caxley incident. According to her window cleaner, the rumpus started sometime after nine, when Ern, a little the worse for drink, arrived at Mrs Fowler's front door and demanded admittance.

Mrs Fowler's reply was to shoot the bolts on front and back doors, and to go upstairs to continue the argument from a bedroom window.

Ern called her many things, among them 'a vinegar-faced besom', 'a common thief' and 'a right swindling skinflint'. He accused her of trapping him into living there, and then taking possession of his rightful property, to wit, chairs, a table, pots and pans and a brass bird-cage of his Aunt Florence's.

Mrs Fowler, giving as good as she got, refuted the charges. He had given her the chattels of his own free will, and a poor lot they were anyway, not worth house room, and if he continued to molest a defenceless and respectable widow, whose husband had always been a paid-up member of the Buffaloes she would have him know, she would call for help.

After a few further exchanges, Ern, incensed, picked up the first handy missile, which happened to be an empty milk bottle standing in the porch, and flung it at his adversary's head. Mrs Fowler's screams of abuse, and the crash of glass, roused her neighbours, who until then had been hidden but fascinated observers of the scene, to open protest.

The window cleaner threatened to send for the police if they didn't pipe down and let honest people sleep and, amazingly enough, he was obeyed.

Ern, still muttering threats, slouched off, and presumably walked out to Springbourne in the darkness, and Mrs Fowler slammed the window and presumably went to bed.

'Obviously,' commented Amy, 'neither wanted the police brought in. I suspect that Mrs Fowler knows jolly well that she's hanging on to property that isn't hers, and Ern doesn't want to be run in for causing an affray, or whatever the legal term is.'

'I thought it was something to do with "behaviour occasioning a breach of the peace"!'

'Comes to the same thing,' said Amy carelessly. 'I feel very sorry for our window cleaner.'

'I reckon Ern is going to have a job to get his stuff back,' I said. 'Mrs Fowler was always avaricious. The Hales had trouble with her when she was their neighbour at Tyler's Row.'

'The best thing he can do,' replied Amy, 'is to cut his losses, find a job, and get Minnie to take him back.'

'Some hope,' I said. 'I can't see Mrs Pringle allowing that, even if Minnie would.'

'We must wait and see,' said Amy, quoting Mr Asquith.

The first day of March arrived, and came in like a lamb rather than the proverbial lion. Balmy winds had blown gently now for a week or more, a bunch of early primroses adorned my desk, and the blackbirds chattered and scowled as they trailed lengths of dried grass to their chosen nesting places.

With all these signs of Spring to cheer one, it was impossible to worry about such things as schools closing, and I made my way to the village hall that evening in a mood of fatalistic calm. What would be, would be! I had got past caring one way or the other, after all the weeks of suspense.

There were a surprising number of villagers present, and all the managers, with the Vicar in the chair. Mr Salisbury had been invited and sat in the front, with an underling from the office holding a pad for taking notes.

The meeting was scheduled to start at seven-thirty, but it was a quarter to eight by the time the last stragglers arrived, puffing and blowing and excusing their lateness with such remarks as: 'Clock must've been slow' or 'Caxley bus was late again'.

'Well, dear people,' said the Vicar at last, 'I think we must make a start. You know why this meeting has been called. So many people have been concerned about the possible closure of our school that it seemed right and proper for us to hear what is really happening, and to put our own views forward.

'We are lucky to have Mr Win – Mr Salisbury, I should say – here with us, to give us the official position, and I know you will all speak frankly about our feelings. He will, of course, answer any questions.'

He smiled at Mr Salisbury, who looked solemnly back at him.

'Perhaps you would care to outline official educational policy before we go further?' suggested the Vicar.

Mr Salisbury rose, looking rather unhappy, and cleared his throat.

'I am very pleased to have been invited to meet you all this evening but I must confess that I am not at all sure that I can help a great deal.'

'Must know if the school's closing or not, surely to goodness,' grumbled old Mr Potts, who is somewhat deaf, and speaks as though everyone else is too.

'Our general policy,' continued Mr Salisbury, ignoring the interruption, 'is to provide the best service possible with the money available. Now you don't need me to tell you that times are hard, and we are all looking for the best way to stretch our money.'

'But what about the children?' called someone at the back of the hall.

'Exactly. As I was saying, we want to do our best for the children, and we have been looking very carefully at ways and means.

'A small school, say under thirty pupils, still needs two teachers and sometimes perhaps a third, for extra work. It needs

cleaning, heating and supplying with all the hundred and one pieces of equipment found in a school.

'Now, it does seem sensible to put some of these smaller schools together, to make a more workable unit.'

'When's he coming to the point?' asked old Mr Potts of his neighbour.

'And so, for some time past, we have been going into this question very carefully. There are several small schools, such as Fairacre, in the area, and we think the children would benefit from being in larger ones.

'Let me add, that nothing definite has been decided about closing this particular school. There would be consultations all the time with the managers, and parents too. That is why I am so glad to be here tonight, to answer your questions.'

'I've got one,' said Patrick's mother, leaping to her feet and addressing Mr Salisbury directly. The Vicar, as chairman, made an ineffectual attempt to regularize the situation, but is so used to having the chair ignored that he becomes philosophical on these occasions, and really only intervenes when matters become heated.

'Do you think it's right that little children should have to get carted off in a bus, ever so early, and back again, ever so late – in the dark come winter-time, when they've always been used to walking round the corner to school?'

'I think "walking round the corner to school", as you put it, is the *ideal* way. But we don't live in an ideal world, I fear, and we have to make changes.'

'Then if it's ideal,' said Patrick's mother, 'why change it?'

She sat down, pink with triumph. Mr Salisbury looked a little weary.

'As I have explained, we have to do the best with the money available. Now, if we can put these small schools together to make one of viable size – '

'Now there's a word I *loathe*!' commented Mrs Mawne, in what she fondly imagined was a discreet whisper.

'It would seem the best solution,' continued Mr Salisbury, diplomatically deaf.

'Mr Chairman,' said Mr Roberts, who tries to keep to the rules at our meetings, 'I should like to ask Mr Salisbury about something different from the financial side. What about losing a valuable part of our village life?'

'Hear, hear!' came a general murmur.

'We've lost enough as it is. Lost our dear old bobby, lost half our parson, in a manner of speaking, lost our own bakery, and now it looks as though we might lose our school.'

'He's right, you know,' said old Mr Potts. 'And I mind other things we've lost. We used to have two lovely duck ponds in Fairacre. Dozens of ducks used 'em, and the horses drank from 'em too. And where are they now? Gorn! Both gorn! And the smithy. We used to have a fine smithy. Where's that? Gorn! I tell you, it's proper upsetting.'

There were murmurs of agreement, and the Vicar broke in to suggest that perhaps questions could now be directed to the chair, and had anyone anything else to add?

'Yes,' said someone at the side of the hall. 'What happens to Miss Read?'

'I understand,' said the Vicar, 'that Miss Read would be well looked after. Am I right?' he added, turning to Mr Salisbury.

He struggled to his feet again and assured the assembly that I should suffer no loss of salary, and that a post would most certainly be found for me in the area.

'But suppose she don't want to go?' said Ernest's father. 'What about her house and that? Besides, we want her to go on teaching our children.'

I was feeling slightly embarrassed by all this publicity, but was also very touched by their obvious concern.

Mr Salisbury elaborated on the theme of my being looked after, but it was plain that few were satisfied.

There was a return to the subject of doing away with a school which practically all those present had attended in their youth, and their fathers before them.

I felt very sorry for Mr Salisbury, who was really fighting a losing battle very gallantly and politely. His assistant was busy scribbling down notes, and there certainly seemed an amazing amount to be recorded.

Countrymen do not talk much, but when their hearts are touched they can become as voluble as their town cousins. The meeting went on for over two hours, and Mr Salisbury, at the end of that time, remained as calm, if not quite as collected, as when he arrived.

His final words were to assure all present that no definite plan had been made to close Fairacre School, that should that situation arise there would be consultation at every step, there would be nothing done in secrecy, and that all the arguments put forward so lucidly tonight would be considered most carefully.

The Vicar thanked everyone for attending, and brought the meeting to a close.

'Wonder if it did any good?' I overheard someone say, as we stepped outside into the gentle spring night.

'Of course it did,' replied his neighbour stoutly. 'Showed that chap you can't push Fairacre folk around. That's something, surely!'

19. *Dr Martin Meets his Match*

Whatever the long-term results of the village meeting might be, the immediate effect was of general relief.

We had made our protest, aired our feelings, and those in authority had been told clearly that Fairacre wished to keep its village school, and why. We could do no more at the moment.

We all relaxed a little. The weather continued to be seductively mild, and all the gardeners were busy making seed beds and sorting through their packets of vegetable and flower seeds, with hope in their hearts.

I was busy at the farthest point of my own plot when the telephone bell began to ring one sunny evening. My hands and feet were plastered with farmyard manure, but I raced the length of the garden to get to the instrument before my caller rang off. Too rushed to bother to take off my shoes, I grabbed the receiver, dropped breathless upon the hall chair, and gazed with dismay upon the new hall carpet.

'What a long time you've been answering,' said Amy's voice. 'Were you in the bath, or something?'

I told her I had been in the garden.

'Picking flowers?'

'Spreading muck.'

'Muck?'

'Manure to you townees. Muck to us.'

'Lucky you! Where did you get it?'

I told her that Mr Roberts usually dumped a load once a year.

'I suppose you couldn't spare a bucketful for my rhubarb?' said Amy wistfully.

'Of course I can. I'll shove some in a plastic sack, but I warn you, it'll make a devil of a mess in the boot of your car. You should see my hall carpet at the moment.'

'You haven't clumped in, straight from muck spreading, all over that new runner?'

'Well, I had to answer this call.'

'I despair of you. I really do.'

'You didn't ring me up to tell me that old chestnut, surely?' Amy's voice became animated.

'No I've just heard some terrific news. Guess what!'

'Vanessa's baby's arrived.'

'Don't be silly, dear. That's not for months yet. Try again.'

'I can't. Come on, tell me quickly, so that I can get down on my haunches to clean up this mess.'

'Lucy Colgate's engaged to be married!'

'Well, she's been trying long enough.'

'Now, don't be waspish. I thought you'd be interested.'

'Do you think it will come to anything this time? I mean she's always been man-mad. Remember how she used to frighten all those poor young men at Cambridge? And I could name four fellows, this minute, who rushed to jobs abroad simply to evade Lucy's clutches.'

'You exaggerate! Yes, I'm sure this marriage will take place.'

'Well, my heart bleeds for the poor chap. Who is he anyway?'

'He's called Hector Avory, and he's in Insurance or Baltic Exchange, or one of those things in the City. This will be his fourth marriage.'

'Good heavens! What happened to the other three?'

'The first wife died in child-birth, poor thing. The second was run over, and the third just faded away.'

'He doesn't sound to me the sort of man who looks after his wives very well. I hope Lucy knows about them.'

'Of course she does. She told me herself!'

'Ah well! Rather her than me. I take it she'll stop teaching?'

'Yes, indeed. He's got a whacking great house at Chislehurst which she'll be looking after.'

'I bet she won't have muck on her hall carpet,' I observed.

'I'm going to ring off,' said Amy, 'and let you start clearing up the mess you've made. Don't forget the contribution to my rhubarb, will you?'

'Come and collect it tomorrow,' I said, 'and have a cup of tea. We never seem to have time for a gossip.'

'What was this then?' queried Amy, and rang off.

*

Spring in Fairacre takes some beating, and we took rather more nature walks in the exhilarating days of March and early April than the timetable showed on the wall.

At this time of year, it is far better to catch the best of the day sometime between ten in the morning and three in the afternoon, so Fairacre saw a ragged crocodile of pupils quite often during that time of day, while the weather lasted.

The birds were flashing to and fro, with feverish activity, building their nests or feeding their young. Mr Roberts had a score or so of lambs cavorting in the shelter of the downs, and in the next field was a splendid lying-in ward, for expectant ewes, made of bales of straw. Sometimes, when the wind was keen, the children suggested that we sheltered in there, and it was certainly snug enough to tempt us, but I pointed out that the ewes, and Mr Roberts, would not welcome us.

Polyanthuses, yellow, pink and red, lifted their velvety faces to the sun, and the beech leaves were beginning to show their silky green. Friends and parents would straighten up from their seed planting to have a word as we passed, and this brought home to me, very poignantly, the strong bond between the villagers and their school.

Joseph Coggs attached himself to me on one of these outings.

He was obliged to walk at a slower pace than the others for the sole of his shabby shoe was flapping, and he had secured it with a piece of stout binder twine tied round his foot.

'Do you think you ought to go back, Joe?' I asked, when I saw his predicament.

'It'll hold out,' he said cheerfully, as he hobbled along beside me. He seemed so happy, that it seemed better to let him take part with the other children and if the worst happened we could leave him sitting on the bank, and collect him on our way back to school.

'That lady come again last night,' he volunteered.

'Which lady?'

'The office one. Comes to see Mum.'

I realized that he meant the Probation Officer. Naturally I had heard from several sources – including Mrs Pringle – that the officer in question was doing her duty diligently.

'She brung us – '

'Brought us,' I said automatically.

'She *brought* us,' echoed Joe, 'some little biscuit men. Gingerbread, she said. They was good. The leg come off of mine, but it tasted all right. His eyes was currants, and so was his buttons.'

Joe's eyes were alight at the happy memory. My opinion of this particular officer soared higher than ever. It looked as though the Coggs family had found a friend.

'We've got a tin now,' went on Joe, 'to put money in. When we've got enough, my mum's going to buy me some more shoes.'

Looking down at his awkward progress, I observed that he would be pleased when that happened. His eyes met mine with some puzzlement.

'It don't *hurt* me to walk like this,' he explained. He was obviously troubled to know that I was concerned on his behalf, and anxious to put me at ease.

I realized suddenly, and with rare humility, how much I could learn from Joseph Coggs. Here was a complete lack of self-pity, uncomplaining acceptance of misfortune, delight in the Probation Officer's generosity and thoughtfulness for me.

I wished I had as fine a character as young Joe's.

*

Mrs Pringle arrived one sunny morning, bearing a fine bunch of daffodils lodged in the black oilcoth bag which accompanies her everywhere.

'Thought you'd like some of our early ones,' she said, thrusting the bunch at me. I was most grateful, I told her. They were splendid specimens.

'Well, yours are always much later, and a bit undersized,' said Mrs Pringle. 'It always pays to buy the best with bulbs.'

'What sort are these?' I inquired, ignoring the slight to my own poor blossoms still in bud.

'King Alfred's. Can't beat 'em. I likes to have King Alfred's, not only for size, but I likes his story. Burning the cakes and that, and fighting them Danes round here. Some time ago, mind you,' she added, in case I imagined the conflict taking place within living memory.

I was still puzzling over the reason for this unexpected present when Mrs Pringle enlightened me.

'And talking of battles, I've just had one with Dr Martin, and feels all the better for it!'

'About the dieting?'

'That's right. Half-starved I've been all these months, as well you know, Miss Read, and fair fainting at times with weakness. And yet, to hear doctor talk, you'd think I'd done nothing but guzzle down grub.'

'I know you've been trying very hard,' I said diplomatically, admiring my daffodils.

'Well, it all come to a head last night, as you might say. Got me on that great iron weighing machine of his, up the surgery, like some prize porker I always feels balancing on that contraption, when he gives a sort of shriek and yells: "Woman, you've gone up!" *Woman*, he calls me! *Woman*, the cheek of it!'

Mrs Pringle's face was flushed, and her pendulous cheeks wobbled, at the memory of this outrage.

'So I gets off his old weighing machine, pretty smartly, and I says: "Don't you come calling me *Woman* in that tone of voice. You takes my money regular out of the National Health, and I'll have a bit of common courtesy, if you don't mind!" And then I told him flat, he was no good as a doctor, or I'd have been a stone lighter by now, according to his reckoning. He didn't like it, I can tell you.'

My heart went out to poor Dr Martin. I remembered Minnie's remark about Auntie always winning when it came to a battle.

'What did he say?'

Mrs Pringle snorted.

'He said I'd never kep' to my diet. He said I was the most cantankerous patient on his list, and the best thing I could do was to forget about the diet, and go my own way. What's more, he had the cheek to say that for two pins he'd advise me to go to another doctor – '

She stopped suddenly, bosom heaving beneath her purple cardigan.

'Yes? What else?'

'Go to another doctor,' repeated Mrs Pringle, quivering at the memory, 'but that he wouldn't wish any such *trouble maker* on any of his colleagues. Those was his very words. Burnt into my brain, they is! Like being branded! A *trouble maker!* Me!'

'I shouldn't let it worry you too much,' I said soothingly. 'You were both rather heated, I expect, and after all, Dr Martin's only human.'

'That I doubt!'

'Well, getting old, anyway, and rather over-worked. He's probably quite sorry about it this morning.'

'That I can't believe!'

She sniffed belligerently.

'Anyway,' she went on more cheerfully, 'I felt a sight better after I'd had my say, and I went home and cooked a lovely plate of pig's liver, bacon and chips. It really set me up after all that orange juice and greens I've been living on. Had a good night's rest too, with something in my stomach instead of wind. I woke up a different woman, and went to pick some daffodils afore coming along to work. Sort of celebration, see? Thrown off my chains at last!'

'It was kind of you to include me in the celebrations.'

'Well, you've looked a bit peaky off and on, these last few months. Thought they might cheer you up.'

There was no trace of a limp as she made her way to the door. Discarding the diet had obviously had a good effect on all aspects of Mrs Pringle's health, and we at Fairacre School might benefit from this unusual bout of cheerfulness.

George Annett was buying a sweater in Marks & Spencer's in Caxley when I saw him next. He seemed to be in a fine state of bewilderment.

'Which would you choose?' he asked me.

'What about Shetland wool?'

'Too itchy round my neck.'

'Botany wool then. That washes very well.'

'Not thick enough. What's the difference between wool and nylon?'

'How? In expense, do you mean?'

'No. The stuff itself.'

I looked at George in surprise. Surely, he knew the difference.

'Well,' I began patiently, 'wool is a natural fibre, from the sheep's back, and nylon – '

'I know all that!' he said testily.

He really is the most impatient fellow at times.

'Say what you mean then!' I answered.

'Which wears better? Which stands up to washing better? Is one warmer than the other? Will one go out of shape quicker? *Which*, in fact, is the better investment?'

I began to get as cross as he was.

'All Marks & Spencer's stuff is good,' I began.

'Have you got shares in them?' he demanded suspiciously.

'No. I wish I had. Honestly, I think I'd choose a woollen one, but some people like a bit of nylon in with it.'

George flung down a rather fetching oatmeal-coloured confection he had been fingering.

'Oh, I don't know. I'll let Isobel choose for me. It's all too exhausting, this shopping! Come and have a cup of coffee.'

Over it, he asked if I had heard anything recently from the office.

'The usual flood of letters exhorting us not to waste anything,' I replied. 'Not that I get much chance at Fairacre, with Mrs Pringle keeping her hawk-eye on me. She handed me an inch stub of pencil she'd found in the wastepaper basket only yesterday, and she certainly sees that we don't waste fuel.'

'We're going to need more drastic cuts than that,' said George. 'Since these government announcements about making-do and cutting-back and so on, in education, I've seen nothing more of the chaps who were measuring the playground for those proposed new classrooms.'

'You mean we shall all stay as we are?' I asked, the world suddenly becoming rosier.

'Well, nothing definite's been said yet, but I've had no reply to a whole heap of numbers I was requested to send to the office, "without delay" a term or two ago.'

'What sort of numbers?'

'Oh, footling stuff like estimated numbers on roll if the Fairacre children came along. How many were leaving? How many desks were available, and what sizes were they? How many children could be seated at school dinner? How many trestle tables were in use? You know, the usual maddening questions involving us crawling about with a yard stick, and counting dozens of pieces of furniture.'

'I've heard nothing,' I said cautiously.

'That's the point. It's all delightfully negative at the moment. I think we shall have to hear one way or the other pretty quickly. After all, if the county is going to go ahead with re-organization as planned, it will need to give plenty of notice. If not, we should be told very soon. Either way we ought to know where we are before next term, I should think.'

'Mr Salisbury said we should be consulted at every stage,' I agreed. I suddenly felt extremely happy.

'Have a chocolate biscuit,' I said, offering the plate to George, the dear fellow. Any passing irritation with him was now forgotten, for was he not the harbinger of hope?

When Amy came to collect a second sack of manure for her garden, I told her of my encounter with George Annett.

She looked thoughtful.

'As you've heard nothing definite, I imagine that some committee or other is going into which would be cheaper – to take yours to Beech Green, or to hang on as you are.'

'That shouldn't take long to find out.'

'Well, you know what committees are,' said Amy. 'Sometimes vital decisions get lost in transit between the steering committee, and the pilot committee, and the finance committee, and the general policy committee and Uncle-Tom-Cobley-and-all's committee. James talks about these things sometimes, and what with all the complications, and the Post Office thrown in, I wonder if it wouldn't be simpler to be completely self-supporting in a comfortable peasant-like way with just a potato from the garden to eat, and a goat skin to wear.'

'Smelly,' I said.

'Unless your children can be squeezed into Beech Green without any building being done, I can't see Fairacre School closing,' said Amy. 'And surely, the building programme will simply cease to be, with the country's finances in the state they are.'

'Well, it's an ill wind that blows nobody any good,' I said. 'I certainly shan't bother to apply for any other jobs. I'm glad I didn't do anything about Mrs Allen's. Things look so much more hopeful now.'

Amy rose to go.

'Your trouble is that you are too idle to arrange your own life,' she said severely. 'You simply let things drift and when they appear to be going as you want them to, then you start congratulating yourself on doing nothing. I warn you, my girl, the fact that you haven't heard anything yet, one way or the other, doesn't automatically mean that you are out of the wood.'

'No, Amy,' I said meekly.

'One swallow doesn't make a Summer,' she went on, opening the car door.

'You sound as though you'd swallowed *The Oxford Dictionary of Quotations*,' I shouted after her, as she drove off.

It was good to have the last word for a change.

20. Relief on Two Fronts

The end of term came, without hearing any more definite news from the office. The Easter holidays were an agreeable mixture of work in the house and garden, and occasional outings with Amy and other friends.

Earlier in the year, I had been pressed to go with the Caxley Ornithological Society on a lecture tour in Turkey. It all sounded very exotic but, apart from the expense, which struck me as too much for my modest means, I was too unsettled about the fate of Fairacre School to make plans so far ahead, and I had turned down the invitation to accompany the Mawnes, and several other friends, when they set off in April.

I did not regret my decision. My few trips abroad I have enjoyed, and one with Amy to Crete some years earlier was perhaps the most memorable of all. But Easter, when fine, in Fairacre is very beautiful and there were a number of things I wanted to do and see which were impossible to fit in during term time.

Mrs Pringle offered to come an extra day to give me a hand with spring cleaning upstairs. I received this kindness with mixed feelings. Left alone I could have endured the condition of the upper floor of my house with the greatest equanimity. Mrs Pringle however confessed herself appalled by the squalor in which I seemed content to live.

'When did you last dust them bed springs?' she demanded one day.

'I didn't know that bed had springs,' I confessed.

Mrs Pringle swelled with triumph.

'There you are! When I does out that room, I expects to strip the bed, pull off the mattress, and get a lightly oiled rag into them cup springs. That's what should be done weekly, but as it is there's always some excuse from you about "leaving them". Now, Mrs Hope when she lived here – '

'Don't tell me,' I begged. When Mrs Hope, wife of an earlier head teacher at Fairacre School, is brought into the conversation, I just give in to Mrs Pringle. According to that lady, Mrs Hope was the epitome of perfect housewifery. The furniture had a light wash with vinegar and warm water before polishing. Everything that was scrubbable was done twice a week. Sheets were never sent to a laundry, but every inch of linen used in the house was washed, boiled, clear-starched and ironed exquisitely.

My own slap-dash methods scandalize Mrs Pringle, and I sometimes wonder if the spirit of Mrs Hope ever returns to her former home. If so, no doubt I shall see her one day wringing her ghostly hands over the condition of the house under my casual care.

We were washing down the paintwork together one sunny morning when I inquired after Minnie's affairs. I had not seen her on the previous Friday, having spent the day with Amy, and returned just in time to lift the wet dusters from a row of upturned saucepans on the dresser before going to bed.

'Ern's back,' said Mrs Pringle.

I looked at her with dismay.

'Oh no! Poor Minnie!'

'There's no "poor Minnie" about it,' replied Mrs Pringle, wringing out her wet cloth with a firm hand. 'She's a lucky girl to have him back at Springbourne. You can't expect her to bring up that gaggle of children on her own. She needs a man about the place.'

I was bewildered, and said so.

'Yes, I know Ern left her, to go to that Mrs Fowler who's no better than she should be, as we all know. But it's no good blaming Ern.'

'Why not? I think he behaved very badly towards Minnie. Dash it all, half those children he left with her are his own!'

'Maybe. But he's a man, ain't he? Men do go off now and then. It's their nature.'

'I'm sure Mr Pringle doesn't,' I dared to say, attacking a particularly grubby patch of paint by the door.

'I should think not!' boomed Mrs Pringle. 'He's nothing to go off for, living peaceable with me!'

'But is Ern behaving properly?' I said, changing the subject. We seemed to be skating near very thin ice.

'As nice as pie. He'd better too. He knows he's got a bed to sleep in at Minnie's. That cousin of his give him the push after a few days. The springs of the sofa give way, and she's trying to make Ern pay for the repairs.'

'And is he in work?'

'That's not for me to say,' said Mrs Pringle, buttoning up her mouth. 'There's a lot going on at the moment, I'm not to speak about it. No doubt you'll hear, all in good time.'

'I didn't mean to pry,' I said apologetically. 'I beg your pardon.'

'Granted, I'm sure,' said Mrs Pringle graciously. 'And if you'll give me a hand with these 'ere pelmets, I'll take them outside for a good brushing. They can do with it.'

Term began in a blaze of sunshine, and I returned reluctantly to school.

The children appeared to be in the highest spirits, and attacked their work with even more gossiping than usual. I do not expect dead silence in my classroom, when work is in progress, as did my predecessors at the school, but I object to the sort of hubbub which hinders other people and gives me a headache.

It took a week or more to settle them down again to a reasonable level of noise, and a reasonable rhythm of work, so that I did not think about Minnie's affairs until I discovered that she was in the house, when I returned one Friday afternoon. She was scouring the sink with considerable vigour when I approached.

'You're working overtime, Minnie,' I told her. 'It's nearly ten to four.'

'Don't matter. Ern don't finish till five, and we don't have our tea till then.'

I remembered Mrs Pringle's secrecy about Ern's employment. Presumably, all was now known.

'Is he working at Caxley?' I asked.

Minnie put down the dishcloth and sat herself on the kitchen chair, ready for a gossip.

'No. He don't go into Caxley no more. That Mrs Fowler and his cousin are after him. He's best off at home.'

'Where is he working then?'

'Working?' queried Minnie, looking dazed, as though the word were foreign to her. Then her face cleared.

'Oh, *working*! Oh, yes, he's *working*! Up the manor.'

'At Springbourne manor?' I said. It seemed odd to me that Ern should go to work at the same place as his erstwhile rival Bert.

'That's right,' agreed Minnie. She found a hole in her tights at knee level, and gently eased a ladder down towards her ankle. She concentrated on its movement for some minutes, while I wondered whether to pursue the conversation or simply let it lapse.

Curiosity won.

'But doesn't it make things rather awkward,' I said, 'with Bert still there? After all, they are both – er – fond of you, Minnie.'

She smiled coyly, and removed her finger from the ladder.

'Oh, Bert's been and gone! The boss sent him packing.'

'Mr Hurley did?'

Minnie looked at me in amazement.

'There's no Hurleys now at Springbourne. Mr David was the last, and he sold up to these new people. Name of Potter.'

I remembered then that I had heard that the last of the old family had been obliged to part with the house because of death duties, and had gone abroad to live.

'Of course! And why was Bert dismissed?'

'Pinching things. He had a regular job selling the vegetables and fruit and that, to a chap in Caxley. Made quite a bit that way.'

Minnie spoke as though it were to Bert's credit to be so free with his master's property.

'I'm glad he was found out.'

'Oh, he wouldn't have been, but for Mrs Potter goin' into this 'ere greengrocer's for some lettuces, because Bert told her that morning there wasn't none ready for the table yet.'

'What happened?'

'She said what lovely lettuces, and where'd they come from and the man said he got a lot of stuff from Springbourne manor, and it was always fresh, and everyone liked it. So, of course, she come home and faced Bert with it.'

'I should think so!'

'A shame, really,' commented Minnie. 'He was doin' very nicely till then. Anyway, Mr Potter packed 'im off pronto, with a week's wages and no reference. Still, he done him a good turn really, seeing as Bert's got a job laying the gas pipes across the country, and they makes a mint of money.'

'So Ern has got Bert's job?'

'That's right! Mr Potter come down to me one evening and talked about Ern coming back and settling down to be a good husband and father, and what did I think?'

'What did you say?'

'I said I wanted him back. He never hit me nor nothing, and as long as he behaved proper to me, he was lovely.'

'So you've forgiven him?'

'Well, yes. And Mr Potter said he could have this job, and free fruit and veg. as long as he behaved hisself. And if he didn't, I was to go and tell him, and he'd speak sharp to him.'

'Well, it all seems to have turned out very satisfactorily,' I said. 'But look at the time! You must hurry back.'

Minnie began to twist her fingers together.

'I waited to tell you. Now Ern's back, I don't need to come out so much, and I wondered if you could manage without me.'

'Manage without you?' I echoed, trying to keep the jubilation from my voice. 'Why, of course I can, Minnie! I'm just grateful to you for helping me out these last few months, but of course you need more time at home now.'

'That's good,' said Minnie, getting swiftly from the chair and collecting her dues from the mantelpiece. 'I've really enjoyed coming 'ere. You just say if you ever wants me again.'

She looked around the kitchen, her brow furrowed.

'I've never done the dusters,' she said at last.

'Don't worry about those, Minnie,' I said hastily. 'You hurry along now.'

I watched her untidy figure lope down the path, her tousled red hair gleaming in the sunshine.

Relief flooded me, as I gently closed the door. Long may Ern behave himself, I thought!

One morning, soon after the happy day of Minnie's departure, a letter arrived from the office in the usual buff envelope.

I put it aside in order to read more important missives such as my bank statement, as depressing as ever, a circular exhorting me to save with a local building society, pointless in the circumstances, and two letters from friends, which made ideal breakfast reading.

After washing up and dusting in a sketchy fashion, I took the letter from the office over to the school. No doubt another tiresome directive to save equipment, or else measure it, I thought, remembering George Annett's remark.

It remained unopened until after prayers and register-marking. It was almost ten o'clock, and the children were tackling some English exercises, when I slit the envelope and began to read.

It was momentous news. The gist was that because of the devastating cuts in government spending, all local authorities must make do with the present buildings, apparatus and so on. There would be cuts in staff, both teaching and domestic. Re-organization plans were shelved until the country's finances improved.

There were two more pages after this first staggering one. This circular had obviously been sent to every head teacher. But in my envelope there was a covering letter signed by Mr Salisbury, making it clear that there was now no need to have any fears for the closure of Fairacre School, in the light of the accompanying directive, and that the status quo both at Fairacre and Beech Green would remain until such time, in the far future, when the matter of combining the two schools could be reviewed again.

I put down the letter on the desk, securing it under the brass inkstand, and wondered why my legs were trembling. It would have been more rational, surely, to have capered up and down the aisles between the desks, but here I was feeling as though I had been hit on the head with Mr Willet's heavy wooden mallet. I began to realize just how desperately I had been worrying all these months. This, presumably, was what medical men called 'delayed shock'.

My teeth began to chatter, and I held my jaw rigid in case the children heard. Perhaps I ought to make a pot of tea, and have lots of cups with lots of sugar? Vague memories of First Aid procedure floated through my mind, but before I had time to dwell any longer on my symptoms, a diversion arose.

The door was open, letting in the scents of a June morning, and at this particular moment Tibby entered, bearing a squeaking mouse dangling from her mouth.

As one man, the class rose and rushed towards her. Tibby vanished, followed by half the class, and by the time I had restored order my weakness had passed.

Ernest was the last to return, looking triumphant.

'Got it off of 'er!' he announced. 'It run off into your shed. Old Tib's waiting for it, but I reckon it's got 'ome all right.'

'Thank you, Ernest,' I said with genuine gratitude. People I can cope with – even Minnie Pringle, in a limited way – but not mice.

'I think we'll have early playtime today. Put away your books and fetch your milk.'

When they were at last in the playground, I told Hilary the good news, and then went indoors to see if I could get George Annett on the telephone. He has an instrument in his staff room, a rather more convenient arrangement than my own.

'Isn't it splendid?' roared George, nearly deafening me in his enthusiasm. 'I bet you're pleased. And so am I. The thought of building going on in term time was beginning to get me down. Frankly, I think we're all a dam' sight better off as we are. I shall have to lose one teacher, I think – perhaps two – but the main thing is I shan't be cluttered up with your lot.'

I felt it could have been put more delicately, but was far too happy to voice objections. All my shakiness had gone, and I returned to the classroom in tearing high spirits.

It seemed a good idea, bursting as I was with unaccustomed energy, to tackle one or two untidy cupboards, and I set some of the children to work on this task.

The map cupboard is always the worst. Patrick grew grubbier and grubbier as he delved among the piles of furled maps, bundles of raffia, odd tennis shoes, a set of croquet mallets bequeathed us by the Vicar, innumerable large biscuit tins 'which might come in useful' and, right at the back, a Union Jack.

Patrick shook it out with rapture.

'Look! Can us put it up?'

It seemed to me, in my state of euphoria, to be sent straight from heaven to be put to its proper use of rejoicing.

'Why not?' I said. 'You and Joe can stick it up over the porch.'

They vanished outside, and could be heard dragging an old desk to the porch. By standing on it, I knew they could reach comfortably a metal slot which Mr Willet had devised some years ago, for holding the flag stick.

The flag met with general approval when the children had finished their tidying inside and went to admire Joe and Patrick's handiwork. I managed at last to get them in again, and we spent the rest of the morning wrestling with decimals of money.

The children worked well, glowing with the virtuous feeling of having tidied cupboards and desks.

And I glowed too, with the relief which that plain buff envelope had brought me.

That afternoon, when the children had gone home and I was alone in the quiet schoolroom, I opened the bottom drawer of my desk, and took out the weighty log book which holds the record of the school.

I heaved it up on to the desk and turned to the last entry. It had been made a few weeks earlier, and recorded the visit of the school doctor.

I took out my pen, and put the date. Then I wrote:

'Today I received official notice that Fairacre School will not be closing.'

As I gazed at that marvellous sentence, the door-scraper clanged, and Mrs Pringle appeared, oilcloth bag on her arm, and an expression of extreme surprise on her face.

'What's Fairacre School flying the flag for?' she asked.

'For mercies received,' I told her, shutting the log book with a resounding bang.

Discover more about our forthcoming books through Penguin's FREE newspaper...

Penguin
Quarterly

It's packed with:

- exciting features
- author interviews
- previews & reviews
- books from your favourite films & TV series
- exclusive competitions & much, much more...

Write off for your free copy today to:
Dept JC
Penguin Books Ltd
FREEPOST
West Drayton
Middlesex
UB7 0BR
NO STAMP REQUIRED

READ MORE IN PENGUIN

In every corner of the world, on every subject under the sun, Penguin represents quality and variety – the very best in publishing today.

For complete information about books available from Penguin – including Puffins, Penguin Classics and Arkana – and how to order them, write to us at the appropriate address below. Please note that for copyright reasons the selection of books varies from country to country.

In the United Kingdom: Please write to *Dept. JC, Penguin Books Ltd, FREEPOST, West Drayton, Middlesex UB7 0BR*

If you have any difficulty in obtaining a title, please send your order with the correct money, plus ten per cent for postage and packaging, to *PO Box No. 11, West Drayton, Middlesex UB7 0BR*

In the United States: Please write to *Penguin USA Inc., 375 Hudson Street, New York, NY 10014*

In Canada: Please write to *Penguin Books Canada Ltd, 10 Alcorn Avenue, Suite 300, Toronto, Ontario M4V 3B2*

In Australia: Please write to *Penguin Books Australia Ltd, 487 Maroondah Highway, Ringwood, Victoria 3134*

In New Zealand: Please write to *Penguin Books (NZ) Ltd, 182–190 Wairau Road, Private Bag, Takapuna, Auckland 9*

In India: Please write to *Penguin Books India Pvt Ltd, 706 Eros Apartments, 56 Nehru Place, New Delhi 110 019*

In the Netherlands: Please write to *Penguin Books Netherlands B.V., Keizersgracht 231 NL–1016 DV Amsterdam*

In Germany: Please write to *Penguin Books Deutschland GmbH, Friedrichstrasse 10–12, W–6000 Frankfurt/Main 1*

In Spain: Please write to *Penguin Books S. A., C. San Bernardo 117–6° E–28015 Madrid*

In Italy: Please write to *Penguin Italia s.r.l., Via Felice Casati 20, I–20124 Milano*

In France: Please write to *Penguin France S. A., 17 rue Lejeune, F–31000 Toulouse*

In Japan: Please write to *Penguin Books Japan, Ishikiribashi Building, 2–5–4, Suido, Tokyo 112*

In Greece: Please write to *Penguin Hellas Ltd, Dimocritou 3, GR–106 71 Athens*

In South Africa: Please write to *Longman Penguin Southern Africa (Pty) Ltd, Private Bag X08, Bertsham 2013*

BY THE SAME AUTHOR

'Miss Read, as a country dweller, has been blessed with a love of nature, a taste for every one of the dramas with which rural life is fraught, and a sense of humour' – Elizabeth Bowen in the *Tatler*

Miss Read's books about village life are written with charm, humour and charity to delight readers everywhere.

Published in Penguin are:

Affairs at Thrush Green
At Home in Thrush Green
Battles at Thrush Green
Changes at Fairacre
Christmas at Fairacre
The Christmas Mouse
Chronicles of Fairacre
Country Bunch
Fresh from the Country
Friends at Thrush Green
Further Chronicles of Fairacre
Gossip from Thrush Green
The Howards of Caxley
Life at Thrush Green
The Market Square
Miss Clare Remembers
Mrs Pringle

More Stories from Thrush
  Green
News from Thrush Green
No Holly for Miss Quinn
Over the Gate
Return to Thrush Green
The School at Thrush Green
Storm in the Village
Summer at Fairacre
Thrush Green
Tiggy
Village Centenary
Village Christmas
Village Diary
Village School
The White Robin
Winter in Thrush Green

And two volumes of autobiography:

A Fortunate Grandchild
Time Remembered